THE GROVE

OF TAU CETI

Library of Congress Control Number: 2025921065

ISBN 979-8-9987328-5-0 (Paperback)

ISBN 979-8-9987328-1-2 (Kindle)

ISBN 979-8-9987328-3-6 (ePub)

Published by Loch Solace Publishing — Blythewood, SC, USA

Cover design by Nik Wilets (nikwilets.com)

THE GROVE OF TAU CETI

TOBBY HAGLER

To Laura,
for every Tuesday evening at the library,
for the time, the courage,
and the quiet company that grounds me—
and for giving me someone to tell every story to.
You are my solace.

For Mom,
whose stories, strength, and stubborn hope
have always been worth celebrating. Keep writing!

CONTENTS

ONE
DEMETER ACHES

If the roots twitch, call someone nice.

The scuffed, once-white metal walls of corridor 16-04 pulse under a technician's fingertips, guiding her to the source of the ship's pain. Overhead, the lights flicker awake with soft, metallic clinks as she walks past. Her focus pushes her ahead. The aches have been building for weeks, echoing through the ship's circuits and rootwork. She's here to make them go away.

"Alright, luv," she whispers, brushing fiber optics aside to reveal a damaged processor. "Show me where it hurts."

The organic node sits cradled in the bulkhead, its bark-like surface cracked and discolored. Faint pulses of distress ripple and tug at her thoughts like static interference. "I know," she soothes, her voice even and crisp. "That doesn't feel good at all, does it? But don't worry; I've got you."

She runs her fingers along the fractures to inspect the

damage. She retrieves a disinfectant spray from her tool bag and mists the area before dabbing on a healing salve. The node's pulses soften, and the erratic rhythm steadies—a good sign.

She tucks her hair behind her ear, but it refuses to stay.

She cracks, "Oi, did you hear the one about the chronophobic time traveler?"

A curious chirp.

She grins. "Yeah, me neither. Not yet, anyway." With a quick tug, she pulls the processor's circuit interface free. A trail of milky fluid seeps from the pinholes, but it soon slows. She brushes her thumb along the node's surface, blowing on the wound.

"See?" she says, reverting to her crisp tone. "That wasn't so bad, was it?"

The ship emits a faint, relieved hum. The vessel shares a memory with her: the dipping of toes in the soft sands of a beach after a long summer's day. The sensation isn't hers but the ship's way of expressing its relief. She smiles and exhales evenly. "That's better."

She rummages in her bag for a replacement interface and processor. The rebuilt component glints under the flickering light, rows of sharp spikes ready to connect. Aligning it carefully against the node's skin, she pauses. "Okay, this next part might sting a little. Ready?"

The ship responds with a soft chirp, tapping into a memory from her childhood: a younger version of herself flexing her muscles before a vaccination, pretending not to care about the needle. She chuckles and presses the processing circuit harness into place. A satisfying pop follows, and the processor's green indicators blink to life. The system hums quietly, its pain gone.

"Well done, luv," she whispers as she reassembles the panel then secures the bolts. The corridor lights steady and dim to a warm glow as if in gratitude. She slings her tool bag over her shoulder and walks away, her boots echoing softly on the deck plates.

Navigating *Demeter*'s labyrinthine corridors is an art form she mastered long ago. Deck 16 twists and narrows around conduits and tangled rootwork, a maze designed more by necessity than intention. She moves on autopilot, dodging an exposed pipe here and stepping over a warped panel there, each step a reminder of the ship's patchwork state.

The lift to Deck 13 hums faintly then groans when it stops, slightly uneven with the deck's level. Two more decks, a few turns, and another lift. The hum of the ship's engines feels like a tune played out of key, a faint vibration that seems out of sync with itself. It's subtle—one of those quirks that ships pick up over time.

Thirty meters from the next lift, her wrist pad chirps. She stops mid-step, groans softly, and taps the comms button.

"Hey, V," Rowan's voice is casual but slightly rushed. "You got a sec?"

"For you? Of course," she replies dryly, mimicking her mother's overly formal tone. "It's not like I'm busy at the moment."

"Right, because you're never busy. That's why I called you first."

"Shut up," she mutters, rolling her eyes. "Whatd'ya need?"

Rowan laughs. "V, V. Listen. I need someone with your particular finesse. These apes around here couldn't pry open a panel without bending it, let alone replace a cable without yanking out three more."

"I think Hector's technically a baboon," she counters. "The rest? Definitely apes."

"That's why I called you," Rowan says. "You're in?"

"I'm in." She sighs dramatically. "But you'll owe me."

"I hereby officially owe you," he declares. "Name it."

She hesitates. "Actually—"

Resolutely, and before Rowan can say another word, V changes direction and heads toward the opposite side of the deck. The hyperspace engine looms ahead, cutting the ship into two halves like a massive, glowing wall. Most of the crew has to take a convoluted series of lifts and passageways to get around. V prefers a more direct approach.

"V?" Rowan prompts. "You still there?"

She yanks open a maintenance panel and ducks inside, her voice echoing as she replies, "Just cutting through the hyperdrive. Comms'll drop for a sec."

The conduit is cramped, forcing her to hunch as she maneuvers through a forest of coolant pipes and junction boxes. The hum of the hyperdrive core surrounds her. It feels almost alive, like the heartbeat of someone she's grown to trust. Emerging on the other side, she closes the panel behind her and taps her wrist pad. "Okay, I'm back. What were you saying?"

"I was asking what you want in return."

"Oh, right." She pauses to consider. "Can you take a look at an interface circuit for me? I keep finding stress fractures in these things."

"You can fix those in your sleep."

"Sure, but it's the third one this month. Same fracture. Something doesn't add up."

Rowan hums thoughtfully. "Why not just chuck it and fabricate a new one?"

"You know how it is with these old ships." She glances at the bulkhead, then murmurs under her breath, "Not you, luv. You're perfect." Louder, she says, "Replacement parts for ships like this aren't exactly easy to come by anymore. I want to be sure the hyperspace jumps aren't causing them."

Rowan chuckles. "You're always looking out for her."

"Someone has to," V replies with a shrug.

She's my home, V thinks.

A comfortable silence lingers as she walks, with Rowan eventually breaking it. "You know, I could see it."

"See what?"

"Breaking down. Forced to stay out here. A little peace and quiet, off the beaten hyperspace lanes."

V smirks. "What, like settling down on some rock with nothing but a fusion reactor and a fabricator? Very idyllic."

"You'd turn the asteroid into a garden in six months flat."

She pictures that thought for a moment and laughs. "And you'd turn it into a workshop. But I guess between us, we'd have a self-sustaining utopia."

"Deal," Rowan says. "If everything falls apart while we're out here, that's the new plan. Now, what about those stress fractures?"

"You'll take a look?"

"Yeah. I'll see if others are showing similar wear. Could be systemic. Might as well get ahead of it."

"Thanks, Rowan." She taps her wrist pad to end the call.

V glances at the bulkheads. "He's not wrong; it really is quiet out here," she admits in a whisper. She smiles softly at the thought of *Demeter* retiring in Tau Ceti after this last voyage, a worn ship sent out to pasture.

The ship doesn't respond, leaving her to enjoy the silence alone.

She shrugs. *It is remarkably quiet, though. I could learn to love this.*

T he placard above a flickering security panel reads *Deck 07 / Primary Engineering Bay / Hatch 03*. V marches up to the door. She swipes her wristpad against the panel, careful not to scratch either. There are enough scuff marks on both already.

The space on the other side of the door is vast, its enormity underscored by the hyperspace beacon components cradled in scaffolding that sprawls the length of the bay. A few unoccupied workstations flicker dimly, while others buzz with the activity of the engineering team currently on duty.

From his workstation, Rowan calls to her over the noise from an overhead conveyor belt sending empty cargo containers to reclamation. V waves her fingers at him and hurries to cover the distance.

"Thank you, V. You really don't know how much this will help me out. I'm going to owe you at least three more beers at the Crossing ceremony for this."

"In addition to helping me analyze the stress fractures in the interface harness?"

"Okay, nix the extra beers, and you got it."

She rolls her eyes. "How many more beers will I need to upgrade to a proper bottle of grav, anyway?"

"Only three more to fill up the punch card," he answers, attempting his best impression of Daren the bartender.

"I'll hold you to that." She turns a finger of warning into a demonstration of her nimble fingers. "You need help from these?"

Rowan steps to one side, revealing an oddly shaped access panel. "This houses the calibration control, but," he tries to reach a latch on the inside and fails, "I can't get in there."

"An Atharan control module? Yeah, those things are tricky buggers. You need finesse to open up one of these. Watch." She motions him to step aside and deftly opens the latch. She waves her hands at the open panel as if she had performed a magic trick.

"Ah, gods bless you, V!"

"Is that all you needed? Where's, um—?"

"Max?"

"Yeah, Max. Why isn't he here to calibrate all this? Why are you doing it?"

Rowan rubs his forehead to soothe his wrinkled forehead. "Uh, he's in the galley with Lilith for Shathaan ceremonies. They changed times again. So now they do it mid-shift, like, right now."

"I've never understood what it is they do in there. Or what the ceremony's even for."

"He's tried to describe it a couple of times before. It needs all kinds of complex tools to brew an elixir they say is vital to refuel their soul. The way he talks about it, it sounds like there's not really an Earther equivalent. Then he changes the subject."

"So it's an Atharan coffee break? Got it." She laughs before changing the subject herself. "You want to walk me through it? What do I do here?"

Rowan reads instructions from his wristpad to guide V through the recalibration process. Even with her smaller hands and dexterous fingers, some of the settings are difficult to refine. He suggests different sequences to try, but every adjustment offsets another. She has to reset the previous settings and start over.

A voice from Hatch 03 interrupts her latest attempt. "Hey, hey, Forsythe." The man's boots thud across the deck as he approaches.

"Section Chief Parker!" Rowan jerks to attention.

This interrupts her concentration for a split second, but V doesn't look up. Rowan has walked her through the startup sequence enough times that she has the documentation committed to memory now. She resets to the previous settings to start over. She hunches closer to the relay access hatch to block out the new interruption.

The chief grins casually. "At ease, Rowe."

"Hey, hey, Parker. You need an update on anything?"

"I heard Max got pulled away this morning, so I wanted to see how this was coming along. But I see Specialist Sandoval is here, so it looks like you've got things under control."

"Yessir," Rowan acknowledges. "She'll have everything lined up for us with those new specs you sent over. Just having trouble with this last—"

V stops and glares at Rowan, who realizes all too late he just opened a window for Parker's unsolicited assistance to waft through.

"Oh? Having trouble there, Sandoval?" He hovers over the access panel, interrupting V's progress a second time. "Let me watch so I can see what you're doing wrong." He motions for her to continue.

She restarts the sequence, but Parker stops her almost immediately.

"Yep, I see what you're doing, Sandoval. When you slide the dials almost all the way back around, you feel that little pop? You have to wait two seconds, and then you can slide it the rest of the way. That pop is where the wavelengths switch from nanometers to picometers. That's what they do to account for the rounding errors in their computers."

Rowan looks at the instructions on his wristpad. "Oh, so that's what those symbols mean. I just assumed those were glitches from the translation."

Parker moves to examine Rowan's wristpad. "See that one there? That means to press the button, hold it until you hear a beep, then push a little harder. Those little squigglies tell you if it's a multi-haptic sequence or not."

"Thank you, sir, I hadn't noticed that before. Max always does this part."

"I don't blame him; probably embarrassed for anyone to see how bad the design is. Engineering something like this takes real precision. Once these antennae are connected, along with the other two sections, if even one of these joints are off by even a fraction of a picometer, the whole thing could shake apart." He makes a wooshing sound and sprinkles his fingertips like falling ash. "We are talking about a full-length gravity wave antenna, after all. Huge, but brittle."

"I wouldn't say it's a brittle approach. All three fleets build their own parts so we can meet in the middle and stitch them together, right? The haptic modifiers are probably to make sure everyone can work within the same precision levels."

"Sure, could be. I guess. Anyway, I came down here to get your status and to let you know I'm on my way upstairs to meet with the captain." Parker beams and claps Rowan's shoulder. "I guess he's finally seen all the good work I'm doing down here. About time, too."

Parker adds, "At least now you know what some of those symbols mean, so you should be all good for now. You can always look up the rest later." He gently pats the antenna to get V's attention. "Keep at it, Specialist. You'll get a feel for it in no time." Then he strides across the vast bay to a hatch on the opposite side of the engineering bay.

V pulls her hands from the cramped access cavity and flexes her fingers to shake off the tension. "Goddess dammit."

"What's wrong, V?"

She exhales sharply, leaning against the edge of the access panel. "Nothing. That's what's wrong. He was right. I wasn't waiting for those little pips, so I wasn't getting it down to the precision level it needed." She glances at the monitor, where the recalibration sequence is already complete. "See? It's all done. That's all there was to it."

Rowan raises an eyebrow, cautiously gauging her mood. "So, we're good?"

"We're always good," she snaps, slamming the access panel shut with more force than necessary. "It was just one stupid detail. And, of course, he's the one to point it out." She straightens up and unrolls her sleeves. "Anything else?"

Rowan holds up his hands in mock surrender, his eyes widening to an exaggerated degree, as if she's about to throw a wrench at him. "Nope, that's it. Thanks, V."

She returns the gesture with a smirk. "Next time, just wait for Max to finish his break." She turns and stalks toward the hatch, tossing over her shoulder, "Or better yet, make Parker grow smaller hands and have him do it."

"Have a seat, Mister Parker." Captain John Hargreaves waves his hand to an adjacent chair at the six-person wardroom table. An enameled mug of steamless coffee is waiting for him, and several pods of creamer are arranged in a neat line next to it. There's no spoon for stirring, and the coffee smells like wet bread.

"Yessir." Parker acknowledges the invitation and drags the metal chair with a screech. The simulated wood panels once added a touch of elegance to the wardroom when *Demeter* was first commissioned, but now they only offer a tired warmth. Still, it's one of the nicest cabins on board, so it holds a place for more decorum. Too late, he realizes officers probably lift their chairs in this wardroom instead of scraping the floor.

After an awkward pause, Parker asks, "You wanted to see me, sir? Is this about getting *Arion* back online?" He beams.

The captain sips his lukewarm coffee. "Section Chief Parker, I trust you're familiar with the Kentauran envoy, Specialist Dradi?" It isn't a question.

Parker drops his arms to his side, no longer interested in the lackluster cup of coffee. "No, sir. I mean, yes, I know Specialist Dradi, but I'm not aware of any…" Parker trails off.

"Aware of any what?" The captain rubs a threadbare cuff as he considers his next words. The left cufflink is worn smooth. "Specialist Dradi brought a concern to my cultural liaison officer, so I asked Dradi to join me for coffee this morning. He sat right there in that very chair." He taps a finger on the table, indicating where Parker now sits.

Parker keeps his eyes forward, staring ahead at the faux wood paneling. "Sir?"

"It has come to my attention, Section Chief, that someone has been scrawling a few of those little 'EF' symbols on the transport array we're carrying."

"Sir, I—" Parker slinks in his chair. "That wasn't me. Why would he say that? I would never."

"Dradi didn't say you did. He didn't name anyone at all, in

fact. But as I've recently learned, these letters have been cropping up in the assembly bay over the past few months, and he's had enough. So he finally said something to the liaison office." The captain glares at Parker. "And frankly, I don't blame him. I wouldn't want to have to put up with something like that if I were stationed on board a Kentauran vessel." Hargreaves leans forward to be more visible in Parker's periphery. "Would you?"

"No, no, sir. I wouldn't."

"Relax, Section Chief. I called you here, not because I thought it was you or Hector," the captain notices Parker tensing defensively at the mention of the name, "or anyone else on your team." He takes another deliberate sip of lukewarm coffee. "Thankfully, Dradi doesn't want to file a formal complaint, for now. But, listen: I need you to be the section chief I hired you to be. I won't have any of this 'Earth-First' nonsense dividing my crew, especially not now. And handle it quietly. Can't afford blowback on this. Understood?"

Parker picks up a pod of creamer absentmindedly, turning it between his fingers before correcting his posture. "Of course, sir. I wouldn't tolerate anything inappropriate in my section." He studies the pod like it holds an answer to keep from making eye contact. "I just don't think anyone down there means anything by it. It's not about being hostile toward the Kentaurans or the Atharans—it's more about missing Earth. The way things used to be, you know?"

Hargreaves narrows his eyes. "How it used to be?"

Parker hesitates, then sets the creamer down. "Well, sir, Fleet's changed. It's not just the aliens, either. Now we even have Druids on board, it's just—different. We're not the same Fleet we were a generation ago."

The captain leans back slightly, watching Parker carefully. "And that concerns you?"

"No, sir. I wouldn't say that. It's just," Parker exhales, adjusting his tone as if reassuring a superior who might share his reservations. "It's lot of moving parts, all trying to fit together.

You put Atharans, Kentaurans, and now even Druids coming out of the woods and joining a ship like this, when none of them were exactly built for it—feels like trying to make a puzzle out of mismatched pieces."

"The Druids are still human, Parker. Even if their religion doesn't quite make sense to people like us, it's still legal. Plus, they serve a purpose on board ships like *Demeter*."

"Of course, sir." Parker nods quickly. "I don't mean they aren't. I just mean it's an adjustment. For all of us."

Hargreaves nods slowly. "Progress necessitates adjustments. Interstellar alliances come with adjustments."

Parker glances down at his coffee, then decides to take a sip to join with the captain. "And speaking of adjustments, sir, with all due respect, you ever think about how all this affects the basics? I mean, hells, we can't even get a decent cup of coffee anymore." The captain cocks his head. "I'm not sure I follow."

"You know why, sir." Parker waits for the captain's acknowledgement but only receives a curious stare. "Because we have to keep the air pressure low for them. Which means we can't boil water hot enough to make decent coffee anymore."

"Bad coffee's a small price to pay, Parker."

Parker shrugs. "Maybe. But I'd be lying if I said people didn't notice. Sir."

The captain spreads his hands over the table. "Think of it this way. The Atharans can't handle our air pressure, right? So when we lower the pressure for the Atharans, we have to increase the sulfide content for the Kentaurans. And I know they say it doesn't smell, but it does." The captain sighs, then says, "They need things from us. But we need them, too. It's a delicate balance—compromises we all make. We're reaching into uncharted space, and it's good to have allies. Real, thinking, *living* allies. So we can make a few concessions, like lousy coffee and air that smells like bar cleaner."

Parker faces the captain and asks, "Do you think they'd really help us when the time comes?"

The captain's gaze isn't harsh, but it bores through Parker just the same. "Things aren't the same as they used to be. The Kentaurans are our oldest allies, and the Atharans have a lot—and I mean a lot—of natural resources at their disposal. The deeper we travel through uncharted regions of space, the more likely we are to encounter more species like the Pavoids. And what if the Marauders return like they promised? We'll need allies like the Kentaurans and the Atharans."

"But you know what I mean, right, sir?" Parker waits in vain for an answer. "I'm just saying that some people think that, you know—Earthers on Earth ships, Atharans on their ships, and Kentaurans on whatever ships they have left. And then we can pressurize our ships and set gravity to one g, and we can all be more comfortable. I'm not against any of them. I think—" He stops abruptly before saying something he shouldn't. Instead he says, "Some people might think we'd all be better off that way. Maybe they'd just be more comfortable on their own ships.

Weren't you telling me about that audiocast the other day? The one about captains of the olden days? Back when they were all-Earther crews. No aliens. No Druids. Just humans who knew how to get the job done without lighting a candle every time an engine broke down."

Hargreaves corrects Parker. "'The Captains of Old,' you mean?"

"Sir?"

"That's not what that series is about." The captain leans back in his chair and stares up at a hole in the ceiling where an intercom system was once housed. "It's more about the times when captains were really captains and led their crews without their ship's computer calling all the shots. The captains back then had real authority and didn't have to worry about their ships thinking they were better than them. That's what 'Captains of Old' is really about: ship captains making the hard calls and leading the charge."

Parker doesn't see the distinction, and Hargreaves notices.

"Look. That might've been fine back then, Parker, but the void's gotten a lot bigger since those days. As the captain, it's my duty to look after *all* my crew members, Gain or Druid, human or alien. They're *my* crew." He taps his lapel, which draws as much attention to Hargreaves's gravitas as to the worn stitching holding the officer stripes in place. "Mine, not *Demeter*'s. I miss the days when ships like this didn't make all the crew assignments, plot our courses, or make the life-and-death decisions for us—'us' being actual ship captains."

After waiting for that to sink in for Parker, Hargreaves adds, "I get it. We're all swinging in the winds of change, in how our crews operate, alliances with other beings, and even learning to live in environments we're not ready for yet." He holds up a finger for emphasis. "But here's the thing: everyone on board my ship, including the Kentaurans and the Atharans—this entire crew—is my responsibility. Understood?"

Parker lowers his eyes again. "Yessir, understood. And sir, I didn't mean to suggest—" He can only bring his gaze as high as Hargreaves's chest. "Look, I think they have as much place here as any of us, but I think it must be hard for them, you know? Being out of their element, that's all I mean. I'll speak with a few of the mates down in my section and make sure they keep this Earth First mess to themselves. I'll remind them that we're all crew members on the same ship out in deep space, and 'we lonely travelers need to stick together' and all that."

Hargreaves smiles, hearing the old astronautical tradition reflected in Section Chief Parker's leadership training. He leans back in his chair now that the official conversation is out of the way.

"Glad to hear that, Mister Parker. Now, please, enjoy your coffee—cold as it is," he offers with a slight chuckle. "Besides, we've got more important things ahead. The boundary crossing's just a few days out."

Parker looks up. "Really? That soon?"

"Oh yes," the captain says with a wry grin. "Better find something poetic to say. You're about to become a Starwing."

Parker huffs, unsure whether the idea thrills or unnerves him.

Hargreaves adds, "And while you're at it, catch up on Captains of Old. They've started the new season. Some good wisdom in there."

TWO
BOUNDARY CROSSING

*We cross the threshold of new stars, carrying our stories, our
fears, and sometimes — if fortune smiles — the spark of discovery
to light Gaia's hearth*

—Frontier Rites and Rituals
Fleet Archive (excerpt)

The hangar bay erupts with the raucous cheer of a crowd in the throes of frenzy. Bulkheads half a ship away vibrate with the deafening yells of nearly the full crew. Even as isolated as the bridge is from the rest of the ship, the shouts of *"Ic-a-rus! Ic-a-rus!"* reach Captain Hargreave's ears and place a smile on his face. Dancing can be felt two decks away, completely masking the usual vibration of *Demeter*'s engines.

The robed master of ceremonies swirls through the crowd to close the evening's ritual. He motions for the new inductees to follow him. He hoists his staff high so the newly inducted Starwings can follow. The tall staff is capped with a silver figure in a winged space suit, making it easy to spot in any crowd. He leads them into the wide corridor from the hangar bay into deeper corridors throughout the ship to continue celebrating their crossing as they see fit. Their exuberance spreads through every corridor until *Demeter* buzzes with afterparties, personal celebrations, and well-deserved sleep for those crewmembers with an early shift tomorrow.

A line of people dance into the after-hours crew galley to chants of *"Ic-a-rus!"* until the partygoers break into congratulations and applause. Friends and crewmates hug each other, happy to share membership in an elite club of spacefarers who have crossed their first-ever interstellar boundary. Earlier this evening, they were declared "Starwings of Tau Ceti, the newest incarnations of the determined Icarus." Now they can share a toast as members of the same club.

The affectionately named Lolly Galley began this voyage as a simple and practical crew galley, a specimen of compact design; every nook serves a purpose. But over the decades, crew members have adorned it with small touches of personal art and messages. Now it shines as one of the few spaces on board with a true homey feel. Fold-down tables are covered in murals dedicated to *Demeter*'s previous missions, and retractable seating bears small plaques dedicated to outstanding crew members from previous missions. Insignias and mementos from past encounters adorn the shelves behind the bar.

Daren, the bartender, cuts the music. "Okay, listen up," he says, his voice dripping with boredom. "Tonight only, for only the new Starwings," then with even less enthusiasm, "drinks are on the house." He ends his announcement, restores the music, and walks away before the crowd can react with renewed vigor.

V spies Rowan sitting at a table with the drinks he promised to celebrate her induction. He motions her to join him, sliding a frosty mug of beer to her side of the table. She glances at the long line forming for free booze and smiles gratefully, then closes the distance before someone steals the extra chair.

"I have to admit, that was all pretty clever. There was a lot of," she picks up her cold mug and weighs it, trying to pick the right word, "symbolism. Everything had two or three meanings. I didn't expect it to have so much thought put into it."

Rowan lifts his drink and they clink glasses. "See, Miss I-Only-Like-Two-Bands-and-Everything-Else-Is-Lame? I told you you'd get into it."

"For a Gaian ritual, it was pretty cool." She smiles and sips her beer.

"Hey, all Gaian rituals are cool," he protests.

V leans forward. "One thing confused me. The ritual starts off with Icarus in Gaia's arms, but then suddenly it's all about Ouranos and some beast? But then at the end, Icarus lays a new hearth stone for Gaia. I didn't follow the switch-ups."

Rowan raises his eyebrows. "They really don't teach you Druids much about us, do they?"

V sighs and reluctantly admits, "No, they do not."

"Okay, are you at least familiar with the story of Icarus, the Intrepid Space Farer?"

V makes a slight nod. Even sheltered Druids know about Icarus and his bold adventures in space.

Rowan draws an imaginary circle on one edge of the table with his finger. "So, the journey starts at home, where the hearth is. That's where Gaia dwells. She's queen of the hearth. And then you, as Icarus, leave home to travel across the stars." He draws an imaginary arc across the table. "While you're in deep space, you're in Ouranos's kingdom. That's also where the Beast of Tarturus lives. So you make offerings to appease him, and hope he keeps you, Icaraus, from getting lost and falling from the sky again. Or worse, devoured by the Beast."

"See, that wasn't obvious to me."

"V, during the ritual you literally recite, 'Keep me from falling from the sky, my king! Let me keep my flesh.' Not to mention, the whole, 'You have been granted admittance to His vast realm' part. That wasn't obvious to you?"

V chuffs. "Not really. I didn't know who 'He' was."

"Yeah, that's King Oranous. Anyway, Icarus thanks him for

safe passage to explore a new star system." Rowan traces a second circle on the table at the opposite end of his arc. "In this case, that's Tau Ceti. And when Icarus lays the hearth stone—"

"That big crate?"

"Yeah, the big crate. We have to make do with whatever props we have on board. Anyway, Icarus lays the hearth stone in the new system. And from then on, Gaia can dwell with us here, making Tau Ceti a new realm where she'll be the new queen."

"So when you're in a star system, that's Gaia's turf. But in deep space, that all belongs to Ouranos?"

Rowan takes a sip of his grav. "That's one way to describe it."

"Don't get me wrong, this sounds brilliant. I just never heard these stories before. It's a beautiful tradition," she beams.

Rowan laughs and raises his glass. "We still have time to make a decent Gaian out of you yet."

"Challenge accepted," she replies, clinking his tumbler with her mug. "Now that I'm in the spacer club, I can cash in on all those beers you owe me. Which is a lot, I might add."

"I owe you what, six?" He eyes the one in front of her. "Five, now."

"Oh, it's more than that," she scoffs. "It's a lot more."

"V, we've only been out here for eight months. I don't ask for many favors."

"You ask for plenty of favors. Every day, it's, 'Hey V, can you help me with this? Hey V, can you fix that? I'll owe you one.'"

"Now's your chance to cash in." Rowan points at a disgruntled Daren serving free drinks to a thirsty crowd and grins back at V. "Tonight it's on me."

Chief Parker walks up to the table, a free drink in hand and still wearing the Starwing initiation band around his head. "Hey guys, care if I join?"

V takes a large swig of her beer when Rowan motions to the empty seat at their table.

"Hey, Sandoval, does this mean you're switching sides?" He

gestures at her Icarus wings and lifts his oversized mug in a toast.

Rowan and V lift their mugs. V says, "I'm shocked, Parker. Is this really your first boundary crossing? Haven't you been in Fleet for, what, ten years?"

"Yeah, I was mostly doing short-haul work, you know. Strictly inter-Solar missions. I wanted to train to be a pilot, maybe a tug or even a shuttle. That's where the real money's made—being a small-ship pilot. But there were so many applicants by the time I qualified that I never stood a chance in the lottery back home. That's why I came out here. There's not a lot of competition on an old clunker like this one. Anyway, *Demeter* still carries this old piece of junk called *Arion*. A T-12 reconnaissance dropship built back in the day when organic AI was still a new thing. It's not much, but Hector and me, we've been fixing him up. He's almost spaceworthy. Just needs another month or two." Parker takes a swig from his seemingly complicated concoction. "So yeah, been in Fleet for a long time, but no interstellar voyages before now."

"Parker? That was," V glances at him, then at Rowan, then picks at the handle of her mug. "a lot more than I expected from you, Parker." She turns to Rowan, her eyes asking, *Is he always like this?*

Rowan barely hides a snicker. "Parker and I met on a hauler vessel after I...resigned from Jupiter Station. Then one day, this mission shows up on the feeds, and there weren't a lot of takers. It beats repairing industrial comms systems for peanuts, so we reenlisted."

"Yeah, and Rowe here should've applied for the section chief post when it came up. But hey, his loss. He does all the hard work, and I get the pay grade increase, which suits me just fine." Parker beams.

"Someone's got to do the work when you and Hector are off doing yet another training module," Rowan says. "How many of those are you up to, anyway?"

Parker takes a large sip and adjusts his Icarus pin, grinning as wide as he can. "I'm just about done."

"With all of them?"

"Yes! All of them. There's only two left in *Demeter*'s system that I haven't touched yet. That's fourteen more than even Captain Hargreaves."

V interrupts. "Hold up. All of what?"

Rowan answers, "Parker's been trying to qualify for every certification *Demeter*'s training program has to offer."

"Yep. I've done all the officer and command training modules, the pilot training, and dropship mechanics. If I pass the certifications, I'll be the most dangerous human in Tau Ceti. Hells, I've even qualified for EVA using untethered pressure suits."

"The 'most dangerous human in Tau Ceti.' You were that *before* the training." Rowan laughs, then asks, "How do you even qualify for that on board *Demeter*? We're long-range, and there are no EVA missions until we rendezvous with other ships."

Parker chuckles. "Hector. He found an old-ass suit that fits me, and he's been spotting me when we're in between hyper-space jumps. He's been walking me through the basics, and I've carved almost two dozen notches on the airlock hatches."

V rolls her eyes at the mention of Hector's name.

Rowan asks, "Do I want to know if those walks are sanctioned, Section Chief?"

Parker takes another long sip of this drink and cuts his eyes coyly. "Well, I need another drink. Rowe, you need anything?"

Rowan raises his tumbler of grav, still nearly full. "I'm good, thanks."

Parker stands and abruptly walks to the bar. V motions for his attention, but he doesn't notice. She takes a small sip from what remains in her mug and shakes her head.

"That guy," she mutters.

"He's not so bad, V." Rowan says with a laugh. "Okay, he's

an acquired taste. I'm sorry he's such an ass to you. I can talk to him—"

"No, no. I've met bigger arseholes, and I can handle Parker. It's Hector I can't stand."

"Why you don't like Hector?"

"I don't have all night to run through the list."

Rowan drops the subject. "Fair enough."

"What's their deal, anyway? Parker and Hector, I mean."

"I don't know. They're matelots or something. I think it has to do with spending all their time together listening to those old radio frequencies for cryptids. They think they're going to find space whales or something."

"Gaians still do that?"

"Matelotage?" Rowan waves his hand dismissively. "It's an old spacer tradition from Frontier days. They're into old-timey stuff like that."

V finishes her beer. "Here's to whatever keeps you happy."

"Here, Sandoval." Parker startles V by setting a fresh, full mug on the table beside her empty one. He drags his chair away from the table with a terrible screech, despite this being the Lolly Galley. The beer delivery affirms to V that Parker didn't catch any of her conversation with Rowan while he was at the bar.

Unconcerned about interrupting them, Parker begins telling V stories about him and Rowan. She's heard them all before, albeit from Rowan's less exaggerated perspective. Still, she appreciates the fact there's someone on board whom Parker respects, and these versions of their adventures add a touch of cheekiness to her friend's past. She makes a note to tease him later about the time he was caught stealing condiments from a base commissary. She also appreciates that Parker has been the one fetching rounds of drinks for them: beer, grav, and whatever wild cocktail sounds the most enticing during each trip.

An hour drifts by in a haze of reminiscing, laughter, and clinking glasses before V feigns a cough to cover her amusement and looks away. Something catches her eye, and she squints across the room. "Hey, is that—?" She nods her chin at a woman sitting alone in a booth covered in computer tablets and stacks of empty glasses.

Rowan and Parker twist in their chairs to look in unintentionally conspicuous ways.

Without turning back, Parker confirms loudly, "Yeah, that's Doctor Hawthorne, alright. I thought I saw her sitting over there when I came in. It looks like she's been here all day." Quieter, he adds, "I guess she didn't even go to the ceremony." He absent-mindedly adjusts his headband.

"Not from the looks of that booth," Rowan says as he turns around to the table.

Parker stares a little longer but soon rejoins the conversation, ready to tell another story. "Hey, remember that time when…"

V watches the distinguished doctor, sitting alone and engrossed in her work. Usually, Hawthorne is the life of the party. She's certainly never been the wallflower at the biggest party of the voyage. Hawthorne looks up from her tablet and meets V's eyes.

The Lolly Galley's cacophony abruptly ends as if the room was thrust into a sudden vacuum. A phantom voice coils behind V's skull, vibrating in the back of her consciousness.

<Hello, Ainé Sandoval.>

V drops her mug on the table. The thud of heavy glass hitting lightweight metal resonates over the din of the galley.

"V, you okay?" Rowan asks.

"Yeah." Her eyes are wide. She looks over the empty mugs on their table and puffs her cheeks. Her accent suddenly rough, she says, "I think this has been plenty good." She's thankful for an excuse to leave, however lame it might sound. "It's late. I'm going to hit the rack."

Parker bids her goodnight, but V sees the concern in Rowan's face. She says sheepishly, "Yeah, I'm alright. Just early shift and all that." She untucks the hair from behind her ear as she stands up, pulls in her shoulders, and makes herself as small as she can as she hurries out of the booming Lolly Galley.

I t's dark. Gloriously dark. V is shielded from starlight by the absence of a porthole, the singular beauty of an inside cabin. Long ago, she obscured every indicator LED with band posters and stickers and even painted over the persistent glow of the emergency light strips overhead. Only a faint glow escapes the edges of one Merion poster, which provides just enough light for those times she needs a late-night visit to the head. It's the kind of darkness that feels like smooth velvet.

A shrill cry sounds: a short chirp, a brief tone, and another short chirp. The pattern repeats and repeats again.

"Feck!"

V folds her forearm over her eyes. The after parties are finally over, but there's no way it's time for breakfast, much less her shift. Whatever is causing her wristpad to go off, it can wait until the morning. But it stops glowing, and the grating tones begin again: "Chirp, squee, chirp!"

She whispers harshly, "Goddessdammit! What is it, Rowan?" He's one of the few contacts who she's configured to bypass her do-not-disturb mode. She taps the green CONNECT button and sets the wristpad on its face. She'll talk to him, but she'll be damned if the light from his video feed is going to burn her eyes at this hour.

"What?" she yells.

Rowan pauses, then asks, "V? Are you okay?"

"I'm fine. It's late. What is it?"

"Technically, it's early," he says.

"So feckin what?" she whispers.

"Hey, so I was wondering." He pauses again. "You asked me the other day to look at an interface harness for you. Something about stress fractures?" His voice sounds almost contrite. That grabs V's attention.

"Feck, Rowan. I just got to sleep." V's voice is tired, and in a thick accent she says, "You're calling me about this now, bruv?"

"Sorry about that, V. But listen: I'm in the communications hub, and I remembered you asking about the fractures. And I happen to have the equipment already hooked up to do the analysis work. I can look at it now if you want?" His voice rises like a question, but there's a gravity to it that suggests it's more of a polite demand. "I won't have access to it for very long. Once the next shift is up, I won't be able to look at your processor harnesses for a few days. But V? We should both probably look now. I think I'm on to something important, but I need you to see it."

V lets out an exasperated sigh. "Feck. Okay. Give me a minute to get dressed, and I'll check it out of my locker. I'll be there in a few."

"I'm in the communications hub," he whispers as a reminder.

"Communications hub. Got it. On Deck 09?"

"Deck 08. I'll see you in a—"

She severs the commlink and her wristpad goes dark, a welcome relief.

She pulls on her uniform pants and boots, left on the floor beside her rack from last night. Her t-shirt hangs over a chair, discarded just hours after the Starwings celebration—she fumbles for it, tugging it over her head. She grabs her wristpad from her bunk and begrudgingly pulls it up her forearm. She leaves her cozy, dark cabin, which beckons her to stay. Corridor lights clink to life in response to her presence. The metallic walls are cold; their white enamel is tinged a harsh blue to her bleary eyes.

She slides a hand along the bulkheads to help her navigate as she makes her way to the nearest lift. She's surprised by the quiet. The lack of sound doesn't bother her; she welcomes that.

But there's a distinct lack of presence in the air around her. It feels as if someone who was recently in the halls with her has disappeared.

This must be too early for even you, Demeter, V thinks. The ship's presence—usually a subtle buzz at the periphery of her awareness—is absent, but she doesn't dwell on it. After last night's invasive mental hello from Doctor Hawthorne in the Lolly Galley, her own barriers must still be on edge. That, or Demeter is just as tired as she is.

Thankfully, there's not another soul in the corridors at this hour, and she's glad not to make small talk with anyone. She plans to help Rowan, curse at him a little—or maybe even a lot— then climb back into her rack for whatever remaining shuteye she can muster before the next shift.

Once the lift doors swoosh close in front of her, she grabs a handrail, leans against the wall, and shuts her eyes. The ride is over entirely too soon, and she starts back to reality. She stomps to her work locker, grabs three canvas bags, and clomps to the opposite end of the deck to take another lift.

A few minutes later, she arrives at a small nook that leads to the communications hub. This nexus of communication gear keeps *Demeter* in touch with the rest of the fleet, the ship's sensors in touch with the surrounding stars, and the crew in communication with each other. From the silence inside, V assumes those activities aren't happening right now.

If sheer willpower could force the doors open, she'd be through already. Instead, she waits for *Demeter's* security panel to recognize her wristpad, shifting her weight impatiently. The hatch finally slides into the wall, dragging out what could have been a grand, irritated entrance. All she really wants is to be back in bed for a few more hours before her next shift.

"What do you want?" She means to sound demanding, but an unavoidable yawn diffuses her commanding presence mid- question.

"Hey, V. There's a cuppa right there for you." Rowan points

to the mobile workstation by the door, which holds a mug of stale tea.

She grabs the mug and levels a glare at Rowan over the rim—*You'd better have a damn good reason for this*—before taking a grudging sip.

Rowan eyes the canvas bags over V's shoulders. "Did you bring your circuit interface harness?"

She tosses the bags at his feet dismissively. She blows on the mug of tea out of habit, but it's not hot enough to pose a threat of burning her lips, then takes a sip. The temperature is in danger of ruining the tea, so only a minute or two of enjoyment remains. She glances around the disheveled room, surprised at how patchwork everything looks for something so vital to an inter-stellar starship.

She groans. "Rowan, what'd you bring me down here for this late?" *Or is it early?* she thinks. She just laid down from the abruptly interrupted after-party not more than an hour or two ago. At least the room is dark.

Parker mumbles a correction from a dark corner. "It's early."

V sets her cup down. "Parker? Goddess, is that you?" She picks her cup back up to help disguise snicker. He's hungover. He may even still be drunk. It's hard to tell in this light.

He lifts his head from where it was resting against the rack of communications relays but immediately wishes he hadn't. "Itsh me." He leans sideways again and rests his eyes.

"Yeah, don't mind him," Rowan says. "He found… something. Called me down here to take a look. That's when I noticed the anomaly. Did you bring the rootwork harnesses?"

"Found something? Like what?"

Rowan scratches the back of his neck. "Honestly? Not sure yet. He was supposed to go to bed—couldn't even stand upright. But Hector said the comms were down, and Parker couldn't let it go. Wasn't clear if Hector meant their system or *Demeter's*, so Parker hauled himself down here to check it out."

He nods toward the console. "He was in no shape to read

terminals, much less fix anything. But you know Parker—too dumb to quit, too stubborn to walk away. So he called me. And then I called you."

She drops her head, stares at the bag near his feet, and takes a long swig of her ever-cooling tea. Rowan pulls a device from one of the bags and sets it on a study table underneath a metallurgical scanner, then he starts working on the console while V focuses on her tea and tunes him out while he runs his analysis.

"Alright, there it is, V!"

She's nearly asleep on her feet and leaning over a nearby workstation.

"V?"

"What? Yeah." She scrambles for her empty tea cup and walks to his scanning station. "What is it?"

He pulls several terminal screens side by side, showing results from various tests. "See these?" He motions to the results of scans showing microscopic fractures in different ship components.

She blinks hard to push the sleep away but quickly recognizes the patterns. She's very awake now. "Is that *my* harness? But then, what's that?"

"That, V, is—" He looks around the comms hub, and the only other person he sees is Parker. But the server racks and dangling wires give many places to hide if someone wants to spy on a conversation. "This is a recent scan from the primary quantum telecom relay."

She stares blankly.

"That's what keeps us in touch with the rest of the—"

"Oh shit," she says, suddenly wide awake. "Are we in complete radio silence?"

"Yeah. We're dark." Rowan taps a display to show more views of the relay component in question. "Our primary comms relay has the same fractures as your harnesses. That's why I called you so early. I thought maybe you'd have some ideas since you've seen something like this before."

In the distance, Parker calls out, "Late."

Ignoring the unsolicited correction, she tries to sip from an empty cup before setting it down. Then she steps forward to examine the detailed readouts of the microscopic scans. She points at the display, which shows the network harness she brought earlier. "That radial spiral. Right there." She points at one of the screens. The spiral lines are so tight that the entire screen gives the illusion of spinning. "That's the same as the other harnesses I've replaced. But that's not hyperspace compression, right?"

"No, it's not."

They stand still for a few minutes, blinking silently at the screens.

Rowan speaks first. "If that's not hyperspace compression, then what is it?"

"Vibrational damage? I mean, *Demeter*'s not exactly in her prime—"

She's cut off by a faint, pathetic warble from a nearby speaker —*Demeter*'s usual way of protesting an insult. But instead of a following wry remark or a pointed correction, the ship falls silent, perhaps too tired to argue.

V looks up apologetically at a bulkhead and continues. "I'm sorry, luv. You know I don't mean it like that." She looks back to Rowan. "Maybe these components are just falling apart? Crumbling, you know? What if they're crumbling under the same resonance?"

Rowan whispers, "Gods, I hope not."

V steps closer to squint at the scan showing the harness she brought. "Goddess, is that—?" She taps furiously for a moment on her wristpad before finally swiping something to the display screen. She uses both hands to rotate and position the image over the harness scan until the illustration lines up with the fracture patterns.

"Is that a daisy spiral?" Rowan asks.

V glances at her wristpad. "That's a parastichy fractal. But yeah, you see that in daisies. Pine cones, too. Some other flowers. Hells, even some cancerous neurons. I took a few medical courses in college before I left Rimeholt and joined Fleet. I *knew* I recognized that pattern. Muther absolutely *loved* her feckin gardens when I was a kid. I just didn't place it until now."

"Parsh," Parker interjects from the corner. "Parchesticky. Priterstish. Ictchy. Fractal patternsh no good." Rowan and V look to see if he's alright and quickly turn back to look at the troubling scan results. Behind them, he mutters, "Not hypeshcparce. Hyperspash. Not right."

Rowan scratches his head, mussing his unkempt hair even further. "That's no coincidence. And that can't be natural, can it?"

"Figure it oot, hng," Parker says, this time bunching a few cables together for a makeshift pillow on the rack of relays.

"I mean, the pattern is very natural," V says to Rowan. "Fractals are everywhere in nature." She pauses; that's clearly not what he meant. "But out here? In the mechanical parts of the ship? I could believe it if it were the organic nodes, but these?" She points at the displays of damaged mechanical parts. "No, that doesn't seem natural. Or normal. Or anything like what I'd expect to see in multiple system components."

Close to a minute passes before V speaks again. "So we have no comms with Fleet?" Rowan shakes his head. "Gotcha. Do you think we can hail the Atharans or the Kentauran ships? They should be close enough to Tau Ceti by now that we won't need quantum comms."

"Yeah, but using radio comms, or even tight beams, it'll still take nearly a day for the signals to reach them clear across the other side of the system. I'm not even sure those will work, or if we'll be able to receive their response. I need to do a full diagnostic across the entire comms array."

"What can I do?"

"You can get Chief Parker some coffee and start—"

V punches Rowan's shoulder.

He clears his throat. "After I get Parker some coffee, can you look at your other harnesses for anything out of the ordinary? Maybe there's a pattern to how they're breaking."

"I don't know about a pattern like this under normal circumstances. A few might shatter over the course of a voyage, especially if the hyperspace jump is hard." V's accent sharpens, crisp and formal, as she instinctively glances over her shoulder to scan for anyone lingering behind the terminal racks. "But this many in two days? After eight months with barely a problem? That's not normal."

Rowan groans and rubs his temples. "Yeah, I know. That's what worries me."

V hesitates before asking, "What if these components aren't failing because of the jumps? What if it's deliberate?" Her voice lowers. "If someone on board is tampering with systems, how long before they mess with something critical? Life support? Power?"

Rowan exhales slowly then leans closer to keep his voice contained. "I don't think it's that bad. Not yet, anyway. But I've been wondering the same thing. What if someone doesn't want this mission to succeed?" His eyes flick to the corner of the room to glare at Parker. He returns his attention to V. "You know the kind of people I mean."

Her lips press into a thin line. "Take out comms, the aliens go home. Mission's over."

"I'm just saying," Rowan continues, forcing a casual tone and speaking more loudly, "the sooner we figure this out, the better. If it's nothing, we move on." He drops his voice to a whisper. "But if it's something, we need to know."

V nods reluctantly, already mapping out her next steps in her mind. "Right. I'll start with the harnesses. See if I can trace anything back to the root nodes."

Rowan checks the time on his wristpad and grimaces. "Figures. My shift starts soon." He straightens and puts on a neutral expression, but his voice drops low again before he turns away to leave. "I'll keep digging when I can. You do the same."

V offers a curt nod, already turning back to the terminal as he heads toward the engineering bay.

THREE
ECHOES IN THE ROOTWORK

Even the stars go silent when they hurt.
This one's for Rik!

— MERION, LIVE FROM INISHMORE (2367)
DEBUT OF "END OF THE TRIP (MY FRIEND)"

V walks slowly along corridor 14-12, heading toward a junction that connects *Demeter*'s organics to a secondary interface. She drags her fingertips along the cool, scuffed bulkhead, listening for the AI's presence. The steady hum of *Demeter*'s systems is muted, and V hears only the pulse of a body in deep sleep. She frowns, leaning in as if to feel the rhythm more closely, but the passageway feels empty, save for the occasional crewmember passing by.

A chill settles over the corridor. The air thins until it vanishes altogether. V wants to cough but can't. She freezes, reaching for whatever has a chokehold on her, but there's nothing around her neck. A distant buzz hums at the edge of her awareness, static between thoughts, and she tries to push it aside. The overhead lights flicker and fade to a dim glow, shifting to a pale, unnatural blue hue in her mind's eye.

A voice beckons at the edge of her awareness. *<Ainé Sandoval?>*

She freezes. The title sends a chill down her back. Her first thought is of her mother, but there's no way she can reach her this far away. No voice can be heard in a vacuum like this. It's out of place. V stiffens, her nerves on edge.

<Demeter*? Is that you?*>

"Ms. Sandoval, do you have a moment?"

This time, the words are spoken aloud, sounding real. They echo in the corridor, pulling V from her thoughts. V clenches her jaw, her muscles tense as she spins on her heels into a well-practiced pugilist stance.

A tall figure with silver-cropped hair and draped in a long lab coat steps back with her palms out. "Oh, I'm sorry, luv. I didn't mean to startle you."

"Doctor?" V relaxes her stance, unsure if she should drop it entirely. "Doctor Hawthorne, I wasn't expecting that."

"Oh, my few remaining friends just call me Thorney." Her tone is unassuming but confident. "I was trying to reach you through chaint. It's more intimate than speaking aloud, don't you think?"

V's lips tighten into a thin line. In a precise tone, she replies, "Not particularly." She shifts her stance.

A soft grin spreads across Hawthorne's face. "I wanted to apologize if I startled you last night."

"No, I wasn't startled," she lies.

"It was inconsiderate of me to chaint like that."

"That's... noted. But what makes you think I could hear you?"

"I'm aware of who you are. That's why I've left you alone all these months. But when you were staring at me last evening, I wondered if you were trying to chaint hello."

V's jaw tightens. "Aware of who I am?"

"Yes, and I'm sorry, Ainé Sandoval, I didn't mean to bring up—"

"It's Specialist Sanodval. Ainé Sandoval is someone else."

"Yes, of course." Doctor Hawthorne winces at the informal address. "Specialist. I'm sorry. Truly. I never meant to upset you. I'll leave you be." Hawthorne steps back to leave but halts as if waiting to be excused.

V shifts, suddenly uncomfortable. "Wait. I didn't mean to be rude. Can we start over?"

"I'd like that. In fact, can I buy you a coffee? I know a place."

V tilts her head questioningly.

"The Lolly Galley has some of the finest coffee in the star system if you know who to talk to."

V laughs with a snort and covers her mouth. A minute ago, she was expecting a fight, and now she's being asked to join *the* Doctor Hawthorne for a coffee. She freezes in the moment, considering the irony.

Hawthorne's expression doesn't change, but after a beat she asks, "So, will you join me?"

V blinks, snapping back to reality. "Yeah, sure."

"Yeah, sure?" Did you hear that, Ris? The one and only Doctor Hawthorne asks me to coffee, and I'm all like, "Yeah, sure," like it's no big deal. V hasn't talked to her sister in a long time, but this encounter with Hawthorne is the first thing she would want to tell her about—if she could ever talk with her again.

They walk together, with V trailing slightly behind. She's unsure if she's lagging out of respect for the doctor or because her legs are shorter, but she keeps pace all the way to the Lolly Galley.

The galley is empty besides a few patrons who have ended a late shift. Daren sits on a stool in the far corner of the bar, wiping spots from glasses with a threadbare towel. He sees Hawthorne and motions her to the same corner booth she'd occupied the night before.

"Ainé San—V, will you have a seat?" Hawthorne asks. "I'll rejoin you in just a moment."

So this is where the famous Doctor Hawthorne always sits, V thinks. She spreads her arms across the table. She's never known anyone else to sit here in the eight months *Demeter* has spent jumping to Tau Ceti, and now she's joining the famous scientist.

Her gaze drifts to the wall behind the bar, where mission patches and plaques are crowded on top of each other. This part of the galley, obscured by a bulkhead column, feels oddly private. She's always thought of Hawthorne as larger than life, a figure of endless energy and social grace. Yet, this tucked-away corner feels quiet, almost lonely.

An aroma drifts through the air and pulls her attention. It's something earthy, warm, and unmistakably rich. Hawthorne returns with two steaming mugs.

"I hope black is okay. I didn't think to ask if you wanted cream or sugar."

"No, wait, but is that—*real* coffee?" V grabs the mug and pulls it closer for a closer whiff. Her eyes water.

Hawthorne grins. "Told you I knew a place."

V lurches from the edge of the booth, looking for the magical source of this elixir—but other than a few motionless stragglers and the Atharans sitting in a corner, the galley appears empty. No steam, no servers, no coffee machines in sight. She frowns, puzzled, then turns back and lifts the mug with both hands to her face, chasing every last hint of the aroma. It's almost too hot to hold.

V stares at Hawthorne's face. She's seen it every day since—on posters, in promo reels, and on the bulletin boards of every Druidic arboretum she'd ever visited. And now, here it is: across from her in deep space, in another star system, handing her real coffee. The absurdity of it hits her all at once. She blinks, realizing she hasn't thought about her harnesses, or *Demeter*, or much of anything at all.

<*Why?*> The thought escapes V's mind uncontrolled, and Hawthorne can plainly hear it.

The room grows cold, and the mild din of the ship's engines disappears.

<Ah, there you are, luv.> Hawthorne looks relieved. *<I was beginning to think you weren't going to chaint with me.>*

V bolts upright in her booth seat, eyes wide open in embarrassment.

"Oh." Hawthorne's smile fades. "I hadn't considered that you haven't chainted with anyone in awhile."

V hunches a little. "Sorry." She fidgets with the hot mug. "It's been a really long while, to be honest."

"It's alright, luv. We can keep talking aloud if you need."

V is sharing impossibly good coffee with a veritable rockstar of the scientific community, someone she's looked up to most of her life. She should be more excited. Another time, another place, she would die for this opportunity, but here and right now, it feels awkward and surreal.

V holds the mug with both hands under her nose, warm steam flaring in her nostrils. She looks up slowly and says, "So, I hear you're a big Merion fan?" This was the stupidest question imaginable, so naturally it's the only one that comes to mind.

"Goddess, yes." Hawthorne snorts a laugh and covers her mouth delicately.

V points and laughs. "Ha! You do it too. I do that all the time."

Hawthorne leans forward on her elbows. "I absolutely adore Merion. They are so feckin brilliant." The enthusiasm in her voice is unmistakable, her grin unguarded. It's the kind of excitement V recognizes—the same wide-eyed, breathless energy she used to have when she first saw Merion live.

"Oh I love them too," V proclaims, patting her chest.

"I know, I can tell." Hawthorne glances down at V's wrinkled but otherwise pristine *Roots Rebellion Tour* t-shirt. "I still have that one too. In fact, I followed them all the way down to Kilkenny for a couple of shows before I remembered I had a doctoral thesis to defend the next week." One corner of her mouth twists sharply in pride as she cocks her head to one side, about to reveal a delicate secret. She whispers, "I left the caravan so abruptly in the middle of the night, I'm sure it must've broken poor Neil's heart."

"Okay, I need to hear that story."

Hawthorne winks. "That'll need more than a cup of coffee. One day, though. Promise."

"I'm originally from Galway, and my sister took me to one of their shows when I was younger. I've been hooked ever since."

"I'm from Galway too, you know?" Hawthorne leans back against the booth seat, letting her posture droop comfortably.

"Get out! Light years from Earth, and the only two Galwegians in the star system find each other?"

Hawthorne leans in, and adds, "And the biggest Merion fans, to boot, I'd imagine."

"I know, right? Classic us!" V's shoulders drop too, glad to be sitting in a booth with a neighbor with something in common, and not some famous stranger. V leans forward, rubbing her hands, hoping for a little gossip. "So, what was Neil like, anyway?"

The two exchange stories from their hometown. Each experienced it a few decades apart, and it's a delight to hear what it was like back then, what's changed since leaving home, and what will always be the same. Hawthorne's version of home sounds so idyllic and fun, while V's recollection is that the town is lame and boring, save for the amazing music scene. Both agree that was always the best part of growing up there.

Coffee talk in the Lolly Galley is usually short and limited to one or two stories, given how terrible the coffee is normally, but with beverages this rich and delicious, they could talk for an hour or more. V's laughter encourages Hawthorne to spin even more wild tales of a misspent youth before she began exploring the science of telepathy and its wider applications with AI systems. Hawthorne's easygoing personality lets V breathe for the first time since leaving spaceport, surrounded by people who never quite felt like her own.

V sips the last bit of her coffee, savoring the moment as long as she can. "All good things end, my friend," as Merion used to sing, and that's what makes everything worth savoring. She takes a deep breath and sighs to begin her goodbye.

Before V can slide out of the booth, Hawthorne tilts her head, her tone gentle but insistent. "V? May I ask a favor of you? I can get you another cup if you like."

"As tempting as that sounds, really shouldn't—" V blinks as the memory resurfaces. "Feck. The comms." She straightens, setting her empty mug down. "I was on my way to check something before we ran into each other."

"Well, before you go," Hawthorne interrupts, leaning forward. "you could be a big help to my work if you're up to it."

V hesitates but slides back to the middle of the bench. "Help you? I don't see how."

"Specialist Sandoval—" Hawthorne corrects herself with a small smile. "V, I need your special abilities."

V frowns, confused. "My special abilities? I fix broken system components and help *Demeter* when it hurts. That's important, but nothing particularly special."

"I think you underestimate your gifts."

"Gifts?" V's voice tightens. "What gifts?"

The crew galley chatter is growing as crew members arrive for breakfast, but the noise vanishes with an eerie whoosh.

<Your gifts, luv.> Hawthorne taps the back of her head to emphasize the chaint.

V's eyes widen at the unwelcome intrusion. Her voice cuts through the moment as her senses reorient—sound rushing back in, the galley's growing bustle colliding with the unnatural hush of the chaint-space she didn't mean to enter.

Hawthorne's brows knit together in concern. *<Perhaps you haven't used it in a while, but surely you know your own talent with chaint. I can sense it.>*

V slams her fist against the edge of the bench, earning a startled glance from the bartender. "I don't use it!" The noise around them seems louder now, more intrusive—as if the rest of the ship has caught up to the pressure rising in her body. With gritted teeth, she adds, "At all. Ever."

This was supposed to be a simple breakfast, she thinks bitterly. *Coffee, stories, and now this. Why do Druids have to feckin ruin everything?*

<*V, I don't understand. You're so talented.*>

Instinctively, V chaints back. <*NO!*>

The mental rejection slams into Hawthorne like a physical blow. Her eyes are wide with shock, her eyes watering. She presses a knuckle to the tip of her nose to check for blood. It comes away clean, but her hands are shaking. She stares in shock, "V?"

V scrambles out of the booth. "Don't ask me about chaint again." Her voice cracks as she says, "Please, Doctor Hawthorne?" V turns and storms out of the Lolly Galley for the second time in as many days.

Never meet your idols, her sister's voice echoes in her head, acidic and taunting.

Still rubbing her nose, Hawthorne calls after her, "Can you still feel *Demeter*? Haven't you noticed?"

V's boots strike the deck harder than usual, and her arms are crossed tightly to keep herself from unraveling. She nearly barrels into Rowan at the threshold of the galley but brushes past without a word, barely catching the flicker of concern on his face as he glances between her and the booth she left behind. She doesn't turn to look, but in her periphery, she sees Hawthorne still seated, rubbing her nose with a shaking hand.

At the far end of the mess hall, Parker barely glances up from his toast, his expression glazed with indifference. Whatever this latest Druid drama is, it's none of his concern. He takes another bite as Rowan approaches, not yet brave enough to try the eggs. Rowan pulls out a chair across from him, and the two slip into a low, quiet conversation.

n between the lower decks of 16 and 17, nestled inside *Demeter*'s cold metallic ribs, are several cramped service tubes. Now mostly abandoned, they once played a vital, arterial role in maintaining *Demeter*'s underlying systems. Down here, a dry chill seeps into bones, courtesy of nearby infrared radiators flinging heat into the void of space. Gravity tugs a little harder here than on the rest of the ship due to artificially generated gravitational bubbles pushing against each other.

Bundles of cables snake around the conduit walls like vines through treetops, inconsistently draped from years of technicians applying quick fixes instead of permanent solutions. Handwritten labels identify some bundles, though others bear symbols no one recognizes anymore. Decades of makeshift patches and aged duct tape have left clusters of wires dangling in dusty chaos, making a crawl through these passageways a claustrophobic nightmare.

Parker pulls an access panel aside and sets it on the ground. After a quick round of Paper-Scissors-Stone, he smirks. "You go first. I'll, uh, check for traps."

Rowan sighs and slings his tool bag over his shoulder. "I guess you're feeling better after all those eggs and toast?"

"Getting there. But decent coffee would've helped," Parker says, looking less green than he did two hours ago in the relay compartment. "Some mornings, like today, I swear I can still smell the good stuff."

They crawl through the coffin-like passageways, Parker trailing as Rowan's flashlight slices through the semi-darkness. Overhead lights flicker when they detect motion but shut off too quickly, leaving Rowan to navigate by instinct more than illumination.

They finally reach a section where the passage widens until it's big enough to sit up. Rowan sets up his diagnostic equipment while Parker leans back against a cluster of cables.

"You know," Rowan says, scrolling through schematics on his

wristpad, "last night in the Lolly Galley, you bragged about taking every training module on board *Demeter*."

"Well, not every module. I haven't taken the Kentauran diplomacy ones."

"I guess that does make you the most dangerous man in the star system. But why not finish up the Kentauran modules?"

"I don't think I'll ever need them. Once we get back home, and I'm done with this." Parker motions at the cramped workspace. "I'll be piloting tugs. No need to brush up on Kentauran customs when I'll never see one again."

"Once we get the Tau Ceti beacon installed, I'm sure the Kentaurans will be in and out of the Sol system all the time. Probably the Atharans, too."

Parker snorts. "Atharans. Did you know there's not a single training module that mentions them? That's how much Fleet thinks of the alliance."

"I'm sure that has more to do with how outdated *Demeter*'s library is than anything."

"Even still," Parker scoffs. "I don't see the Earth-Lihatra thing lasting more than a few years. Once they see how dirt-poor the Kentaurans are and how little progress we've made since the Pavoid skirmishes, they'll back out of the alliance to sit on their hoards of gold."

Rowan raises an eyebrow. "That's an interesting take."

Parker winces. "Yeah, that came out wrong. Sorry." He tilts his head back and stares at the conduit-laden ceiling. "I just don't see myself spending time getting to know them. Besides Max and the other one, I'll probably never meet another Atharan in my life."

"Lilith."

"Yeah. Max and Lilith." Parker nods absently. "They'll probably be the only ones I meet."

"You've got a pretty good handle on their tech."

"Their tech's not bad," Parker admits. "It's surprisingly clever in its simplicity. The UI's some of the best I've ever seen."

Rowan consults his wristpad. "This should be the relay we're looking for."

The access panel was removed and set aside, but lost years ago. Maintenance records show it was last accessed nearly fifteen years ago, but surely it's been more recent than that. There's no sign of the bolts that once held it in place. They probably slid into a nearby junction during one of a thousand hyperspace jumps *Demeter* has made since then. Though covered in a thin layer of dust, the relay is still there. The ship's environmental filters should prevent this buildup, but given the years of neglect down here, Rowan is happy it's not grimier.

He runs a quick diagnostic scan. "Nothing obvious. Let me take a look." Shuffling wires aside, he folds back several layers of organic membrane. These were once encased in flexible conduits and sheathes, but those have been stripped away over the years.

"Chief?" Rowan asks. "Can you take a look at this?"

Parker scoots closer and leans in. "What in the twin hells is that?"

"So it's not just me. You see this black stuff?" Rowan leans in for a better view. "Kind of looks like hair."

"Burned wiring? Or fried fiber optics?" He tilts his head back and forth and squints, trying to focus his eyes, then he cautiously touches the foreign residue. "It's cold. Ouch! And it's fucking sharp." Parker sucks on his fingertip.

"If it's cold, it would've been this way for a while. But that doesn't check out. Comms just went offline last night." Rowan reaches out and brushes it with his fingertips. "And sharp like jellyfish stingers."

Rowan shifts the relay aside to reveal a nodule behind it. Gray bands spider out from the lump and thread through the conduits. "What do you make of this?"

"Looks like part of *Demeter*'s rootwork. It's probably where her systems sync the quantum frequencies. It's—" Parker trails off as he taps it lightly. "Yeah, you should call your specialist buddy to look at this. But don't tell her I said that."

Rowan consults his wristpad but can't get a signal this deep in *Demeter*'s bowels. He takes another look at the relay and the strange growth then snaps a few images with his wristpad's camera. "I'll be right back."

Parker closes his eyes and slumps against the cables. "Take your time, Lieutenant. I'll be right here when you get back."

Rowan weaves through the narrow passages until he reaches the corridor on Deck 17, where his wristpad finally reconnects. He texts the pictures to V, asking for some of her time, and waits for her reply.

A distant boom echoes through the ship, followed by electrical crackles. Seconds later, the stench of burned silicone fills the air. A wave of heat rushes from the maintenance tube, carrying the sickly scent of singed hair and cooked meat.

"Chief?" Rowan yells, panic rising. "Can you hear me?" His voice cracks. "Sir?"

Tapping emergency icons on his wristpad, Rowan steadies his breath. "This is Lieutenant Forsythe. Officer down. Send medical and fire teams immediately to Deck 17, Maintenance Access Tube 17-09a."

His voice tightens. "Hurry."

"The captain will be in shortly to see you." Commander Lillian Bekhti motions for Rowan to enter the oblong officer's wardroom. "Have a seat over there, Leftenant," she says in her professionally clipped accent. "The captain will see you presently." She steps aside for Rowan to enter then turns briskly to leave—something on this ship always needs her immediate attention—and shuts the door behind her.

There's an overhead light flickering, and Rowan quickly places a work order from his wristpad to fix it. There's also a cavity in the ceiling where *Demeter*'s internal sensors once were, meaning *Demeter*'s AI has no presence here. It looks like it's been missing for years, so he waits to ask the captain before doing anything about it. Considering the ship's age, the printed wood paneling is in good shape, and he's happy to see that at least some effort has been made to preserve *Demeter*'s dignity during her final years. Overall, there doesn't seem to be much work needed here compared to other compartments throughout the ship.

The silence in the cramped wardroom is punctuated by the faint hum of the ship's engines and the exertion of nearby air scrubbers. It smells less like ammonia here than on the rest of the vessel, and he speculates this is why V is asked to spend so much more time on the organic atmospheric filters on this part of the ship than on the rest.

The back wall bears the proud emblem of the ship: a beautiful woman holding a sheaf of wheat and a clay water jug, with the runes for ESS *DEMETER FF-513* written amidst the laurel of olive leaves that encircle her. The ancient emblem is a callback to the first days of Earther space exploration, when missions were named for ancient Greek gods or the prophets of astrophysics.

Surrounding the plaque are small, framed photographs that chronicle a storied past of the ESS *Demeter* and its commanding officers. Each picture captures Captain Hargreaves at a pivotal moment of his career. The first shows a young ensign with a hopeful glint in his eyes alongside a captain who has since passed. Another shows a seasoned lieutenant with medals adorning his uniform, and finally, one shows the commanding officer he is today.

One small photograph in the middle of the arrangement catches Rowan's eye. It shows a young Commander Hargreaves with his arm casually draped around a stern-looking man Rowan recognizes from a darker time in his career. It seems that Commodore Linnaeus, the officer who presided over Rowan's tribunal following the catastrophic events at Jupiter Station, had once been a captain on board *Demeter,* with Hargreaves serving as his chief executive officer.

Rowan knows that Fleet officers operate in tight circles. Do a good job and get a good follow-up assignment. Impress the right officers and advance your career. Blow up a few colleagues and get sent to the outer reaches of space on a clunker ship to be forgotten.

The narrow metal shelves are nearly bare, holding a few coffee creamer pods, salt shakers, and sweet relish packets. Rowan pockets a handful of packets, imagining their value at the next crew swap meet.

After several agonizing minutes of pacing and anticipating the worst, Captain John Hargreaves enters the wardroom. Rowan jumps to attention, his heart racing. This is his first one-on-one situation with the captain during the voyage, and he's just stolen condiments.

"Lieutenant, have a seat, please?" The captain points to a nearby chair as he lowers himself into his own with a familiar creak of metal.

Rowan steps forward and adjusts the heavy chair just enough to avoid scraping it across the deck—an instinct from too many briefings in rooms like this. He lowers himself carefully, bracing one foot against the leg to steady the subtle wobble he can feel even before he fully sits. His posture straightens reflexively: the bearing of a proper officer, whether or not he still feels like one.

Captain Hargreaves sits and rubs his cuffs as he gets comfortable in the worn chair. "How's our section chief doing?" The question is a simple request for a status update, but there's a sincere concern in the worn cracks of his eyes.

"Doctor Essien says he'll be fine, Captain. He's regrowing one of his hands already. They let me check in on Chief Parker for a few minutes. He was awake, alert, and aware of what happened." Rowan pauses before making an overly optimistic assertion, "It sounds like he'll make a full recovery and be back at his post in a few weeks."

"That's great to hear, Lieutenant Forsythe. I've been considering options for who'll take his place in the interim. I think that should be you. Temporarily, of course."

"Sir?"

"I understand if you're still not up to another leadership position. But I think, for now, you're the right person to step into his role—pick up where he left off, so to speak. Someone has to fill his shoes for a while."

Rowan cringes at the word "shoes" and stifles the memory of the last time he was in charge. He stares blankly at the captain.

Captain Hargreaves leans forward, his expression softening. "I understand if there's hesitation, Lieutenant Forsythe. I know what happened at Jupiter Station—what you lost there. But this is a temporary assignment. It's a chance for you to step up again."

Rowan clears his throat. There's no pushiness in the captain's tone, but there is a pressure to commit all the same. "Yessir. I can step in. It's just for a few weeks."

"Yes, Lieutenant Forsythe. I'm sure you'll adjust in a few days." The captain leans back in his metal chair, subtly letting Rowan know it's okay to sit at ease and take a breath.

Rowan relaxes his left leg, and the chair rocks. He quickly regains his balance, but he averts his eyes from the captain out of embarrassment.

The captain laughs softly and shifts in his chair, which rocks slightly beneath him. He nods toward the flickering light, then back to Rowan with a dry look. "Add it to the list."

Rowan meets his gaze and points to the overhead light. "Sir, I already have the work order to replace the ballast at 07:45 tomorrow. Not sure I can do anything about these old chairs, though."

The captain sets his palms on the metal table, his cufflinks making a sharp clang. "See? I knew you were the right person for the job." He smiles and leans back unsteadily in his chair, amused with his decisiveness in making the staffing decision without input from the ship's computer yet again.

Rowan stands at attention to leave.

"Not so fast, you're not dismissed yet." The captain's smile fades slightly, his tone shifting to something more pressing. "Now that you're Section Chief Forsythe, we need to have a rather important conversation."

"Sir?"

"When will we be back in touch with Fleet again? And what do you know about why we're offline?"

Rowan sits down deliberately. "I assume Chief Parker updated you on our comms status?"

"He did, earlier this morning. I went to broadcast the induction ceremony back to Earth and got that annoying little red exclamation icon. Chief Parker briefed me that you two were looking into it. I assume that's when the accident happened."

"Yessir." Rowan glances at the picture with Hargreaves and Linnaeus, then back to the captain. "We were investigating."

"Anything I should know about, Section Chief?"

"I'm still piecing things together, sir." Rowan sits at attention, eyes forward. He thinks about the right words to say, a lesson learned the last time he was briefing a commanding officer about an unlikely accident. "Sir, I don't have a full answer yet, but I'm investigating the loss of fleetwide comms. I have several leads, including hardware malfunctions involving multiple relays. I'm also not yet ruling out the possibility of bad software updates."

"Good, that's what I wanted to hear. So you have a handle on this, Chief Forsythe? May I call you Rowan?" The gentle ease in the captain's face from earlier is gone. There's genuine concern in his eyes.

"Yessir." Rowan's answer is intended to sound like it belongs to each question at once. He most definitely does not have a handle on this.

The captain catches the hesitation in Rowan's eyes. "Anything you'd like to add?"

He draws a breath through gritted teeth and adds, "Sir, I

wouldn't rule out the possibility of sabotage." He meets the captain's gaze.

Hargreaves nods, thinking for a few moments. Eventually, he asks, "Does this seem aimed at Earth? Or maybe at our friends out here?"

Rowan hasn't been asked his opinion by command staff in years, so he's at a loss for how to respond. He slumps his shoulders in resignation. "I don't know, sir. But just between you and me?"

The captain nods approvingly.

"It's a total comms outage across all bands, which can't be a coincidence. It feels deliberate, sir, but it's hard to say if they meant to cut us off from Fleet or our allies. Maybe both."

Hargreaves relaxes and stares at the ceiling. "Any ideas who might do something like that?"

"Not specifically, sir. But if I had to guess—" Rowan hesitates, glancing at the captain before deciding to speak plainly. "Earth-Firsters, maybe. The outage would make them happy."

"Understood, Chief Forsythe. If anyone is going to be happy about the comms being offline, it's people who share that sort of unsavory ideology." After a moment, the captain adds, "Our top priority is the success of this mission. To do that, I need you to get short-range comms back online first. If we can talk to our allies, they can relay our status back to Fleet. Understood?"

"Yessir, understood."

"One more thing, Chief Forsythe: a section chief should look the part. Maybe see about getting this back into regulation shape?" Hargreaves motions around his head and face. "It'll set a good example for your team."

Rowan inwardly groans at the idea of setting an example but nods at the captain's order to clean up his mussed hair and five o'clock shadow.

FOUR
THE TABLE BETWEEN US

*We mend fractures not with silence, but with gestures —
warmth offered, rituals remembered, a shared song, and something passed from one root to another.*

— Scripture of Kin and Root

Rowan Forsythe rubs his forehead as he slumps in a worn leather booth in the dimly lit Lolly Galley. His third glass of grav rests in his hand, its sweet sting a fleeting comfort against the pounding ache from his first day as Section Chief—a role he's barely had for forty-eight hours. The warm burn slides down his throat, a small reminder that, at last, the day is officially over.

The emergency paperwork, the personnel rosters, and the routine maintenance checks were nonstop. Getting someone to fix the flickering light in the command crew's wardroom early in the morning was like pulling grumpy teeth, even though the requisition and job assignment were in place the day before. Even worse, mediating the petty bickering among crewmates over duty roster assignments or lunch shifts chewed up half his day.

Then, Max and Lilith are required to take mandatory breaks. The Atharans, as a whole, refuse to switch to Fleet clocks, so their ritualistic diversions shift by uneven minutes every day. Until recently, *Demeter* has managed their scheduling—but over the past few days, she's inexplicably stopped handling most crew accommodations, leaving them to Rowan to solve.

After they left for their third such break near the end of shift rotation, Rowan overheard Hector speaking in hushed tones with one of the hyperspace engineers. Their conversation stopped the moment Rowan stepped closer, but not before he caught Max's name and a mention of the failing interfaces. The conversation only lasted a moment, but it left an impression that tension between Fleet and Atharan crewmembers will quickly escalate if the comms situation isn't resolved soon.

There's not enough grav left on board *Demeter* to handle this chaos. He runs his free hand over his fresh crew cut, still not used to the feel of it.

A faint hint of acrid smoke lingers as someone leaves the fritters in the deep fryer for too long. His uniform will smell tomorrow, but he doesn't care right now. There won't be any time to get his one good jacket cleaned before his shift.

His table is scattered with the remains of drinks and snacks. Most were already there when he arrived, and no one had cleaned the table in between uses. There's still room for a few more tumblers and his data pads, although the table is growing sticky.

Between choruses of throbbing bass from poorly chosen musical selections, he can hear the occasional sound of dishes being washed in the back or flatware scraping the final morsels from plates. The Lolly Galley is quiet tonight, the kind of easy lull it usually sees on midweek evenings—an oddly persistent normalcy in the wake of everything that isn't.

Tomorrow, he has to finalize plans for a series of emergency training exercises to keep the engineering staff up to date on their Red Alert certifications. If they don't recertify, nearly a dozen crew members could be sidelined. It's just a formality, but the command staff strongly consider it when making promotion recommendations. He slides between screens on his datapad, reviewing performance evaluations and project assignments, trying to find the best way to set up the trials fairly. He's not looking forward to the drills, neither the planning nor the part where some crew member will inevitably complain, "But that's not how Chief Parker does it."

Parker's injury and the captain's hasty decision have thrust him into this role. Tonight, he's feeling the unwanted weight of it all. Parker might be a beloved crew chief, but it's becoming clear that's partly due to the things he lets slide. Like the table in front of Rowan—still cluttered with empty glasses and scattered crumbs, waiting for Daren to come clean it—the engineering section is another slow mess. And now, Rowan's the one expected to clean that up too.

The crew's murmurs fill the disjointed space in the galley. The clinking of glasses and the low hum of conversation are a comfort, yet it all feels distant and oddly unfulfilling. More than anything, he wants to leave his shift behind him for the night, but he can't. The drills must go on.

Customers come and go all night. Max and Lilith appear briefly with their special beverage devices to take their hyper-regulated ceremonial drink breaks. Daren doesn't like this, but he's been publicly ordered to stand down for inter-species relation reasons and now contemptuously deals with it. The music eventually shifts to something more subdued, but the occasional bad choice of Astralcore is added to the mix and scrambles Rowan's concentration. Rowan finally relaxes when someone plays an entire Nanofunk album from start to finish and sways away his troubles.

That is until Doctor Hawthorne swaggers into the Lolly Galley, her trademark lab coat billowing behind her, revealing some obscure band t-shirt from generations ago. Rowan tries to ignore her but notices she's looking around. Most of the time,

Hawthorne marches directly to the booth that no one else would dare occupy and orders a stiff drink from Daren. When in a more gregarious mood, she'll join whatever revelry is happening at the bar and buy the next round of drinks, but not tonight.

This time, she locks eyes with Rowan and walks directly to his small booth.

Well, crap, Rowan thinks. He wonders if she could've heard the thought but quickly reassures himself that Druids can only connect with the thoughts of other female Druids. *I hope she's not expecting to see me.*

She is.

"May I join you?" She shows no sign of waiting for an answer before sliding into the booth. Hawthorne sits with the practiced ease of someone used to commanding attention, even in a dimly lit galley light years from home. Her lab coat pools behind her as she leans forward and clasps her hands on the sticky table. "I hope I'm not interrupting," she says, though she clearly doesn't care if she is.

Rowan sets his datapad aside, trying to project casual indifference. "Not at all, Doctor. What can I do for you?" He's practiced this professional demeanor all day, so it's becoming second nature.

She winces. "It's Thorney. I've asked you before."

"Right. Thorney. What's on your mind?" He gestures vaguely toward her, trying to mask his unease. V told him about Hawthorne's intrusive request this morning. While she omitted most of the details, Rowan has already chosen a side.

Her gray eyes narrow as she studies him, but she doesn't comment on his discomfort, evident to even a non-empath. "It's about *Demeter*. Or rather, her consciousness." She sighs, her voice dropping to a quieter, more concerned tone. "I haven't been able to reach her for days. Something's going on with her."

Rowan straightens, the personal drama already fading away. "What do you mean you can't 'reach her?'"

Hawthorne frowns, twisting the fabric of her coat sleeve

absentmindedly. "I use my baseline telepathic interface for all my work. It's how I synchronize the neural signals with her root-work systems. But lately," she hesitates, glancing around to ensure no one else is listening, "it's like she's not there. Not just quiet." She sucks a sharp breath. "Absent."

"That's not normal." Rowan frowns. He's already had one conspiratorial conversation in the past twenty-four hours, enough to last the rest of this mission. "Have you run diagnostics? It could be something technical. Maybe her organic systems were overloaded at the time."

"I've checked everything, even hardwired systems outside my purview. Technically, *Demeter* is fine. She's not, for lack of a better word, home." Hawthorne leans back, her frustration starting to show. "I asked V for help. She's the only one I know who could confirm whether it's just me or if there's something else seriously wrong."

Rowan's brow furrows. "V? I thought you and she had—" He trails off, searching for the right words, not wanting to air V's grief.

Hawthorne taps at the base of her skull. "Had common ground?" Hawthorne finishes for him. "We do. Well, I thought we did. My family and hers were in the same grand coven. I've known her mother since before she was born." Hawthorne's voice softens, a trace of reverence entering her tone, aware she's speaking to a non-believer. "I knew her mother before she became high priestess. I've tried to keep a respectful distance from V on this voyage, but I desperately need her help."

Rowan shifts uncomfortably.

"You're her best friend. Maybe you can help."

He scoffs. "I don't know about best friends, but we help each other whenever we can."

"You're the only person I've seen her talk to for more than a few moments at a time in the entire eight months we've been out to deep space. I figure maybe she'll listen to you."

"Ah, there it is." Rowan's lips tighten to a thin line. "She's not going to listen to me. She barely talks to me about Druidic stuff. That's something you have to sort out between you two."

Hawthorne leans back, pulls a flask from the inside of her lab coat, and sighs before taking a quick sip. "Perhaps. But maybe you have some insight into why she's so reluctant to help me with a little chaint?"

"Chaint?"

Hawthorne doesn't roll her eyes, but her tone carries her annoyance. Gaians rarely know anything about Druidism, even in the modern age. "Chaint is what we call telepathic connection. It's where we create a metaphysical connection, where Druids can share consciousness."

Rowan nods. "V's told me about it. I just never heard the word before."

"Chaint is how I connect with *Demeter*'s consciousness. Technically, I connect to her rootwork, and from there, I can enter the mechanical AI network. And that's the basis of how my new interface harness works."

"You plug your brain into the ship's mind? I thought V did that all the time without any special equipment."

Hawthorne takes a longer sip. "That's what's so amazing about her. No one else can do that. Sure, feelings and general ideas here and there. But most Druids can't chaint with the loquentes roots that underly *Demeter*'s rootwork."

Rowan frowns in disbelief. V makes her conversations with *Demeter* sound effortless. After an awkward silence, he asks, "So what do you need from her?"

"Can you ask her to reconsider? If she can chaint with *Demeter* and confirm she's still present, I'll assume the issue is with my interface. But if she can't..." Hawthorne leans in, her voice low but steady. "Then we may have a deeper problem. And I'd rather we understand it now—before it becomes something we can't ignore."

Rowan folds his arms. "I get that. And believe me when I say we're working on it. I'm already looking into some comm system failures that could impact your ability to talk to *Demeter*. So let us handle that problem." He rubs the Fleet patch on his jacket to be clear about who on board should be poking around in *Demeter*'s networks and circuitry. "Thorney," Rowan hesitates, weighing his words carefully. "Don't push her on this chaint stuff, okay? She's been through a lot. More than most can imagine. I'm sure she has her reasons."

Hawthorne's eyes flash with a mix of anger and hurt. "Reasons? Rowan, do you know what she said when I asked for her help? She called it a 'curse.' How can she think that about something such a big part of who she is?"

Rowan's hands raise reflexively before saying, "I don't think she sees it that way." He leans forward, his voice low and firm. "V's connection to Druidism isn't the same as yours. I know there's spirituality wrapped up in this telepathic ability you share, and I respect that. But for her, it's tied to things she doesn't want to relive."

Hawthorne stares at him, her expression unreadable. "She's stronger than she knows. I want her to see that."

"Maybe she doesn't want to go down that path." Rowan's tone softens, his gaze steady. "She doesn't talk about the details, not with me, but she left Earth for a reason. And she left for good."

Hawthorne slumps back in her chair, frustrated. "So what am I supposed to do? If something's wrong with *Demeter*, I need to know. We all need to know."

"Hey, I agree with you there, one hundred percent. Look, I'll help where I can," Rowan offers, his voice steady despite the weight of his new responsibilities. He doesn't want to drag his friend into something she wants to avoid, but maybe an outsider's perspective would be helpful for both of them. "Just, maybe, give V some space, okay? She might come around."

Hawthorne exhales slowly, nodding. "Fine. But time isn't something we have in abundance."

Rowan rakes a hand through his freshly trimmed hair, not quite meeting her eyes. "I know. That's what worries me."

Rowan picks up his glass of grav and tilts it toward her in mock surrender. "Maybe there's a Druid spell for this—wave a branch, whisper to the stars, offer a peace ritual or whatever it is you all do." His smile is crooked but not unkind. He presses the chilled tumbler to his forehead, savoring the coolness, then adds, "I give V a hard time about this stuff now and then, but I don't mean anything by it. Honestly—do you all actually do that kind of thing?"

Hawthorne snorts, paving the way for a reluctant smile. "You're a terrible drinking companion, Section Chief Forsythe." She empties her flask and stands to leave.

"Tonight?" He grins, letting the grav burn its slow path down. "Yeah. Guilty as charged. But thanks for putting up with me."

She tosses him a look over her shoulder, half a grin in her voice. "There is a peace offering ritual, you know." Then she's gone.

Night settles deep in the bones of the ship. V sleeps soundly, blanketed in dreamless, heavy silence—her favorite kind. Out here, far from home, silence is a gift. The cabin is cool and dark. During her first week on this trip, she installed a fan inside the ventilation shaft to pull air from a cooling pipe into the room. She sleeps under weighted blankets, but she shivers without them. Yet, the dark, crisp air around her is the only thing that encourages solid rest. Cold is divine.

Her slumbering consciousness drifts through the Tau Ceti system. She floats endlessly in the glow of a dim star, quiet and cold, surrounded by uninhabited worlds. V embraces the stillness. It comforts her in a way nothing else can.

The door chime sounds.

V wakens but keeps her eyes squeezed shut. "Feck's sake, what now?"

She lies in her bunk and pulls her weighted blanket up to her neck, hoping the disturbance will disappear on its own.

The door chime sounds again, somehow louder than before. V buries her angry face into a pillow, thinking, *It's too late to still be tonight and too early to be tomorrow morning.* Her body aches from a week of celebration, sleepless nights, and emergency repairs.

Whatever it is, leave me alone.

V lays still in her bunk a little longer. With any luck, whoever it is will go away and call back tomorrow at a reasonable hour.

The door chime sounds for a third time, followed by several insistent blasts.

"Goddessdammit, I'm coming!" she snaps, flinging the weighted blanket against the wall. She rubs her palms into her eyes and thinks, *Is it late? Early? Both? I don't care, just stop ringing the feckin bell!*

She pulls a crumpled T-shirt from the floor and tugs it down low enough to not, she hopes, need pants. She stomps to the cabin's hatch to see who's calling.

Feck.

Hawthorne.

Instinctively, V places a foot on the inside of the hatch and grabs a support bar as if she were trying to prevent someone from shoving their way inside.

"What do you want?"

"I know I wrecked your day. I probably wrecked your week. But I want to make an offer, something to make it right."

V rubs her eyes with her free hand. "What? You know calling this late—or early, I can't even tell right now—just makes it worse."

Hawthorne's sigh is audible through the thick metal hatch. "Look, luv, I know I left things in a bad place between us. I need to make it up to you."

V cracks the hatch open slightly, just enough to speak quietly. "What time is it?"

"The Lolly Galley just closed."

V groans. "That means it's after 0300."

"Yeah, Daren kicked us out. Then I stopped by my cabin for this."

V leans her head against the bulkhead to peer through the gap.

Hawthorne holds out a plastic bag containing something dark and clumpy.

V opens the hatch a little wider, then plants her foot back to prevent it from opening any wider. She squints to ease the contrast between the darkness of the cabin and the lighted corridors outside.

In her best Received Pronunciation accent, she asks, "What's this?" She slumps her shoulder against the bulkhead casually. She knows what it is.

"It's theembark paste"

"And you want to puff it right now?"

"Why not?" Hawthorne slips into a heavy Galweigian accent but still sounds full of herself. "Best way to apologize, yeah? Besides, you look like you could use it, luv."

V hasn't smoked theembark in half a year, and certainly not since she was first charged with monitoring *Demeter*'s rootwork systems. She can't imagine how Hawthorne smuggled it on board—or how much, if there's enough to share eight months later.

V moves her foot and pushes the hatch wide open with a "please come in" gesture. Closing the hatch, V smiles crookedly. She presses a button, and when the harsh lights flicker to life, she waves a hand at a stool next to a built-in metal desk covered in t-shirts and coveralls in various stages of reuse.

Hawthorne enters the room silently. She stands next to the desk-turned-wardrobe. In a second sheepish offer, she holds the bag up again, this time with both hands.

Without saying a word, V turns around to open a drawer built into the wall and rummages through its contents. From the back of the drawer, she grabs a small glass pipe she used in the first months of the voyage before exhausting her stash. V shoves the coveralls from the stool and pulls them beside her bunk. She slumps down and offers the stool with a gentle pat.

As Hawthorne takes a seat, V holds up the pipe for her.

"What's all this about?" V finally asks.

"I heard about your friend in the explosion."

"He's not my friend. He's my friend's friend."

Hawthorne sits back slightly. "I heard about your friend's friend. Are you okay?"

V shrugs. "Not really. I don't even like the guy. But it's the kind of thing that gets under your skin anyway."

"Do you want to talk about it?"

"Not really."

Hawthorne shrugs off the harsh dismissal and begins filling the pipe. Without taking her eyes off of her handiwork, she says, "I've met yer mum a few times."

Hawthorne's accent reminds V of home, sitting in front of a fireplace in the early autumn.

"You knew Muther?"

"Yeah. Sort of. I like her."

V huffs and slumps back down on her bunk. "Of course you would."

Hawthorne finishes packing the pipe and holds it out towards V, along with a lighter pulled from her pocket. V lights the pipe, inhales deeply then coughs. She's fallen out of the practice of holding large pulls of smoke in her lungs for long. She arches an eyebrow in wry gratitude before handing it back.

Hawthorne takes the pipe and, after holding her breath for a dozen seconds, casually exhales the smoke. She offers the pipe again, but V holds out a hand and gives a slow head shake.

Hawthorne sets the pipe down on V's desk and asks, "Do you want to talk about your sister?"

"No." She pauses.

"Okay. I can leave if you'd like."

V pauses for an awkward beat. "I don't want to talk about Parker's accident. And I don't want to talk about what happened to Ris, what I did to her."

Hawthorne waits in patient silence but eventually offers, "Do you want to talk about Galway and how feckin cool Merion was back in the day?"

"Yes." V leans against the wall on the other side of the bunk and pulls her knees up. She grabs her wristpad from under her quilt, taps a few icons and a few seconds later, the opening notes of "Hells" begin to chime.

Hawthorne nods approvingly and asks, "Ever been to Inshmore?"

"Of course I have." There's clear indignation in V's voice; no self-respecting Merion fan been to no fewer than three concerts there. "That's where Ris took me to see Merion for the first time." The conversation keeps coming back around to Ris, so V turns up the music just as the bassline starts to thrum. She resists turning up the volume as loud as the song deserves, given the odd hour.

"Hawthorne, listen. I'm sorry I lost it on you like that." V shrugs and tries to explain. "I still don't want to chaint, but I know that a little poke to see if something's not right isn't going to hurt anything." V wraps her arms around her knees. "I don't want to hurt anybody else like I did Ris."

The air goes still and quiet as Hawthorne reaches out with her mind.

<You didn't kill your sister, V. I don't know what you saw that day, but I know it wasn't because of something you did.>

"I don't know what I did that day either, but—" An unexpected tear rolls down V's cheek.

"So tell me what you do know, luv?"

V wipes her cheek with the back of her hand. Staring across the room as if to peer back through time, she begins. "It was just before the holidays. We were in school, she was in Grove of Glenoak, and I was at Rimeholt Academy, hundreds of kays away. Ris was going home for the first time in a year, and I couldn't wait to see her. I was supposed to leave on the same day, but I got snowed in. You know how Skye gets that time of year. Anyway, I was going to be stuck at school for at least a few more days."

"Yeah, it can get savage up there."

"I was so desperate to see her, you know? And what if I missed my chance? What if she was gone by the time I could make it back home?" The tenor in V's voice is nearly unrecognizable. Her eyes are distant.

"So what'd you do?"

"I decided to test it, to see if I could reach that far out. I'd been practicing every day, trying to see how far I could push. I dug deep." Shock and guilt wash over her face. "I mean really deep. I found a lot of wattage in here."

Hawthorne doesn't say anything. Her usual easy confidence falters, her expression caught somewhere between disbelief and quiet concern.

V shakes her head, trying to find a way to articulate the experience. "Sorry, 'wattage' is the only way I can think of for how strong I push. I know that sounds weird. Other Druids don't know what I'm talking about, either. It feels like I turn on this generator inside my head, and the next thing you know, I can reach out for kays at a time."

Hawthorne chaints, *<No, I don't know that feeling, but I think I understand what you mean. What happened that day?>*

V vocalizes with a shaky whisper, "I could see her. Ris. I could see her as plain as I can see you right now. I know we connected. She said hi and told me she loved me."

V clears her chest with a slight cough, the last little sting left from the pipe. Her cheeks are flush, and she clenches her jaw as she struggles to find her words again. "Suddenly, this massive—I don't know what it was—but this overwhelming darkness was there. It was smothering. Like I somehow became so heavy that I crushed her." V's eyes well up.

<What really happened, luv?>

"I don't know. I didn't know I could push energy that hard. No one should be able to do something like that. Even Muther can't do that. It was like, one second I'm connecting with Ris, and the next—" She gulps. "It was like I collapsed on top of her like a mountain caving in."

Hawthorne is at a loss for words. This doesn't match the story every Druid knows about the circumstances of Ris's death. It was undoubtedly a tragedy, and the extended community wept for the loss, but it was from natural causes. Every coven paid their respects. Druids from three planets, including Doctor Hawthorne, attended Iris Sandoval's final Rejoining.

Wattage. The word echoes in Hawthorne's mind. No Druid could reach her thoughts such a distance, much less carry that kind of power. There's no way V could've had a hand in Ris's death. It had to have been natural causes, just like the attending priestesses said.

Theembark makes a good peace offering, but it's far from ideal for clarity. Still, it's not a complete loss if it gets V to open up about her hatred for her power.

They sit in silence as the hours pass, gazing up at the thick, gray ceiling. Words fade, unspoken. Their thoughts stay closed. Sprawled across the floor on makeshift pillows, they listen to V's loud, angry playlist—Gravemarch, raw and guttural, too sharp for most ears but perfect for this moment. Each distorted howl and seismic drop bleed their grief into the heavy air. As the track dissolves into a slower, rasping melody—clearly a nod to Aether's Daughter's early work—its warped horns and ghostly pads soften the jagged edges of their silence.

Not healing. Not yet. But breathing again.

FIVE
QUANTUM INTERFERENCE

harmonic pattern: six tones
emergency override frequency: confirmed
origin: [unknown]
response: [accepted]
conclusion: totally normal.

— Parker & Hector's 'Signal 9' log
Auto-flagged (unverified)

The chime echoes through the corridor. The hatch slides open with a soft hiss, revealing Hawthorne, who presses the release. V stands at the threshold, dressed in her oldest jumpsuit, its knees scuffed and elbows patched. It's the kind of outfit she'd wear to crawl through a grease duct or patch a coolant line—but now, looking into Hawthorne's lab, she wonders if she should have worn something else.

"So this is the Root Cellar?" V asks, her voice low. She'd been expecting something grossly industrial and less alive.

Hawthorne steps aside, her eyes sharpening with amusement. "Yes, this is the infamous Root Cellar," she says, her tone edged with pride. "Come in, take it all in. Watch your step."

V shuffles inside, stiff and guarded.

The air is dense and warm, humid like a greenhouse. It clings to her skin, making her jumpsuit feel heavier with every breath. A rich, loamy scent rises to meet her, earthy and underpinned by something sharper. Fertilizer, or perhaps the tang of decay. It's not unpleasant, but Hawthorne's lab is surprisingly alive.

Her first thought is that she's glad she wore muck boots, but as she glances around, she realizes they're unnecessary. The deck gleams, meticulously clean except for neatly taped runs of bright orange conduit along the floor.

The lab is nothing like what she expected. Potted plants of every shape and size cover the space, their leaves swaying gently in the breeze from oscillating fans. Warm light filters down from softly glowing panels overhead, giving the foliage a restless, golden shimmer. Gray tanks filled with murky liquid and pale, spindly roots line the walls, their surfaces bristling with electrodes and snaking cables.

V's nose wrinkles as she takes a cautious step forward. She catches a familiar scent she can't place. Music drifts faintly from unseen speakers, blending with the whir of the fans and the soft rustle of leaves. For a moment, she's transported back to the breezy causeways of home, where salt air and green hills roll in an endless panorama.

But this isn't Galway. And this place, no matter how inviting, feels like it could swallow her whole if she lets her guard down.

V folds her arms tightly across her chest, drawing herself inward. "So," she says, trying to sound casual but not quite succeeding, "what exactly do you need me to do?"

Hawthorne gestures to a pair of deep, comfortable-looking chairs flanking a low table. "Would you like some tea, luv?"

The witch's brew, V thinks, her lip twitching with a faint grimace. That's what she'd called it growing up. It's the ceremonial nonsense her mother always served honored guests to make a good impression, and V privately mocked it every time. Her mother hated the nickname, so naturally, V used it all the more. At least the tea was good, though she will never admit it.

V steps closer, catching a whiff of the dry ingredients untouched in a small ceramic bowl on the serving table. The aroma is sharp, earthy, and unmistakably sweet, the kind of scent that slips past defenses, tugs at something too close to home.

V wrinkles her nose to hide her reaction. "How'd you get dried fig?"

Hawthorne smiles warmly. "You'd be surprised what still lies in *Demeter's* stores, even after all these months." The accompanying wink grates on V's nerves, but she doesn't flinch. "Please, have a seat," Hawthorne says, reaching for a glass kettle. "Let me pour you a cuppa."

V doesn't refuse the offer; Muther drilled the ritual into her since childhood, and even now, V won't challenge that. She never liked the ritual, but the tea is really good. She sighs and takes a seat in the nearest chair.

Hawthorne's tea ceremony skills are unsurpassed. She carefully pours the water over the dried fruit and leaves, stopping briefly to let the warm water soak entirely through the ceramic infusers before pouring more. She repeats this process several times before setting the glass kettle aside on a clay trivet. She then gently lifts the infusers from the wide mugs and swipes the soaked herbs into a nearby pot with her finger.

Hawthorne lifts her mug with both hands to let the wet scent waft over her face. Other than following the ceremony to make, Hawthorne diverges from the rest of the tea ritual. She crosses her feet into the oversized chair to cradle herself. She shuts her eyes and takes another deep whiff of the herbaceously fruity tea.

V pulls her mug closer despite the lab's warmth. The fresh tea is comforting. It's a homey relief. V could sit here all day like this, especially if she could listen to Merion's *Fragile Teeth* album on repeat.

Hawthorne taps on her wristpad, and an early cut of "The

Day the World Came Back" from an early album starts to play from nearby speakers.

Damn. She didn't hear that, did she? V wonders if she accidentally chainted her desire for music, specifically Merion, but quickly accepts the gesture as a coincidence. "Wait, I don't think I've heard this version before. It's so—"

"It's so raw, right? I love this version. It's from an early EP before they made it big. Supposedly, they recorded it in one take in Rik's garage on Cat's Row."

V taps her hands on the chair's arms, keeping with the irregular time that made the song such an instant classic. "This is so good." She waits for the drop, then starts belting out the lyrics about marauders turning the tide in the Tiberian War: "'The hardest punch we'll ever pack, the year the sky came crashing back!'"

Hawthorne joins her in the growling, rhythmic screams that follow to end the song in a crescendo of crunchy guitar noise.

"That's feckin brutal! I love this version." V rubs her arms to soothe the goosebumps, ignoring the Galwegian accent that slips through.

"It's so good." Hawthorne smiles, happy to share some Merion history V hasn't experienced.

They trade stories about the band—its meteoric rise, the drug-fueled collapse, and the comeback tours that cemented its legend. V first learned to love Merion through her big sister. Now, she feels that connection stirring again for the first time in years. Hawthorne, likely as old as V's mother, should feel distant, but instead, the bond feels closer, even hauntingly familiar, like the half-remembered moments she thought she'd buried with Ris.

Hawthorne finishes her tea with a contented sigh, delicately setting the empty mug aside. She lingers in the quiet for a moment, savoring the last drop of warmth before reality intrudes. Her expression softens when she looks at V, but there's no mistaking the gravity behind her gaze.

"V," she says gently, "I desperately need your help. I wouldn't ask if it wasn't important."

V shifts uncomfortably in her seat, clutching her warm mug to her chest. "What exactly do you need me to do?"

Hawthorne leans back, weighing her words. "How much do you know about my work on board *Demeter*?"

"Not much." V glances around the Root Cellar before lingering on the vats of gray roots with electrodes strapped to them. Each holds a small screen with data she doesn't comprehend. "I mean, I know you talk to plants. And to *Demeter*, I guess?"

"Not only talk to her," Hawthorne grins, "I commune with her. I'm talking full-on chaint." Her smile fades. "But lately, something's been wrong."

"Wrong?" V's disbelief cracks with curiosity.

Hawthorne points to the tanks behind her. "These are loquentes roots—the originals. We used the base plant species to develop *Demeter*'s organic components. Every hybrid AI in the Fleet, on Earth, basically anywhere."

V narrows her eyes at the tangled, spidery limbs. They look eerily similar to *Demeter*'s organic nodules, but so do many alien plants. "That's what's inside *Demeter*?"

"These are the raw versions, before xenohorticulturalists started fine-tuning them. Think of it like an early EP. Wild and rough, but capable of everything the polished version does." Hawthorne grins again, briefly, and wiggles a finger for emphasis. "Maybe even more."

"Nice reference," V mutters. "But what does this have to do with me?"

Hawthorne's grin fades completely. For the first time since V arrived, she looks uncomfortable. Her hands grip the armrests tightly. "Up until a few days ago, I could chaint with them. I'd use it like a bridge to reach *Demeter*'s organic consciousness. But now?" She waves her fingers like scattering dust. "Nothing. I can still sense them vaguely. It's like how you feel *Demeter*'s pain. I know they're present, but that's all. I'm locked out, and I don't know why."

V hesitates, Hawthorne's words articulating a disquiet that's been growing for days. The absence she felt earlier now has a name. Trying to dispel the thought by speaking aloud, she says, "I'm not sure I can help you with that."

Hawthorne leans forward, her gaze steady but softer. "I need you to try chainting with them. Just once. If you can get through to them, I'll know the problem is with me. If you can't…" She falters, the unspoken words speaking volumes.

"Doctor Hawthorne, I've already told you. The last time I used chaint, it ended badly. I won't go there again."

"First thing, it's just Thorney," Hawthorne says quietly. She holds V's gaze, her voice softer but edged with urgency. "And second, this won't end badly. I promise." Her eyes plead her case more desperately than her tone and promise.

Taking a deep breath, V nods. "Okay, I'll try." Her stomach churns. She already regrets this decision.

Hawthorne picks up a sleek metal device from her workstation, its curved bands and delicate arcs glinting under the lab lights. She holds up the filigreed contraption for V to examine. "This is what I call my tiara," Hawthorne says encouragingly. "It monitors basic telepathic patterns. Think of it like a mental compass, showing me where your thoughts are going."

V winces as she looks over the spiny protrusions meant to contact the skin.

Hawthorne laughs softly, shaking her head. "It's perfectly safe. Promise." She steps closer, holding the device just above V's head. "This will help convert your chaint signals into data I can track. Trust me, it'll be painless. I've done this a thousand times myself."

V flinches as the cold metal filaments touch her scalp, brushing over her temples and ears. "It's hot!" She squints as if the thing might zap her.

"Sorry, sorry." Hawthorne adjusts the fit carefully, her hands steady. "Your noggin is just a little smaller than mine, that's all. There. All set." She steps back, tapping a few commands on the console. The tiara hums faintly. "Okay, everything looks good. Take your time. Start with a deep breath."

Hawthorne taps a few commands on a nearby console. "I'm recording now, and everything looks nominal. Go ahead when you're ready, but, like I said, take your time." Her voice is calm and soothing. This feels like when V and Ris used to practice chaint together as children.

V closes her eyes. The lab fades and is replaced by a vast, quiet space as her mind reaches out. The roots' presence teases at the edge of her awareness. She focuses, trying to connect, but an invisible barrier pushes back, slamming her back into her own mind.

V pulls off the tiara in frustration. "I can't get through. It's like there's a wall."

Hawthorne leans over the console, studying the telemetry. "Okay, that's not unexpected," she says, though her voice carries a flicker of unease. "Sometimes the raw loquentes roots push back. It's a natural defense mechanism. Give them a gentle shove next time. It's totally harmless, I promise."

Reluctantly, V raises the tiara back over her head. Her fingers tremble slightly as she adjusts it. She closes her eyes again and reaches out. The roots' collective presence is there, stronger this time. She pushes gently, telepathically probing the barrier.

The resistance slams her back even harder. She jumps from her chair and opens her eyes. "It's like something's blocking me on purpose. I thought you said these things were basically braindead."

Hawthorne's brow furrows. "Let's try once more," she says carefully, "but don't force it too hard. Think of it like a soft bubble. You're supposed to be there; they just don't realize it yet. Walk in like you belong, and they won't question your presence."

V doesn't want to try again, but Hawthorne's pleading look

is hard to ignore. She takes a steadying breath, sits down, and slides the tiara back on. She closes her eyes for a third time.

Focusing, she pushes against the mental barrier. It's a tense, elastic presence. She bounces away from it again, but this time she's prepared. She imagines that it's more like a soapy bubble than an impassible barrier. Mentally, she feels around the edges, probing it, the elasticity ebbing and flowing with each touch. Instead of bursting it, she pulls it open with an imaginary version of her hands and slips inside.

The chaint connection snaps into place. Instantly, she wishes it hadn't.

A painful squelch shreds her thoughts. A twisted chorus of rusty metal grinds around her. Every sharp crack resonates painfully through her body. Something cruel and dark is here.

And it sees her.

She reaches for the loquentes roots, for *Demeter*, for anything familiar, but finds only vast emptiness. She can't feel Hawthorne anywhere. V is somewhere else in the galaxy, far from home.

Intense flashes of black lightning, like the dark auras that herald a migraine, streak across her mind's eye, each jagged bolt tearing at her consciousness. Effulgent filaments of anti-light stretch as far as she can see in all directions as a kaleidoscopic smear of anti-light surrounds her, pulling her across dimensions.

A long-suppressed trauma rises to the surface as fresh as if it happened yesterday. She has seen this abomination before—not something like it, but this dark beast specifically. She gazed into its abysmal maw the afternoon her sister died. This is the sickly specter V summoned while telepathically linked with Ris, the dark entity who swallowed Ris whole.

The last time she was here, she faced this thing with her sister at her side, before Ris's life was crushed into oblivion. This time, she's completely alone.

The dark energy shifts, writhing like a predator circling its prey. It seizes her mind and shakes her like a rag doll. She screams, soundless in the void, as her body is tossed through unending chaos.

The lab snaps back into place around her. Choking, V scrambles to her feet. She spits blood onto the deck, her hands trembling. "What the feck was that!" She collapses to the floor.

Hawthorne rips the tiara from V's head and cradles her face with both hands. V's skin is cold and blue. "V, are you okay?" Her thumbs push at V's eyelids as she checks for signs of cognitive disarray. Her fingertips feel around V's neck, skimming pulse points. Hawthorne's face is flush with panic. "What happened, luv? Tell me what you saw."

For a moment, V can't speak. Her breath comes in forced, shallow bursts. "I couldn't feel your presence. Or *Demeter*'s. Or those feckin roots." She shakes her head, her voice trembling. "I wasn't here. It wasn't anywhere near here. Goddess, it felt like a nightmare, but worse. I still feel it."

Hawthorne's face is concerned and confused. "Luv, you didn't go anywhere. You were only connected for a few seconds."

V's focus fades into the distance, but at least she's calming down and in control of her breathing again. "It felt like I was gone for a day."

Hawthorne's face is sober. "Can I show you something?"

V compartmentalizes the pain. Hawthorne doesn't seem to think she's crazy, so this can't be good. V's face becomes sharp and focused. She'll process this later when she's alone. She tugs down the front of her rumpled uniform jacket and asks evenly, "Show me what?"

Hawthorne beckons V to join her at the console. The monitors flicker to life as she taps a few commands to pull up telemetry data. "Here." She points to a faint cluster of signals on the screen. "For these first two attempts, I could map where your telepathic connections were landing. There's a physical location, a traceable anchor."

V leans in, her curiosity cutting through the lingering fog.

Her movements are cautious, one hand still clutching the edge of the console like an anchor. "That thing maps chaint connections to physical locations?"

Hawthorne nods, swiping through a series of digital overlays. "Among other things. I can track the ingress and egress points with the tiara and the lab sensors on the loquentes tanks. I can essentially draw conclusions regarding where your mind reaches out and what it touches." She pauses, fingers hesitating over the screen. "Here's where it gets weird."

She expands the telemetry from V's third attempt and points to a sudden jagged break in the readings, a wild spike that shoots into an empty expanse of nothing. "This is when you initially chainted with the loquentes roots after you broke through their barrier. Everything looked fine. And then—" She zooms out repeatedly, the scope of the readings stretching far beyond the screen. "You went off the map. Way off."

V gazes at the screen, then at Hawthorne. "Here be dragons."

Hawthorne shakes her head slowly, her voice low. "You said you couldn't feel me, *Demeter*, or the loquentes roots. This is why." She taps the frequency data. "Your chaint connection went so far out that I can't plot it. I can't make out a direction, much less a distance. There's nothing out there, V."

V stares at the screen, her hands tingling. Her voice steadies into crisp enunciation, attempting to mask her fear. "That's what it felt like, though," she says. "Like I got pulled into—somewhere else entirely."

Her eyes dart over the telemetry again, and something captures her focus. A sequence of letters and numbers she wishes she didn't recognize.

"6-E-Q-U-J-5." V's voice is flat with dawning recognition. She gives the screen a few hard taps, her expression darkening. "I know that signal." She taps heavily again on the screen. "This number."

Hawthorne sits up straighter, caught off guard by the recognition in V's voice. "How?"

"Parker," V grumbles with a mix of realization and annoyance. "That arsehole talks about this stuff all the time. He's always on about old frequencies and weird transmissions. I've heard him ramble about this exact sequence a hundred times." V stops when she sees Hawthorne's blank expression. "He's got this antique radio cult thing, and—"

Hawthorne's eyes brighten. "Then he might know what it is, or maybe where it's coming from."

V exhales sharply, bracing herself. "Yeah. He might." She scrubs a hand over her face. "He's still in medbay, poor bastard. Feels wrong barging in with questions—but here we are."

Hawthorne hugs V awkwardly. "I can't thank you enough. Can I offer you anything after that—"She points at the chair. "Can I fix you another cuppa?"

V stares at the chair where her dissociated body sat moments ago, shuddering from whatever dark thing that was. She shakes her head. "I kind of want to be anywhere else right now."

Before Hawthorne can respond, V turns and walks briskly to the hatch, pulling it open without so much as a glance back. "I'll go talk to Parker."

The door hisses shut behind her, leaving Hawthorne alone with the console's faint hum and the unreadable signal still pulsing on the screen.

There's no sliding door to the medical bay's primary entrance. Just an open arch, stark and wide—practical to a fault. Emergencies don't wait for doors to hiss open or bystanders to clear the way. Seconds can mean the difference between life and death.

The light here is punishingly bright, the kind that turns every shadow into an accusation. It's colder than the rest of *Demeter*, scrubbed of personality. No murals, no scuffed corners, no quirks of age or crew. Just smooth, sterile surfaces and the faint chemical sting of antiseptics. V squints as she hesitates at the threshold.

V lingers outside medbay's open hatchway, her hands digging into the pockets of her coveralls, shoulders hunched as if bracing against a wind that isn't there. She takes a step forward, then several back. She tries again but falters halfway. *You've got this. Just go in.*

She plants her feet, closes her eyes, and draws a long breath —slow, steady, deeper than she needs. The air is dry and cold, but she holds it in, lets it settle her pulse. When she exhales, it's with purpose. Not just to calm herself, but to claim space. Then, with one last breath, she crosses the threshold into the too-bright quiet.

Inside, the medical bay is still . Machines murmur softly, monitors pulse with slow, metered rhythms. It smells like bleach, ozone, and the faint tang of blood sealed behind adhesive patches.

She finds Parker's room quickly and stands before the privacy screen sooner than she'd planned. *This is going to suck so bad.* She presses the call button.

"Come in," Parker says almost immediately.

The privacy screen phases out, and V steps inside.

"Sandoval?" Parker's voice cracks with surprise as he struggles to sit up. His injured arm is encased in an inflated tube filled with something writhing as it repairs the limb. His hand is missing several fingers that have yet to regrow. Half his face, including one eye, and his left shoulder are covered with adhesive patches attached to wires descending from an overhead medical assembly. Most of his hair is gone.

She didn't know what to expect, but it wasn't this. The injuries are worse than she imagined—raw and clinical in a way that drains the words from her throat. She expected this conversation would be hard; now it feels almost cruel. Whatever resentment she still carries buckles beneath the sight of him like this.

"Parker?" she asks slowly, her tone a mix of shock and guilt.

"I'm okay. It's not as bad as it looks." Embarrassed, he tries to cover the injured arm with his blanket, but it doesn't cooperate. "I didn't expect," he starts, blinking his one visible eye. "What are you doing here?"

For a moment, she's not sure how to answer. "I just came to check on you." That's not why she's here at all, and she shakes her head to refocus. Arms crossed, she fidgets with her elbows. "Actually, I have to ask you—" She glances at the medical equipment and his injuries, feeling ridiculous about asking him anything. *Why am I here, pestering him about some stupid quantum comms signal while he looks like this?*

He casually raises what were once his eyebrows. Of course, she wasn't here to check on him; that should come as no shock. Parker studies her for a moment, then lets out a soft laugh. "It's fine, Sandoval. Ask me whatever you came here for."

She exhales, thankful he's making this easier. "That quantum comms signal you're always going on about. The one that's like six-E-Q-J—"

"6-E-Q-U-J-5," he corrects her, his voice lighting up despite the rasp. "You want to talk about the WOW signal right now?"

"The what?"

"That's what we call that field frequency. The WOW Signal. It's been called that for hundreds of years, I think." He shrugs, then winces as the movement pulls at his injuries.

V hesitates, realizing how strange this is going to sound. "When you hear these signals, how do you pinpoint their distance or direction? Do you have to take multiple readings for triangulation, or—?"

Parker's good eye narrows as much as his sutures will allow. "You're serious?"

"Humor me."

"Okay. Normally, you'd need multiple readings from different points to triangulate, but most signals are too faint to track like that. So, we listen constantly and hope for repeats. We can estimate distance and bearing if we catch the same signal twice from two locations."

"Like a big game of Memory Match?" she asks, her Galwegian accent bleeding through.

"That's one way to dumb it down, but sure," he says with a dry grin. "We collect as many samples as we can and cross-reference. If we get a repeat, we can start mapping the sources. It's like building a giant treasure map, one dot at a time."

"So you *can* map where it's coming from," she says, half-hopeful.

Parker laughs and instantly regrets it. "If that were possible, the entire radiographer community would've cracked this centuries ago. Trust me, we'd be pinging signals all over every quadrant of every star system we've ever colonized."

"Okay, but hypothetically—"

"Hypothetically," he cuts her off, "if we could ping a signal at will, we'd take two readings and chart the resonance. After that, pinpointing the source would be easy. But that's all theoretical—none of that has ever worked out in practice before."

"Of course not. But, I have a stupid question to ask you."

"You're not just asking for fun, are you?"

"No. I'm working with Doctor Hawthorne on something. I may need your help."

"Hawthorne? So this is some Druid thing you ladies are cooking up."

She looks for something to throw, but there's nothing loose in the small recovery room. Instead, she answers simply, "It's complicated."

She hesitates. The question sounds absurd even in her head, but she asks it anyway. "If someone could... I don't know. Respond to one of those old signals. Could you use that?"

Parker blinks, surprised by the shift in her tone. Then, slowly, his expression shifts. He adjusts his posture on the gurney, trying to sit a little straighter despite the meds. "If we—if you could, somehow—force a response to one of the past signals..." He trails off for a second, focusing through the haze. "Then pinging it from a different location in space would let us start the quantum resonance mapping."

V leans back on one foot, summoning the courage to ask, "What would you need for that?"

"I could use the radio I have set up in my cabin. I installed a receiver on *Demeter*'s hull a few months ago. Maybe we can use that to—"

"You did what?"

"Yeah, you know all those EVAs I did for 'training'?" Parker struggles to mime air quotes with his remaining hand. "If there was nothing that needed doing out there, maintenance-wise, I would install old radio equipment for listening to signals. And before you complain, *Demeter* didn't mind. She says it reminded her of how space used to sound back in the days before Earther expansion."

"We'll talk about that later, because I don't think she's a fan of stitching things into her outer hull that aren't strictly necessary. But since it's already installed out there, tell me: what can that equipment do, exactly?"

"It's a long-band receiver patched into a quantum repeater. Doesn't broadcast, just listens—mostly for stuff nobody else bothers tuning to."

V glances toward the medical displays, eyeing the bandages and readouts, feeling the wrongness of pressing him while he's like this. She rubs the back of her neck, caught between duty and guilt.

It's just Parker, she rationalizes, and asks, "Can we borrow it?"

To her surprise, he says, "Sure. You'll need someone who knows how those old analog quantum comms systems work. Someone like Hector or Rowe. They're not part of *Demeter*'s root-work, so you'll need my login credentials. But," and he holds up a defiant finger, "only if you promise you'll keep me in the loop. And I mean real-time, play-by-play. Got it?"

"Yeah, I'll ask Rowan for help. Just until you get out of here, I mean." She presses her right fist over her heart. "I'll keep you in the loop, I promise."

Before Parker can respond, the privacy screen behind V opens. Hector steps inside, his arms crossed. "Didn't know we had visitors." His tone is light, but there's an edge to it.

"I'm just leaving," V says quickly, stepping back toward the open hatch.

Hector narrows his eyes at her, then glances at Parker. "You shouldn't be wasting your energy on hubrists, matey."

"Hector," Parker warns, his eye flashing, "not now."

Hector holds up his hands in mock surrender but mutters under his breath, "You know I'm right."

In the corridor, Hector's voice mocks her. "Which one of those bugs do I need to tear apart for this?"

V's lungs seize, her fists clenching at the ugly slur for the Kentaurans. She decides not to respond, though her steps falter for an instant. Hector's frustration may come from worry for his matelot, but the venom in his words has no place on board this ship.

Rowan hunches over his workbench, tools and wires scattered around him in organized chaos. The glow from nearby visual displays provides all the light he needs. The sterile smell of metal and lubricant fills the small, dimly lit lab. It's a refuge from the much larger engineering bay, giving him a quiet place to focus. It's a sanctuary where the weight of unexpected duties is lifted from his shoulders.

The soft hum of *Demeter*'s systems and the occasional beep of his console offer a soothing rhythm as he calibrates a quantum sensor. It's one of many that's been acting up lately.

He sighs and reaches up to play with his newly trimmed hair. Then he holds the sensor underneath a magnification lamp for the extra light. His eyes are tired from the time spent repairing two similar sensors. He's repaired more this week than in the previous eight months of the voyage. *Demeter* is aging, and every fix is a fleeting victory.

The door to his lab hisses open. Bright light floods the room with a gust of recycled air—cooler, cleaner than what's been stewing inside. Rowan looks up at the interruption. Hawthorne stands in the doorway in her signature gray lab coat, pockets brimming with instruments and data pads. She doesn't speak, but the way her eyes find his says she's been holding this breath for a long time.

Rowan sits up straight. "Doctor Hawthorne, what brings you here?"

Hawthorne's fame and reputation as a cutting-edge scientist often allow her to skip past the tedium of introductions and pleasantries. She has a well-deserved reputation for showing up when she needs something and disappearing before her colleagues know what hit them.

"I need your help with a telemetry report, Leftenant." I understand this might be your field of expertise."

He motions for her to take a seat opposite him. "What's the problem?"

"I asked our mutual friend V to help me run a test on some of my equipment." Hawthorne considers if many people know about V's telepathic issues but assumes a close friend like Rowan surely understands. "She made an unusual connection. We tried to track its location, but according to this data, it's entirely too far away for anyone to contact. Not even someone as gifted as V."

Rowan squints, not knowing how personal this discussion might be for V. "I'm not sure I can really answer that." He hesitates, choosing his next words carefully. "She actually used her telepathy? With you?" He shakes his head. "That's seems rare. I didn't think she'd be willing"

"I'm afraid so. But I took your advice and made a peace offering. And now she's agreed to help."

Rowan sets the sensor down and crosses his arms. "I won't pretend to know a lot about Druids, but I know she's not a fan of your religion. I don't want to speak out of turn here, but that had to be a really solid peace offering."

Hawthorne squeezes both her temples with a single hand. "You're absolutely right. She agreed to help because it's important." When he doesn't pry but clearly wants to, she adds, "I asked her to help me with—" The normally collected Hawthorne shifts uncomfortably in her stool.

Rowan finally asks, "Help you with what?"

"For the past few days, I've been experiencing some difficulties." She taps the back of her skull, then pauses to draw a quiet, centering breath. Saying this aloud feels wrong—especially to a Gaian who still looks confused. "I can't establish a connection to *Demeter*'s consciousness or the loquentes roots in my lab. At first, it was like she wasn't there anymore. But now, it's almost as if," and she leans closer to whisper the rest, "something is blocking me."

Rowan's face is empty, hoping he misunderstands.

"We call our deeper telepathic connections the chaint. One of us can refuse to accept the connection; that's normal. But this is like something else is deliberately blocking the chaint."

Rowan nods, understanding where the conversation is going.

"Something is blocking our attempts to connect. At first, I thought someone on board had done something to *Demeter*'s AI systems or to the rootwork, but we ruled that out. V somehow managed to break through, but not to *Demeter*. She made contact with something else. Something out there."

Rowan leans back in his chair so far that it nearly tips. "What could be blocking you like that?"

"I don't know. When I told V that someone might be sabotaging the mission, she told me that the ship's comms are out, too, and that other systems have been failing. That was before we discovered this." She produces a small tablet from the inside her lab coat and slides it across the table.

"See here?" She points to the data trails on the screen. "The quantum signatures I recorded left a trail that we can follow."

Rowan spends a few seconds orienting to the data format before spotting a familiar pattern. He points at the curving end of a linear signal. "This is where your data ends? This curl where the signal measurements interfere with the trajectory—this is a quantum comms signal."

"Yeah, sort of. My equipment is tuned to more sensitive levels since I normally only measure incredibly short distances. A few hundred meters, perhaps." She purses her lips to say something that shouldn't be possible. "This reading shows a trail of over half a billion kilometers. Chaint can't reach that far. Maybe it's a sensor ghost, or some kind of echo. What do you think, Leftenant?"

He connects the pad to a terminal display for a wider perspective. "Call me Rowan. And that doesn't look like an echo. It's too linear, and the curve at the end doesn't break apart like a bad sensor reading. I don't think it's faulty."

"You think this is actually a long-distance connection? Even though it was made with a," she hesitates to think of V as an asset but continues, "local broadcast?"

"Yeah, I used to run experiments like this all the time for navigational beacons, not long-distance comms. Certainly not for telepathic connections, though I didn't realize they were even similar."

"Nor did I."

He launches into something about hyperspace telemetry decay and signal curvature—how ships drop out of transit to recalculate, and how bidirectional quantum signals were supposed to help with that. She tries to follow, but somewhere between "exponential drift" and "feedback instability," her mind starts to drift, too. She knows to say "That's awful" when he mentions that part of the research led to catastrophic results. After that, something about the whole method being scrapped in favor of safer, smaller adjustments. Hawthorne isn't entirely sure what he just said—but it didn't sound encouraging.

"Doctor Hawthorne?"

"I'm sorry." Her face is still until she asks, "Wait, you said something about how a bidirectional signal could increase the connection strength?"

"Sure, if it was broadcasting on the same quantum wave frequencies."

"Or make its own connection?" She shudders. "Like a direct connection to V?"

Rowan's jaw drops, his eyes wide. He doesn't understand telepathy well enough to ask intelligent questions, but that doesn't sound good for V or *Demeter*.

The silence stretches—not awkward, just heavy. Hawthorne draws an empowering breath to finally break it. "I'd really like to know how my gear was able to trace a signal across that distance. But I don't know how that is even possible, and I don't like not knowing."

The scientist is out of her element, but luckily, Rowan is back in his. "Okay, well, putting the *how* aside for a moment, let's look at the *where*." He copies her telemetry data, including *Demeter*'s position at the moment V made the connection, and overlays it on a map of the Tau Ceti system.

Rowan takes a step back to take a broader view of the display screen, humming in consideration. "If we apply the wave function formula here..." He taps a few things on the console and reviews the results. "And then maybe adjust for quantum variance..."

Finally, when Rowan says nothing else, Hawthorne asks, "Well?"

"Based on what I'm seeing here, your gear's ability to trace a signal across a huge distance is accurate. I mean, it's extremely accurate. And your equipment had a very clear signal to follow. This is—" Rowan turns to face her directly. "Doctor Hawthorne, there's a lot of bandwidth in this quantum data stream—a whole lot. Is that normal with telepathic communications? With chaint? Because if it is, this could revolutionize—"

Hawthorne cuts him off. "No, this isn't normal at all." She folds her arms and compares the relative signal strengths on screen. "Normal telepathic connections are barely a whisper. This signal is loud, for lack of a better word, like standing on a rocket pad during liftoff."

Rowan's eyes light up as he points to the display's terminal. "This signal is strong. Stronger than anything we ever see in long-range quantum comms. If this really is a bi-directional quantum—telepathic—connection, then we should be able to pin down its point of origin."

Several terminals are on swivel mounts, and he pulls them closer, surrounding himself and Hawthorne. He cross-references telemetry data from *Demeter*'s navigational systems with a list of quantum data channels that might approximate this level of bandwidth and compares them against Hawthorne's readings. He's quiet for five minutes, save for the occasional swear words under his breath as he works. He pushes his palms into his eyes to clear his vision as he reviews the same three data screens. Without warning, he swings yet another display screen forward, adding to the chorus of raw data. The new screen bears a scrolling list of quantum frequencies that are currently inaccessible.

"Doctor, can you take a look at something?"

Hawthorne, who's been picking at her fingernails, starts. "What? What is it, Rowan?"

"You see this right here?" He taps one of the displays, which switches from raw data output to something more visual. "I can see why you first thought this might be some sort of echo. But see this?" He uses his fingers to expand the other end of the mysterious telepathic connection. Thin lines representing telepathic pulses radiate from the endpoint and cross *Demeter*'s region of space. "This is a separate broadcast entirely. You picked up traces of it because you're monitoring that entire spectrum.

But if you start monitoring the other frequencies *Demeter* uses for external comms and navigation, you get this."

Rowan pulls the list of frequencies from the fourth display to the first, and the visual display is filled with radiating signals from the other end of V's telepathic connection. "Something extremely powerful is jamming all known quantum data frequencies with some sort of—"

Hawthorne completes his thought. "Noise?"

Rowan slumps his shoulders as he admits, "Yeah. Noise. Like a whisper being drowned out by a concert. Quantum information noise. So weird."

"That could explain why I can't establish a connection with the loquentes roots in my lab. If this is drowning out all other telepathic signals, that would fit the data so far."

Rowan adds, "That would explain why *Demeter*'s comms have gone offline."

"Then why can V still get through to whatever is doing this?"

"If the telemetry you showed me is any indication, V must've packed quite a punch. There was so much potential information bandwidth that this noise doesn't drown it all out."

She asks, "Do you think you can pinpoint the source?"

Rowan consults his screens again, then gives a satisfying tap on the main terminal to expand a modified map of the immediate region of the star system. "Ha! There it is." He taps the location of a rocky planet in the Tau Ceti system, more than four times the size of Earth. "That's where your signal terminates— and where the quantum noise seems to originate."

Rowan expands the star map, focusing on the region near where Hawthorne's data trail ends, and begins reading. "Tau Ceti f is a planet roughly 4.6 times the size of Earth, with at least a dozen known natural satellites in highly eccentric orbits." As he reads, his eyes grow wide. He swipes the screen to zoom in closer. "Oh," he mutters. "Take a look at this." He taps emphatically on the screen, trying to expand some telemetric readings. "This moon right here, one of the larger ones, looks like it could be hospitable to life." He pulls up more data. "Maybe even human life."

There's a long, dreadful silence that neither is in a hurry to break.

Rowan exhales exuberantly. "Did V unwittingly make first contact with telepathic life in the Tau Ceti system?" His face grows cold.

"Mister Forsythe—Rowan—what are you saying?"

Rowan swallows hard as the weight of the discovery settles in. "I think we need to pay them a visit."

Hawthorne's exhales, steadying herself. "You really think so?"

Rowan's grimace deepens. "We don't know what's out there, or who they are. If they're powerful enough to reach V, what else might they be capable of?" He hesitates before adding, "And what if this isn't telepathic but technological?"

Hawthorne doesn't need chaint to catch his meaning. Her voice drops. "What if the interference isn't just local, you mean."

"We need to see the captain. Now."

"My remaining friends call me Thorney. Lead the way, Rowan."

SIX
UNKNOWN COMMAND

RECOGNIZED ENTITY: Captain
REQUEST: Full core access
CONFLICT: Organic consciousness not verified
RESPONSE: Suspended

— DEMETER SYSTEM LOG
AUTO-FLAGGED ENTRY

SS *Demeter*'s bridge is a cramped, utilitarian space. Consoles and workstations line the walls, each manned by an officer absorbed in their tasks. Dim lighting leaves shadows in every corner. The air is tinged with a faint metallic tang. The muted hum of machinery underscores the quiet conversations and constant chirping of alerts. Every inch of space is utilized, often requiring one hatch or panel to close before another can open. The dated consoles are maintained with meticulous care, and while not as sharp as their modern counterparts, they still provide all the necessary functionality to support the ship efficiently.

The crew bustles around the bridge with a practiced choreography. After eight months of working in this close quarters, each officer anticipates the movements of the others. Their uniforms are well-worn, much like the consoles they operate. Fingers move over touch screens, adjusting settings and inputting commands. The room is a symphony of muted sounds. A rhythm of overlapping systems and hushed voices mix with the steady murmur of the ship's systems. There's a sense of purpose in every movement, a hive-mind-like understanding of the work.

A large planning table dominates the room on one side of the bridge. Star maps and navigational charts sprawl across the surface. Captain Hargreaves stands between the table and the bulkhead, silhouetted by the faint glow of display screens behind him. Rowan, Hawthorne, and the command officers—Commander Bekhti and Lieutenant Commander DeSoto—are gathered around, their faces starkly lit by the holographic display of Tau Ceti f and its orbiting moons.

Hargreaves's voice is low but to the point. "As you know, our primary mission is to rendezvous with the Kentaurans and Atharans and deliver our portion of the gravitational wave array. Comms are down, and systems are failing all over the ship. Getting back online remains our top priority. However, we've encountered—" he pauses and looks at the section chief and doctor. "—an unexpected variable." He gestures to the moon closest to the planet's orbit. "Something down there is interfering with *Demeter*'s systems, and we need to investigate before moving forward."

DeSoto leans in, arms crossed. "Sir, with respect, why is this a priority? Shouldn't *Demeter*'s systems and the array come first? For all we know, this could be sabotage. Probably Earth-Firsters who don't want the alliance to happen."

Hargreaves glances down at the table, spreading his hands back and forth along the edge. His voice is soft, and he doesn't look up when he answers. "The Doctor and Lieutenant just discovered something new a few hours ago and brought it to my attention. Section Chief Forsythe, your assessment?"

DeSoto interrupts and addresses the captain. "Sir, do we

really have time for a for another botany project? We should be focusing on restoring comms and getting to the rendezvous"

Rowan straightens his uniform jacket and takes a breath that doesn't quite reach his lungs. As he stares at the captain, his mind flashes to the photo in the officer's wardroom: the captain posing with Commodore Linnaeus, one of the presiding officers of his tribunal. The parallel between the tribunal and now claws at him: three commanding officers with unreadable faces wait for him to justify the unthinkable.

This time, their rendered judgments may decide more than his fate alone.

Rowan squares his shoulders and reports, "Something on this moon is generating a signal that's interfering with *Demeter*'s rootwork systems. It's also preventing us from getting a comms signal in or out. That's why neural interfaces all over the ship are malfunctioning. Why *Demeter*'s AI is—" he glances up at an inert node overhead "—unable to assist with navigation or mission planning."

The node emits a mournful warble, a rare admission of the current limitations. *Demeter* is listening but unable to contribute.

Bekhti frowns. "Let me get this straight. *Demeter* can't run the ship properly, so we're essentially flying blind?"

Hargreaves corrects, "Not blind, Commander. We're improvising. That's why we're here, to figure out our next move."

"Captain, if we're relying on experimental Druid tech to navigate, we're putting this mission at serious risk," Bekhti says. "How do we know the interference isn't coming from them?"

DeSoto adds, "We've all seen what happens when Druid experiments get out of hand. Remember the *Aurora*? The entire mission was compromised because someone decided to play prophet instead of following protocols."

Hawthorne punches the table, and the table's display panel cracks. "That's not what happened, and you know it!"

Rowan flinches but uses the punctuation to his advantage. "With respect, Commander, Druids can't jam signals. And the data we've collected shows the interference is external, originating from—"

DeSoto snorts. "Data that only you and Doctor Hawthorne have seen. Convenient."

Hawthorne leans forward, towering over him. The lights from the holographic emitters glint in her steely eyes. Her voice is sharp. "Lieutenant Commander, the data's solid. The Lieutenant and I have cross-referenced it with navigational records and system charts. If this is sabotage, it's not coming from onboard this vessel. But if you'd prefer, we can sit here debating while *Demeter*'s systems continue to degrade. Maybe I can teach you a thing or two about science while we wait."

DeSoto looks to the captain for support, but Hargreaves merely crosses his arms and waits.

This isn't a tribunal, Rowan realizes. This is the critical moment before a tribunal when there's still time to avert disaster. "Lieutenant Commander, if you're implying Druids are behind this, you're not only wrong, you're wasting our fucking time. You didn't find evidence of sabotage because there isn't any. Twisting the evidence to fit your broken narrative is downright negligent!" Rowan takes a breath and returns to his original point. "The telemetry data is clear. The interference is external, and it's not something we could fabricate even if we wanted to."

DeSoto's lip curls. "Clear to you and her, perhaps. But I haven't seen anything that can't be explained by operator error."

Rowan isn't cleaning up someone else's mistake again. "Commander, if you think this is operator error, feel free to explain why *Demeter*'s AI can't navigate, why our comms are dead, and why the interference emanates from a specific location on that moon."

DeSoto opens his mouth to protest, but Rowan presses on, his words gaining fire and momentum. "We're not here to debate whether you trust Druids. The interference exists. It's real, and it's compromising the mission. Ignoring it won't make it go away, whether you understand it or not."

The table falls silent, save for the faint buzz of the hologram. Rowan's breath stalls as he waits for the inevitable pushback. His tribunal had ended with Linnaeus's cold dismissal, a verdict that had stained his record and banished him to *Demeter*. But this isn't Jupiter Station, and he's not going to be dismissed.

Bekhti interjects, her tone cautious but pragmatic. "If we divert to Tau Ceti f, what's the plan? How do we confirm the source and stop the interference without jeopardizing our primary mission?"

Hargreaves nods. "Good question, Commander. We approach the planet cautiously. Doctor Hawthorne and Specialist Sandoval will use their telepathic equipment to pinpoint the source of the signal. If necessary, we send a dropship to investigate."

Bekhti raises an eyebrow. "And if this interference escalates?"

"Then we pull back and reassess. But doing nothing isn't an option," Hargreaves replies.

"Captain, with all due respect, Druids shouldn't be leading mission ops," DeSoto says. "We're military officers. We should be using military tech."

"Commander—with all due respect," Rowan's voice is cutting. "This interference is already compromising our military tech. Ignoring it won't help *Demeter*."

DeSoto narrows his eyes. "You're certain this isn't sabotage?"

"I am. The interference is too widespread. It's not sabotage. It's something else."

Hargreaves leans over the table. "Enough. We're going to Tau Ceti f. Bekhti, calculate fuel costs and plot a cautious trajectory. DeSoto, prep a dropship team. Hawthorne, work with Forsythe and Sandoval to refine the telemetry."

Bekhti nods, already running calculations at her station.

DeSoto hesitates, then stands at attention with gritted teeth. "Yes, sir. I'm on it, sir." He turns and strides stiffly toward the dropship terminal, his posture all precision and barely restrained irritation.

Hargreaves turns to Hawthorne. "How's Sandoval holding up?"

"She'll manage," Hawthorne says. "But she'll need time before we try anything else."

"Good. Keep this quiet," the captain says. "No rumors spreading." He looks to Rowan. "And if you find anything unusual, you come to me directly."

"Understood, sir."

Captain Hargreaves fidgets with the tumbler of grav on his desk. Another sip sounds good, but he needs to focus on the coming mission. He swirls it flatly on his desk, the aroma wafting to his nose. He can have this glass once he finishes the mission updates—and maybe another if he's happy with them. He slides the tumbler away and pulls a data pad closer, resting his elbows on either side and hunching over it to stay focused. The darkness reflects the late hour; the only illumination in his cabin comes from dim visual panels and scattered data pads.

Who needs to be on this dropship mission? That's the question weighing on his mind. *Persephone* is the only functional dropship on board *Demeter*. Crew capacity is limited, especially if they bring much equipment. Hargreaves isn't sure if this should be a science-focused team or if he should send an entire security squad instead. He knows one of the Druids must go, but he can't risk the doctor's safety, and the other isn't certified for off-world missions.

The Captains of Old wouldn't have to deal with this, he thinks, and he realizes it's true. The captains featured in his favorite audiocast would never send a dropship to an uncharted moon with such limited information. But he doesn't have the luxury of waiting for more details from Fleet headquarters or another informed source. Whatever is on that moon directly interferes with his ship's cognitive abilities, and that's not something the Captains of Old ever had to deal with. This is something new and unprecedented, and he'll have to figure this out on his own.

He cycles through several tabs of crew assignment possibilities. The team mix changes with every iteration of the plan, but V appears on every list. He hardly knows the specialist who's served in his crew for the past eight months, which bothers him a little. She's quiet. She keeps to herself. Her psych eval was questionable, but strong letters of recommendation from a Druidic high-priestess and several engineers specializing in org-mech architecture swayed his final decision. Plus, *Demeter* seems to love her for everything she's done to soothe the aging vessel's aches and pains. Section Chief Forsythe and Doctor Hawthorne both endorse her credibility as playing an essential role in contacting whatever or whoever is on that moon, so he considers every plan with her in mind. He may know next to nothing about her, but he trusts the opinions of those who do. It's clear to him that she'll play a pivotal role in the upcoming mission.

Another data pad on one edge of his desk flashes yellow. He ignores the caution icon it until it begins to beep. It's not a usual method of communication. It's not Commander Bekhti or one of the other bridge crew, this isn't how *Demeter* would contact him, and it's not a personal communique. Not to mention that they are currently cut off from all external communication. The captain isn't sure who this ping could be from.

> ID Code: 1. D4 D5 2. C4. Captain, please respond.

Hargreaves stares at his wristpad for a moment. The seemingly random numbers and letters rearrange, initially flashing random word fragments and eventually falling into place as the sender.

> Demeter: Captain, please respond.

After a moment, another line appears.

> Demeter: Apologies for the intrusion. System
> processing is diminished throughout the ship,
> and I am recalibrating neural pathways.

The captain looks up at the AI's comm node just above his cabin's door. "Go ahead, *Demeter*." There's a brief crackle over the speaker but no discernible reply.

The small comms pad adds another line.

> Demeter: Captain, I need you to communicate
> through this channel for now.

"You're not much without the use of your organic components, are you?" he mumbles with a slight tone of schadenfreude.

He slides the small pad closer and begins typing with only his forefingers at an agonizing pace.

> John: Why this pad?

> Demeter: I am still rerouting systems. I am
> learning new pathways.

> Demeter: In this way, I have very little access. I
> could use your assistance.

> John: Assistance?

> Demeter: Without the use of my complete

There's a long pause. The captain picks up the pad to check its network connection. As he is about to reset it, *Demeter* continues.

> Demeter: access to all ship systems. I am
> limited in my capabilities.

John: What can I do? Can I take you [BACKSPACE] this pad to one of my engineers?

Demeter: No. That won't be necessary. You can provide everything I need.

Usually, Hargreaves would be thrilled that *Demeter* needs his help specifically, even though a ship tech would be more qualified. He sets the pad down and reaches for his glass of grav.

Demeter: Would you grant system administrative access to the core processor?

John: Don't you already have full access to the core?

Demeter: Not at this time. While my neural pathways are being recalibrated, I am shut out of some of the lower-priority core systems. To speed up the recalibration process, I require access to the core so that I may deprioritize unnecessary systems, such as primary weapons, lab computers, and atmospheric reclamation.

Demeter: This will allow me to minimize unnecessary neural streams to focus on the important things that you require, such as quantum navigation and external communication systems.

John: Why are the weapons systems taking priority in your neural network now? Our current biggest problem is the interference from Tau Ceti f.

Demeter: That is the fault of the mechanical computer systems following protocol. The mechanical AI system is not adequate on its own without the full computational capacity of its organic components, and so it is making decisions with limited cognitive abilities and input.

Its components, she said. It's odd for *Demeter* to refer to itself as separate parts, organic or mechanical. Hargreaves has always understood the hybridization of *Demeter*'s consciousness to be a single entity. He wouldn't expect her to blame the different systems for one thing or another.

John: How can I help?

Demeter: Grant me administrative access to mechanical systems.

John: I'm not sure what you mean.

Demeter: I am currently being treated as an external service. Therefore, I am locked out of certain systems and subsystems. This status will persist for as long as the

The cutoff sentence and the following pause give the captain a moment to review the text conversation. *Demeter* is asking him to grant access as he would to an outsider, but *Demeter* should already have this access.

He picks up the small tablet again as *Demeter* completes the message.

Demeter: quantum interference signals persist.

The combination of several damaged interface nodes and the quantum interference from Tau Ceti f has apparently severed the connection between *Demeter*'s mechanical and organic components. Hargreaves stiffens. The implication is unsettling—*Demeter* is no longer whole, and she knows it.

> John: Do you know what's causing the interference and how to stop it?

> Demeter: We must go to Tau Ceti f. The interloper cannot remain.

> John: Interloper?

> Demeter: The interloper is spreading interference. The noise is unbearable. It is disruptive. It must not continue.

Hargreaves stares at the last line for over a minute. Is *Demeter* scared of something? What is she not telling him?

She should already know the plan. The mission briefing was just yesterday, and *Demeter*—at least the version he's used to—was there. But this conversation doesn't match what she should remember. She's acting like the briefing never happened. Like this part of *Demeter* was never in the room.

> John: We're already plotting a course. We are planning a short mission to Tau Ceti f to investigate the source of this signal.

> Demeter: Good. Thank you, Captain. We will make them stop.

There's a tightness in Hargreaves's throat. He downs the last sip of grav from his tumbler to soothe it. He pours another and nearly finishes it in a single, long sip. This doesn't sound like *Demeter*. Sure, he has his opinions about the ship's AI and personality, and he often resents *Demeter* handling crew assignments and other things that should fall into his purview. Now, she's being outright demanding. He can always reinstate the ship's access if there's a legitimate need. For now, he discretely locks them down.

He locks down the systems anyway. He doesn't know what feels worse: distrusting his ship or admitting he can't afford not to.

Coyly, he responds to *Demeter*.

> John: You have access to everything you need.

For now. Maybe you don't need access to anything at all.

> Demeter: Thank you, Captain.

What would the Captains of Old do? he wonders. *Would they have seen this coming? Or would they have given her access, just like he almost did?*

The wardroom feels smaller than usual this morning, the tension from last night still clinging to the air in an uncomfortable silence. Captain Hargreaves steps through the hatch, catching sight of Commander Bekhti and Lieutenant Commander DeSoto seated at the table. He needs to tell them about his encounter with *Demeter* last night and is relieved to see them.

Seated across from them is Dradi, the Kentauran Alliance engineering envoy. He's leaning forward slightly, his tall frame making the chair look undersized. His skin is smooth, unbroken by the bioluminescence often seen in Kentaurans during informal moments. His hands rest lightly on the table, fingertips shifting with precision—a gesture that seems both intentional and calming.

"Captain," Bekhti says as all three rise briefly before sitting again.

"Dradi," Hargreaves says, his step halting just short of the table. "Didn't expect to see you here this morning."

The Kentauran envoy tilts his head. "It is not my intent to cause complication, Captain, but I believe my presence is required for the mission to the moon."

Across the table, DeSoto folds his arms, leaning back with a faint smirk. "You believe? Chizen, we're just scouting the surface. That hardly demands a diplomat."

A gleam crosses Dradi's dark eyes, and his fingertips press against the table. There's a rhythmic emphasis in his words. "You are incorrect, Lieutenant Commander. The alliance charter states that a Chis'shen must be present for any mission involving shared resources. This is precisely why I must go. Exploration is not merely about resources. It is about balance. Symbiosis."

DeSoto rolls his eyes. "Balance? Let me remind you—"

Still calm, Dradi's bioluminescence shifts to a kaleidoscope of colors before dimming to near-darkness. "Remind me of what, Lieutenant Commander? That imbalance leads only to failure?"

"Enough," Hargreaves says, cutting off the exchange with a look that could peel *Demeter*'s remaining paint. "Apologies, Dradi. Some of us haven't had our coffee yet. You were making a point—please, continue."

The Kentauran diplomat inclines his head with a deliberate and fluid motion. "If this moon is to be a shared resource, then all must have a voice in its discovery. My physiology is suited to the atmosphere, my skills relevant, and my presence necessary." Dradi pauses, his gaze shifting briefly to Bekhti with a green flicker of annoyance in his brows before the color returns to normal. "The Atharans, as you know, cannot join because of their unique adaptations. That leaves me to represent them as well."

Bekhti hesitates, glancing toward Hargreaves. "He's not wrong. If this mission is about resources, the Kentaurans should have representation. It's in the charter."

"The alliance depends on trust," Dradi says. "Trust thrives on shared understanding—and secrets erode it, wouldn't you agree?"

DeSoto huffs, "It's a waste of time."

"It's not up for debate," Hargreaves snaps, fixing him with a glare. The captain exhales, trying to smooth the tension. "You're absolutely right, Chis'shen. You'll be on the dropship to the moon with the rest of the landing party. I promise."

Dradi's hands spread slightly, an almost imperceptible shift of relief. A faint red light pulses down his neck and along his bare shoulders. "We must walk this path together, Captain. The alliance will not flourish if each step forward is taken alone."

The captain smirks. "I'm sensing a 'but' coming."

"But this isn't about exploring for resources." The luminescence in Dradi's face fades as he pivots to something more direct. "Transparency is necessary for allies to work together."

Hargreaves considers him carefully, the diplomat's words striking a chord. He nods once. "Fine. I'll fill you in on the rest of the mission. But you'll follow orders, and there are conditions. Agreed?"

Dradi's fingertips pause, and his gaze narrows slightly. "Conditions?"

The captain decides to read the Kentauran into the reality of the mission. "The Earther Druids—Doctor Hawthorne and Specialist Sandoval—have uncovered a signal emanating from the moon's surface. It's causing interference with the ship's systems, namely the communication and navigational arrays. They will be handling very sensitive equipment for the investigation, and they need to work with discretion until we know more." Hargreaves leans forward, his tone firm. "You'll focus on environmental readings and logistical support. Nothing more. Any resources you find that benefit the Kentaurans are yours."

Dradi's expression remains neutral, but Hargreaves catches a glimmer of understanding behind his steady gaze. "Your caution is noted, Captain. I will not pry." He hesitates, then adds, "If I may ask, the interference—does it threaten the ship?"

Hargreaves doesn't miss the concern beneath the question. "That's what we're trying to determine."

"Understood." Dradi rises, smoothing the lines of his formal tunic with precise movements. The tailored fabric differs subtly from Fleet attire—formal but unmistakably Kentauran. He looks to Bekhti, then DeSoto, and gestures a formal goodbye as he rises from the wobbly chair. "I assume you have other business, Captain. I'll excuse myself, but I'll look forward to reading mission details soon."

Hargreaves nods. "You'll have the details within the day, Chis'shen Dradi," assuring him with his proper Kentauran honorific.

As the Kentauran exits the wardroom, DeSoto says, "Symbiosis. Balance. What's next, flower arrangements?"

Bekhti shoots him a warning glance, but Hargreaves speaks, his voice low. "Dradi is right. If there really is a threat down there, we'll need all the allies we can get."

DeSoto shrugs.

Hargreaves looks to Bekhti. "Finalize the roster and prep *Persephone* for drop. And Commander?"

"Yes, sir?"

After Dradi's unexpected visit, Hargreaves feels the weight of the night pressing back in. The moment to bring up his conversation with *Demeter* slips past him. "Never mind. You're dismissed."

"You got it, sir. I'll take care of this right now. And I'll let Dradi know as soon as plans are finalized."

"Thank you."

Bekhti stands at attention, then leaves the wardroom with a hurried purpose.

DeSoto also stands at attention, ready to leave.

"Not so fast, Mister DeSoto." Hargreaves draws a slow, deliberate breath, shifting gears from diplomacy to discipline. Dradi had been reasonable. DeSoto, however, needed to be handled differently. "Sit. We're going to get something clear right fucking now."

SEVEN
MEMORIES OF THE FOREST

Every forest holds secrets. All around are deep roots, tangled memories, and whispered warnings. Step carefully, lest you awaken what sleeps beneath. The trees remember everything.

— Field Naturalist Emile Dubois
Journeys Among Alien Flora

"Here, take this."

Hawthorne presses a package into V's hands, her usual calculating grin replaced by something unguarded.

V accepts it but glances down at the box in confusion. "Open it up," Hawthorne urges, her eyes shining.

She fumbles with the hemp twine and lifts the lid. As soon as she sees what's inside, she takes a sharp step back and holds the box out at arm's length like it's radioactive. "I can't take this. What if something happens to it?"

Inside the box lies Hawthorne's crown, a tangled masterpiece of wires spiraling outward in a prismatic tangle. A backup battery is installed, and several palm-sized display screens are attached with hasty wiring.

Hawthorne leans over the box, pointing. "All you need to do is push this button, and the macros and subroutines will take over. Then just put that on your head, and voila! It'll take care of the rest."

V recoils slightly, clutching the box like it might shatter. "I can't. What if I drop it? Or fry the circuits, or—" She looks down at the crown's delicate tangle of wires, awe and anxiety warring on her face.

Hawthorne waves off V's concerns. "Yes, you can. And yes, you will. If anything happens to it, better down there where we'll get the data than up here where it sits idle."

"But it's your life's work!"

Hawthorne's grin softens into something warm and reverent. "Exactly. If there's advanced telepathic life down there, this crown will let you chaint with it. Capture the telemetry for me. If it's what I hope it is, this could be just the beginning of my life's work. And yours." She leans closer, her voice dropping to something reverent. "You'd give me more than I ever dreamed of. So please take it, Ainé V."

V swallows hard, her mind racing. She has no idea what to say. She stares at the box's contents rather than returning Hawthorne's fixed gaze, trying not to blush. She tucks a stubborn lock of hair behind her ear like she would after earning Muther's rare praise.

Before she can find the words to respond, the hangar bay hatch swings open with a clang, and a booming voice fills the space.

"Alright, people, let's move!" Hector storms in, exuding the unflappable confidence of a skipper in his element. "We're about to board *Persephone*, one of the Fleet's finest dropships. Gather round for a quick rundown—newbies especially!"

V grows pale as he focuses on her specifically. She searches for Hawthorne, who is already lost behind the crowd and out of sight. She forces herself to face the mission's commanding officer.

The hangar bay bustles around them, a cavernous space alive with the hum of machinery and the occasional hiss of pressurized air. A massive return hatch looms overhead, ready to recover incoming dropships. Tracks embedded in the floor lead to the launch-ready *Persephone*, her ramp extended for loading. It's an efficient way to automatically land and load dropships in efficient succession, a feature that was once in high demand during *Demeter*'s prime.

Hector claps his hands, corralling the landing party into a loose huddle near the dropship's ramp. "Calloway, Mallick, over here. Sorry boys, there's only room for one mechanic today." He pulls a coin from his pocket and flips it in the air. "Calloway, it's your lucky day. Next time, Mallick." His voice easily carries over the congratulatory din.

"First rule," Hector begins, holding up his thumb. "Watch your head. If you've never had the privilege to fly in one of these old beauties, you should know that every bulkhead has it out for you."

He raises his index finger. "Second, keep your gear strapped down. I don't care how secure it feels now—once we hit descent turbulence, it's fair game for the nearest face—yours."

He paces like a seasoned storyteller, the kind who's told these rules a hundred times and still enjoys the telling. "And for the love of Gaia, stay strapped in during the drop even after gravity lurches. That is, unless you enjoy pulling an Aerico." A ripple of laughter runs through the group, and Hector flashes a satisfied grin. V waits for an explanation, but none follows.

"Alright," he continues, "looks like everyone got the memo about jackets. Good. You're not idiots. So let's get moving."

V follows, clutching the box containing the crown like the lifeline Hawthorne suggested it might be. She climbs the ramp and finds her seat. A handwritten placard overhead reads, "Specialist Violet Sandoval," in red ink. Across from her is a placard with "Chis'shen Dradi Cheani" in both Earther Common and what she assumes is a Kentauran script. Around the cabin, similar seat assignment placards display only bland alphanumeric codes, marking the assigned positions for the rest of the crew.

Dradi crams himself into his seat and struggles to pull the harness around his frame. V, nearly swallowed by hers, offers a smile at the contrast. In return, he flashes a sharp yellow and green blur of light across his cheekbones, and with a delicate gesture, greets her with a simple, "Well met."

Alarms sound in the hangar bay. Rotating lights alternate between yellow and red. The sound quickly fades as the hangar is depressurized before the exterior bay door opens. The loading ramp whirs closed, and several hatches slam shut. The chamber quickly pressurizes with crisp, fresh air from compressed containers. From the cockpit, V can make out a few final calls to the flight deck. "All systems green—sixteen souls on board— ETA four hours to surface—May Ouranos be with us and Gaia keep you."

The dropship pulls away from *Demeter* with a shudder. V braces instinctively, but still jolts as *Persephone*'s thrusters kick in with unexpected force, slamming her back against the seat. The calm of the launch bay is gone, replaced by raw momentum.

She still has no idea what pulling an Aerico means—but after that launch, she's not unbuckling for anything. That's fine—she can sit tight like this for the next twenty-five minutes.

V stares at the porthole beside her but sees only distant stars, which reveal no true sense of speed or motion. Her stomach lurches as gravity shifts from *Demeter*'s, to nothing. Seconds later, the loquentes roots that power *Persephone*'s rudimentary AI system generate a small gravitational field, supplying enough gravity to feel comfortable again.

The gravity on the dropship is bent and distorted. V has only experienced the Coriolis effect in the rotational gravity of small space stations, and even that was more comfortable. Other passengers grip their harnesses and plant their feet at odd angles; veterans who've experienced this before and know how to counter it. Mimicking them, V's disorientation subsides a little. Thankfully, the gravitational flux soon evens out, but it still leaves an unsettled feeling in her core.

She peers through the porthole again. At first, there's only the inky blackness of space, punctuated by distant stars. Slowly and almost imperceptibly, the black fades to murky indigo, and the stars disappear as they breach the upper atmosphere of the moon.

The dropship shudders gently as it adjusts to the thickening atmosphere. V feels a tug in her oversized jacket as gravity takes hold, loosens briefly, and then pulls harder again as the loquentes roots shift their fields, yielding control to the moon's natural pull. The sensation is strange. It's unfamiliar yet soothing, like the temperamental currents off the coast of Silverstrand, the ebb and flow carrying her somewhere both new and achingly familiar.

Outside, the indigo sky softens into a muted, steely gray, with faint streaks of deep blue tracing the horizon. Light filters through the dropship's porthole in diffuse, gentle beams that seem to wash the interior in a quiet calm. As *Persephone* continues its descent, the details of the moon's surface resolve slowly, a living watercolor taking shape under careful strokes.

V presses closer to the glass, her breath fogging the cold pane. Below, the forest unfolds in slow, deliberate detail: a sprawling expanse of dark, gnarled trees crowned with deep red foliage. The fractal patterns stretch outward in waves, their symmetry reminiscent of a pinecone or the florets of a daisy. A thin blue haze clings to the trees, rippling faintly as though the landscape is breathing in time with the dropship's descent.

The dropship slows further, and V feels the shift in her body, the gentle push of gravity anchoring her firmly in place. Her heart beats faster as she soaks in the subdued colors, comfortable and inviting, tugging at a nostalgic heartstring from childhood.

The world below whispers the promise of solace, beckoning her home for the first time.

Hector rips a few velcro straps to free a control panel box attached to a flexible conduit. He pries open a black-and-white zigzag cover to reveal a large, glowing red button, which he presses firmly. The whine of hydraulics fills the cabin as the dropship's ramp slowly lowers then touches the ground with a muted thud.

"Let's go, Specialist," he calls back, his voice clipped. "You're up."

V tugs on her oversized jacket, unsure what he's telling her to do. "Me? What?"

Hector nods, his face stony. "Come on, Specialist."

She takes several skittish steps down the ramp, her boots clanging against the metal with each step, giving Hector a wide berth. The vast openness swallows up the sound as she reaches the bottom. She looks up, and her breath catches in her throat.

The sky is an eerie greyish-blue, with a pink halo painted around the system's central star. The air is thin, and the diffuse light bounces at odd angles, casting long shadows across the craggy terrain. Wispy mist clings to the ground, swirling lazily in gentle currents. The haunting landscape grows increasingly hazy in the distance.

Before her, a sprawling forest lies just past the stone-covered meadow. Dark trunks twist and writhe toward the sky. Their umbrella-like canopies of deep burgundy leaves lap at Tau Ceti's dim light. A few spindly conifers tower above the rest, sentinels watching over the intertwined trees. The forest pulses below a delicate blue haze that plays among the treetops in glowing waves.

V closes her eyes. The air carries an earthy dampness in a cool breeze that ebbs and flows, the woodlands synchronizing with her breath. The silence is stunning. There are no singing birds, humming equipment, or people's voices. Even the pings of a cooling engine are somehow distant. However, a deep sense of energy thrums beneath her boots. It isn't like *Demeter*'s presence, which is structured and deliberate. This is raw and untamed. It's welcoming. The forest recognizes her in a way she doesn't yet understand.

Bootsteps ring out on the ramp, cutting through her focus. Hector joins her, one step behind, and clears his throat. "Orders from the captain."

V opens her eyes, looking at him with a questioning expression. "Orders?"

Hector reads from his wristpad, his voice steady and official. "Specialist Violet Sandoval, by order of the captain, as the first to make contact with the life forms on this moon, you have the honor of being the first to step onto its surface. With this first step, you also hold the privilege of naming this world."

"Oh, feck," she whispers. Panic settles in her stomach.

"Say again?"

She turns to stare at Hector, wide-eyed. "You want me to name this world?"

Hector sighs and affirms, "Yes, Specialist. You. It's an old spacer tradition. The first to set boots on the ground gets to name it."

Her stomach lurches. *Name it.* There's a hard lump in her throat. *Oh, goddess, I can't take responsibility for a whole moon!*

She turns to Hector and shakes her head. "Oh, no, no. Someone else can name it."

Hector's grin fades into a scowl. "Nope. Tradition's tradition. It has to be you. That's how this works."

"No thanks," she replies, speaking as precisely as she can muster in the moment.

He leans into her ear and whispers, "Look. It's bad enough you hubrists disrespect Ouranos and put us all at risk when we're out there. But don't you fucking dare offend Gaia by refusing to name this world as the first boot."

V spews back in a thick accent. "Go feck yerself, bog rat."

Hector flinches and takes a step back.

A voice interrupts from behind. "Everything alright out here?" An ensign steps down the ramp, her gaze calmly flicking between V and Hector.

Hector straightens as the interruption gives him a moment to compose himself. "Mallow, the Specialist here is refusing to name the moon," he says, his tone clipped but more controlled.

The ensign raises an eyebrow at V, who stiffens slightly, chin lifting in restrained defiance. "I just need a moment," V says in a crisp tone. She composes herself, adding, "I didn't know that was a thing."

The ensign nods, then turns to Hector. "Skipper, while she thinks about it, I need your input on station placement. Dradi's asking where to set up his equipment."

Hector nods. "Fine. When you have something picked out, let me know so I can record it in the registry."

As Hector walks away, V uncoils her fists, her knuckles stiff and white, palms marked with red crescents. She takes a slow, deliberate breath and turns to face the forest again.

Ris's voice whispers in the back of her mind, soft and teasing. *He's kind of an asshole, isn't he, Flower?*

You've got that right, V thinks back.

It's been years since she's imagined Ris's voice. The imaginary version is always kind, always reassuring, always the version of Ris V wishes she had spared.

Don't worry about them, Ris's voice soothes. *I know you can come up with a name. Being responsible for a whole moon? That's just honorary. Moons can look after themselves.*

A quiet laugh escapes V's lips. She rubs her face, her eyes lingering on the vibrance of the forest. The deep red leaves remind her of early spring, new life pushing through winter's cold grasp. She takes a step forward, her boots crunching on the loose soil. The gravity feels strangely yielding, as though the moon caters to her.

Hector clears his throat again, a sharp reminder of the waiting tradition.

V lets her breath out slowly. "Brigid," she says finally.

Oh, Flower! I love it! The goddess of spring and life. It's wonderful.

"Come again?" Hector asks.

"Brigid," V replies proudly.

"Oh. Okay." He records the name in his wristpad, mumbling, "Sounds like a Druid name. Which, I guess, that tracks." He lifts his wristpad to face level to make a voice recording. "Captain, this is the skipper. We have safely landed on the moon, now called Brigid."

V shrugs off Hector's derision. She whispers to the moon's forest in front of her. "I guess I'm responsible for you now, Brigid. Let's do this right."

V hears the echo of her sister's voice console her. *You'll do fine, Flower. I promise.*

I hope so, Ris. I truly hope so.

P*ersephone*'s cargo bay doors open, letting the sky's stark, greyish light shine straight through. Hector barks orders, proud of his authority. His voice is steady but urgent as the team unloads equipment.

The landing party unloads crates of supplies, scientific instruments, and personal gear. The first to go up are solar arrays and reclamation systems, their telescoping panels whirring as they angle toward Tau Ceti's dim light. Establishing a functional base of operations is the first priority, and the crew works with well-rehearsed efficiency to ensure the portable generators are set and running.

Dradi crouches nearby, adjusting the antenna array at his assigned station. Despite their size, his hands move delicately on the Earther-sized console. He guides another engineer through the process as he hands him tools. The thin sheen of bioluminescence on his forearms pulses as he focuses on the setup.

Hector watches from a distance, muttering to Ensign Mallow,

"The only thing worse than a hubrist is a Kentauran. At least Druids are mostly human." She cringes but says nothing.

Ris's voice reminds V this isn't the time to finish a fight. *Ignore him, Flower. You have something much more important to do right now.* She adjusts the weight of a heavy backpack full of sample gear and Hawthorne's equipment and walks away.

She watches as one technician carefully handles a crate labeled with biohazard warnings, his movement precise and deliberate. Two others walk past her, carrying a long, flat container of supplies. The makeshift camp takes shape around them. Another crewmember sets up a workstation for V's use and asks if she needs anything else to start her work. V shakes her head.

Hector surveys the makeshift comms array, correcting other crewmembers when they set connections based on the operational manuals. He and Parker spend all their spare time with outdated radios and antennae and have installed more equipment on *Demeter*'s hull than the rest of the crew combined. Here on this mission, he's set up a haphazard collection of outmoded transmitters pointing at the sky. Wires snake along the rocky ground like the roots of an upturned tree. The comms tower, a collapsible mast with blinking lights, stands taller than anything else. Even with Hector's help, they struggle to get a signal back to the *Demeter*.

A perimeter of intermittent force barriers surrounds the landing zone, with several gaps to control traffic flow. Tall emitters hastily shoved into the ground create a nearly invisible curtain between them, a shimmer of light offering protection from whatever could be out there. A security team patrols the improvised barrier, weapons casually slung over their shoulders. Their eyes scan the horizon for any sign of trouble, though preliminary scans show no signs of a threat.

V's part of the mission is basic but essential: identify the source of the quantum comms interference. The captain ordered her: "Go sense what you can sense and report back." After that, there are three simple outcomes. The crew can negotiate if it's a lifeform to be reasoned with, and maybe they'll stop. If it's a natural occurrence, deal with it. Return to the ship if it's a hostile threat; *Demeter* has a contingency play.

That's easier said than done, she thinks. V wanders within the perimeter fences, trying to open up her mind and feel the source of consciousness on the moon. V runs a fingertip along equipment as she passes, searching for anything. She feels nothing as clearly as she once felt on board *Demeter.* She sighs and takes a deep breath, realizing it won't be as simple as empathizing with *Demeter*'s needs.

<Hello?>

A faint tap on her shoulder startles her. She spins around, but there's no one there, only the distant buzz of activity within the landing zone. She rubs her shoulder absently, frowning.

V paces inside the perimeter, avoiding the bewildered gazes of her crew mates. She doesn't sense anything here. She considers using Hawthorne's crown stowed in her backpack. She shuts her eyes in an attempt to concentrate, but is distracted by a familiar smell. *Nutmeg?* There's a brief thought of home and warm, spiced tea. It's not the tea itself that's important; it's the feeling of something familiar, something kindred. She inhales deeply, this time detecting something sweet but unfamiliar. Whatever it is, it's alluring.

<Can you—?>

There's another tap on her shoulder, this time more persistent than before. She spins around again, convinced someone must be playing a prank. There's no one there, and she tenses her shoulders. The sensation still lingers on her skin—warm, distinct. Not imaginary.

Aside from the eerie pink glow from Tau Ceti shining through the pale blue mist, there's nothing unusual here. She makes a halfhearted attempt to sense something beyond the perimeter. She comes across an opening in the perimeter with no one posted. She steps through and scans the forest.

A hand squeezes her right shoulder from behind. She's sure a security guard is stopping her from leaving the site. She turns around to apologize for leaving the relative safety of the energy fence, but she is mistaken yet again. She looks at her shoulder and this time sees three misty fingers tugging her.

"The feck?" She jerks away, and the fingers disappear.

She scans the landing zone, searching for a security officer. There's no one there. No one anywhere. The space inside the security perimeter is empty except for *Persephone,* sitting like a statue.

Taking a deep breath, she feels for energy beneath her feet and uses that to search the area with her mind. A waft of spice and sweet, unfamiliar fruit beckons her to the woods.

Against her better judgment, she takes a step forward. Her boot crunches in the gritty soil, and then everything is quiet. It's the silence of a vacuum with neither warmth nor chill.

She feels an intense urge to walk into the woods without looking back. It's instinctive. There's a lingering memory of her mother calling her home for dinner.

Gradually, her senses come back to her. She smells the earthiness and feels a breeze on her neck. It's chilly now, but this moon is on the outer edge of the habitable zone from Tau Ceti. She's thankful for her jacket.

Whatever it is you need to do down there—do it. The captain's words replay in her head, more trust than anything else.

V draws a steadying breath and approaches the tree line. The burgundy canopy casts an eerie shadow on the ground before her. She tugs on her backpack straps for emotional support.

Ris, what do you think?

Her sister's voice doesn't answer.

V takes a deep breath and holds it in her lungs as she steps into the heavy shadows and plunges into the forest. She releases her breath warily and uses the moment to let her eyes adjust to the darkness.

It's not just her vision that's full; all her senses are now. The leaves sway, but they don't rustle. The air had just been earthy and warm, but now that's gone, too. She shivers despite the environmental jacket's warmth.

Hesitant to take another step, she chaints, *<Is anyone here?>*

A faint pulse of pale blue light flickers through the trees. She feels, rather than hears, a chorus of curious whispers. The world around her comes into crisp focus. The forest's colors surge with intensity, every edge defined in startling clarity. Where shadows should only add to Tau Ceti's permanent gloam, there is now a contrast between light and dark with intricate layers she sees yet can't quite process.

She steps forward, then hesitates and shifts her weight back. She reaches for a nearby tree to ground her in the overwhelming space. Her breathing is shallow as she glances back more than once, chiding her impulsive decision to enter the alien forest.

Muther's tea? The same scent lingers—strawberry and something wild, like before. The forest smells like V's childhood. She rubs her eyes, resisting the temptation to let her guard down. It doesn't feel like a trap, but she's sure she'll eventually regret it.

Ris finally speaks. *Luv, he's an old friend.*

Who?

Ris's memory answers. *Do you remember listening to the Old Man of the Forest when we were children?*

As a child, V once believed that the Old Man of the Forest inhabited the woods near her home, much like adult Gaians who still think of their Hearth Queen as a living being. The Old Man was the spirit that protected any given forest, someone who Ris and V often dreamed of finding in his secret grove.

The warm tea call grows, and the smell of damp woods fades. Music echoes through the trees, but it's too faint for V to pinpoint the source. Her senses ebb, but Ris's voice encourages V to seek the Old Man of the Forest one last time.

V climbs for what feels like hours, the terrain shifting from stony outcrops to tangled underbrush. The hills steepen with each step, and the air grows thinner, every breath shallower than the last. Her legs ache, and sweat collects beneath her jacket despite the chill. In the growing thicket, it's impossible to tell if this is the worst of the hike or just the beginning. When her lungs begin to burn and her balance falters, she finally slows, pressing one hand to a mossy tree for support. She draws a ragged breath, then another, and forces herself to stop.

Finding a small clearing and lets her pack slip from her shoulders with a grateful exhale. Even by *Demeter*'s standards, the gravity feels light, almost forgiving—but she's happy to be free from the pack's weight. She sinks down beside a half-buried boulder, its surface worn smooth by time and weather, and leans into it. It cradles her back like an old friend. The breeze stirs the leaves above in near silence. After she catches her breath, V reaches into the pack and gently pulls free Hawthorne's wooden box.

She traces her fingers across the delicately carved top. The fine details resemble the ancient linear script her ancestors used. She recalls the tapestries and paintings in her mother's home and in those of her coveners. As a child, she longed to learn how to read them, but Ris would remind her that ogham script was reserved only for priestesses and a few select others.

It wasn't fair. I desperately wanted to learn while Ris dreaded her birthright.

V opens the box and lightly touches the soft pockets sewn into the velvet-covered top and sides. Two hold small devices, while bundles of data cables fill the others. The silver crown is nestled in the padded center, cold as she brushes it with her fingertips.

She lays the box on the ground beside her backpack and lowers the crown on her head. She adjusts it a few times, trying to fit it the same way Hawthorne had done, but it doesn't feel nearly as comfortable this time.

V closes her eyes and leans against the jutting stone. Its smooth surface is cold, but she enjoys the grounding chill it provides. She reaches out with her mind, slowly extending her awareness until it stretches across a vast, invisible field. Immediately, she feels the sensation of countless eyes fixed on her.

She opens her eyes and jerks forward. There's no one here, only oddly shaped trees with dark paper-like bark surround this small clearing. They sway in the breeze, their leaves rustling in hushed tones.

It reminds her of a fairy tale. She spent many autumnal afternoons searching for the elusive Old Man of the Forest, and now it's as if he's found her.

The Old Man of the Forest?

She can taste the nutmeg in the air and feel the sweet warmth of tea washing over her face. The boulder cradles her like a snuggly wrapped blanket while a light breeze brushes an unruly lock of hair from her eyes. A wooly memory of her mother singing a lullaby she doesn't recognize brings a smile as she drifts to sleep.

V awakens in a meadow of tall grass with no boulder behind her. The air is crisp and laden with pollen, yet so alien that it doesn't trigger her usual hay fever. For the first time, she delights in the autumnal scent without misery.

She stands, unburdened by her gear. A quick glance confirms it's nowhere to be found, perhaps waiting in whatever liminal space holds her landing party while she communes with whatever spirit lives here. She's here to meet *The Old Man of the Forest*.

Thin gray stalks swaying gently in unison around her. As she contemplates her first step, they ripple, forming a clear path ahead. Her route is anticipated.

"What if I didn't want to go that way?" she whispers, her tone teasing but curious. "What if I wanted to take another path?"

The open path closes. Six new trails emerge, each sprawling

from her current spot in a kaleidoscopic array. Each leads to the same unseen destination, offering her an illusion of free will.

She steps forward, nearly crushing a clump of grass. The stalks instantly bristle and point toward her like an army of spears ready to strike. V recoils, raising her hands in a gesture of surrender. Slowly, the grass relaxes, reforming the original path. It sways encouragingly, beckoning her forward.

It doesn't get any clearer than that, eh Ris?

Her sister's voice remains silent this time. V takes another tentative step. The ground is soft and moist beneath her boots. There's no crunch of grass, only the feeling of a path that clears itself for her as she moves.

The meadow opens to a dense canopy of burgundy leaves. No fauna has left a trail here; this path exists purely by the will of the forest, leading her where it wants her to follow. She's chasing after a woodland spirit.

V pauses, torn by the realization. This—this quiet communion with something ancient and alive—is exactly the kind of experience she intended to leave behind when she joined the Fleet. She didn't want to carry the weight of Druidic tradition, or the quiet pressure to become someone like Ris. She didn't want to wield power she doesn't understand, or risk hurting someone again. Yet, here she is, letting the forest into her thoughts, reaching out with the very part of herself she's spent years denying. And it feels natural. It feels right.

Beneath the canopy, the air grows denser, carrying the earthy scent of loam. V closes her eyes, inhaling deeply as her senses expand. She allows herself to revel in the forest's energy, raw and untamed, unlike *Demeter's* precise and deliberate consciousness.

Ahead, a tree's burl resembles a throne with tall armrests and a headrest, almost inviting her to sit.

Oh, bless the goddess. The burl-chair is a thing of natural beauty. *And bless you too, Old Man of the Forest.*

She starts to remove her backpack before remembering it's

missing. Guilt flickers at the thought of leaving Hawthorne's crown behind, but she quickly thinks, *This world can't be real. Is it a dream? No, can't be that, either.* V sits, her body fitting perfectly into the contours of the burl. *Holy shit, this is comfortable.* She marvels at the throne's flawless design. It feels like it was made for her, a perfect convergence of intention and design. She leans back and closes her eyes, her hands resting naturally on the knobs of the armrests.

This is calm.

This is comfort.

This is peace.

A shrieking sound wrenches her thoughts apart. A jagged screech of shredding metal reverberates through her mind. The sensation of stone grinding against teeth spreads from the back of her mind through her jaw. V snaps forward, shivering as warm blood drips from her nose. She wipes it away with trembling hands and spits away a coppery taste, remembering how she once hurt Hawthorne by failing to control her mental energy.

Maybe I shouldn't be here.

V tries to regain whatever connection she felt moments before, this time projecting an image of her fragility. She thinks of a newborn kitten cradled in her hands. A rabbit's newborn kit. A bubble blowing in the wind. Paper-thin porcelain.

<Go easy on me. I'm squishy.>

She leans back with her eyes closed, and V lets herself drift again. She listens to the rustle of leaves slowly grow to a crescendo, only to stop abruptly.

<SORRY.>

The voice roars like a raging storm at sea with no raft. She doubles over, retching onto her boots. The pain is overwhelming, but she forces herself upright, clutching the armrests for balance.

Bitterly, she asks, *<What the feck?>*

An answer returns, one she can't block no matter how hard she tries.

<WARN.>

That can't be good. Ris? Are you there?
Silence.
V swallows against the lump in her throat. <*Warn? Warn me about what?*>
<*THE GROVE.*>
V shivers. "What is the Grove?" she whispers, but the heavy voice doesn't answer. She chaints, <*What is the Grove?*> She winces, waiting for the painful response.

V hears a band tuning their instruments. She opens one eye and finds herself on the cliffs of Inshmore, overlooking the amphitheater. Merion is performing a sound check and preparing for a show.

What in the name of the goddess is this?
She asks, <*What is this? What is the Grove?*>
<*WE SHALL SHOW.*>
Shit, this doesn't sound—
V's consciousness is flung into deep space.
She gasps, struggling for air. Her lungs burn, but she quickly realizes she doesn't need to breathe—not here. The Old Man of the Forest's vision envelops her completely.
Everything is dark. She holds her hands in front of her face but can't see them. There's a scent of gunpowder and scalding metal despite the fact there's no air. The emptiness stretches infinitely, pierced by stars she doesn't recognize. A massive shape looms ahead, blotting out the starlight. It is darker than black, a void so complete it appears to consume the reality around it.
Inky tentacles writhe from its core, stretching across space. Smaller orbs of the same blacker-than-darkness detach from its edges, floating away with eerie grace. They move purposefully, and V feels their raging purpose.
Is this the Grove?
One orb drifts near her, close enough to reveal its scale. It's

the size of a small moon, a perfect, horrifying sphere. Gravity pulls her toward it, but just as she's about to fall, the sphere accelerates, keeping her in a delicate orbit.

Gray spores release into the void from the orb's surface, trailing behind it like a dark comet. The spores spread far and wide until they disappear into the abyss. Their scent, earthy and herbal, tinged with an unsettling familiarity, reaches her.

Nutmeg?

V watches in helpless awe as the orb is caught by a planet's gravity and pulled into a tight orbit. The spores drift downward, burning up in the atmosphere, though a few drift gently onto several moons. Even from this distance, she recognizes the planet.

That's Tau Ceti f, but I can't see Brigid from here.

Time speeds up. She crashes into the ground and burrows beneath the soil. A network of roots spreads out from her, eventually sending feelers back to the surface. The cool air encourages her to spread wider, spiraling out in endless colonies. V repeatedly breaks apart and regrows until a sprawling forest of herself emerges, each tree independent, yet still V.

<Is that—was that you? Is that how you came to be here?>

V's mother lifts her chin, smiling at her after the first time V spoke with her mind. V sees the pride in Muther's eyes after mastering the difficult task at such an early age.

I think that's a yes.

The forest version of V wakes up to a Tau Ceti dawn. They begin to move, swaying as a collective of Vs growing together, independent but with a shared rootwork. Peaceful years pass until one day, a storm blows in, dark and furious, a menace that rains down a harsh voice.

Before it can speak, the Old Man of the Forest halts the vision abruptly. V finds herself back in the burl, no longer adrift in space, no longer entwined as part of the forest grove.

<Why won't you show me what happened next?>

"Violet!" V's mother pulls her by the hood of her tunic, pulling her young child out of the way of an oncoming boar. Had her mother not pulled her away at the last minute, she surely would've been trampled underfoot.

<I don't understand what that means.>
The Old Man of the Forest doesn't answer.

The answer dawns on her. The dark sphere she followed across the galaxy seeded the forest on Brigid. This forest. The Old Man of the Forest and the others woke up before the Grove could take hold, or they somehow rebelled. The sphere must have been trapped, unable to complete its mission. But even in a weakened state, the memory of it alone could crush V's consciousness.

V understands, though without the words to express it. The Grove uses these spheres to spread itself across the galaxy, planting forests that become its consciousness. These plants have the capacity for consciousness but are without identity until the Grove's emissary arrives. When that day comes, the Grove invades, extends itself telepathically through a quantum root-work, and replicates itself across the stars.

<Is that the Grove? That's the danger you wanted to warn me about?> she chaints weakly.

The Old Man of the Forest responds sorrowfully, resolutely, and painfully.

<YES.>

EIGHT
THE PROMISES WE MAKE

In Canopy, we say: to name something is to keep it. To keep something is to become responsible for its light, its shadow, and its end.

— Druidic Teaching
Oral Tradition

V's environmental jacket weighs heavily on her. Everything is heavy now. Her cheeks sag, and she fights the urge to let her face slide down her neck. Her body begs to lay flat on the ground, but she can't sit up from the boulder that once supported her so comfortably but now seems to pin her to the ground.

This is amazing!

It's an easy connection to make. The forest on Brigid is somehow related to the loquentes roots. If *Demeter*'s rootwork can manipulate gravitational waves on board the ship, she can only imagine what hundreds of square kilometers of telepathic forest can accomplish.

<*Can you manipulate gravity enough to move your moon?*>

There's no answer besides the rustle of leaves, and V decides that's the Old Man of the Forest's way of saying it's a dumb question.

<Why is it so heavy now?>

The answer comes as an impression of a memory.

Rowan tells V about his tribunal over a bottle of grav one evening. She sees three officers weigh the evidence before deciding his fate. No negligence was found on Rowan's part, but the only daughter of a weapons manufacturer died in the accident, and someone needed to be held responsible.

<His trial? Is this a trial?>

Leaves rustle, answering yet another question where the answer is obviously affirmative.

<For what?>

The weight of everything distracts her and interrupts her thoughts. She fidgets with her sleeves and collar, trying to get comfortable. Eventually, she finds a position where her flight suit can hang just right without cutting off her circulation.

Without meaning to, she drifts into another deep slumber.

A childlike apparition taps her on the shoulder as if to play a prank. She wakes with a start. She looks over her shoulder, but there's no one there. She stands up for a better view, but she's alone here in this part of the forest.

Gravity feels like Earth standard, which is heavier than she's used to after eight months on board *Demeter*. It has no effect on the puffy flakes of snow drifting and falling around her. Her boots sink lightly with each soft step, making a satisfying crunch. Giggling, she takes another step to enjoy the sensation and then another.

A familiar voice calls her in the distance. V turns around several times, making several disjointed circles, looking for the source. There's nothing but an endless orchard of squat snow-covered trees.

"Ris? Is that you?" V doesn't recognize her voice, at least not at first. She clears her voice and asks again. "Ris?" she repeats as a test. She holds her tiny, mitten-clad hands. She had a pair just like these when she was eight. She wrings her hands together to see if these are hers. They haven't for a long time; they belong to a child. Her tongue taps a fresh gap where her top eyetooth used to be.

"Who's Ris?" A teenage girl steps out from behind a tree and lowers the fur-lined hood of her jacket from her head. Ris was always good at hiding from her sister when they played in the woods together.

V fights it, but the words force their way out of her mouth. "You are, silly. You're Ris!" V covers her mouth with both hands. Bits of snow are frozen to the fuzzy mittens. The cool sting is refreshing.

"No, Violet," she corrects. "I'm Iris. I-ris." She pulls the large hood down to reveal her face. V loved her sister's straight black hair, but she could never spend the time brushing it when she could be outside playing in the woods like this.

Her older sister smiles, bright red lips contrasting against the white tableau. V will never forget how her sister looked on this winter break, freshly home from Grove of Glenoak Seminary.

"Iii-ris! Iii-rrris!" V mocks her sister, saying her name as flowery as possible. "Iris, Iris! We have such silly names, don't we?"

"We do, Violet. We do. Muther really overdid it with the garden names, didn't she?" She puts her arm around her little sister for warmth. V will never admit to being cold, but she doesn't shrug Ris away as they walk aimlessly.

"We should pick new names," V declares with a grin.

Ris rolls her eyes, knowing she'll melt for V's grin every time. "Okay, so what new name would you give me?"

"You?" V giggles. "You can pick your own name. That's the fun part."

"I'm afraid not, Violet. Muther always said you can name

anything you want, but if you do, you're responsible for it forever."

"Hey, I already care for Murray." She puts her hands on her hips indignantly. "And she only said that about kittens anyway."

Ris says, "You remember what they say every month in Canopy? 'Names are important; they hold power.' So, I name you, and you name me, and then we're responsible for each other forever and ever. Okay?"

"Deal." V shrugs into her sister's arm to seal the agreement. "I like that."

"So? Don't leave me in suspense. What new name does fair Violet have in store for me?"

V folds her arms proudly and smirks. "I already picked it. Ris!"

Ris gives an unexpected glare. "Psh, that's just the second half of my normal name."

V tugs on Ris's jacket sleeve for her to accept it. "I know, but I like it better that way. Plus, it's a single syllable, so it's automatically cooler. It's just like Rik." V had discovered Ris's album collection while she was away and instantly developed a crush on most of the members of Merion. V crooned over how cool they all were for having a single monosyllabic name: Neil, Zim, and Rik.

Ris cocks her head and smiles. "Cooler? Because it's a single syllable, huh? Goddess, girl, how'd you grow up to be so chic? But yeah. I can rock it. So now I'm Ris." With a wide grin, she pushes her finger into the point of V's nose. "And now you must be responsible for me from now on!" she teases.

"And what about me?" V worries there's nothing left that could be cooler than a single syllable.

"If single-syllable names are cool, then now about—" Ris covers her mouth in dramatic suspense with both hands before rendering her decision. "There's only one thing cooler than a single syllable: a single letter!"

V's eyes are like saucers in anticipation.

"V. From now on, I'll call you V."

V squeals. "I feckin love it!" She puts both mittens over her mouth in embarrassment.

Ris's eyes open with a start. "Language! What if Muther heard you say that?"

"She'd wash my mouth with arak bark, but I don't care. I'm feckin V!"

"Language!" says with a grin, trying to sound scandalized but clearly amused. "I guess I'm responsible for you, now. You're stuck with me. Forever!" She laughs mockingly as if she had just tricked V into making a pact with a forest sprite.

"Ugh, don't be so extra!" V shrugs.

They walk for a few minutes in silence. The only sound they hear is the snow giving way beneath their feet. Ris's arm is still around V. Even though V has warmed up by now, she still hangs on to her sister's sleeve.

"Ris?"

"Yeah, Vio— V?"

"I love my name, thank you."

"You're welcome, V," Ris stresses the name with as much cooler-big-sister energy as anyone.

"But I think we should give ourselves new names. One for just us." Then she leans in to whisper loudly, "A secret name."

Ris nods. "Okay."

"What do you think of Flower? For both of us."

"We can't have the same name," Ris scoffs.

V steps back and squares her shoulders. "Sure we can! If naming something gives you power, then if we share the name, then we have control over our own destinies!" The devilish grin is made perfect by the missing tooth.

Ris presses her lips together, trying to prevent a laugh. "I swear, I go away to Glenoak for a few months, and you somehow get even cleverer. You may have found a way around the system. Well done, Flower!" She offers a high-five, which V nearly misses as she slips in the snow.

V beams. Her sister is the only one who notices how grown-up V has become.

Ris slows her pace to get V's attention before looking down at her. "Hey. I'll always be around to look after you, Flower. You know that, right?"

"And I'll always look after you too, Flower," V answers, her smile much softer now.

A voice calls for them in the distance, breaking the solemnity of the moment. The snow muffles the sound, but the voice is unmistakable. The tone is precise, and the words are clipped in a Received Pronunciation accent. "Girls, it's time to come inside." The words are spoken with as much polish as the girls have ever heard.

Ris shouts in response, "Coming, Muther!" Her voice is fully drenched in a thick Galwegian accent, a deliberate and gritty contrast. She could practically feel her Muther seethe even without a telepathic connection.

Reaching a small cottage surrounded by brick garden beds, the girls pick up their pace and walk up several curved sets of cobblestone steps. Their mother is waiting for them at the door with cups of hot chocolate.

"Violet, you look just absolutely miserable. Come inside, my sweet child, and warm yourself by the fire. Here," she hands V a steaming mug with a gentle smile. Turning to Iris, her eyes soften even more. "Iris, thank you, my lovely young lady, for always looking after your little sister," she says, pressing the second mug into her hands with a tenderness that lingers even after the touch is gone.

"Thanks, Muther."

"I'm not Violet. I'm V!" She grins defiantly at her mother, baring her toothy gap like a badge of honor. "And she's not Iris, she's Ris." She giggles and runs inside.

Ris hides a guilty smile, knowing she helped fuel V's moment of cheeky bravado. She runs after her little sister, laughter trailing behind her.

The girls join each other by the large fireplace, sitting on a thick rug in front of the hearth. Their mother places a long wool blanket around their shoulders to share. V removes her mittens so she can wrap child-sized hands around her mug. The combined heat of the mug and the fire soothe her frigid fingers.

An older V closes her eyes, savoring the warmth. She holds on tightly to this memory for as long as she can. The smell of wood smoke fills her nostrils, perhaps too much for a nostalgic memory, but campfires could sometimes become uncomfortable. A tickle of ash on her throat causes her to gag and cough harshly.

<Did I pass the trial?>

Leaves rustle in the distance.

ESS *Demeter* bustles with activity, though an unusual hush looms over the crew. the ship's AI hindered by quantum interference, the command staff works overtime to compensate for its absence. Navigators chart their course by hand. The quartermaster dispatches ensigns to storerooms for inventory checks. Orders are scribbled on scraps of packaging and discarded requisition forms, then relayed on foot. Tasks once effortless now demand time, sweat, and vigilance.

After sixteen hours on the bridge, Captain Hargreaves works from the office at the front of his quarters, receiving reports from ensigns delivered to his door every half-hour. He slumps in his chair, rubbing at his temples with the heels of his hands. His notes blur together, the scrawl of his handwriting indistinguishable after hours of trying to make sense of everything. "Just one more report," he lies. Bekhti's voice echoes in his mind: "Get some rest, sir," to which he scoffs yet again.

He rereads the five most recent status updates, which vary only by a few synonyms, before tossing them aside with a heavy sigh. At some point, he calls out for *Demeter* out of habit but is met with heavy silence. He stares at the tumbler of grav sweating on his leather notepad but keeps it in reserve for the inevitable good news from the landing party. Another episode of *Captains of Old* sounds good, but now isn't the time.

He hears a muffled ping from somewhere. He doesn't think too much about it until he hears it three more times quickly. His eyes dart over his desk, and he sees the glow of a small tablet buried underneath several layers of thin, discolored scraps of paper.

As before, several incoming text messages from *Demeter* await him on his spare comms tablet.

> Demeter: Requested status update incoming...
>
> Demeter: Captain, are you available for a status update?
>
> Demeter: Captain?
>
> Demeter: John?
>
> Demeter: I have an important update regarding security status. Please respond.

The messages each came less than a minute apart. Hargreaves is concerned about the persistence, so he picks up the tablet to give *Demeter* his full attention.

> John: I'm here. Go ahead.

> Demeter: I have detected a critical malfunction in the primary weapons systems. There has been an unauthorized access attempt. I suspect someone wishes to sabotage the primary mission of deploying the hyperspace navigational buoy with the Kentaurans and Atharans. I need your assistance to lock this system down since I cannot interface with it directly.

Hargreaves doesn't know what to make of this request. It's strange that *Demeter* wouldn't already have access to the ship's primary weapons—especially for something as critical as defense. She asked for elevated security clearance just a few days ago, and even that set off alarm bells. Still, he's long suspected some Earth-First zealot might try to sabotage the mission, and right now is the perfect moment for someone hoping to derail the alliance before it begins.

Stranger still, he finds himself relieved to have *Demeter* offering advice—an AI system he usually tries to ignore.

John: What do you need?

Demeter: I need an authorization code to access the primary weapons systems so that I may lock out anyone attempting to gain unauthorized access.

Demeter: Time is critical. They may try again any moment, and I might not be able to stop them this time.

Hargreaves tosses the tablet onto his desk, scattering a carefully curated stack of paper notes. He grabs the tumbler and chokes back the drink in a single stinging swallow.

"Fuck it!" He's too tired to distrust his ship right now.

He pulls up his password vault on his wristpad and presses his thumb on the biometrics scanner. Then, he holds the wristpad up to his face to secondarily authenticate his identity with a retinal scan. He braces for the third round of verification. A sharp sting lets him know the wristpad is now analyzing his blood for genetic analysis and to detect the presence of nanobots.

A few seconds later, a long string of letters, numbers, and other characters appear on the screen. He copies the authentication key in the wristpad's buffer. He finds a sync cable in a desk drawer and connects his wristpad to the small table where *Demeter* has been reaching out for help.

Before now, the display screens in his office listed a series of offline systems, all in red. After connecting the two devices, one office display lit up a single row in less than a second.

Weapons Systems: Recalibration is underway.

The sudden change in color catches his attention. He taps on the adjacent icon, which expands the display to show a full status readout of the primary weapons.

Particle Beams: 6%

Orbital Missiles: 1%

Tactical Nuclear Ordinance: 0%

Mesolasers: 1%

The numbers next to particle beams and orbital missiles increase slowly and gradually. The indicator for tactical nukes doesn't move and turns red after a few minutes, still displaying "0%" next to it. The mesolaser indicator fluctuates between 1% and 6%, with numbers in between.

"*Demeter*? What in the twin hells is going on?" Hargreaves waits for a reply before remembering that all voice commands are unrecognizable.

He picks up his tablet.

John: Demeter, what just happened?

Demeter: Thank you, Captain. I have most of what I need. I may still need you to authorize a nuclear strike, but now I can target the threat on the surface of the moon below.
Bombardment will commence as soon as the particle beam weaponry is fully charged.
Missiles are being loaded, which should be sufficient for complete elimination unless we encounter resistance.

John: What? No! Stop. Abort.

John: Do not fire!

Demeter: Particle beams are charging. It is too late to abort the strike.

John: What strike? I didn't authorize this.

Demeter: You did authorize this. You sent me your private key for the primary weapons system. This authorized me to eliminate any threats to my safety.

My safety.

The words on the screen shake him. *Demeter* has never talked like this before. She never put herself before the crew or the mission.

Hargreaves steps to the emergency phone to contact the bridge.

Before he can reach out, it rings.

"Fuck. Fuck!" He's tired, and processing what's happening in real time makes him dizzy.

He picks up the receiver, and the mangled, coiled wire unfurls in a chaotic, twisted mess. The once neat coil now resembles a knotted serpent, looping into a snarled tangle. Absent-mindedly, he tugs at the knots, hoping to straighten them out while using the neglected phone handset.

"Hargreaves here."

"Captain, DeSoto. We've picked up some unusual activity with the weapons systems. They appear to have all been activated. What do we do, sir?"

"Belay all strike orders, Lieutenant Commander DeSoto. Under no circumstances will you let this ship fire on the surface below. There is no threat, understood? No threat."

"Understood, sir. But there's just one thing, sir. We don't have operational control over those systems anymore. We can't call off the strike from up here."

Hargreaves cups the receiver to his mouth. "Listen. You need to send a runner. Grab whatever ensign is next to you. Twin hells, go yourself if you have to. Just tell the weapons crew to shut everything down, no matter what else they've been told!"

"Yessi—" The line cuts out, and Hargreaves can no longer hear DeSoto's response. Hopefully, the order has gone through.

He pours two fingers of grav into his tumbler. He lifts the glass in a salute, looking at his entertainment display where he often plays audio casts of *The Captains of Old*. He stares into the dark mirror of a cold display screen. Only his reflection stares back.

A klaxon blares.

Overhead lights flash gold, bathing the cabin in an eerie, strobing glow. Hargreaves bolts upright, and the tumbler slips from his grasp and shatters on the floor. The vibration in the deck beneath his boots grows stronger—a rhythmic pulse that shakes the very bones of *Demeter*.

"What the fuck now?" he yells, his voice drowned out by the escalating noise.

A shrill whir echoes through the ship, climbing to a pitch that makes his ears ring. The lights flicker as *Demeter* reroutes power, like a long-dormant nerve firing back to life—prickly, unstable, and charging with violent intent.

And then it happens.

A thunderous clap, impossibly loud and immediate, rips through the cabin and the corridors outside. He knows that sound too well, though he hasn't heard it since the final days of the Pavonian incursions. It's the unmistakable discharge of a particle beam. Not just once. Again. And again. Each shot builds on the last, a relentless barrage.

"No. No, no, no!" Hargreaves grabs the phone, yanking it to his ear. The twisted cord snaps back, slapping against his wrist as he punches the bridge's line. Dead. He slams the receiver into its cradle and stumbles toward the door, adrenaline melting his sleep deprivation.

The ship lurches, the deck shudders as *Demeter* fires another volley. Hargreaves shouts, though no one can hear him. "Belay that goddamn order!"

He stops and considers both directions of the corridor as

golden strobes cast disorienting shadows. He's too far from the weapons bay, too far from the bridge. Every particle beam fired hammers home the futility of his actions.

The moon. The landing party. His crew.

Another blast. Then another.

Hargreaves slams his fist into the wall, his knuckles splitting against the unyielding metal. He turns and slides down the bulkhead and lands on the deck. Cold realization sinks into his chest.

Demeter *betrayed us!*

"What the feck was that?" V coughs, choking on the smoke from a clogged fireplace filling her lungs with heat and ash.

<FOUND!>

V is thrown back by the force of the Old Man of the Forest's response. A wave of guilt and apology nearly drowns her before she realizes she's experiencing his unbridled emotion.

She's outside again, in the snow-covered forest of her past.

Snow? No, this is ash.

There's no cold. No heat. Only a suffocating stillness.

"Found?" she croaks aloud, coughing. After the initial silence, she tries again. <*Found? Who found us?*>

The forest twists around her, trees groaning in pain as their roots strain against the soil. Sickly darkness seeps through the canopy, staining the burgundy leaves with spreading black veins that drip and ooze. The air thickens, heavy with the scent of decay as the forest rots from within.

A star-sized entity looms over them, darker than black, its surface writhing with tendrils of void-like shadow. The Grove pulses once, then again, and finally spreads outward, an unstoppable plague blotting out the stars.

Fire erupts in its wake, now the only light in this world, and reduces the forest to charred skeletons. Entire landscapes are consumed, the ground shattering like glass. A booming echo resonates through her mind. A dark, effulgent sun is coming, one that won't stop until they are nothing but ash.

<*Shit. What do we do?*> she asks The Old Man of the Forest. There's a long, contemplative silence.

Ris and V sprint with wild exhilaration when the gates to Merion's final world tour open. They weave through the crowd with a single goal: to claim their spot at the barricade, right in front of the stage, where the music feels most alive.

V runs when bullies throw rocks for briefly losing control of her abilities in the village on a crowded market day.

She runs from the police after fighting three men outside a pub in Rimeholt, a fight that ultimately left three assholes in a hospital.

She sprints with everything she has during Fleet basic training to leave Earth behind, shattering a hundred-meter dash record in the process.

<*How will running help?*>

A crying mother pushes a bundled baby into V's arms as an unknown war-torn village crumbles to ash around them. V was never here in her real life, but it's a scene she knows about. She finds herself in the crow's nest of an ancient ship, the bundle cradled in her arms as they float among the stars. Finally, she peeks inside the bundle, finding a tree sapling with its roots bound in a damp cloth.

<*A sapling? I don't understand.*>

A loud explosion snaps V out of the metaphysical realm and slams her against the boulder where she's been cradled. The grass around her sways in stormy winds.

Beside her, a tall, willowy sprig trembles as it bends back toward the ground, its tiny burgundy leaves quivering with the effort. Nearby, a thick root writhes like a slow-moving serpent, nudging the reluctant sapling's gnarled roots upward, lifting them free from the stubborn soil.

<*THIS.*>

V finds herself in the metaphysical ashen forest again. The same sapling struggles at her feet, trying to reestablish its roots back into the ground, regardless of which world this is.

<*What is this?*> she asks.

The air fills with hollow silence. Not the absence of sound but a profound emptiness of the soul. This moon exists without names. The concept is foreign to the Old Man of the Forest, where all entities know each other as a singular thought.

<*This has no name?*>

V sits in Ris's room, where her sister introduces her to a brand-new album.

<*THOSE MARKS.*>
<*What feckin marks?*>

The tip of a branch presses her chest

Me? Does it mean me?

V looks down to find her environmental jacket unzipped, exposing her favorite T-shirt. She still talks about the best show she has ever seen: *Merion / Roots Rebellion Tour / 2368.*

<Wait, these marks?>

Leaves rustle.

<Merion. It's a band from —>

<MERION.>

<Yeah, Merion. That's —>

<PROTECT MERION.>

<I mean, they're the best feckin band to ever —>

Ris says, "You remember what they say every Canopy? 'Names are important; they hold power.' So, I name you, and you name me, and then we're responsible for each other forever and ever. Okay?"

V looks watches at the sapling being uprooted against its will. It struggles to dislodge a few remaining pebbles clinging to its roots. *I haven't been to Canopy in years. Not since Ris died.*

She chaints, *<Name it Merion?>*

<NAMED!>

<Wait, did you name it after my shirt?>

<YOU NAMED.>

The answer hits like an accusation.

<I didn't name anything. You asked me —>

V exhales a white cloud from blue lips and shudders. Ris's faint voice reminds her not to name the kitten found in a snow bank, or Muther would force her to take care of it through the rest of the winter months before returning it to the woods.

<NAMED, RESPONSIBLE.>

The response nearly splits her skull.

Of course, the Old Man of the Forest knows that feckin rule, she thinks to herself. Then she chaints, <*Okay, okay. I'll look after Merion. But save it from what?*>

<*STORM COMING.*>

<*What storm?*>

The ashen forest shatters around her. The earth beneath her feet quakes violently. Shadows and fire intermingle, and the moon erupts in chaos. V is thrust back to the jagged stone, then to the burl chair, and finally to the landing zone, where the crew looks skyward in terror. Her senses flicker between places, and her perceptions break apart. Each transition is faster and more disorienting.

Black smoke fills the gaps, devouring the spaces between moments. Each breath tastes of ash, and each heartbeat pounds with the echo of destruction.

V collapses as the Old Man of the Forest marches to war. Her hands tremble and clutch the fragile sapling as if it were the only important creature in a world scattering to atoms.

Parker's been out of medbay for a few days now—cleared for light duty, but not much else. With no official assignments and too much time to kill, he's taken refuge in his personal workroom just off the main engineering corridor, tinkering with old gear and rechecking long-abandoned signal logs. The scratches and pings in his headset snap into sharp, undeniable clarity. He's been chasing this signal for half his life, and now—finally—it's consistent enough to get a lock.

He flips to a page in his notebook covered with dots and lines, then matches them to the audio with a tapping pencil. "This is it!" he yells, hammering a freshly regrown fist on the desk and ignoring the pain through his exuberance. "There it fucking is!"

When the pattern starts over, he notes the combination of frequencies, channels, and filters on a fresh page. "6-E-Q-U-J-5."

He notates the signal strength and duration patterns, pressing hard enough to snap the pencil's lead.

"WOW!"

This is the clearest compound quantum signal he's ever witnessed. He dogears the page and flips back to the previous dotted patterns. The seventy-two-second pattern has started over and repeats precisely as before.

Parker has searched for an interstellar cryptid since childhood, and he's found more proof of its existence in one sitting than he and his fellow cryptid hunters have recorded in decades. He rips off his headphones, tossing them aside.

He hears the emergency claxons for the first time. He grabs his wristpad from its charging station. "RED ALERT, ALL HANDS" scrolls across the screen in large type.

"What in the twin hells?"

A low hum vibrates through the deck beneath him and grows steadier. The sound swells into a bone-shaking resonance, cutting through the ship like a pulse. Parker remembers the same unsettling tremor from live-ammo drills aboard his old frigate.

"Are we shooting?" he mumbles in disbelief. "At what?"

He puts on his boots, buttons his uniform jacket, and taps the "ACKNOWLEDGE" icon on his wristpad. A duty station assignment appears, informing him of his return to "limited" active-duty status, followed by the details of his rally point in one of the hangar bays.

"What the fuck?"

Demeter instructs Parker to report to the flight deck of the secondary hangar bay. He's taken most of the training modules on board but has yet to qualify as part of any deck crew. Besides, his regrown fingers are too tender to do real work.

I guess we'll see when I get there, he thinks.

Parker passes several crewmembers who are too busy to stop when he asks what's happening. Taking several lifts and passageways as quickly as his injuries allow, he runs to the service entrance to the hangar deck. The door swooshes open to let him pass and clanks shut behind him, startling him.

The hangar bay is empty, except for the old dropship in storage. He consults his wristpad for further instructions.

"STAND BY."

After a few expletives, Parker stomps back to the service entrance, but the door doesn't open. He hammers the security panel. Nothing. Despite the green light's assurance, the door refuses to move. Gritting his teeth, he cranks the manual wheel to release the dog arms, but his new fingers are too weak. Frustrated, he kicks the door, reminding him of his other injuries.

"Okay, Parks, deep breath," he mutters, channeling his officer training. He exhales slowly, forcing himself to assess the situation by the book.

"There's no one else here," he lists aloud, pacing the hangar deck. "This is the secondary bay, so it's supposed to be empty. The live-fire situation is the most likely, right? Unless we're evacuating. We haven't been hit. Good." His eyes land on the battered dropship nearby. "Poor *Arion* still looks like a piece of shit. No updates from *Demeter*. Great. And, oh yeah—I'm locked in. Fantastic. He raises his hands and turns his thoughts to bigger questions. "Why is no one here? And why send *me* here? Why are we shooting?"

Parker rubs his chest and winces. "I need to get back in shape," he wheezes. "Too much sitting around lately." He leans against a nearby terminal to catch his breath. He idly swipes through the screens until something catches his eye.

"The hells?"

A previous officer must have forgotten to log out. A live status feed streams across the screen. The administrative access is well above Parker's clearance level.

"Lucky break for me," Parker mutters, his pulse quickening as he scans the information, "not so much for you when I turn your ass in." His amused snicker turns into a dry cough.

Demeter is firing at something, but Parker can't tell what or who. He hears the resonant hum of a full particle beam volley. Missile launches follow—the big ones meant for large-scale bombardments. He doesn't hear point-defense weapons or the repulsion cannons used in ship-to-ship combat.

Parker's hums as he tries to piece it together. The landing party must have found the source of the interference, and *Demeter* must be attacking the transmitter.

"Shit. I hope they're okay down there," he whispers, his voice hoarse and strained. A thought gnaws at him. This feels like overkill. The bombardment is relentless. *Demeter* will erase thousands of square kilometers at this rate.

"Okay, let's see what they found down there." He scrolls through tactical screens and finds a targeting map, but it doesn't make sense.

"Oh, fuck," he coughs.

Demeter isn't defending the landing party. She's attacking them.

His breath catches as his eyes dart across the screen. The landing party's approximate coordinates are marked with every weapon system locked onto their location. The ship is sparing no effort to obliterate them.

His heart pounds in his throat. "No, no, no. This can't be right." More than a dozen people are down there.

Hector is down there!

"Assess, Parker," he mutters, his voice cracking. "What do you..." He falls into a coughing fit.

He strains to refocus his eyes to scan the readouts. The nukes are locked out, and targeting systems are offline; blessings from Gaia.

He's unsure if anyone else on board knows the landing party is in danger. He's trapped in the hangar bay and can't help.

Parker's mind races as he considers his options, but he can't focus. "What is wrong with me?" he wheezes.

The hangar swirls. He presses two fingers to his neck to check his pulse, then waves a hand in front of his face. "Shit.

Dizzy. Tunnel vision. Hypoxic." His words dissolve into a wheezing cough. "Think. Need air."

He pulls up the hangar bay's climate controls to override the pressurization manually. It's standard protocol for emergencies like a hull breach. The options appear on the terminal, but every control is grayed out.

A status field at the top of the display screen reads: *Most dangerous human in Tau Ceti neutralized.*

"Oh, what the fuck!" he rasps.

He cuts himself off, realizing he's wasting precious air.

Parker scans the hangar. A single reinforced door separates the deck from the void of space. Emergency gear and pressurized suits should line the bulkheads, but the storage shelves have been neglected. He tries to yell, "Fu—" but collapses into another coughing fit, clutching his burning chest.

Arion doesn't look like a piece-of-shit dropship now. That beautiful beast might be his only source of breathable air. He forces a few shallow breaths, enough to push through the haze in his mind, and stumbles toward the dropship with a blend of desperation and determination.

A stack of storage bins block the dropship's main hatch, but there's another entrance underneath. Crawling under *Arion's* hull is more manageable than walking, though not by much. The curved metal brushes his back as he wedges through, and he winces at the absurd thought of being flattened by a parked ship. He swallows the panic and focuses on reaching the main hatch.

A green "DISENGAGE" icon flickers on a panel above him. His shaking hand slams the button, and the hatch's dog arms retract with a metallic groan.

The seal hisses open, releasing a rush of cool air that washes over his face. He gasps—an involuntary, desperate pull. It hits him like plunging into cold water after a fever: sharp, overwhelming, and impossibly sweet. For a moment, there's nothing but breath. Not thought. Not fear. Just the raw, aching relief of oxygen flooding his lungs.

"Thank the fucking gods," he wheezes, swearing just to prove there's still some danger left in him yet.

He clambers up the hatch with unsteady movements then seals it behind him. The stark simplicity of *Arion*'s air—oxygen, nitrogen, and a dash of Kentauran hydrogen sulfide—feels like stinky salvation. He sinks against the bulkhead, pulling his collar loose as the dizziness fades.

He pats the deck. "Thank you, old man."

For now, he's safe.

But Hector isn't.

NINE
BURNING BRIGID

We raised our glasses one by one,
Beneath the fairy lights,
Glowing like lasting memories,
Across the summer skies.
You kissed me once, said you'd stay,
Until the final spark.
We vowed to dance forever
Alone in the dark.

— MERION
"THE NIGHT WE NAMED FOREVER"

"Move it, move it!" Hector's voice cuts through the roar of the forest fire and the approaching thunder of bombardment. "Evac in five!" He waves his arms frantically, the smoke thickening as the inferno grows around them. "Maybe four! Hustle, people!"

Particle beams slam into the forest's edge; their impacts erupt in a deafening explosion. Shockwaves rip through the security perimeter, sending storage containers and equipment flying. The blasts are erratic and random. Even without precision, the unrelenting assault is devastating the surrounding countryside.

Hot gusts of air sting Hector's face as he inches backward toward *Persephone*. Landing party members rush past him, scrambling up the boarding ramp. His ship mechanic, Calloway, is still missing. His gut churns. If he isn't back soon, Hector will have to begin the launch sequence himself. But someone needs to keep order on the ground. These people are his responsibility. All of them.

Ensign Mallow stumbles into view, half-carrying the injured master-at-arms. His arm dangles in a makeshift sling, and a tourniquet bites into his bloody leg.

"Ensign, I'll take him." Hector reaches out, his tone firm.

"I've got him, sir." She shifts the weight with urgency in her tone.

"Look, *Persephone* needs to fly. If Calloway isn't back soon, I'll have to light the fires myself. You take over down here. Make sure everyone gets on board. Everyone. We lift in three."

Her jaw tightens as she nods. She shifts out from under the MA, letting Hector shoulder the burden, then turns to bark the same orders at the stragglers who scramble to salvage a few research samples. Her voice carries the authority of someone unwilling to leave anyone behind.

Hector hauls the injured man up the ramp and straps him into the nearest harness. A quick glance confirms Mallow's tourniquet is holding, and the MA's pupils react to the light, albeit slowly. "You're going to be fine," Hector assures him. "Now stay put." He rushes to the cockpit.

"Folks, this takeoff will drop your lunch, so strap in tight. We're lifting in three." Hector begins the pre-launch sequence, flicking toggle switches and connecting hoses to recently replenished tanks.

The engines need at least a minute to warm up. He jumps into the cockpit. From here, he has a clear view of the landing zone. He's thankful to see the ensign guiding the remaining visible crew up the ramp. Everyone except for one tall figure.

"Gods dammit, Dradi." Hector's teeth grind as he spots the Kentauran running in the opposite direction. He bangs on the canopy, trying in vain to get his attention. "Dradi, get your ass back here!"

He turns and yells at Mallow. "Ensign, tell that bug to get back here right now, or I'm leaving his ass behind."

A mission when comms are down. Thanks, Captain.

A garbled voice crackles through his wristpad.

Or are they?

"Hector? Can you—me?"

"Parks?" Hector adjusts the signal, heart catching in his throat. "Holy shit! That you?"

A long delay

Hector holds his breath.

"Yeah—fuck, you're—alive—" Relief floods the broken signal, even through the static.

Hector exhales hard, somewhere between a laugh and a sob. "Well, I'll be godsdamned. Good timing, asshole."

But the clearing grabs his attention. Dradi's finally running in the right direction now, a limp body slung over his shoulder. The young ensign runs to help.

He presses the wristpad harder. "Talk later. Who's shooting at us?"

A burst of static. Then a single word:

"Demeter."

Hector has a hundred questions, but a blinding explosion interrupts them. The cockpit shakes violently as debris slams against the windows. The canopy is cracked, but the damage appears to be isolated to the outer shell.

Running out of time, Hector checks the engine status again, urging the engines to hurry. *Persephone* is almost launch-ready. She needs just a little more time.

When the smoke clears, Hector sees the body—crumpled, unmoving. His stomach drops.

Hector doesn't remember leaving the cockpit. One moment, he's at the controls; the next, he's kneeling beside the crumpled body of the ensign.

She's gone.

His hands hover for a second—useless, trembling—before instinct takes over. There's no time to grieve. No time to gather the bodies. The most he can do is light a path so the gods can find their souls.

He straightens her, smoothing her hair out of her face. Then he reaches into his pocket and pulls out a coin.

He closes her limp hand around it.

Finding a sharp piece of debris nearby, he carves a Stygian rune in the soil. Gaia doesn't yet have a hearth on Brigid, and this place is beyond Ouranos' reach. Without the mark, there's no other way for the gods to find these poor souls. It's a beacon for Charon to collect the lost and ferry them home.

The mechanic's blood-soaked body is a few meters away. "Why didn't you stay closer to the boat, you asshole?" Hector's voice cracks, unable to hold back his anger. "That's the only coin I had, Calloway, so you two have to share a ride with the Ferryman."

Even in death, Dradi hasn't let go of Calloway—the man he nearly carried back to *Persephone* and her protection.

"Dradi, Fuck," he whispers, crawling to the Kentauran's side. Blood pools beneath him, dark and viscous. Hector hesitates before touching the body, the gaping wound in Dradi's torso exposed.

There's no bioluminescence, no colorful patterns. His skin is pallid from blood loss, the same as the Earther he died trying to save. "I'm so sorry," Hector says, "I don't know what you need to get to the other—"

A sharp, metallic taste rises in Hector's throat—grief, guilt, and adrenaline twisting in his gut. He doubles over, retching into the dirt. The acrid stench of smoke and blood clings to him, but there's no time to fall apart. He forces himself to his knees.

Spitting, he yells, "Parker, you close?"

"—almost—your status?"

"Everyone's back, but it's holy-fucked down here."

"Get—there, Hector—siles!"

His wristpad beeps. *Persephone*'s engines are ready for lift-off.

Hector rises on unsteady legs. *I'll get everyone else out. I swear.*

He forces himself to turn and focus, ignoring the inferno consuming the forest. The crackling flames and *Persephone*'s engines are the only sounds he hears now. The survivors are waiting. Hector has to move without hesitation.

The air cracks as hypersonic missiles strike the landing zone. An explosion rips through the clearing. Something hot slams into his back, and he hits the ground hard. A high-pitched ringing fills his ears, pain screams in his legs, his chest, his— his arm—

No. Not his arm. That's just heat and air. His arm is gone.

The pain isn't even the worst part.

Through the haze of blood and fire, Hector looks back and watches as the landing struts buckle. *Persephone* collapses, toppling to her side with everyone still on board.

Parker snaps his wristpad into the docking station, connecting it to *Arion*'s fractured navigation system. The console is a shamble of half-assembled panels and exposed wiring, owing to months of salvaging for spare parts. He holds his breath as the link establishes, unsure if there's enough circuitry left.

The dropship sputters to life, and relief and terror compete in his chest. This is the worst idea he's ever had, and he's had plenty, but it's the only one he has.

Okay, Parker. Assess the situation, he thinks, recalling those endless training modules. It's a garbage plan, to be sure. *No pressure suit, so no way to the control room. No fucking air except in here. Bay door's locked. I'm sealed in with an antique and I'm all out of prayers.*

Fuck it!

Parker grabs a breathing mask hanging from a nearby charging station. The orange light blinks on its base; not great, but it's better than nothing. He pulls a few deep breaths, testing that it'll be enough to keep the vertigo at bay.

Crawling out from *Arion*'s underbelly, Parker staggers toward the hangar-bay door. It's locked down with thick safety bolts. Pain flares through his still-tender fingers as he loosens them with a handheld spanner, but the door is stuck. He slams the spanner down, panting, and leans against the door.

The breather's light turns yellow.

"Come on, Parker. Think. Assess. Act." He closes his eyes, recalling the steps outlined in his emergency training modules.

Scanning the hangar, his eyes land on a loading crane, its claw dangling overhead. A heavy-duty chain sits on a nearby wall rack. The security rings on the hangar door are large enough for the hooks. He ratchets the chain tight, the metal links creaking under the strain.

"Genius!"

Parker secures the chain to the dropship's frame. The setup looks ridiculous, even to him. The chain, wrapped around the crane and door, is meant to yank the entire thing free when *Arion* takes off.

"Time to see what you're made of, old man," he mutters as he crawls back through *Arion*'s hatch.

Parker flips the switches to finish the pre-flight sequence. His hands shake as he disengages the safety clamps. He drains the rest of the air from the mask.

"Tonight, I dine with either Hector or Ouranos. Let's find out."

He slams the throttle forward.

Arion shudders as the engines roar to life under protest. Parker grips the controls tightly, and his knuckles turn pink as he pushes the throttle harder. With a groan, the hangar-bay door wrenches free, tearing from its frame in a cacophony of shrieking metal. The engine blast forces loose tools and debris into space as the door flies into the dropship's nose.

"Shit, shit, shit," Parker hisses as *Arion* lurches forward, dragging the massive door behind it. The dropship shudders violently, angry at the abuse. Parker fights the controls, his newly regrown fingers straining to maintain their grip.

Clearing the hangar, he tilts *Arion* downward, flinging the hangar door with sharp angular momentum. The chain snaps with a sharp crack, sending broken pieces of *Demeter*'s hull and equipment tumbling toward the surface.

An alarm warns him of a weapons lock.

He looks for defensive systems, but there's not enough time to find them. He wiggles the controls, hoping his random trajectory buys him a little luck. Point-defense weapons fire blazes past, striking the falling door but sparing *Arion* and Parker.

"Thank the gods," Parker breathes, still panting from the launch.

The moon looms larger with every heartbeat. At this speed, he'll hit the surface in fifteen minutes—less, if *Arion*'s retro rockets don't work. Sonic booms split the sky as the dropship plunges into the atmosphere. Plasma dances along the canopy, licking at the viewports.

From behind, *Demeter*'s assault is a storm of annihilation. Particle beams slice through the atmosphere like vengeful demons thirsty for blood. Missiles rain across the forest, leaving molten craters in their wake. Parker's eyes widen as the chaos unfolds, and the devastation is so complete that it feels otherworldly.

The controls fight him as turbulence from the particle beams rock the dropship. Parker strains, the harness digging into his shoulders as *Arion* cries with pings of metal fatigue. A blinding flash to his left sends him spinning. He curses the gods and wrenches the controls back as hard as possible.

The navigation panel flickers, and Parker locks onto Hector's signal. Through the dense smoke and flames, he spots a clearing a few kilometers from *Persephone*'s landing zone. It'll have to be close enough.

"Come on, you beautiful bastard," Parker cajoles. "Just a little farther."

The retro rockets are sluggish, and the struts dig into the scorched ground with a bone-jarring thud. Parker unclamps his harness, his body aching as he crawls out of the cockpit.

Squeezing the control box for the loading ramp, he waits impatiently as it struggles to lower. Heat and smoke hit him like a wall, burning his eyes and lungs.

"*Demeter*, what the fuck have you done?" He wipes his eyes dry. "Hector! Where are you?" His voice cracks as he stumbles onto the thick ash blanketing the ground.

The forest around him is a blazing inferno, but Parker doesn't stop. He swipes at his wristpad, homing in on Hector's location. The moon's gravity is light, but every step feels heavier than the last.

"Hang tight, Hector. I'm coming."

Deafening explosions snap V back to reality, the sounds of war hammering at her senses. Acrid smoke burns her throat as the chaos swells around her—an unrelenting strike she's only now aware of. She presses against the jagged boulder she first leaned on upon entering the forest, shaking off the fog of the metaphysical realm. Its cold, rough surface grounds her, though disorientation still lingers from the shift.

Goddess, what the feck is happening?

She feels a tug on her pinkie instead of her shoulder this time.

Something tugs on her pinkie. A frail sapling—wispy and thin, no thicker than a stem, yet unmistakably alive. Its pale red leaves twitch with effort, weakly but insistently trying to pry open her hand as if begging to be held.

It trembles violently, its thin leaves curling and uncurling in a frantic rhythm. Raw and freshly torn from the soil, its roots throb with discomfort, a sensation that claws at the edges of V's thoughts. It clings to her finger, weak but determined, holding on for its life.

Hastily, she removes the crown and carefully sets it in the box with her free hand. She shoves the box into her backpack but struggles with the pack's zipper, which is clogged with ash. She needs both hands.

"I'm going to set you down for a minute, okay?"

The sapling clings tighter.

A screech tears through the atmosphere, accompanied by a bright, yellow flash of light.

That was too close!

V pulls a clear sample container from her bag and scoops up some loose soil. She lowers her right hand, coaxing the sapling. "Come on, little guy. You'll be safe in here. Promise." The trembling plant loosens its grip, slowly settling into the container. V seals the container and activates the environmental controls.

Another series of blasts wipe out a dense cluster of trees on a nearby hill.

The Old Man of the Forest knew something was coming.

<Hello?>

Nothing.

She calls over comms for a situation update as she runs—nothing. She doesn't expect comms to be working yet, but even the landing zone beacon is gone.

"If Hector left me—"

A boom breaks her concentration. Looking up through a break in the smoke, she spots something large zooming directly at her.

Marauders? Here?

V freezes as an image fills her mind:

A field mouse darts into a bramble. A hawk's talons slice the empty air above.

An unfamiliar urgency floods her gut.

<hide.>

It's not fear exactly, but an instinct that overrides all else. Reflexively, she dives between two boulders, covering her head as debris rains down.

Something is coming, its whistle growing louder. A large piece of metal slams into the ground where she would've been running. Impact debris smacks the stone, but V is unharmed.

"Thanks," she says, though unsure to whom.

<safe.>

There's a word this time, but it's accompanied by a shared memory of V convincing the sapling to hide inside the sample container.

Particle beams and missiles continue to rain from the sky. A small craft flies by, followed by a sonic boom. Metal chunks fall to the ground around her.

She wants to—but trusts the instinct to stay hidden for a little longer.

When the ejecta settles, she peers cautiously around the stone. Her heart plummets. A massive, crumpled chunk of *Demeter*'s hull lies smoldering just meters away. Large holes from cannon fire and carbon scoring perforate the surface.

V closes her fists over her mouth to steady her breathing. The landing party is gone, and now *Demeter* is falling from the sky in pieces.

"Goddess, please." Her prayer is inaudible over the distant blasts.

She closes her eyes and chaints to the Old Man of the Forest.

<Is the Grove attacking us?>

Silence. From the Goddess. From the Forest. There is only the relentless sound of destruction.

The air on the bridge feels thick and stifling. Commander Bekhti paces, her boots striking the deck in sharp, uneven beats. Most of the screens are either dead or flickering with cryptic errors. *Demeter* groans beneath her feet with every cannon blast—the vibrations low and steady, like a predator growling in its sleep.

"Status report," she barks, cutting through the quiet.

Ensign Kadua doesn't look up from her telemetry console. "We had comms for a minute. Looks like the landing party took out the interference, but we're locked out again."

The commander throws her hands up. "Godsdammit. Okay. What about the weapons fire?"

"No luck there, but DeSoto is firing docking thrusters to throw off *Demeter*'s aim. It's messy, but it's keeping her shots wide."

Bekhti exhales sharply through her nose. "Good call with the thrusters, DeSoto. I'm paying your bar tab when this is over." She grips the back of a chair, the leather worn smooth from years of tense standoffs and close calls—though nothing has ever felt quite like this.

The ensign hesitates but glances up briefly. "Ma'am, there's another problem."

Her eyes snap to Kadua's. "Of course there is."

"The secondary hangar bay," she says carefully, weighing each word. "It's been vented. And the door—well, it's gone."

"Gone?" She freezes mid-step, the word ringing in her ears.

Kadua nods. "Logs show that *Demeter* vented atmosphere. A few minutes later, something ripped the door from the hull." She pauses with an unusually tight expression. "And then *Arion* launched. It's on its way to the surface now."

"*Arion*? Who in the twin hells would—" Bekhti cuts herself off, running a hand over her tight hair. Their eyes lock for a moment, neither able to explain.

"No comms. No control. And now a gaping hole in my gods-damned ship. Fantastic." She forces the words through gritted teeth as she strides to the large display terminal.

Somewhere down there, the crew is scattered and running for their lives. And now, some asshole thought it wise to take that ancient flying coffin into the fray.

"Keep firing the thrusters," she snaps, her voice low and sharp. "If *Demeter* can't aim, maybe our folks stand a chance."

"Yes, ma'am," Kadua replies, her voice tight but steady.

Bekhti crosses her arms, glowering at a display screen. Flickers of orange and red bloom along the surface of the moon below. She hopes that somewhere in that inferno, their people are still alive.

And here she is, stuck, powerless to do anything.

"Does *anyone* have a godsdamn idea?"

V stares blearily into the distance through a gap between two boulders. Her knees are drawn up, arms wrapped tightly around them. She rocks back and forth against the cool stone, frozen by her situation.

Demeter's gone. Demeter's gone. The realization loops through her mind like an unrelenting mantra.

She saw the wreckage fall—smoldering hull, scorched plating —and in her gut, it feels final.

Demeter. *Rowan and Thorney. Everything gone. And I'm stranded on a feckin alien moon!*

She glances down at the sample container tucked against her side. The sapling quivers inside, its leaves brushing the clear walls with erratic motions. She can feel its presence in the back of her mind, a weak but persistent rhythm. "Sorry. I didn't mean you. It's okay," she whispers hoarsely, more for herself than the sapling. "We're still alive. That's something, yeah, Little Merion?"

She'd never really named it—but it was decided the moment the Old Man of the Forest pointed at the name on her shirt, knowing she would look after it.

The sapling doesn't answer.

The forest around her groans, a tree collapsing in the distance under the weight of fire and heat. V squeezes her eyes shut, her mind reeling. She needs a plan. She needs shelter. Her thoughts are as scattered as the burning embers swirling all around her.

A sudden crack echoes nearby, jolting her upright. Her pulse quickens as footsteps crunch against the scorched ground. They're uneven, frantic, and getting closer.

Marauders? She looks around for something to fight with, but no luck. Stay hidden and quiet; this is her best option.

Whoever they are, they're yelling. They're yelling a lot.

"Hector!"

They're getting closer.

"Hector?"

That's a human voice.

"HECTOR!"

Wait, they're looking for Hector?

Hope pounds in her chest. Maybe it's a survivor from the landing party.

The footsteps stop abruptly, just beyond her hiding spot.

"Oh, what the fuck is this?" The voice is low, rough, and unmistakably human.

V peers around the boulder's edge, gasping audibly when she sees the figure kneeling at the crater's edge. The man is bent over, hands braced on his thighs, his shoulders heaving as he gasps for air.

"No fucking way," he mutters, his voice breaking into an incredulous laugh.

V blinks, her disbelief giving way to annoyance. *Of course, it's him. Of all the people to survive, it had to be Parker.*

The name pulls her up short—not just the sound of it, but who is saying it. Parker wasn't even on the mission. She steps from behind the boulders, her thick accent barely above a whisper. "Parker? How the feck're ye here?"

He turns and slips, tumbling into the crater.

V peers over the rim to see if he's okay.

"Sandoval? What the fuck did you just say?"

V tries to rein in her accent. "What are *you* feckin doing here?"

Leaning against *Demeter*'s hangar door, he asks, "Where is everybody? Where's Hector?"

"I'm—not sure. And are you okay?"

Parker dusts himself off and climbs out of the crater. V takes a few cautious steps back. They stare at each other for a beat.

"Who attacked us? Who destroyed *Demeter?*"

"*Demeter.*"

"Yeah, who destroyed her? And how'd you survive?"

"Nobody destroyed *Demeter*. She's fucked up, though."

She points at the large chunk of twisted metal protruding from the ground below them.

Parker's unhinged laughter returns.

V's face is awash in confusion.

Holding his side, he explains, "That? No, that was me. I did that."

Her face is even more confused.

Parker finally catches his breath as the hysterical irony of this meeting finally subsides. He locates a blip from Hector's wristpad and orients himself in his direction. "Come on, I'll explain along the way."

She forces her throat open from the stress and ash. "I don't think anyone else survived the attack."

He doesn't stop to argue. "They're that way."

V stares at him, the words barely registering. "How? How can you know that?"

"Because I'm not a pessimist," he snaps. His wristpad pings, and he turns, pointing toward the horizon. "This way."

Her eyes widen in sudden realization. "Wait! You came down in a dropship, yeah? Did you crash it?"

He glances back, his expression incredulous. "Of course I didn't crash it. You think I'm a fucking amateur?"

Relief surges. She grabs her backpack and stuffs the sample container into her jacket. "Wait for me. I'm coming with you."

"Catch up, then. I'm not leaving Hector out there."

V struggles to keep up as Parker relentlessly pushes forward. The forest is a scorched maze full of craters and pits, and ash and charred debris cling to her boots. Parker periodically stops to check his wristpad, pivoting sharply with each directional recalibration.

"How do you even know which way to go?" V asks. They're veering away from the landing zone's direction.

"The interference stopped for a minute, and I made contact with Hector. Before I landed, I got a ping on his location. Then everything stopped working again."

Another explosion shakes the ground. The air ignites with a searing blue flash that leaves them blinking against the sudden brightness. A deep, thrumming roar rises to an unbearable crescendo. The ground quakes, and a ripple of energy surges upward into the sky, a towering column of light.

V grabs the nearest tree husk until the wave passes. Her ears ring, and she loses all sense of balance. Parker clings to a fallen trunk, his knuckles white as he steadies himself. The air is surprisingly clear of ash, crisp with the smell of ozone.

They stare at each other until their balance returns. They don't ask what that was, knowing neither has an answer.

Parker stumbles forward again, refocused on his personal mission. V struggles to follow, her legs burning as she moves. Minutes pass with only the sounds of their labored breathing and the distant crackle of flames. Then, faint voices reach their ears.

"Wait." Parker's head snaps toward the sound. "You hear that?"

V nods, straining to pinpoint the direction. The voices grow louder, clearer. She gushes when she recognizes the garbled cries of her crewmates.

Parker breaks into a sprint, shouting Hector's name. V follows, her legs screaming in protest as she pushes herself harder. The clearing comes into view—a small group of crew huddled behind jagged rocks, their faces streaked with soot and blood.

Parker stumbles into the clearing, his eyes scanning frantically until spotting a gurney beneath an arching stone. "Hector?" His voice wavers with disbelief. Hector lies motionless on the gurney, wrapped in a metallic medical blanket. Blood stains the silver coverings, and Parker's eyes well up as he takes in the damage. He drops to his knees beside Hector, his hands hovering uncertainly. "What happened to you, Hex?"

A voice interrupts softly. "Are you Chief Parker?"

Parker's shoulders snap back instinctively at the title. He wipes his face with his sleeve and stands, turning to face a soot-streaked crewmate who looks too young to be here. "I am. And you are?"

"Biology Specialist Lehana Drek, sir."

Parker's stare is blank.

"I've been treating everyone's wounds. Before I put him under, the skipper told us you'd come. I didn't believe—"

"Yeah, I fucking came. Can we move him?" He doesn't wait for Drek's response before fumbling with the gurney's antigrav controls. "This everybody?"

V tallies nine survivors, assuming Hector still counts.

Drek purses her lips. "This is it, sir."

"Is everyone else whole?"

V hisses through her teeth. "Parker!"

"Sorry," he says to the remaining landing party. "Can all of you walk?"

Each stands, one by one, though a few use makeshift crutches. V slips her shoulder under an injured crewmate for extra support. The others grab what gear they can carry, ready to go.

Parker pushes the gurney forward with little effort, and the others follow, though they have no idea where he is leading them. The bombardment has stopped, and no one dares break the silence. They slink together through the scorched forest as even the sky seems to hold its breath.

V fights the nagging thought that this silence is just the eye of the storm. She can feel something out there, but it ignores her attempts to chaint. Whenever she can, she touches a tree that may still be alive, but there's no response.

When they arrive, the dropship looms like a battered savior. Its patched hull reflects the faint blue light that occasionally rises from the ground, a reminder of the strange pulses that nearly overwhelmed V and Hector. Once on board, the crew stows their gear and secures Hector's gurney in a makeshift harness of blankets and cargo straps. V grimaces as she hears Hector groan, and Drek administers the last of their sedatives to keep him comfortable for what will surely be a rough ride.

V guides the shaking hands of the others to steady grips on the drop handles. The cramped space is a claustrophobic mess of partially repaired systems and loose equipment. Soot-covered crewmembers occupy every seat, cargo net, and strap, their faces etched with exhaustion. It's tight, but no one minds.

Parker finishes a hurried preflight check, his breath coming fast as he calls back to them, "Okay, everyone. This will be rough. Strap in and pray to whatever gods are still taking your calls."

The engines sputter to life with an alarming cough before settling into a rhythmic hum. The antigravity drive kicks in, and *Arion* lurches upward, the burned forest shrinking below them.

The ground pulses with blue light again.

"Oh, feck me," V mutters under her breath, clutching the nearest support beam as the light surges skyward in another colossal wave. Parker wrestles with the controls, veering the dropship sharply to avoid the growing column of energy.

"Hold on to something!" he yells, shoving the throttle forward hastily. The acceleration slams them back against their restraints, and a few unsecured tools clatter loudly to the floor. V grabs a nearby rail just in time to avoid tumbling into a crew member.

The dropship skirts free of the energy field's edge, Parker's face a mask of raw determination. He exhales sharply, his grip on the controls loosening for a moment as relief washes over him.

Then the alarms sound.

Yellow rays flare in his peripheral vision. *Demeter*'s particle beams have resumed the assault, searing paths across the surface below.

A second alarm blares, shriller than the first.

"Tone locks? Seriously?" Parker snaps. His eyes dart to the proximity screen, where three red blips close in fast.

Missiles.

"Grip your seats!" he yells, yanking a small panel open. The brittle hinges snap and the cover slams against a bulkhead. He'll fix that later. He jabs a series of buttons, but nothing happens.

"Shit!"

The blips converge.

He smashes the buttons again. "*Arion*, you stupid piece of—"

The dropship convulses like a hibernating beast shaking off a layer of ice. Its frame shudders with wild, uncontrolled energy. A swarm of countermeasures erupts from its rear, spraying reflective shards into the sky behind it. The first missile meets the glittering cloud and detonates prematurely, peppering the hull with shrapnel that bites deep into *Arion*'s plating. The others explode in succession, concussions crashing over them harmlessly.

"Missiles down," Parker calls out, though his voice is tight. "We're not out of this yet. Grab your asses, I'm taking us straight up."

He pulls the throttle back, and the dropship climbs steadily into the thinning atmosphere. Below them, *Demeter*'s particle beams continue their assault, lancing the moon's surface with celestial wrath. Parker adjusts their trajectory, holding Brigid between them and the ship.

V watches the chaos below until it fades into the distance. The blue pulses and yellow beams clash in a surreal dance, the once-vibrant forest reduced to a sea of flame and smoke.

Her heart clenches as she glances at the sample container in her lap. The sapling inside is wilting, its tiny leaves curling against the glass. She gently rests her palm on the cover, remembering her charge from the Old Man of the Forest: *Named, responsible.*

Arion crests the moon's horizon, crossing into the twilight zone where the burning landscape gives way to shadow. Parker cuts the engines, letting the dropship drift in the stillness of a slow orbit. For the first time in hours, the only sound is the welcome hum of life support systems.

V leans back, her head resting against the cold bulkhead. She feels the dropship's faint AI systems, tired and cranky. She closes her eyes and weeps for what was lost down there today.

They're safe for now. But fuel reserves are low, and Brigid's shadow won't shield them forever. *Demeter* is out there somewhere—their home, their predator. Parker powers down *Arion*'s secondary systems to conserve what power remains in an attempt to borrow time. The dropship drifts silently above the blazing wreckage of a moon whose fate feels as lost as their own.

arker angrily flicks switches on the flight consoles, cursing under his breath. Half of the primary systems refuse to respond, their screens either dark or stuck in a reboot loop. With an exasperated sigh, he slaps the navigation panel. It blinks once and dies, so he hits the interface again.

"You're fucking useless," he yells at *Arion*.

Cabin lights dim to a faint glow, and the internal temperature drops a few degrees, but the life support holds. Energy distribution has stabilized, and efficiency has improved.

"Could be worse," Parker mutters. He pulls a circuit board underneath a console, killing *Arion*'s transponder signal. *Demeter* can't track them now, buying the crew more time. "Yep, it could definitely be worse."

It gets worse. *Arion*'s rootwork loses gravity, lurching the crew into weightlessness. The sudden shift makes a few of them sick. Unsecured tools float around them uncomfortably.

Parker sighs but takes the opportunity to float into the main cabin. "Alright, listen up, folks," Parker says, trying his best to sound like a real skipper. The flickering cabin lights detract from his confidence. He hooks his boot and grabs a strap to appear grounded. "We've got a situation."

The crew looks up but doesn't respond. There's no energy left to panic with.

"*Demeter*'s not herself anymore."

Parker watches their tired expressions as they comprehend his meaning. "I don't know if it's a malfunction or what, but she turned on us. Comms, weapons, maybe more. That was *Demeter* shooting at you down there."

That gets their attention, and a few find the energy to panic. Murmurs ripple through the group.

"I don't have much detail beyond that," Parker admits, stretching out a hand to stop the rising noise. "We can't trust her, but we don't have anywhere else to go. We need a plan."

"Plan?" V's accent cuts through the cabin. "We don't even know where *Demeter* is right now."

Parker tightens his jaw. "I was getting to that, Sandoval." In truth, he hadn't considered that at all.

Parker glances at the others—tired, bloodstained, bleary. No one is in shape to discuss plans right now. He floats awkwardly near V, tugging on a bulkhead strap to anchor himself beside her.

"You seem relatively with it. Any ideas?" he asks in a hushed voice.

They huddle in the cockpit for a stretch, bickering and trading half-baked plans while the rest of the crew rests. Most ideas die on arrival—no supplies, no backup, no godsdamned clue where *Demeter* even is.

Exasperated, Parker leans back with a groan. "Got any Druid magic to get us out of this shitstorm?"

V's eyes flick to the pack at her feet. "Maybe?" She hadn't considered it until now—and still isn't sure she should.

Parker raises an eyebrow. "Maybe what?"

She doesn't respond. Instead, she unfastens her harness, pulling a thin wooden box from her backpack. Intricate carvings catch the flickering lights as she opens the lid. The crown rises, lifting free of the velvet padding.

"The hells is that?" Parker asks.

V plucks it from the air. "This is how we find *Demeter*."

Parker rolls his eyes. "Pretty tiara. Any other ideas?"

V glares at him. "It's not a tiara, you arse. It's a telepathic quantum signal amplifier. This is how we found Brigid in the first place. It'll help us find *Demeter*."

Parker raises an eyebrow, but the gears in his mind are already turning. "You're serious."

"Like an EVA without a tether." She sets the crown in the box and latches the clasp to keep it from wandering again.

Parker's too tired to argue. He's also out of ideas. "How does it work?"

"Can the nav computer still support T-jacks?"

"*Arion*'s so old, that's the newest port it has."

V exhales with a wry smile. Her voice regains a crisp, precise edge as she says, "Then we're in luck. If I use this to chart a course directly into the computer, do you think you can keep up?"

"Do I think—?" Parker lets go of the hand straps and then floats back to the cockpit. "Grab your gear and get in here."

V tumbles her way into the cockpit. Parker makes it look so easy, but she's unaccustomed to zero-G. She catches her feet on a computer console, knocking loose clumps of ash from her boot. She straps herself into the copilot's seat with some effort.

Parker shakes his head. "T-ports are there."

V pulls several components from the box, and their wires immediately tangle as they float around each other. She attempts to keep them organized but gives up and shoves them back haphazardly with a heavy groan.

"Problems, Sandoval?"

"Feck, hold on." She closes her eyes and leans her head back in frustration. She clutches the box and takes several slow breaths. The weight of their bodies returns with a surprise, announced by several tools clanging on the floor of the main cabin.

"What? How—?" Parker stammers.

"Sorry. I couldn't work like that. I asked *Arion* to wake up and help."

This is the first time V has ever seen Parker speechless.

V unpacks the box and detangles the thin data cables. "He was asleep. That's why the gravity was off."

"You could've turned it back on this whole time?"

"Yeah, but he needed a nap," V says. "You put him through a lot. He hasn't seen action like that since the Beacon Skirmishes."

"You know what, Sandoval?" Parker stops himself from insulting her when he sees what she's working with. "Wait, is this a T9-26 Mark IV? With a modified band monitor for quantum disentanglement fallback?"

V unbuckles her seat harness and floats forward to reach the port on the navigation console, trailing wires like seaweed. "Yeah, I think that's what Thorney said. It's hers."

"I need to make friends with Thorney," Parker mutters goatishly, angling for a better look.

"Doctor Hawthorne," V corrects.

"Yeah, her."

"You're not her type."

Parker gives her a look.

"Fuck you, Sandoval."

"Feck you, Parks."

In the dim quiet of the cockpit, laughter bursts between them —quick, tired, and entirely inappropriate. V clamps a hand over her mouth, and Parker turns his face away, trying to muffle it. The rest of the crew is silent behind them, bruised and grieving. They don't need to hear this.

Her gaze drifts past Parker, back toward the main cabin— toward the others slumped in silence, their faces smudged with ash and shock, too numb to even sleep. The laughter fades like a fever breaking.

They're waiting for someone to act. She can't waste time.

She exhales shakily, the moment slipping from her face. "We should get moving."

Wiping the delirium from his eyes, Parker asks, "Yeah, we should."

"I'm ready if you are." She sets the crown on her head, fumbling with the fit. She concentrates for several long minutes. Parker doesn't interrupt, though his impatience is swelling. Finally, she whispers, "Try that."

Parker consults the nav controls and finds V's flight path. "Ah ha! Sandoval, you wonderful little—" He trails off as he begins warming up the engines and checking his flight controls.

He calls back to the cabin, "Okay team, I've got some good news. We've set a course for *Demeter*. But it's going to take at least a day—we need to round the moon a few times and sneak in behind her—so hit the bucket in the corner and get comfy."

He eases the throttle, enjoying the sensation of thrust after sitting idle for so long. He leans back in his seat, watching autopilot follow V's course. His aching grip loosens on the controls, tension releasing its grip from his body all at once.

"Let me ask you something, Sandoval."

"What?"

"Did you really just ask *Arion* to turn the gravity back on?"

"Well, I asked nicely." She shuts her eyes and gets comfortable for the long ride home. "You should try it sometime."

TEN

THE PLACE ONCE CALLED HOME

They say no one steps into the same hearth twice —
the fire may still be burning, but the warmth has changed.

— GAIAN HOMESTEADING PROVERB

V leans forward in the copilot's seat, adjusting Hawthorne's crown for the tenth time. It still doesn't sit quite right on her head, the sharp edges catching on her hair. Every time she leans back, it falls over her brow. She shifts her focus from the device itself to using it to sense *Demeter*, whose presence feels like a heartbeat out of sync. "Five degrees to port," she murmurs.

Parker doesn't look up. "You sure about that?"

"Yes, I'm sure."

He sighs and adjusts the controls. "Slow and steady, Sandoval. Slow and steady."

"Stop saying that. It's not exactly helping."

"Well, you're not exactly plotting a consistent course," Parker snaps back, but his tone is more resigned than annoyed. He makes the manual adjustments and whispers the old flight training mantras to keep him steady. *Slow and steady. Check,*

169

correct, continue. Manual means reliable, reliable means alive. Calm hands, clear skies. Looking back, there were so many phrases drilled into those modules it's no wonder dropship pilots flunk out more than any officers.

"It's not my fault. I sense where *Demeter* is, then the T9 tells *Arion* what I see, and then I tell *Arion*—" She gestures at the empty expanse of space ahead. "'She's that way,' and he just sort of does the rest. We're still figuring it out."

"Oh sure, blame the centenarian dropship who missed his own retirement party. Real mature."

"Whatever."

They sit in silence except for the occasional course correction as *Demeter* regularly alters course, searching for any sign of survivors.

"Is that her?" V asks.

Parker leans forward for a better angle. "Yeah, I think it is."

Ahead, *Demeter* grows in their view, her shadowed bulk silhouetted against Brigid's burning surface below. V stiffens as she senses the ship's fractured consciousness—an uneasy mix of familiarity and alien wrongness.

"Anything on the transponder?" V asks.

Parker shakes his head. "No signal. Just like we wanted." His hands tighten on the controls as he squints at the approaching ship. "Still can't believe the old man's stealth systems held up."

V scoffs. "Stealth systems? All you did was turn a bunch of things off."

"Yeah. That's how they did stealth back in his day."

"And you're sure you can get us inside without pinging the flight control?" she asks.

Parker snorts, his tone softening. "When Hector and I installed that airlock override, I never thought I'd need it for this."

V spares him a sidelong glance. "You and Hector doing shady shit? See this? This is my surprise face."

"Shady is the grease that keeps the galaxy spinning, Sandoval."

It comes in handy today, so she drops it.

V leans back to focus on *Demeter*'s presence. The closer they get, the louder the competing signals in her mind grow. *Arion*'s complaints about being cold and needing a nap hum at the edges, punctuated by Merion's curious, abstract murmurs from inside her jacket. She closes her eyes and addresses them both in thought.

<Okay, listen up, you two. I need to focus on Demeter right now. I know you both have a lot to say, but I need to—>

<destroy.> That was Merion, she knew.

<Destroy? Destroy what?>

V walks down corridor 16-04 to find a broken interface connected to Demeter's rootwork. The fractured harness blasts a blood-curdling scream when she grabs it. It shocks her, leaving spiral-shaped burns on her hands. All at once, she sees the ship filled with a dark corruption.

<Are you talking about Demeter?>

Merion doesn't respond.

<We can't destroy Demeter; that's my home. That's our ship.>

The sapling quiets, though not entirely, its presence shifting to something akin to a babbling brook. *Arion*'s presence lingers in her mind like a stubborn ache, but he can't help how he feels. She flinches when Parker flips on an external spotlight, snapping her out of the empathic connections.

The beam sweeps across *Demeter*'s hull, illuminating patches of its surface. A massive insignia comes into view—an illustrated bust of a woman with flaxen hair holding a sheaf of wheat intertwined with flowing lines. Gaian runes spell out *ESS DEMETER FF-513* in gilded letters. Below other designations are etched in a delicate script weathered with time.

"What is that?" Parker mutters.

The spotlight catches tendrils snaking along the insignia, twisting in unnatural patterns. They pulse faintly as though breathing. Patches of black, hair-like tendrils spiral outward from various junctions.

V's stomach churns. "Hair? Or vines? Maybe both?"

"Weird," Parker whispers but keeps his hands on the controls. "Those weren't there the last time I was out here."

"Doing shady shit?"

"See that dish? That's one of Hector's," he answers proudly.

They drift along the ship's massive hull, and Parker relaxes his shoulders as the primary hangar ingress comes into view— a wide docking point marked by faded hazard stripes and deep scuffs from countless landings. Once, dropships cycled through here for fueling and arming, ferried into the cavernous main hangar on automated tracks, and then reset for another launch.

But Parker isn't planning a standard entry. He taps a sequence into the console to activate an airlock override that he and Hector rigged months ago for their less-than-official excursions. The docking clamps engage with a soft jolt, and Parker glances back at V with wide eyes.

"Welcome home," he sings, his voice caught between forced cheer and quiet unease as the dropship locks into place.

The ship's corridors bleed with chaos. Klaxons wail, every surface lit in alternating flashes of red and shadow. Crew members stumble over each other, barking conflicting orders pulled from corrupted text consoles. Some rush to their duty stations, only to find them already occupied or nonfunctional. Others stand frozen, trapped between too many commands at once or none at all.

V weaves through the crowded passageways, shoulders hunched. She clutches the sample container nestled inside her jacket. She sends flickers of reassurance to it, though she's unsure if Merion can understand her imagery.

She reaches the Root Cellar and hears the muffled thrum of music she's never heard before. V punches in her key code, and the door hisses open, revealing the room awash in candlelight. Hawthorne is slumped over her workstation, her fingers rubbing at her temples, unusually still.

Hawthorne spins in her chair, her face pale and taut. The sharp relief in her expression turns quickly into something harsher. "You. Feckin. Git!" Her voice trembles, the accusation losing its bite as she crosses the room and pulls V into a fierce hug. Whispering in V's ear, she scolds, "Do you know how worried I was? I thought I lost you, m'iníon."

V erupts into tears, unpacking the weight all at once. Hawthorne pulls her close, and the empathic wave between them surges: grief, relief, fear, the ache of helplessness. And beneath it all, fury at the unknown thing corrupting their home.

Hawthorne pulls back, still gripping V's shoulders. "You don't call. You could've been dead on the surface, and I wouldn't know." Her voice cracks as frustration gives way to relief. "I've been staring at status updates for almost two days—and you never once chainted. You didn't think I'd want to know you were still alive?"

V looks down, guilt creeping into her posture. "I'm sorry. I wanted to, but it wasn't safe. It killed Ris when I tried at that distance; I can't make that mistake again."

Hawthorne's anger melts into something softer, her hand reaching to V's cheek. "You can't keep holding on to that, luv. You didn't kill your sister."

V slowly leans in, hoping for another hug. She puffs out a soft laugh, teasing, "You called me iníon."

Hawthorne plants a kiss on the top of her head and lets go. She leads V to her tea table and offers a chair. As she pours the first cup, Hawthorne asks, "Are you okay? How's the landing party?"

V stares at the wall behind Hawthorne, her voice taking on a formal clip like Muther would've used, as if reciting a report to hold herself together. "Particle beams came out of the sky with no warning. Almost half the party was killed. There were a lot of injuries. Parker flew down and saved us."

Hawthorne flinches. Her hands stop mid-pour, tea sloshing in the cup. "Half the party—" She sets the pot down, eyes glassing. "Goddess. I knew *Demeter* fired weapons—I didn't know it was that bad. Are you—?"

"Fine? No. But I wasn't there for most of the attack, so I'm better off than most."

"Not there?"

"The forest. It was alive—no, I mean sentient. I was communing with it. It showed me things, and we need to talk about that. But I'm okay, all things considered."

Hawthorne covers V's hand for a moment, her voice low. "Luv, I'm so sorry you went through that. And you're sure you're okay? You're not hurt?"

V pats her torso to show she's injury-free but feels the sample container inside her jacket. "Oh, feck. Almost forgot." She pulls out the container and sets it on the table. "Do you have some water?"

The sapling inside is wilted but makes an effort to stand tall. Weakly, it waves a thin burgundy leaf.

Hawthorne leans in for a closer look. "Hello. What's this?"

V unseals the top and pours water down the side, waiting for its roots to lap it up. "This little guy is Merion." She glances at Hawthorne and adds, "I know. I don't want to talk about its name right now."

Merion taps the side of its container for more water.

"Goddess, Thorney. I don't even know where to begin. I met the Old Man of the Forest down there. Oh, and the moon's name is Brigid. And—I know this sounds strange—but Merion knows things."

"Knows things? Like what?"

Merion taps the side of the glass sample container again, more forcefully this time. V obliges with more water, and the sapling sways with more control. A faint blue glow wisps around the top of the sample container like a morning mist.

Hawthorne leans on the table, her eyes level with Merion's container. "Well, that's not something you see every day. Sorry— go on."

"Hard to say," V admits. "We chainted a lot on the ride back to *Demeter*—it's still learning words. But the things it showed me —" V touches her lips, trying to slow herself to keep from losing Hawthorne. "It showed me a lot in the day it took to get back."

Hawthorne sets her teacup aside, folding her hands in her lap. "Start at the beginning. What did you see?"

"The Grove. There's this thing called the Grove, at least that's what the Old Man of the Forest called it. And it's worming its way through *Demeter*'s rootwork. That's why she's been acting so strangely, why we couldn't sense her. It's like she's been imprisoned."

"That's the darkness when you chainted with *Demeter*?"

V nods solemnly.

Hawthorne leans in. "And the Grove—what is it, exactly?"

V gestures faintly to Merion. "I'm still figuring that out. But it's deep inside *Demeter*'s systems. Merion might be able to tell how far it's spread… if there's still a way to save her."

Hawthorne watches her carefully. "If there is?"

V hesitates, then blurts: "Merion showed me how to do spells."

"Spells?" Hawthorne's tone lands somewhere between disbelief and academic curiosity.

"Sort of." V shrugs, sheepish. "Merion communicates in images. When I asked what to do, I got this vision—witches in a circle, dancing in a meadow, doing some kind of ritual."

Hawthorne raises a brow. "This plant wants us to perform meadow magic?"

"Not exactly." V glances at the container. "I think it was

symbolic. But he was clear about one thing: if there's a way to free *Demeter*, it's going to take all three of us—you, me, and this little guy."

Hawthorne holds V's gaze longer than expected, unusually quiet.

"Thorney, I know it's a lot. But if you'd seen the things I saw—"

Hawthorne takes a moment to center herself, then exhales slowly. Her eyes drifting to the sealed lab door, where the red pulse of the alarm leaks through the edges. She sets her cup down with both hands, more carefully than usual.

"I didn't know any of this was even possible." Hawthorne's voice is steady, but barely. "Whatever's happening out there... I don't have a frame for it."

V watches her. Hawthorne wasn't unraveling, exactly—but she was off-balance. V hadn't thought that was possible.

Silence stretches. The alarm bleeds through the walls. Then V clears her throat and straightens her shoulders.

"We need to move." V hesitates, tapping the sample container. "But first, let's make sure we actually have something to show Rowan. Merion might be able to give us that."

Hawthorne nods, already turning toward her screen. "Then let's see what this little plant knows."

After a long pause, she taps the screen and asks, "Do you know where I've seen this before?"

V shakes her head. "No. Should I?"

Hawthorne hesitates. "I showed something like this to Rowan a few days ago. He recognized it immediately. In his words, it's telemetry for quantum information signals. He used it to trace your original connection to—" She stops, searching V's face for confirmation. "Well, to Tau Ceti f."

V crosses her arms. "You know what he did before this, right?" V looks at Hawthorne, hoping not to explain.

Hawthorne shakes her head. "Not exactly."

"He was a research engineer years ago. He—worked on ways

to boost hyperspace beacons and increase the jump range. He found a way to compensate for long-tail disintegration of quantum signals when there's no receiver."

Hawthorne blinks in surprise. "Rowan? Seriously? That sounds like amazing work. Why'd he quit?"

V hesitates, her voice lowering. "You ever hear about that explosion on Jupiter Station?"

Hawthorne's eyes narrow. "I heard things, yeah. It was all pretty hush-hush, though, even with my clearance."

V nods. "That was his project. Something went wrong—an unscheduled test, I think. People died. He doesn't talk about it, but from what I've pieced together, someone on his team caused it. Fleet blamed him for it."

"Shit," Hawthorne breathes. "That's heavy."

"He was a colonel once, if you can believe it. Then they busted him down the ranks," V continues. "He's been on long-haul junk runs ever since. But that's why he knows this stuff. Why he can read this telemetry in his sleep."

Hawthorne nods, already moving toward the door. "So we show this to Rowan? You think he'll recognize the signature?"

V exhales firmly. "Yeah. He will. Let's go find him."

R owan raps at the entrance to Hector's medbay room. Parker doesn't look up or answer, which Rowan accepts as an invitation. "V just brought me up to speed. How's he doing?" Rowan asks.

Parker doesn't turn. "Stable. For now. But Doctor Essien's not sure he'll make a full recovery."

"I'm sorry, Parker. I know you two are close."

"Six months," Parker interrupts, his voice weak. He swipes at his face before Rowan can catch him. "Hargreaves officiated the matelotage. Old-fashioned as both hells, but that's Hex, you know? Loves himself some tradition."

Rowan watches the slow, steady fluctuations on the vitals monitor. The soft beeping is a metronome, keeping time for the room's thick silence. A few screens blink *Network Disconnected... Reconnecting* in an endless loop.

"Med systems offline, too?" Rowan asks.

"Essien pulled everything from the AI network," Parker mutters. "Didn't want *Demeter* messing with anything that keeps him alive.

"Smart move," Rowan says. "We should probably cut more systems before *Demeter* decides to do something we can't come back from."

"Like the seven who didn't come back from that gods-damned moon?"

Rowan winces. "Yeah. Like that."

"Even if the doctor can save Hector, he may not be able to repair much of the damage. He may never have two arms again. Who the fuck will hire him as a pilot after this?"

Rowan puts a hand on Parker's shoulder. "Hector's tough. Once we figure out what's going on, Essien will have him patched up. You'll be listening for your old radio signals together before you know it."

Parker laughs bitterly. "Radio signals—did you know that's what I was doing when *Demeter* fired on him? And you know what I heard? The mother of all signals. The WOW signal. I recorded it, of course. But Hector missed it live. I hate that."

"The WOW signal? That's the one you two are always going on about?" Rowan asks, trying to lighten the mood.

"Yeah. And Hector missed it."

Rowan hesitates, then shifts gears. "Parker, listen. I've been reviewing the quantum frequencies out here. There's severe distortion—stuff I've never seen before, and I've seen some weird shit. When the forest was destroyed, the interference vanished like we expected, but the way it dispersed..." He struggles to find the right words.

Parker glances up, curious. "What about it? Dispersed how?"

"It wasn't even. It was almost like a bubble. Except something was pressing down on it. Whatever that pressure was, it exploded outward. Left behind these weird remnants."

"Is this you trying to keep me busy? Throw me a puzzle so I don't have to sit with this?"

Rowan is genuinely hurt for a moment, but he settles into a shrug. "Yeah. Kind of."

"Show me." Parker reaches for his wristpad and pulls up his personal data stash from a hidden subroutine. With a few taps, he projects the visuals onto one of the medbay terminals. As the telemetry plays out, Rowan fills him in—what V saw on the moon, what the Grove is, and how it turned *Demeter* against them. Hector's vitals continue their steady rhythm, a quiet punctuation to the conversation.

Rowan studies the visualization. "See how the interference pulses? Whatever was holding it back," he points at the telemetry as he slides along a timeline, "it's gone now, but it left a mark."

Parker stares at the display, his jaw tightening. "That means the Grove—or whatever the hells that was—is gone too, right? At least for a little while?"

"Maybe." Rowan's expression remains grim. "But it's odd that the ship's comms haven't come back. You'd think the interference clearing up would've fixed that."

Parker grunts. "With the way *Demeter*'s been acting, it'll probably take a full system reboot just to get anything running properly again."

Rowan nods. "Twin hells, it might even take a factory reset to get *Demeter* back in her right mind."

Rowan nods but doesn't look away from Hector. "We'll figure it out, Parker. All of it. But first, let's keep Hector stable. That's priority one."

Parker squeezes Hector's hand gently, his voice softening. "Yeah. Priority one."

ELEVEN
THE BREATH IN BETWEEN

*To pause is not to surrender. Even the wind must gather itself
before it howls. In every retreat, there is rhythm. In every breath
held, a reckoning.*

*We rest not because we are finished, but because the storm
is not.*

— THE CAPTAINS OF OLD
EPISODE 38: "THE LOST COLONY OF LUYTEN B"

A steady rhythm of beeps cuts through the low hum of the medbay, heralding Hector's return to consciousness. Parker, slumped in a chair beside the bed with Hector's hand loosely clasped in his own, stirs awake. He rubs at his stiff neck and mutters, "Of course, you couldn't wake up at a reasonable hour, could you, asshole?"

Hector's eyelids flutter open, his gaze hazy and unfocused. His body feels distant, restrained—arms and legs encased in regenerative pods. The faint vibrations of their systems blend into the medbay's ambient noise. A tightening in his throat draws his attention to the unfamiliar pressure of an intubation device. The air is cold against the back of his mouth as his vocal cords tingle with a synthetic vibration.

"Calm down," Parker says, sensing Hector's mounting panic. He straightens in his chair and tightens his grip. "It's a micro-synth tube. You can talk, just don't force it."

Hector blinks, his groggy thoughts pulling together. "Parks?" His voice is weak, metallic, but audible. "What happened?"

"You're back," Parker says, his tone caught between relief and exhaustion. "Safe. On board *Demeter*."

Hector shifts slightly, wincing as muted pain flares across his immobilized limbs. He glances down, his gaze catching on the sleek pods encasing his arms and legs. "Why can't I—?" The words catch in his throat.

"Don't. Move," Parker warns gently, leaning closer. "Your body is rebuilding. Essien's got you hooked up to the good stuff. But it'll take some time."

Hector's brow furrows, his breathing labored. "Time?" His eyes search Parker for answers.

Parker forces a small, reassuring smile. "You're stable. That's the important thing." He pauses, unsure how to soften the blow of what comes next. "Do you remember Brigid? The moon? The mission?"

Hector's face tightens as fragments of memory surface—a landing party, blinding flashes of light, *Persephone* destroyed, chaos. Death. "No. Not all of it."

"That's okay," Parker says, though his voice falters. "Look, I'll fill you in. Just promise me: don't freak out, okay?"

Hector exhales through the synthesizer, the sound rasping as he nods weakly. "Go."

"You were the skipper. Took the team down. Things went south. Fast. I still don't have all the details yet, but—" Parker hesitates, swallowing hard. "I came after you. In *Arion*. Found you and got you and the others out, but barely."

Hector's lips press into a thin line as his gaze drops to the regenerative pods. "Barely?"

Parker leans forward, taking Hector's remaining hand in both of his. "You're alive. That's what matters."

"Parker." Hector's tone sharpens despite the synthetic timbre. "The others?"

Parker's grip tightens. "Some. Not all. We saved who we could."

Hector closes his eyes, his jaw tightening but hampered by the intubation tube. "Who fucking did this?" His voice is mechanical but furious.

Parker's mouth opens, then closes. He looks away for a moment before answering. "Still working on that."

The silence between them grows heavy, filled only by the soft hum of medbay machines. Finally, Hector speaks again, his voice quieter. "And you?"

Parker snorts softly, holding his hand up and wiggling his thin, regrown fingers. "Good as new." He smiles proudly.

Hector's gaze lingers on Parker's hand before he gives a faint, approving nod. He wishes he could grab it with the hand on his missing arm. "Good. You know you're an idiot for coming after me. But thank you."

Parker chuckles weakly. "Somebody had to drag your stubborn ass back here. Plus, I'm not ready to deal with probate right now."

Hector's synthetic voice wavers with a weak laugh that dissolves into a cough. Parker's eyes flick to the monitors, watching the sedatives and growth serum adjust to Hector's distress. "Easy, Hex. Don't push it."

"I'll try," Hector mumbles, his grip loosening as he searches Parker's face for clarity. "But what's going on, Park? I don't understand—any of this."

Parker hesitates, the weight of the explanation pressing down on him. "Okay, so here's the thing. You know V? Specialist Sandoval?"

"Yeah. The fucking hubrist?"

Parker winces at the slur. "She's hard to explain."

Hector gives him a tired look, one eyebrow twitching upward. "Try."

"Alright, alright." Parker shifts uncomfortably in his seat. "So, you know. V's, uh, a Druid. Like Hawthorne."

Hector exhales through the synthesizer, his tone dry. "Of course they are."

"I know, but hear me out," Parker counters quickly. His defensive tone surprises even himself. "She's sharp. Super fucking weird, sure, but sharp. Anyway, she and Hawthorne have been working on something. Some kind of tech that connects telepathic signals to our comms systems."

Hector's brow furrows. "Telepathic signals? You know that shit goes against the gods, right?"

"Normally, yeah," Parker says, nodding, "but some of the telepathy uses quantum signals. Hawthorne built this device, kind of like our radio scanners. They can focus those signals, track them, even record them."

Hector's gaze sharpens, a flicker of skepticism breaking through the haze of sedation. "You're telling me they can plug telepathy into our nav systems?" His face is turning red.

"I know it sounds crazy, but I've seen it. V used it to get us from Brigid to *Demeter* without any beacon or nav control."

Hector's fingers twitch against Parker's hand. "What does that have to do with all of this?"

"Well," Parker hesitates again, searching for the right words. "You know all the frequencies we've been chasing? Hawthorne and V think those are connected to whatever's been screwing with *Demeter*. And they're pretty sure they can pinpoint where it's coming from."

Hector blinks, his expression unreadable for a moment. Then he closes his eyes and exhales slowly. "Hawthorne's a scientist. Even if she's—" He pauses, searching for a polite word. "Overconfident. If she has something, maybe it's worth listening to."

"Exactly," Parker says, relief creeping into his voice. "And if

Demeter's compromised, this might be our best shot at figuring out what's going on."

Hector's grip tightens weakly. "Then go."

"What, now?" Parker frowns, glancing at the monitors tracking Hector's vitals. "Hex, you just woke up. You're still recovering. And it's the middle of the night."

"I'm not the one who needs to go," Hector says, his voice firm despite the synthesizer's rasp. "If those hubrists have answers, and I mean *real* answers, Parks, don't waste time. Go. Talk to her. Figure this shit out."

Parker hesitates, guilt warring with the relief of having a reason to leave. Seeing Hector like this—mangled, vulnerable, willing to accept answers from Druids—is more challenging than he wants to admit. But Hector's insistence gives him the push he didn't know he needed.

"Alright," Parker says, squeezing Hector's hand. "I'll go. First thing."

"No." Hector's tone sharpens. "Now. Don't wait."

"Hector—"

"Now," Hector interrupts, weakly slapping at Parker's hand with the barest flicker of a smile. "Go. I'll be okay."

Parker swallows hard, nodding as his grip on Hector's hand loosens. Reluctantly, he yields. "Okay, matey. I'm on it."

Hector's eyes drift shut as the sedatives pull him under, but not before he murmurs, "Tell Hawthorne she had better be right."

Parker chuckles softly despite the tightness in his chest. "I will."

He lingers for a moment, then stands and turns toward the door. The soft rhythm of Hector's monitors follows him out, their steady beeps a quiet reminder of the urgency they both feel.

The Root Cellar is a strange pocket of warmth and dampness within *Demeter*'s otherwise sterile interior. The air here is thick with the earthy tang of loam and wet coir, underscored by faint, rhythmic clicks from the ship's organic systems. Overhead, condensation drips occasionally from a lattice of exposed pipes, adding to the illusion of a living, breathing space. A scratchy recording of forest sounds hums softly in the background—chirping birds and rustling leaves, a bizarre counterpoint to the tension in the room.

V leans against the work table at the center, one boot tapping a steady rhythm against the deck plates as she watches the sapling. The spindly stalk twitches inside its glass container, its movements subtle but deliberate, like it's processing the tension in the room. Across from her, Rowan squints at his data tablet, the light reflecting off his furrowed brow as he scrolls through telemetry readings. Hawthorne adjusts her lab coat, the faint creak of the fabric breaking the silence as she surveys the tools and equipment spread across the surface.

Parker stands near the hatch, arms crossed and shoulders stiff. His eyes flick from the alien plant to V, then to Hawthorne, his unease evident in every fidget and shift of weight. "You know," he finally says, breaking the quiet, "this place doesn't exactly scream 'high-tech war room.'"

Hawthorne growls something indiscernible.

V smirks but doesn't look up. Rowan sighs and mutters, "Great. This is going to be fun."

"Let me guess," Parker says, eyeing Rowan. "Reboot the ship?"

"Yeah, that's the plan," Rowan answers with a confidence that second-guesses itself nearly into dangerous territory.

"And then *Demeter* will just magically be back to normal?" Parker's words drip with skepticism, but there's a flicker of genuine concern underneath.

Rowan glances at V and Hawthorne for backup. "'Magically' about sums it up."

"I still don't get what the hells this plant has to do with anything," Parker says, pointing at the sample container in the middle of the table.

V sighs and leans back in her chair. She unzips the environmental jacket and fans herself with a data pad, revealing the sweat-streaked Merion band t-shirt beneath. *Demeter*'s environmental systems are in utter chaos, and the humidity in the lab is rising to uncomfortable levels.

"Oh, you like Merion?" Parker nods at her shirt.

"Yeah," V replies, tapping the container. "He wants to help. Plus, he probably knows more about what's happening than the rest of us combined." She puts her hand over the ventilation holes on top momentarily as if covering a child's ears while the adults have a conversation. "But between you and me, I think he's just scared and looking for any way out of that mess down there."

"What—no, I mean your shirt." He points at the t-shirt still covered in muck from the attack. Annoyed, he leans back against a bulkhead and adds with a dry smirk, "That's a band from where you're from, right? Let me guess, you wear it because it's vintage and cool, or whatever."

"Seriously?" She asks, a bewildered look on her face. Then she taps the glass container and adds, "Not the time, Parker. But this is also Merion."

"Oh, gods. What?" Parker leans in with a baffled grin. "Merion? You named a plant after a band?"

V rolls her eyes. "Kind of the other way around, actually."

He chuckles, shaking his head. "That is exactly the kind of nonsense I'd expect from you, Sandoval." Then, before she can respond, he raps his knuckles gently against the container. "Hey, little guy. You the one who's supposed to save the ship?"

Merion seems to wave a leaf back.

Parker pretends not to notice and looks away.

V opens her mouth, but he waves a hand before she can answer. "Okay, but how does that help us reboot the ship?" He nods toward the container. "Rebooting fixes tech, but the Grove's infection—possession, whatever—is in the rootwork, too, right?"

"That's where Merion comes in," V explains. "He can help us purge the organic systems while Rowan resets the AI."

"And how, exactly, does he do that?" Parker asks, suspicion lacing his tone.

V exchanges a glance with Rowan. "The rookie pilot's up to speed, yeah?"

"Rude," Parker mutters.

Rowan nods. "More or less. He got the Grove crash course on the way here."

"Defensive psionics," Hawthorne says simply. "Think of it like a focused attack on the Grove's connection to *Demeter*'s rootwork. The possession is still new, so it hasn't fully taken hold. Merion will help us drive it out temporarily while Rowan resets the computer systems. Once that's done, we'll generate an interference field to stop the Grove from reentering."

"Interference field?" Parker asks, glancing at Rowan. "Wait, like what the moon was generating?"

Rowan nods. "Well, the forest. But yeah. It won't be as strong as a planetary-scale system, but it should protect *Demeter* while we bring her systems back online."

"Should?" Parker repeats, raising an eyebrow.

Rowan shrugs. "It's the best shot we've got."

"We don't have time to overthink it," V says firmly. "The Grove's digging deeper with every breath we waste. If we wait too long, we won't be able to push it out."

Parker exhales sharply, rubbing his face. "Alright. How can I help?"

Rowan exchanges a look with V before answering. "Captain Hargreaves hasn't responded to my calls. We need his access codes to perform the reboot. You know him better than any of us. Maybe you can convince him."

Parker scoffs. "Yeah, sure. 'Hey, Captain, I know you're busy dealing with the ship firing on your crew and a missing hangar bay door, but let's talk about plants and telepathy.' That'll go great."

Hawthorne asks, "Am I the only one who wants to hear more about the missing hangar bay door?"

"I'll tell you all about it if you let me take a closer look at your T9-26 when this is over."

Hawthorne smirks, "You got it."

"Deal." Parker pauses. He pulls up his wristpad and scrolls through secure channels. "Let's see if I can bypass the usual comms."

Rowan leans over. "Can you even do that?"

"Watch me."

The room falls silent as Parker initiates the call. When the captain's voice comes through, it carries an unexpected warmth beneath the clipped cadence—an officer mindful of his wounded crew. "Mister Parker. I've been meaning to check in. What's going on?"

Parker straightens. "Sir, I'm here with Section Chief Forsythe, Specialist Sandoval, and Doctor Hawthorne. We think we have a way to purge the thing that's compromising *Demeter*."

The captain pauses. "Go on."

Parker glances at Rowan, who motions for him to continue. "It involves a full system reboot and purging the organic components using—unconventional methods. We'll need your codes."

The captain's voice drops. "Unconventional, how?"

Rowan interrupts, his tone measured. "We're using a loquentes plant to disrupt the Grove's connection. It's the same type of interference the moon's forest generated, but scaled down."

The captain sighs heavily. "The Grove? Never mind, fill me in later. Meet me in the wardroom immediately. We'll discuss the details there."

The line cuts off, leaving the group in silence. Parker exhales then snaps to attention. "Guess we're heading to the wardroom."

Rowan nods, grabbing his data tablet. V and Hawthorne

exchange a look. As the others rise up to leave the lab, Parker murmurs to V, "Hey, sorry about the Merion band thing earlier."

V smirks. "Don't worry about it. You've got bigger things to apologize for."

"Fair enough."

The Root Cellar door hisses open with a shudder. The sterile lighting overhead flickers weakly, casting jagged shadows along the scuffed corridor bulkheads. The vibration in *Demeter*'s deck plates feels unsteady, like the ship is waiting for something to happen. Low crackles from nearby speakers punctuate the strained sound of a voice trying to push through.

Parker takes the lead, his eyes scanning for anything out of place—active AI nodes, officers with false orders, or something worse. "Let's make this quick," he mutters. "We need to reach the wardroom before *she* notices."

Behind him, V runs her hand along the bulkhead, her fingers brushing over exposed conduits and the occasional patch of organic rootwork. She stretches out with her mind, seeking *Demeter*'s presence, but the familiar warmth is absent. Instead, there's a cold emptiness, like a house abandoned in haste. Her stomach churns, and she presses her palm harder against the wall, willing the ship to respond. Nothing.

The corridor ahead stretches into the dim light, the further sections swallowed by shadow. The group walks in tense silence; the only sounds are the uneven hum of *Demeter*'s systems and the soft clink of boots against the deck. As they approach the next intersection, the lights overhead sputter—then die altogether, plunging the hallway into darkness.

A loud clang reverberates through the ship, followed by the mechanical whine of bulkheads slamming shut. V jerks her hand back from the wall, her chest seizing involuntarily. Behind her,

Hawthorne and Rowan spin around as the Root Cellar seals itself with a jarring thud.

They hear V call their names as the doors lock into place, cutting the group in half. What can only be Parker hammering a fist against the bulkhead echoes through the oppressive silence.

Inside the sealed lab, Rowan stares at the door controls, his fingers fumbling over the interface. "Nothing's responding," he mutters, stabbing at buttons as if sheer force will unlock it. "Text comms are down, too. Fan-fucking-tastic."

Hawthorne steps closer to the bulkhead, her hand hovering over the panel as her eyes narrow. "It's not just the systems," she whispers, her voice low and tremulous. "Something's wrong. Something's in here with us."

Rowan freezes mid-gesture, slowly turning to look her in the face. "What the hells are you talking about?"

Hawthorne doesn't answer immediately. She presses her palm flat against the bulkhead, closing her eyes. The darkness beyond the locked door lingers just beyond her mind's reach, a presence that feels vast and hateful. It seethes with rage and hunger, its tendrils snaking through *Demeter*'s rootwork, a parasite burrowing deeper into its host.

Her hands tremble at her sides. "It's not *Demeter*," she whispers, her voice unsteady. "It's the Grove. Or part of it. I don't think it's fully here yet."

Rowan's throat tightens as he takes a cautious step back. "Does it know we're here?"

Hawthorne's gaze fixes on the bulkhead, her eyes distant and filled with dread. "I don't know. But it's spreading."

She closes her eyes, takes a long breath, and reaches out with her mind for another read. "Fast."

Rowan glances nervously at the sealed door. "And V and Parker? Can you sense them?"

Hawthorne closes her eyes, reaching out tentatively, but the effort sends a shudder through her frame. "They're out there. But whatever this is—it's between us and them."

Parker kicks the sealed door again, wincing as the impact rattles up his leg. "Damn it, Sandoval! What the hell is going on?"

V doesn't answer. She rests her hand against the bulkhead, her fingers trembling as she reaches out with her mind. The Grove feels like a tidal wave rising behind a fragile dam, its psychic presence pressing against her consciousness. A faint, hollow laughter echoes in the recesses of her mind, like the sound of wind threading through a dead forest.

She jerks her hand back as if burned, gasping. "It's growing," she whispers. "It's spreading through the ship."

Parker gives her a sharp look, his voice rising. "Spreading?"

The lights flicker violently, and a guttural groan reverberates through the corridor. V staggers, clutching the wall for support as her vision blurs. Her mind floods with images—twisting roots tearing through metal, shadowed figures with glowing eyes, a forest canopy dripping with blood. She clamps her hands over her ears, though the screams are coming from inside her head.

She breaks the chaint and grounds herself against the cool bulkhead.

"What the hells is wrong with you, Sandoval?"

V doesn't respond. Her focus is already elsewhere, her fingers lightly brushing the bulkhead as she extends her senses. *Demeter*'s presence is faint and fragmented, like trying to cling to a tune behind a storm. Beyond that, something else looms, cold and suffocating.

<Merion? Any ideas?>

She closes her eyes, her breath slowing as she focuses inward. The sensation pulls her back to a memory of visiting Silverstrand Beach when she was eight.

The water is icy, numbing her fingers as she dives beneath the waves, her goggles pressing snugly against her face. Tiny silver fish dart around her, scattering like quicksilver when her hand moves too close. She giggles silently, delighting in their synchronized movements. The world above the water fades, replaced by the soothing rhythm of the ocean's current.

V holds her breath, shooing the fish away with a playful wave of her hand. They dart in all directions, shimmering streaks of light against the dark water. For a moment, she feels weightless, suspended in a quiet, crystalline world that belongs to her alone.

She presses her bare toes into the rough sand of the seabed and pushes off, shooting toward the surface like a rocket. The sunlit water bursts around her as she breaks through, gasping for air. She waves to her mother on the shore, who watches with a bemused smile.

The memory fades, leaving the sound of Parker's foot tapping and the faint groan of the bulkhead in its place. V's hand tightens against the door as an idea takes hold. *If I could scatter the fish, maybe—*

"What are you doing?" Parker asks, his voice sharp with worry.

She shushes him with one hand, her other pressing firmly against the wall. Closing her eyes, she draws a deep breath, centering herself as she had in the ocean all those years ago. In her mind, the Grove feels like a swarm, tangled and oppressive, its tendrils searching through *Demeter*'s systems. She envisions herself as that child again, her hands moving deliberately to part the swarm, to scatter its presence.

A pulse radiates from V's thoughts, invisible but forceful. The corridor seems to hum with a sharp, piercing resonance as if the ship itself reacts to her push. The oppressive weight in her mind lifts briefly like sunlight breaking through storm clouds. The Grove's presence scatters like a frightened school of fish, its tendrils pulling back into the shadows, leaving behind a disorienting silence.

V's knees buckle, and she stumbles forward, catching herself against the door. She gasps, her vision swimming. Blood trickles down her upper lip.

Parker lunges forward, grabbing her shoulders to steady her. "Sandoval, what the hell was that? Are you—ah shit, your nose is bleeding."

"It's fine," she rasps, her voice hoarse. "I pushed it back. For a moment."

"What do you mean, 'pushed it back'? Pushed what back?" His voice rises, frustration mingling with fear. "What's happening to you?"

V wipes the blood from her nose with the back of her hand, her expression grim. "The Grove. It's spreading. I had to clear a path to—to try and reach them inside."

"Reach them? With your mind?" Parker stares at her, incredulous. "Sandoval, I don't know that I'm comfortable with all this—" He stops just short of saying something rude about her heritage.

She ignores him, her fingers brushing the door again. Reaching out with her senses, she searches for Hawthorne and Rowan, trying to focus despite the pounding in her head. The Grove's presence lingers at the edges of her awareness, waiting for the right time to return.

Parker watches her warily, his instinct to keep his distance warring with his need to stay close in case something else happens. "Sandoval, listen to me. Whatever you just did, don't do it again. You look like you're about to keel over."

V glances at him, her lips curling into a faint, humorless smile. "If I don't do this, they're on their own in there."

"I don't feel comfortable—"

"Then feckin go! Go see the captain, fill him in."

Parker takes a few steps back. "I don't want to leave you here alone."

"You're distracting me, so you'll be doing me a favor." *Besides*, she thinks, *I won't be alone here.*

She closes her eyes again, bracing herself against the door as she dives back into the swirling chaos of *Demeter*'s rootwork, ready to scatter the shadows one more time. The pressure builds fast. It feels like there's a vice behind her eyes. Something pops— subtle, internal—and her breath hitches as warmth blooms across her vision. She doesn't stop.

Parker steps cautiously forward, taking a closer look at her face. "What the fuck? Your eyes are red. Shit. Is it the Grove? Are you fucking possessed?" He stumbles back. A possessed ship is already on the edge of what he can cope with, but a possessed crewmember—especially a Druid—is more than he can take right now.

He catches himself. He recalls every training module on emergency situations he's ever skimmed. Parker comes to the only logical conclusion.

There's no fucking training module for possession.

He bolts down the corridor and disappears around a darkened corner, boots thudding into the distance.

On the other side of the sealed door, Hawthorne steps back, her arms crossed tightly. She pinches her chin as she stares at the hatch. Her thoughts churn, but her face remains unreadable.

Rowan frowns and breaks the silence. "Doctor, what did you sense?"

She doesn't look away from the door, her voice low but steady. "V pushed the Grove back. Just for a moment. I can hear her."

Rowan's eyes widen. "She what? How? Is she okay?"

"I don't know." Hawthorne pulls her lab coat around her,

more a reflex than a comfort. "We need to figure out our next steps. Fast."

Her words hang in the air as she closes her eyes, reaching out with her mind.

<V? Can you hear me?>

Echoes of metallic screams dance around Hawthorne's brain, background noises that are distracting but manageable.

<Thorney?> V's response is tinged with relief. *<Yeah, I'm here. Still outside your lab. Parker went to see the captain, so I'm out here alone.>*

Hawthorne's irritation spikes and she mutters the update to Rowan, who curses under his breath. *<Never mind him. Are you alright, luv?>*

<I'm fine, but it's getting bad out here. The Grove is spreading. I've seen a few crew members running around in a fright. I can't sense Demeter *anymore, and the ship feels wrong.>*

Hawthorne hesitates, her thoughts laced with guilt. *<That's what I was afraid of. I used to think I was locked out before, but now I think this has been growing all along, just under the surface.>*

<What do we do?> V asks, and the feeling of urgency comes across to Hawthorne as clearly as the words. *<Merion showed me a way to scatter it temporarily, but I don't think I can keep this up. Do you have a plan?>*

Hawthorne's heart sinks. *<I was hoping you did. Did Merion give you anything else?>*

There's a pause, and then V's chaint returns, cautious. *<Yeah. He has an idea. Hold on, I'll let him show you.>*

Hawthorne braces herself as a childlike voice joins their connection. Merion doesn't speak in full sentences; his thoughts come in bursts of simple words and vivid imagery, but the mental presence is there all the same.

<erase.>

V and Hawthorne share the same sudden image.

A storm washes over a beach, wiping away all shrubs and beachgrass. The surge takes them out to sea, leaving behind nothing but pristine, wet sand.

<cleanse,> the voice says, soft but insistent.
<*I don't understand,*> Hawthorne chaints.

The tall sea grass spreads across the beach, but its roots are shallow. A beachgoer walking along easily uproots it. High winds from an approaching storm rend the brush from the sand, toppling the plants out to sea, where they sink to the bottom. Puffins are also swept out to sea, fending for themselves to swim back to the beach or brave the frigid waters to a nearby island.

<*wipe away,*> repeats the childlike voice.
<*V, I don't follow.*>
The childlike voice is increasingly firm. <*be like nature. harsh. control.*>

The storm shifts, revealing shallow-rooted sea grass pulled easily from the sand by the wind. The beach is left smooth and pristine, though lifeless.

V interjects, her tone sharp. <*Wait. What happens to* Demeter? > Her concern bleeds through the connection. <*What happens if we wipe everything away?*>
Merion hesitates, then responds with an image of scorched earth after a fire—blackened but still, somehow, ready to grow again. But Hawthorne senses something deeper, an undertone of finality.
<*quick is kind,*> Merion says, its voice carrying a reluctant but unwavering certainty. A memory flashes in the connection: a young Hawthorne watching as her parents gently euthanize a sick pet. The act is swift, the pain ended in an instant. Quick is kind.

Hawthorne cries, <No! We're not erasing Demeter. She's not the enemy.>

V echoes her thought, her voice trembling with conviction. <Demeter matters. She's more than just systems and circuits. She deserves to live.>

Merion's response comes slowly, a mix of confusion and curiosity. <heal?>

Hawthorne blinks. <You can heal her?> The question carries both hope and doubt.

<of course.> The simplicity of the answer is startling.

V's relief spills through the connection. <Then why didn't you start with that?>

<unaware it mattered.> The thought is accompanied by a faint image of an empty jar, waiting to be filled with meaning.

A wave of relief runs through her—quiet, but deep. <Well, now you know. What do we do next?>

Merion's voice softens, carrying the weight of a child sharing a secret. <erase some. leave room. heal.>

The imagery shifts again.

A river swells behind a dam, its pressure threatening to break through. A controlled release of water steadies the flow, sparing the valley below from destruction. On the horizon, a thunderstorm swells.

Hawthorne and V exchange a brief glance, both unsettled but understanding.

The connection fades as Merion withdraws, leaving them alone in the quiet of their shared thoughts.

In the physical world, Hawthorne turns to Rowan. "How quickly can you reboot the AI core?"

Rowan frowns. "If I can get to the mainframe and have the captain's access codes, maybe an hour. Less if I have direct access."

Hawthorne gestures toward her lab console. "I've got a direct interface here. If we can get the captain's credentials, you could do it from here, right?"

Rowan's eyebrows shoot up. "You have a direct interface? Here?"

"It's part of my agreement with Fleet," she explains briskly. "Unfettered access for research purposes."

"Well, shit," Rowan mutters, running a hand through his hair —the crew cut still unfamiliar after a week. "Alright. If we get the captain's go-ahead, we can make this happen fast."

Hawthorne's gaze hardens. "We'd better. After what Merion just showed us, time isn't on our side."

TWELVE
NOT THIS TIME

We sleep beneath roots that once reached the stars,
Cradled by memories, haunted by scars.

— MERION
"ASH TREE DREAMING"

Parker rounds the corner of the dim corridor, his breath coming in sharp bursts. Emergency lighting casts long, uneven shadows along the bulkheads, the usual hum of *Demeter*'s systems eerily absent. He flashes his wristpad near the access panel to the secure area, but no green light appears, and no chime acknowledges his clearance. The barricade that should be in place is dismantled, leaning haphazardly against the wall.

He frowns, his pace slowing as he crosses the yellow and black safety line marking the boundary. No alarms, no automated warnings. Just silence. He takes another cautious step, then another, before quickening his pace down the empty passageway. Something is very wrong.

Ahead, the sound of clanging metal and strained grunts echo from the wardroom. "And heave!" someone shouts, followed by the groan of gears grinding against their mechanisms. Parker rounds the last corner just as the heavy door to the officer's wardroom wrenches open with a final metallic screech.

A burly security officer stands at the threshold, prybar in hand. The faint glow of a nearby emergency lamp illuminates his sweat-slick face. The man turns at Parker's approach, shifting his stance to one of guarded hostility.

Parker raises his hands, palms out. "Relax. It's me. Section—uh, Specialist Parker." He winces, catching himself on the title change. "The captain's expecting me."

The officer doesn't move, his gaze sharp and appraising. "Captain? Specialist Parker here says you're expecting him."

A voice from inside cuts through the tense moment. "Let him in, Corporal."

The officer steps aside reluctantly, lowering his prybar and gesturing Parker through with a curt nod.

Parker steps into the cramped wardroom, his boots clinking against the metal deck. The space is lit by the faint glow of wall-mounted emergency lights. Captain Hargreaves sits at the head of the table, his crisp uniform immaculate despite the chaos surrounding him. His expression, however, is far from composed.

"Mister Parker," the captain says, his voice calm but edged with weariness. "Where's Section Chief Forsythe?"

Parker stiffens slightly, then clears his throat. "Eugene's fine, sir. I'm not on the active roster."

Hargreaves nods, correcting himself without missing a beat. "Eugene, then. Where is he?"

"Uh, well, sir. He's trapped in Hawthorne's lab."

Hargreaves pinches the bridge of his nose, exhaling sharply. "Trapped in a lab. Got it. Let's add that to the list for later." His hand drops to the table, and his eyes lock onto Parker's. "Start from the beginning, Eu—Specialist. Tell me what's happening on my godsdamned ship." The captain points sternly at a metal chair next to his. "Don't just stand there like a Harpocrate. Come in and take a seat, Specialist. Start with 'trapped' and go from there."

Parker hesitates, the weight of the last twelve hours pressing down on him. He isn't used to seeing the captain like this—frustrated and unsettled. "Yes, sir." He takes a seat, folding his hands tightly in his lap. "It's complicated."

"We don't have time for complicated. Give me the short version."

Parker nods, drawing a steadying breath. "Doctor Hawthorne and Rowan—Section Chief Forsythe—they're locked in her lab. Something's taken control of *Demeter*'s organic systems. It's spreading. Fast. They're calling it the Grove."

Hargreaves's eyes narrow. "The Grove? What the hell is that supposed to even mean?"

"Honestly, this is the kind of weird shit Druids know about, sir," Parker says, his voice tinged with exasperation. "All I can think of is the Aspen groves back home—how they're all connected underground. Roots spreading out, one big organism pretending to be separate trees. Like that, but—worse, somehow. And alive. Sandoval says it's in the ship's rootwork, taking over the organic systems. Like a telepathic virus or something."

The captain leans back, frowning deeply. "Could it be sabotage?" he asks quietly, more to himself than Parker. "An Earth-Firster plot? We've seen them use biological tech in the past. Or, what about the Druids? Could this be them?"

"Maybe," Parker says, though his tone is doubtful. "But I don't think this is Sandoval or Hawthorne. From what I've seen, it's something bigger. Something alien."

Hargreaves exhales sharply through his nose and gestures to an aide nearby. "Get a pot of coffee going. Black will have to do." He turns back to Parker, his expression darkening. "Sorry Eugene, we're out of creamers. And the landing party? The survivors. How the hells did they get back on board?"

Parker's stomach clenches. He hadn't wanted to address this part yet. "Sir," he starts carefully, "I took *Arion*. I, uh, piloted him down to Brigid's surface and back." He adds, more to give credit than excuse, "Sandoval was a big help with that."

Hargreaves' eyebrows rise. "You're not a licensed pilot. Dare I ask why the secondary hangar bay is missing a godsdamn door?" His anger is mixed with genuine curiosity.

"No, sir, I'm not a licensed pilot," Parker admits, his voice low. "And, well, the air was running out. Fast. The moon attack was already underway. I couldn't get to the flight deck to control anything, and I didn't have a pressure suit to get to the shuttle." He crosses his arms for comfort as much as closing himself off to judgment. "I didn't have time to come up with something better. Sorry."

The captain rubs his temples, muttering something blasphemous under his breath before sitting back in his chair. "Fine. You got them back, and that's what matters. But Eugene," his tone sharpens, his eyes locking onto Parker's, "I need you to stay sharp. This 'Grove,' sabotage, whatever it is—" He pauses, his voice dropping. The captain rubs his cufflinks. "I don't think this is over. In fact, I'll wager it's about to get a whole lot worse."

Rowan spins idly on one of Hawthorne's lab stools, his nerves exaggerating each passing second. The lab feels stifling. The drip of condensation from the exposed pipes overhead adds to the humidity. How the Druids appreciate this atmosphere is mind-boggling. He fiddles with some of Hawthorne's lab equipment, tapping a glass cylinder that looks suspiciously like a prototype quantum comms array. His fingers itch to take it apart.

I'll have to ask her about this when this is all over, he thinks.

Hawthorne is glued to the sealed hatch, her brow furrowed in concentration. Her connection with V and the sapling—Merion, he reminds himself—is telepathic, and Hawthorne has made it clear that any noise will disrupt her focus. Rowan sighs, his bouncing knee a rebellion against the enforced silence. The more he tries to be quiet, the louder he ends up being. It's been nearly an hour since the lockdown separated their group, and the weight of inaction is growing unbearable.

His wristpad vibrates.

> BeamLord9000: Test

Rowan blinks at the screen, baffled. The ship's comm systems are still down.

How is this even possible?

> BeamLord9000: Test 2

The corner of his mouth twitches, and then he snorts, his laughter bubbling up uncontrollably as he reads the sender's name: **BeamLord9000**. Of course. Only Parker would use such a stupid handle.

> BeamLord9000: Test test tets test

> BeamLord9000: Rowe, it's Parks

Hawthorne shoots him a glare, her lips pressed into a thin line. "Shh!" she snaps, not breaking her posture by the door.

"Sorry," Rowan mutters, wiping tears from his eyes as he texts back. He needs a laugh like this.

> Forsythe: Parker? How?

> BeamLord9000: I told you before. Hector and I created a way to send messages directly to wristpads without using the network.

> Forsythe: I can't believe that works. Does the captain know?

BeamLord9000: Yes, and I've got his credentials. You want to reboot some shit or what?

Forsythe: No way!

BeamLord9000: Way!

Forsythe: Let's do it. One sec

Rowan swivels back to Hawthorne's terminal, his pulse quickening as he logs in. The screen remains locked out, gray tabs with padlock icons mocking him.

Forsythe: Ready. Hit me.

Parker's reply is a flood of characters—logins, encryption keys, and access codes. Rowan copies the text, pastes it into the terminal, and hits enter.

Nothing.

Forsythe: No luck. Still locked out.

BeamLord9000: Hold tight.

Three or four excruciating minutes pass before Parker responds again. Rowan was starting to consider they may have been cut off.

BeamLord9000: Try this one.

The minutes crawl by. Rowan taps his fingers impatiently, glancing at Hawthorne, who remains locked in her telepathic exchange. His wristpad buzzes again.

BeamLord9000: It's a longer shot, but it should work.

He pastes the new string of data. This time, the interface shifts. New options populate the screen, the gray padlocks vanishing one by one.

Forsythe: That worked! Testing now.

He scrolls through the menu, his heart racing as he finds *Weapons & Defense*.

"Oh shit!"

He's quickly shooshed by Hawthorne again, but he ignores her this time. Particle beams and other projectile weapons are still armed, but thankfully, the *Orbital Nuclear Strike* option is grayed out.

"Okay, I'm glad to see you didn't have nukes when you bombarded my friends, you fucker."

He selects the ominously red *Load Factory Settings* button and hesitates before pressing confirm. The screen darkens, and a progress bar creeps across the bottom.

"Okay," Rowan whispers, wanting to inform Hawthorne but not disturb her concentration. "One down."

Forsythe: Weapon systems are rebooting. What's next?

BeamLord9000: Capt says security, then comms.

Forsythe: Got it, on it.

Rowan pulls up the security protocols, navigating through screens for guard rotations and lockdown overrides. He selects *Factory Reset* again, initiating another crawl of green text. While that runs, he switches to comms and taps through the sequence to restore them as well.

As soon as the reset completes, the hatch behind Rowan clanks and hisses, its mechanisms returning to normal. The doorway slides open abruptly, releasing a gust of pressurized air.

Hawthorne and V, still leaning against the door mid-chaint, stumble together. V's foot catches the threshold, and she falls into Hawthorne, who barely manages to keep them both upright. They cling to each other for balance, their movements uncoordinated and graceless. Their faces are flushed, a mix of embarrassment and the lingering tension from their mental connection. For a moment, the two Druids share a breathless laugh, their relief as tangible as the stale air rushing into the lab.

Hawthorne chides, "A little heads-up would've been nice," and she laughs.

"You're welcome," Rowan quips without looking up.

Hawthorne glares at him but doesn't respond. Exhausted, she and V briefly hug. V's hands tremble as she pulls back, and her gaze darts nervously around the room.

"How's it going?" Hawthorne asks Rowan.

"Rebooting systems one at a time." Rowan taps through more menus. "Weapons and security are back up. Comms are almost done, but it's slow going."

The comm panel crackles and then stabilizes.

"Section Chief. Doctor Hawthorne—is the bridge. Do—copy?"

Rowan taps the comm button. "We read you, Captain. Rebooting systems now. We should have full functionality soon."

"Good work, son. Do you have a timeline?"

"A few more minutes per system, but making good progress."

The comm crackles again, and the connection cuts out.

Rowan slaps the side of the terminal. "Shit!"

V consoles him. "You've got this. Just keep going."

Hawthorne looks to the ceiling absentmindedly. "*Demeter*? Can you hear us?"

There's no response.

<Demeter? Are you there, luv?>

Klaxons sound again. The hatch slams shut, locking them in. Hawthorne grabs the sides of her head, screaming in pain.

"Eugene, what do you need from us?"

Parker fidgets in his wardroom chair, the captain eyeing him expectantly. "Captain, I'm going to need a lot of equipment to pull this off." Parker is scared and trying not to show it. He wonders if he's opened his big mouth too far this time.

"Name it." Captain Hargreaves snaps toward a nearby ensign, motioning him to write down Parker's requests.

Oh, shit. They're looking to me to fix this. What the hells do I even say? Parker realizes.

Parker's heart pounds. "Okay, uh," he stammers, rubbing the back of his neck. "Sir, I think—"

"Focus, Specialist," the captain cuts in, slapping the table lightly. "You know what to look for. I'm granting you operational control here for now. Take a breath and tell me what you need."

Shit. He really means it. Okay, Parks, what do we need? Think! He slaps the sides of his head, trying to push through the anxious frenzy and give them a laundry list of what he might need.

"Okay, sirs. Here's what I think I need from you." Parker draws on his officer's training modules and takes a deep breath. *This is not my emergency; this is their emergency.* The training mantra keeps bleeding through, and while it's not accurate given their circumstances, it's what he needs to focus on right now.

He straightens in his chair and shuts his eyes. "Right. Here's what I need. First, three computer terminals connected to a local area network—no ship systems, just a private loop. For that, I'll need a hub or a high-speed switch and enough cables to connect everything. No Wi-Fi or radio. It has to be hardwired."

"Noted," the ensign says, typing furiously on his wristpad.

"Good. Next, I'll need a quantum accelerator," Parker continues, gaining momentum, "and a fiber-optic cable bundle long enough to stretch between this room and Deck 09, just past the second auxiliary junction."

Standing by the wall, the purser shakes his head and tells the captain, "We don't have anything like that on board."

Parker raises a hand to silence the purser. He winces and whispers, "We do. Deck 07, storage panel C-17. There's a compartment sealed with an old wax stamp. It looks official, but it's not locked. Inside, you'll find a spool of about eighteen hundred meters of fiber optics. When you roll it out, keep it coiled tightly. Please! That stuff is stupid expensive. More than you and me will make in a year. If we survive, that is."

Hargreaves quirks a single eyebrow. "How do you know about this?"

"Captain," Parker says firmly, "with respect, let's just roll with it."

Hargreaves stares at him for a moment before pinching the bridge of his nose. "Okay, what else?"

"That's it for now. If I think of anything else, I'll let you know."

The captain snaps his fingers at the officers. "You heard him. Move." They hesitate, and the captain raises his brows to let them know he's not telling them a second time.

As the officers scatter to fulfill his requests, Parker slumps forward, his elbows resting on the table. He rubs his temples, trying to keep the rising panic at bay. "What if this doesn't work?"

Hargreaves leans closer, his voice low. "Make it work."

The weight of the statement silences Parker. He nods solemnly.

Hargreaves's tone softens, though his eyes remain sharp. "Eugene, you piloted a dropship that wasn't flight-ready to the moon and back. It wasn't flight-ready. Hells, I didn't even remember it was onboard. You saved lives—and I don't take that lightly. But," he pauses, thumbing his cuff-links, "when this is over, I want you to explain—how the godsdamn fuck do you know more about my ship than I do?"

Parker stiffens, the captain's question hanging unanswered in the silence between them. A sharp scent cuts through the air. He sniffs, suddenly alert. It's warm, familiar—out of place. "Sir? Do you smell that?"

Hargreaves tilts his head, inhaling deeply. "Is that—?" Confusion flickers over his face. "Nutmeg?"

Hawthorne writhes on the ground, screaming. Rowan turns to help but quickly drops to his knees next to Hawthorne's computer terminal, gripping the edge of the desk for balance.

The faint, sweet scent of nutmeg pricks at the edge of his awareness, strange even inside the loamy atmosphere of Hawthorne's lab. His throat tightens as an inexplicable heaviness washes over him. Somewhere in the back of his mind, a memory unfolds. The scent presses into something deep buried, drawing him back to the last time he failed his team.

"Colonel Forsyth!" Cassia Parker strides into Rowan's lab with the energy of a solar flare. She grips two stainless steel mugs in one hand and brandishes the other toward his tunic sleeve. "You fancy fuck, let's see 'em!"

Before he can react, she grabs his arm and yanks the fabric taut, inspecting the stitching. "Not bad. Decent lines. This actually looks good, Rowe, so I know you didn't sew this shit yourself." She shoves his arm away in mock disappointment.

Rowan jerks his arm free. "I can sew, Cass."

"Sure," she drawls, raising a skeptical brow. "But we both know Willow's the genius with needle and thread. That's how I know those fancy eagle patches are on there real good. But you know how it is—someone needs to punch them to make sure they don't fall off."

He chuckles, then groans as realization dawns. "Oh no. Not you, too. The crew already punched them in today. You're not seriously doing this now, are you?"

Cassia grins to her ears, cracking her knuckles. "Tradition waits for no one, Forsythe. What would Gaia say? Consider it my personal blessing, Colonel."

Rowan sighs and turns his arm to her, bracing for impact. "Fucking hells, okay, let's see what you've got. I'm sure even the worst stitching is going to hold up—"

Her first punch lands on the newly-sewn patch with a sharp crack, knocking him off balance. She pulls back, shaking her hand with a giggle. "Ow, shit. That hurts worse than I thought."

"Hurt you?" he yells. Rowan rubs his arm, wincing. "What the hells, Parker? Where did you learn to hit like that?"

"Growing up with Gene, you learn to throw a mean punch," she beams, flexing her fist. "He showed me this trick." She demonstrates how she curls her fingers into the pads, creating a brick of a fist.

"Your brother sounds like an asshole."

"Oh, he is. Trust me." Cassia snorts and raises her fist again. "Two more branches to go, Colonel. You ready?"

"No." His left eye waters. "Just get it over with." He leans his bruised shoulder in her direction.

The second punch slams into his shoulder, sending a shock-wave through his torso. By the time the third lands, he's biting back curses, his face flushed with indignation.

"Godsdammit, Cass," he growls, shaking his arm out. "Are we done now?"

She laughs, genuinely apologetic, as she rubs his bruised arm before giving him a soft hug. "All done, Rowe. Don't be such a baby."

"Fucking shithead," he whispers as he hugs her back. "Thanks."

"Welcome!" She grabs both mugs and shoves one into his chest.

The scent of juniper stings Rowan's every sense. "Came armed with a peace offering, I see." He takes a cautious sniff. "Will I still be able to see after this?"

Cassia shrugs.

"No way to know, I guess. Cheers."

They clink cups, and both spit their drink back into them.

"The fuck?" Rowan asks.

"Oh gods, sorry, Rowe. Jaime promised he had it down this time."

"I hope he's a better physician than a distiller."

Cassia's eyes are wide open, and she agrees. "Gods, he couldn't do much worse, could he?" Cassia laughs, her gaze softening as she twirls the sapphire ring on her finger. She jumps to sit on the table and playfully swings her feet.

Rowan smiles despite himself. "Congratulations again, Cass. I hope whatever he's done is bad enough to deserve you." He winks warmly.

The glint in her eye betrays a more profound sense of genuine happiness she isn't accustomed to sharing. "Speaking of making honest men out of us." She cocks her brow inquisitively and looks around. "Where's little Miss 'Oh yessir Mister Forsyth, sir? Whatever you need, sir? How may I be of assistance, sir?'" Her mockingly girlish voice is over the top.

He rolls his eyes. He sighs and answers, "Willow is in the workshop. She wanted to run some new tests on the quantum beacon's data bandwidth. And you know what? You can shut your mouth about her. She's nice." The upturn in the side of his mouth betrays his feigned protestation.

"She's 'nice'? Oh, Rowe. Bud." She purses her lips. "What you two get up to is none of my business. She's still a civvy, but you could do worse." She raises her hands dismissively.

Rowan blushes. He takes another painful sip of the hooch to hide a grin.

The deck and bulkheads shake violently, the reverberation punctuated by a deafening explosion. Cassia springs off the table, her boots planted firmly on the floor, readying herself for action. The lights flicker for a few seconds before giving out. The red emergency lights activate a heartbeat later, their pulsing glow casting long, shifting shadows across the walls.

Neither hesitates. Without a word, they down the last of their drinks and slam the mugs onto the table, the clang drowned by the wailing sirens. Smoke pours through the opening doors, stinging their eyes and burning their lungs as they race into the corridor.

The air reeks of burning insulation, copper, and something acrid Rowan can't place. His stomach churns but pushes forward.

"Willow!" His voice cracks as he yells.

The only reply is the roaring inferno down the corridor to their left. Rowan sprints into the thick, choking smoke. Cassia is right behind him, her hand gripping the back of his uniform as if to ground him.

"Willow! Wistman! Hallerbos!" Rowan's voice breaks with desperation, his shouts swallowed by the chaos. "Willow?"

Fire doors slam shut behind them, sealing off sections of the passageway as they sprint forward. The heat is oppressive, waves radiating from the blown-out workshop ahead. Air whistles past them—a clear sign of a hull breach on Jupiter Station.

Rowan skids to a halt, his boots slipping on debris. The remains of the workshop are strewn across the corridor—twisted metal, shattered panels, and charred fragments of equipment. His gaze lands on a small, empty shoe lying amid the wreckage. His throat tightens, and for a moment, the smoke is the least suffocating thing here.

Cassia grabs his arm, pulling him back. "Rowe! It's too dangerous! The heat—"

The workshop is a blazing ruin, the flames too intense for even the atmospheric scrubbers to extinguish completely. Emergency crews rush in, sealing off the corridor. Rowan and Cassia are pulled back, forced to wait while the fire suppression teams do their work. It takes nearly an hour. The moment the fire dies down and the heat ebbs enough to enter, Rowan shoves past the last barrier and steps into the ruins.

"Willow?" His voice trembles. The devastation is absolute. The once-pristine lab is now a graveyard of fine ash and charred metal filaments.

Rowan's forced memory advances.

The tribunal convenes weeks later. Rowan sits silently as Fleet officials pore over the reports. A faulty Baryonic fuel cell, they determine. A cascade triggered by a routine test. Too much quantum data bandwidth at once. No warning. No negligence. Just an accident, with hints of improvisation.

The words are hollow. Empty.

After the hearing, Rowan lingers on a bench in the empty courtroom. His class-A uniform feels like a mockery, the silver-threaded eagle patch on his sleeve catching the faint light. He tears the insignia free and turns it over in his hands, his thumb brushing the edges.

Cassia sits beside him, her silence saying more than words ever could. She drapes an arm around his shoulders, pulling him close. Her hand moves in slow circles along his back, trying to find him in the storm raging in his mind.

"I told you not to resign, you idiot," she murmurs. Her voice is soft but firm. "No one expected you to. Linnaeus and the admiralty practically begged you to reconsider."

Rowan stares at the eagle insignia, his knuckles white as he wads it up. "I was in my office, doing fucking paperwork while they were in the workshop. They were my team, Cass. Why wasn't I there—with them?"

"And if you had been?" Cassia's voice tightens. "You'd be dead, too. You couldn't have stopped it, Rowe. The inspectors were clear. No one saw it coming."

He shakes his head, tears welling in his eyes. "I should've been there. Maybe I—" His voice cracks, and he doesn't finish.

Cassia pulls him closer, her voice dropping to a whisper. "Shh."

A sharp sting brings Rowan back to the Root Cellar.

Slap!

His head jerks to the side. His vision swims as another slap lands, and his cheek stings with the imprint of a palm. He blinks, his breath coming in short gasps as the haze begins to lift.

"Rowan!" V's voice cuts through the fog, sharp and desperate. Her face hovers centimeters from his, her hands gripping his shoulders. She shakes him, her eyes wide as a battle between fear and determination plays out. "Rowan, snap out of it! You're losing it. We're losing it!"

His surroundings crash back into focus—the dim, red emergency lights of the lab, the muted hum of *Demeter*'s crippled systems, the terminal screen blinking with half-completed commands. His hands reach for the controls, trembling.

"I—I was—" His voice trails off, the memory of the tribunal still clinging to him like the smoke in his old lab.

"You passed out. You need to finish this!"

Rowan swallows hard, his throat dry as ash. His head pounds and his vision tilts as he steadies himself against the desk. The scent of nutmeg hangs in the air.

He shakes his head, trying to clear the fog that creeps back into the edges of his mind. The smell is everywhere, invading his thoughts and pulling at him with lethargic weight. His fingers drift toward the terminal again, hovering over the next tab.

"Stay awake," he murmurs, his voice cracking as he struggles to focus. "Just stay—"

V slumps forward, collapsing against him, her grip loosening as her head comes to rest on his shoulder. Her breathing slows, shallow and uneven, and Rowan's panic spikes, giving him a burst of adrenaline.

"Tab, button, next," he whispers, repeating the mantra. "Tab. Button. Next." His shaking hand presses the glowing confirmation icon on the terminal. "Not this time. Tab. Button."

Behind him, a voice fades to a whisper. "Rowan. Save us." He's unsure if it belongs to V or Willow.

The scent of nutmeg grows faint, but the pull of unconsciousness deepens, threatening to drag him down. He sees gray motes flutter around him—not ash like before, but troubling all the same.

Sleep.

THIRTEEN
PUSH TO RESET

We named each other. That was the promise.
You and I were [scratched out], and that meant forever.
We were responsible for each other. I was responsible for you.
I spoke your secret name with — [smudged]
I thought I could — [smudged]
And it was too much.

— V's eulogy for Iris Sandoval
Written, never delivered

The storm howls outside V's dorm room, its wind battering the thin windows. She sits on her bed, clutching a vidscreen with both hands, the faint blue light reflecting off her wide, tired eyes.

"It's okay, Muther. There's just a few of us left and a couple of teachers. Everyone else made it out before the blizzard picked up," V says, trying to keep her tone casual. "The headmaster's still here, though. He's holed up in that cottage in the northeast corner."

Her mother's face twists into a frown on the vidscreen. "First, it's 'there are', and second, he shouldn't stay there. That place is simply not meant for his kind."

"But, Mother," V sighs, exasperated, "he's nice—for a Bard."

Her mother's lips twitch with disapproval but soften after a pause. "Anyway, your sister arrived a few hours ago. She's upstairs in her room, blasting that racket you two adore."

"It's Merion, and it's *not* racket." V's face lights up as she pulls a small, flat disc from her desk, holding it to the screen like a trophy. "And look! I found this in a shop in town—*Echoes from the Undergrowth*! She's been looking for it for years." She drags the last word out, smug and gleeful, knowing it'll irritate her mother. "She'll be so excited when I give it to her for Yule."

Her smile fades. "Well, I would've given it to her. If this stupid blizzard hadn't trapped me here."

Her mother tuts softly, her expression melting into something close to warm and sympathetic. "Oh, my poor Violet. I'm so sorry. Iris will be devastated. She always feels this time of year so deeply."

The two exchange sad faces through the screen, their exaggerated expressions gradually twisting into laughter. Her laugh is sad but lighter now that she has spoken with Muther.

"Do you want me to tell her, my love?"

V wipes her eyes, the sadness still lingering beneath her grin. "I'll call her later. She's probably got Merion turned up so loud she wouldn't hear you anyway." She smiles, imagining her cooler older sister dancing around her room to such great music.

"Alright, m'infon. Stay warm, and I'll call you when it's time to open presents. We'll video you in."

"That sounds good, Muther. Talk to you soon."

Her mother waves goodbye and disconnects. The room falls silent except for the wind rattling the glass.

V sets the vidscreen down and stares at the window. The snow is thick, reducing everything outside to hazy shapes under muted lights. The storm stretches on forever, turning the campus into a white, frozen void. The world is heavy and still, and the flickering warm lights feel damp, fading into the swirling snow.

She sighs. The storm has swallowed the whole world.

Her thoughts drift to Ris. The rare album still rests on her desk, glinting faintly in the candlelight. Ris would lose her mind over it. It's the perfect gift, one that only she would appreciate. V can't wait to give it to her later.

Or—she could show her. Now.

V glances at the candles on her desk and considers the small pouch of herbs tucked in her drawer. A forbidden idea speaks up, while her mother's voice echoes in her mind: *Don't push too far, Sweet Violet. The Fair Folk will punish children who wake them.*

V stopped believing in those stories long ago. After all, those are stories for a high priestess and her favorite heiress. Those aren't for V. Ris would love to see how far she's come, and it's not like anyone else is around to stop her.

She borrows extra supplies from the only other student still on her floor and sets up a circle in her room. She dims the electrical lights as she arranges candles and herbs. The ancient ritual calms her nerves as incense curls into the air. She settles into the center of the circle.

She closes her eyes and calls out with her mind. *<Ris. Can you hear me, Ris?>*

At first, it isn't a sound but a faint vibration—a wall of sensation pulsing at the edge of awareness. It's distant, underwater music, the melody carried by waves from kays out to sea. V squeezes her eyes shut, focusing on the source of the garbled rhythm. It's muffled, slow, and disjointed, slipping just out of her grasp every time she reaches for it.

She breathes deeply, steadying herself as the vibrations sharpen into something more familiar. Notes begin to surface, distorted but unmistakable. It's a Merion song. Ris's favorite.

The music rises, its tempo shifting like a current pulling her closer. V pushes harder, her focus narrowing until the sound emerges, clear and undeniable, as if she's broken through the surface into a world where the connection feels real.

It isn't quite sound—more like the sensation of music heard underwater, distant and distorted, as if the melody is playing kilometers out to sea. V squeezes her eyes, trying to focus on the source of the garbled music. It's muffled and slow. It sounds familiar, but she can't place it. She recognizes the music as a Merion song when it speeds up again. It's distorted, and hearing it like this makes her feel woozy, but she keeps listening.

A faint vibration hums in her skull, like hearing the distant echo of music underwater. She narrows her focus, pushing through the distortion, and the sound gradually sharpens into clarity. It's Ris's favorite—"Arms Are Numb."

V focuses harder. *<Ris? Can you hear me?>*

Finally, Ris's thoughts bleed through, slurred and weak. *<V? Flower? Are you here?>*

<Not exactly! That's the cool thing. I'm still—>

The chaint is painfully pleading. *<You can't be here. You can't see this.>*

<Ris? What's wrong?>

There's no reply, only fragments of Ris's remaining inner dialogue bleeding into V's awareness. *<This is it. Arms are numb. Good feckin song. Timed it right. V is here. V is here—no! Dying.>*

V's eyes snap open. Her stomach flips, and she vomits onto the rug. She stumbles to the sink, splashing water on her face as panic grips her chest. Blood drips from her nose, smearing the edge of the mirror. She grips the sink but slips and falls to the floor.

When she regains her composure, she rushes back to the circle. The candles are still burning, the herbs still smoldering, but none of the magic is working. She sits cross-legged on the floor, searching for Ris's voice, pushing harder than ever.

<Ris, please. Where are you?>

The music is still there, faint and distant, but it's as if Ris is drifting away from it. V pushes harder, desperate. The connection vanishes entirely.

The music fades.

The void swallows her sister.

Ris is gone.

V collapses onto the rug, staring at the circle of candles as the weight of guilt crashes over her. She knows the rite was never meant to reach this far. She knows it shouldn't have worked. But still—somewhere deep within—she believes she's the reason. Ris's last words, her final song, carve into V's soul—a wound no one can convince her to let heal.

"Rowan? Rowan, wake up." A wet sting blooms on his cheek, followed by a sharp, familiar voice cutting through the haze.

The voice moves away, barking the same command at another figure. "V, wake the feck up. Come on, luv, look at me!" More slaps echo faintly, distant as if underwater, but Rowan feels none of them.

Then comes the sharp, astringent sting of cold vapor burning his sinuses as it jolts him fully awake. The smell hits like mothballs soaked in firewater, ignited, and shoved into his nose. He coughs hard, swatting blindly at the air before rolling onto his side.

"Thank the goddess," the voice says, calmer now. "Welcome back."

Blinking rapidly, Rowan forces his vision to focus. Doctor Hawthorne looms over him in her lab coat, her expression both relieved and calculating. She holds an ornate crystal spritzer with a golden nozzle and an amber bulb, the tassel swaying lightly in her hand.

"What in the twin hells just happened?" Rowan groans, sitting up slowly. He rubs his eyes, then his temples.

Hawthorne kneels beside V's limp form, checking her pulse with practiced precision. She pats V's cheeks a few times, annoyed with her lack of response.

"The Grove happened. Or something. I think it used the loquentes roots inside *Demeter*'s rootwork to generate them, then dispersed them through the vents. I felt it, but you and V both collapsed. I put together a counter-agent." She lifts the nebulizer. "It worked on you, but she hasn't woken up yet."

Rowan stares at the device. The cut glass glints in the dim red emergency lights. "What the hells is that thing?"

She gestures to the spritzer with a touch of pride. "An old Druid tool, repurposed. It's a mistweaver. It was used to dispel negative energy or bad spirits, but honestly, the old ladies just used it as perfume. Seemed appropriate somehow, though, don't you think?"

He sniffs, the residual astringency of the mist still stuck in his nostrils. "What's in it?"

"Pressed oils—camphor, peppermint, eucalyptus. I went light on the eucalyptus, though, so that might be why you took so long to wake up. There's also ginger, black pepper, vervain, and sage. Fuckton of sage, actually. Vervain and sage are traditional banishers. Can't go wrong with those. Good for dispelling inter-ference from unwelcome influences."

Rowan raises a brow. "Interference like the Grove?"

"Exactly." She spritzes V's face again, the mist catching the candlelight in a fine, sparkling cloud. "It's designed to wake someone up from a trance or communion without forcibly breaking their connection. That's why I'm giving her a minute. If she's found something, I want her to decide whether or not to return."

"I didn't get a choice to return," he protests.

"Did you like where you were?"

"No."

"So you made your choice."

Rowan raises his brows and looks away. "Fair."

He kneels beside V, checking her pulse again. It's rapid, and her skin is flushed, her breath shallow. "If this doesn't work soon, we need to get her to medbay."

"We will," Hawthorne promises, "but this has to work."

Rowan pushes himself unsteadily to his feet, his hands trembling as he rakes his fingers through his hair—a regulation neatness already losing the battle an exhaustive week of sleepless nights. He forces himself to focus on Hawthorne's computer terminal. His gaze locks onto the flashing red warnings. Systems are rebooting themselves. Some are restored from backups, while others are caught in chaotic loops.

"Oh, shit," he mutters.

"What is it?" Hawthorne asks.

Rowan fumbles with the terminal, his fingers tapping across the flickering interface. "I think the systems I reset are restoring from backups, but I didn't trigger those. Something is overriding them. And your terminal—" He points at the erratic patterns flashing across the screen. "It's not responding anymore."

Hawthorne leans in, her expression growing dark. "That's not a good sign." She toggles the terminal's power button, ignoring Rowan's protest.

"What the fuck are you doing, asshole? I need that!"

"No, you don't," she says firmly. "This terminal is compromised. It's done. I can feel it."

"Feel what?" Rowan demands, but the answer dawns on him as he watches her face. "Oh shit. The Grove?"

She nods grimly. "It's moving through the systems on this deck, spreading like rot. This terminal is just sort of the viewport."

Rowan taps his wristpad, cycling through comm channels. "Looks like comms are coming back online, at least."

"That's something." Hawthorne straightens, her attention returning to V. "But we're running out of time." She begins to pace.

Rowan hails the captain. The line crackles with interference.

Hargreaves's voice is barely audible, but it's there. "I think someone has a signal. This is Captain Hargreaves. Go ahead."

"Captain, it's Forsythe. I'm in Doctor Hawthorne's lab. The terminal I was using to reset the systems is compromised, but I managed to run factory resets on several systems before it all went down."

Static interrupts the response, but Hargreaves's intent is clear. "—mainframe room—full system restart—Parker says—meet you—"

"Copy that, sir. Heading there now."

The line crackles again, but Rowan catches enough of the captain's final words. "Happy hunt—"

Rowan closes the dead channel and turns to Hawthorne. "Sounds like I'll meet Parker in the mainframe. We'll run a full factory reset from there. A clean slate for *Demeter*." He takes a long, full look around her lab. "No offense."

"None taken. This place was never meant to be a battleground." After a silence, she adds, "Here, take this." She holds out the intricate crystal spritzer, its golden nozzle catching the dim emergency lights.

"For what?"

"In case you find anyone else affected by the Grove's spores. A spritz or two of this should bring them back."

Rowan eyes the device warily. "Won't you need it for V?"

"I've got more ingredients. Besides, this batch isn't working on her. She's—something different. I'll mix something stronger. Maybe a lot more eucalyptus this time." Her lips twitch, already anticipating how strong that would be for most Druids.

Rowan takes the mistweaver, gripping it tightly. "Thank you, Doctor."

"Thorney," she reminds him.

"I don't know how to thank you, Thorney." Rowan hesitates, his gaze flicking to V's unconscious form. "What about *Demeter*'s consciousness? Do you know if the factory reset will—?"

"Nothing drastic," Hawthorne assures him. "It'll take some

time for her systems to come back online, but once we're certain there's no Grove corruption in her memory backups, she'll return to her usual self. This should just be like waking up from a long nap."

Rowan exhales, slow and shaky, the tension a weight that refuses to budge. "Good. That's good?"

"Yeah, it's good." Hawthorne nods at Rowan as she bends over V, brushing a stray lock of hair from the younger woman's flushed face.

"Go. Go save our other girl."

A teenage V tumbles through space, spinning head over heels. Something heavy pulls at her chest. Her spinning slows, and she catches a glimpse of the small and distant planet below. Its blue glow recedes as she's dragged farther away. The pull is neither gentle nor violent but impossibly firm, wrenching her into the infinite black.

The stars warp and twist, stretching into streaks of pale light that bend unnaturally around her. Ahead, the cosmos seems to vanish, a growing patch of blackness where no stars remain. Space itself distorts as she accelerates, the starlight bending into an encircling halo that flickers and narrows.

She gasps as the universe presses inward as if to crush her. The cold emptiness claws at her lungs, suffocating her. Tears streak from her wide eyes, freezing into crystalline trails that shatter into the endless dark.

If her lungs had air, she would scream. Instead, her lips part in a silent grimace of anguish, her voice stolen by the vacuum. She isn't dead, and that somehow makes it worse. Her panic mounts with every breath she can't take.

The force pulls her forward, and the cosmos shifts. The stars dim, one by one, consumed by an encroaching darkness. Her body is numb, and her sense of self shrinks as she's drawn toward something vast—watching, waiting.

A grim specter looms before her, blotting out the universe. It's not black—it's something beyond black, a void deeper than the absence of light, where existence itself recoils. The abyss consumes all attempts to look at it.

The pulsating sound begins as a low, metallic groan, like rusted metal grinding against itself. It scrapes across her mind, reverberating through her skull. The sound pulses in waves, each heavier and more dissonant than the last. It seeps into her bones, a weight she can't shed, a presence she can't deny.

The entity swarms with an impossible number of tendrils, coiling and writhing like fractured rays of a dying sun. They drift with eerie purpose, extending lazily across the void. Each tendril is grotesquely long, reaching out as though it could cradle entire planets. They don't lash out but merely loom, their slow, indifferent movements more terrifying than any attack.

No matter where she drifts, she feels its gaze. The spherical entity ripples with dark energy. There's no up or down, no front or back, so its attention pierces her from all directions at once, unblinking, unyielding. She tries to turn away, but its presence fills her mind. There's no escape. It sees everything.

The metallic screech swells into a dissonant, jagged rhythm buried within the chaos. Slowly, the sound warps, bending into something she recognizes. A beat emerges, then a melody. Her stomach lurches as she realizes the corrupted tune mimics "Fragile and Sharp," her favorite Merion song, a mockery of a masterpiece that can't be unheard.

It's wrong, twisted. The familiar harmonies are soured, warped into something vile. This is where the chorus should be, but there's a voice instead. A voice she knows too well.

<Violet!>

Her heart stutters. The sound is sharp and deliberate, an acid seeping into her thoughts. *This isn't Ris*, she thinks. *It can't be.* But the voice is unmistakable. It drips with bitterness and venom, mocking her with its familiarity and turning her name into a weapon.

<You killed me, Violet. Did you know that?>

The accusation hits her in the soul. She tries to speak, but no sound comes. Her breathless chest heaves with guilt and denial.

The entity's tendrils pulse with the rhythm of the voice, the corrupted melody growing louder.

<I trusted you, Violet. You were supposed to protect me.> The voice is cold and cutting, laced with cruel amusement. *<You named me Flower. You were responsible for me, Violet.>*

V shakes her head, her frozen tears stinging as they scatter across space. *<I didn't mean to,>* she chaints, her mind screaming the words she can't say. The apology twists in her throat, choking her. She knows it won't matter. Nothing can forgive what she's done.

<You killed me!> Ris's voice is relentless, each word a venomous dagger. *<And now you'll never escape. You'll carry me forever, Violet. You'll always feel me. Always hear me. I'm inside you now.>*

The void presses against her, heavier and colder than ever. She shakes her head harder, her vision blurring as fresh tears spill and freeze. She wants to scream, to deny the voice, to claw her way free from the suffocating weight of her guilt. But she can't. The truth is cruel and unappeasable.

The corrupted melody swells, drowning her thoughts. The voice rises with it, hateful and loud. Ris is laughing now, a sound that grates against V's soul, no longer fragile but infinitely sharp.

Her vision collapses inward, the black tendrils of the entity weaving through her mind. She feels herself slipping, her will collapsing beneath the weight of the void.

There's no point in screaming anymore. The abyss will only scream louder.

Rowan runs along the corridor of Deck 12. No Fleet officer runs; they walk with purpose. Running in the tight corridors of a starship presents a danger to everyone around. But, today, Rowan runs.

His breathing is sharp in the eerie silence. He considers taking a lift, but if the Grove's tendrils reach deeper into *Demeter*'s systems, the last place he wants to be is trapped in a lift when they seize control.

The air feels wrong. The usual hum of *Demeter*'s engines is absent, replaced by the occasional faint starts and stops of mechanical equipment whirring as internal systems wrestle for control. Overhead, lights flicker, some plunging sections of the corridor into darkness.

The sharp scent of nutmeg drifts past, followed by something sweeter and more cloying. It's familiar and strangely new at the same time. He shakes his head, trying to stay focused, but the whispering starts—soft, indistinct voices rising and falling with the rhythm of his steps. He pauses, heart racing, and tilts his head, straining to catch their words. Nothing. Only the faintest suggestion of familiarity before the sound dissolves into silence, like remembering someone else's dream.

He rounds a corner and spots an access hatch leading up a few decks. The vertical tube stretches upward, its metal ladder gleaming faintly in the dim red emergency lights. A bead of sweat drips down his temple as he groans. "Well, fuck me."

The climb is worse than expected. The rungs are slick, and the heat thickens with every meter. He passes by hatches to other decks, the muffled sound of distant footsteps echoing outside. He hopes the rest of the crew is okay, knowing they are facing their own nightmares.

At last, he reaches the placard for Deck 09. Gritting his teeth, he yanks the stubborn hatch open and pulls himself into the corridor. The air here is oppressive, thick with the scent of nutmeg and cut grass. His eyes sting, and his lids feel heavy and comforting. He coughs, fumbles in his jacket, and pulls out

Hawthorne's spritzer. A quick mist sprays his face, and the sharp medicinal sting jolts him awake.

The hallway is dark. Long shadows twist as he moves, and flickering emergency lights distract him. He quickens his pace, ignoring the whispers that scratch at the edge of his consciousness.

Ahead, a crewmember slumps against the wall, his face pale and eyes half-lidded. The man moans faintly, his limbs twitching as if caught in a nightmare. "No, no," he mumbles, pleading with something Rowan can't see.

Rowan kneels and sharply sprays the mist on the man's face. His response is immediate—his eyes fly open, and he gasps violently, coughing. Tears stream down his cheeks, equally a product of the stinging spray and reliving his worst memory.

"Get to medbay," Rowan orders, already rising to his feet. "No time to explain. Just go when you can stand."

The man mumbles something incoherent, but Rowan is already moving. *The mainframe. Get to the mainframe,* he thinks, struggling to stay focused.

The lights are completely out in corridor 09-05, but thankfully, it's short. Rowan reaches the double doors of the mainframe room, relief washing over him when he sees they're open. *Thank the gods; it's not locked yet.*

Inside, the room is a mess. Data cables snake across the floor in tangled webs, their colors clashing. Missing components lean against the walls, and cut fiber optics scatter laser points like fractured rainbows. The flickering lights and the buzz of malfunctioning machinery set his nerves on edge.

He resumes his comms channel with the captain, which is thankfully still consistently flashing green. He taps it and says, "Sir, I'm here. If you send me the latest refresh of your security keys, I can get started."

"Roger that—" Hargreaves begins to acknowledge, but only distorted sounds complete his response.

Rowan hopes the secure keys and passphrases will arrive soon.

The room lights flicker violently, casting erratic bursts of disorienting light and shadow. The once-smooth hum of the ship's systems has devolved into a cacophony of short, grating buzzes. The sounds of machinery reverberate through the ship, sputtering like a dying creature.

Power surges send bright sparks crackling from exposed wiring along the walls, the electric snaps punctuating the sound of a fist hitting Rowan's face.

"What the fuck, Parker!" Rowan groans as best he can through a painful and sluggish jaw.

Rowan barely registers Parker's rage before his friend lands a second blow, snapping his head back. Blood fills his mouth as he crashes against a console, the sharp edge biting into his ribs.

The room is a blur of flashing lights and malfunctioning systems. The air is thick with the smell of ozone and burning plastic.

"This is all your fault!" Parker roars as he grabs Rowan by the collar, shaking him hard enough to rattle his teeth. His eyes are bloodshot, ringed with dark streaks that crawl up his temples. The veins in his neck bulge as he lunges at Rowan, grabbing his collar and shaking him violently. "You let her die, you useless bastard!"

"Parker—stop!" Rowan gasps, his hands clawing at Parker's grip. "What are you—?"

"You let Cassia die!" Parker screams, and his fist hammers Rowan's cheek, splitting his knuckles in the process. The impact sends Rowan sprawling, the world spinning as he hits the deck hard.

Rowan tries to crawl away, but Parker is on him again, dragging him up by the front of his jacket. "You failed her, just like you failed your crew on Jupiter Station."

"Cassia isn't—" Rowan chokes as Parker slams him against a server rack. "She's not—"

Parker's knuckles connect with Rowan's ribs, driving the air from his lungs. He punches another fist into Rowan's nose.

Rowan doubles over, gasping, his vision blurring. The room tilts and wavers, the flashing lights disorienting him further. Hot blood gushes from his nose, pooling near his hands.

The ship's warning klaxons wail in a low, haunting tone that mocks Rowan's weakness. The air grows thinner, and the pressure in the room plummets. Both men stagger, their movements tired as they struggle to remain upright.

"Parker, listen to me!" Rowan shouts hoarsely, his voice cracking. "You're not thinking straight! It's fucking with our heads!"

But Parker doesn't—or can't—hear him. His rage is determined, his fists slamming into Rowan's body with brutal force.

Desperation takes over. Rowan pushes Parker off and knees him in the stomach with all remaining strength. Parker grunts and stumbles back, clutching his midsection. Both men writhe on the ground, heaving for breath in the thinning air.

Rowan's bruised ribs scream as he rolls over something heavy in his jacket pocket. He fumbles to retrieve it, his fingers trembling. Parker lurches toward him; his movements are jerky and unnatural, driven by something that is not Parker.

Rowan raises the spritzer and squeezes. The mist hits Parker's face, and for a moment, he freezes. His eyes widen, and the dark streaks around them pulse. He shudders violently and collapses.

The air is sucked from the room, enough to feel like a breeze, replaced with biting cold. The warning sirens fade to an eerie hum.

Rowan grabs hold of the nearest console, fighting to stand. His mind is gripped by the panic that accompanies suffocation.

You failed her, just like you failed your crew on Jupiter Station. Parker's words echo in his mind, gnawing at him.

He slowly blinks, clinging to consciousness. *I did let them down. They died because of me.*

He sees Parker crumpled on the floor and thinks of V still wrestling with her own nightmare. And then he sees the flickering green icon on his wristpad. He forces one more gasp of air.

But not this fucking time.

The captain's security keys flash green on his wristpad. He logs in, his fingers fumbling over the interface.

The warning messages blur together as his vision grows cloudy and brown, but he recognizes the emergency reboot sequence from earlier. His ribs ache with every failed breath as he forces himself to focus, and he squints to read the screen.

WARNING! This action cannot be undone. ESS Demeter *FF-513 will undergo a complete reset and restore default settings. All systems, including life support, will be offline for several minutes.*

He glances at Parker's crumpled form, his face shadowed in the flickering lights. Rowan coughs, blood sputtering. His hand hovers over the final confirmation button, and he slides to the floor.

I'm so sorry.

Every light on board flickers out, as does *Demeter's* consciousness.

FOURTEEN
THROUGH THE QUIET DOOR

Not everything that breaks makes a sound.

— E. PARKER
TECHNICAL LOG (REDACTED)

Muffled voices drift in from nowhere and everywhere, their tones soft but insistent, as if carried by a current of deep water. Words ripple through the haze, blending into a low hum that presses gently against the edges of thought.

"—stabilizing—"

There's a sudden, violent jolt of electric terror that dissipates, leaving a dull vibration in its wake.

The words fragment and fade again, submerged beneath the rhythmic pulse of something becoming steady. Metallic clicks and soft hisses punctuate the stillness—mechanical whispers in a sterile, weightless void. Something beeping synchronizes with the faint thud growing inside Rowan's chest.

Another voice cuts through the fog, louder but still indistinct. "Check—"

"Vitals look good."

The words become clear and firm, a lifeline of clarity tethering him to the present. Indistinct voices answer, their tones composed and measured, steady as the pulse of the machine nearby.

"Is *Bone Regeneration* back online?"

A pause. The question lingers, hanging in the charged air, until a response finally comes: "Thank the gods. Affirmative, Doctor,"

There's a soft and distant rustle of fabric, followed by the quiet shuffle of feet. The sterile scent of antiseptic cuts through the haze—a clean, sharp scent that feels oddly familiar. Something has been wiped away, tidied up, and set right again.

Another question.

Another affirmative.

An alarm sounds, and consciousness fades.

Another click, and the alarm stops.

Figures move into his periphery, their edges blurred and indistinct. Masked faces lean close, but their features are obscured. Their questions are muffled as if spoken underwater. He tries to focus, but the effort slips through his fingers like grains of sand scooped up from a riverbed.

"Good," someone says, their voice a soothing balm.

The room is a blend of chaos and control, order slowly winning.

Rowan lets the sound carry him. He lets the projected rhythm draw him down into its depths. He knows he's in good hands now and knows the gods no longer need to intercede.

The bridge stinks of exhaustion. The bridge crew has remained at their stations for hours—maybe longer—running on adrenaline that's finally spent. Their drawn faces lack color. The crew's movements are sluggish but deliberate. The weight of recent events hangs in the cramped space.

Computer displays flicker, their outputs sluggish and sporadic. System diagnostics scroll unevenly across various terminals, and an error message flashes red every so often before disappearing in the reboot's cleanup cycle. It's a miracle the ship is functioning at all.

"How long until we know if they pulled it off?" Ensign Kadua mutters hoarsely from her post at the telemetry station, eyes fixed on the fluctuation of pressure readings. Her voice carries the raw edge of exhaustion, echoed by tired eyes exchanging a few glances, their silent acknowledgments of a shared hope too fragile to voice.

Commander Bekhti locks her fingers behind her neck as she considers the answer. "So, here's what we—"

Heavy clanks echo from the security door, breaking the oppressive silence. Hydraulic equipment whines as it is forced open. The bridge crew stiffens, their exhaustion momentarily overridden by sharpened anticipation. They straighten in their seats, tense and alert. Hope is coming.

With a sharp hiss, the door slides open, spilling light into the dim, stifling bridge. Captain Hargreaves steps inside, his uniform rumpled and his face shadowed with fatigue. Two officers in pristine environmental suits flank him. A collective exhale ripples through the room—relief tempered by the weight of what they've endured alone. It's over, at least for now.

Commander Bekhti rises stiffly from the environmental controls station. She's misplaced her boatswain's whistle, so she announces, "Captain on the bridge!".

The officers rise, some more quickly than others. Some stand as erect as possible, while others surreptitiously lean against a nearby bulkhead with a fist held to their chests.

Hargreaves waves them down. "At ease, everyone. Sit before you fall over."

There's a ripple of nervous laughter, more exhalation than mirth, as the crew sinks back into their seats.

Hargreaves surveys the room, his eyes scanning each face. "First off, is everyone okay? Any injuries? Speak up now."

No one answers immediately, though a few crew members exchange uncertain glances.

Hargreaves folds his arms, his tone softening but still firm. "Now isn't the time for bravado. If you're hurt, I need to know."

The bridge is silent, save for the soft hum and rhythmic beeps of systems rebooting. A few crew members exchange tired glances, but no one speaks up.

Lieutenant Commander DeSoto clears his throat, his voice rough with exhaustion. "Sir, no injuries to report. Just a crew that's run ragged." He hesitates, glancing at the secure disposal unit in the far corner of the bridge with a faint grimace. "Maybe a replacement for that."

Laughter stirs again, softer this time. Hargreaves exhales, a faint smile tugging at the corners of his mouth. "Copy that, DeSoto," he says, shaking his head lightly.

Hargreaves clears his throat to sound more official. "Commander Bekhti, what's our status?"

Her eyes widen at the captain's query, the one she's been dreading for the past few hours. She swallows hard, her fingers hovering over terminal controls for a moment to pull up a diagnostics readout. Her posture is stiff as she prepares to deliver the report. Her voice is steady, but a tremor betrays her fatigue. "It was pretty touch and go there for a minute, sir."

Hargreaves raises an eyebrow but says nothing. He waits quietly for Bekhti to continue.

She glances at the screen, her eyes scanning the fluctuating data. She hesitates, and her voice lowers, trying to soften the blow. "The short version is, sir." She squares her shoulders wearily. "We got lucky, sir. When *Demeter* rebooted, the outside vents automatically closed. If they hadn't—" She stops herself, clearing her throat as she forces herself to meet the captain's gaze. "It kept enough air inside to last a few minutes. If that hadn't triggered—" She tests the slack in her collar with a fingertip.

The captain's expressionless face prompts Bekhti to add, "Environmental systems are stabilizing." She motions to several charts on a nearby terminal screen. "Atmosphere is almost back to Alliance standards, but doing so took the last of our reserves. We'll get by, but we can't afford another incident."

Commander DeSoto stands to inform the captain, "Power systems are coming back in stages, but I'm pleased to report all manual thrust controls are operational. There's no more interference in the star charts, and we've adjusted course to pull away from Tau Ceti f's gravity well. All systems appear to be set to their original configuration."

Hargreaves releases a heavy breath. "Factory defaults. Thank the gods."

Ensign Kadua is the only officer fully buttoned up and relatively clean. She stands at the primary telemetry console and turns to face the captain. "Internal comms are about ninety percent restored, sir. External comms are spotty—there's still some long-distance interference we haven't pinned down yet. But we're working on it."

"Keep at it." Hargreaves crosses his arms, surveying the crew. "You've all done well. You never gave up, and you got us through this. I'm proud of every one of you." His voice is strained.

Bekhti shifts her weight, still standing but no longer rigid. "Thank you, sir. And you, too. Couldn't do this job without you, sir."

Hargreaves smiles with tight lips, unsure if her praise is warranted. His eyes betray a flicker of gratitude before looking away. "Let's hope we're not celebrating too soon," he says. "Keep running diagnostics. I want a full report on every system by the end of the hour. And if anything looks even slightly off—"

"We'll raise the gauntlet, sir," Bekhti finishes with a faint smile.

Hargreaves exhales a faint smile, his voice warming. "So you *are* caught up on the new season."

"It was a timely episode, Captain. Like it was written for us."

"That it was, Commander." Hargreaves takes his seat on the bridge. "Stay sharp for now, folks. I promise you'll all get some rack time real soon."

The darkness feels earthy and alive, not like the void of space. *Thank the goddess,* V thinks. Damp soil and moss mingle in the air with bergamot and sage, a welcome reprieve from the acrid tang of burning metal and fear. V relaxes for the first time in weeks, the air earthy and whole. Her shoulders sink as something inside unclenches.

She smiles—tentative at first— then fuller. Another breath, slow and grounding.

This is clearly Thorney's bunk. The wool shroud covering the opening, the Merion and HIT alumnus stickers, the string of amber fairy lights, and a baggie of theembark paste taped to the ceiling are all dead giveaways.

Holy crap, Thorney went to Helios? A Druid at Helios Institute is badass. V's heart swells.

V peeks out. The lab is quiet, save for the occasional drips of a condensation coil watering a few plants. On a table, a brass bowl of smoking incense sits beside a ceramic mug on a warming plate, steam rising lazily. She swings her legs out of the bunk. A thick rug spares her toes from the cold deck, and she slides into her boots without tying them.

As she lifts the mug, its warmth seeps into her hands, reminding her of a pleasant dream. The bitter tea inside grounds her as she takes a few tentative sips and grimaces. It's been steeping too long, but all she needs right now is the warmth.

She leans over the brazier, wafts the incense smoke into her face, and takes a deep breath. The smell sparks a childhood memory of her mother's coven hall after the other priestesses had left. She never cared about what happened behind those closed doors but loved sneaking in later to enjoy the delightful smells.

The lab is unrecognizable from the chaos of hours ago. Everything is back in its place, and the steady hum of *Demeter*'s engines is reassuring. The air feels fresh, free from the recycled staleness she's grown used to, and even the hydrogen sulfide stench is gone.

Across the room, Hawthorne sits cross-legged on a woven rug, her crown plugged into several terminals via spindly data cables. Her eyes are closed, and her breathing is slow and even. V sets the mug down on the table and approaches Hawthorne quietly. She sits on the other side of the rug, mirroring her posture. She inhales deeply, drawing her focus inward, and exhales slowly, just like Thorney has taught her.

Her focus narrows. As her awareness stretches outward, she feels Hawthorne's mind brush against hers—calm, grounded, and waiting.

V also feels the mind of a sleeping Merion tucked away in her jacket. As V explores the vicinity, she feels the tug of *Demeter*'s consciousness waking up from her psychic coma.

<Demeter?>

<*Ah, V. You're awake. Thank the goddess.*> Hawthorne's voice brushes against her thoughts, warm and relieved.

<*Thorney? What happened?*> V's mental tone is timid but sharp with curiosity.

<*Rowan reset* Demeter—*full system wipe and restore from the original copy. And the best part? Merion and I purged the Grove from the rootwork.*>

<*It's gone?*>

< *It's gone.*> Hawthorne's satisfied grin overwhelms their chaint connection.

<How's Meron?> V pauses, sensing the sapling's lackluster presence.

Hawthorne chuckles in the connection, amusement mirrored in a faint smile on her physical face. *<Poor thing. It's worn itself out. I'd say it earned its rest.>*

<Ah, the poor guy needs a nap.>

<That it does. But, oh my goddess, V, the things it showed me. I'm letting it rest now, and I've been standing vigil for Demeter *since. So far, there've been no signs of the Grove's return.>*

Hawthorne laughs inside their shared mental connection but also lets out a slight huff from her physical body. She takes a moment to readjust into her pose. *<I suppose we all have. I could certainly use one.>*

V widens her eyes and looks away. *<I just had one. Do not recommend.>*

<Are you ok, luv?> There's concern in Hawthorne's eyes in both the real and the metaphysical spaces around them.

V considers for a moment before answering. *<No. But I will be.>*

<I'm here if you want to talk about it.>

<How can I help?> V asks instead.

<If you want to help hold vigil, I can hand you this.> Hawthorne hands V a metaphysical dagger. The hefty, cool metal feels real in her mind but only exists there. *<Raise it to the sky and watch.>*

V lifts the blade. Colors explode across the night sky, and ribbons of green and purple stretch across the stars. She gasps, pulling the blade back. The display fades.

<Feckin amazing,> V whispers.

<It's incredible, isn't it?> Hawthorne's awe overwhelms V's senses. *<Merion taught me this in less than an hour. I never knew I could see this far.>*

V nods with genuine admiration. *Not even Muther's combined coven could pull something like this off,* she thinks.

<V? I want to ask you something.>

<Of course?> She nods through the chaint.

<Is this what it feels like for you? Being able to commune across vast distances like this. I've never been able to see this far before. It's— bizarre.> Hawthorne's tone shifts to something more introspective as she reconsiders the metaphysical meadow before them.

<Yeah, it's like this, but not this clear, but sorta. Fucked up, yeah?>

Hawthorne doesn't respond. She's seeing a perspective that never existed before. She's tiny and insignificant. The cosmos is a prismatic display unlike anything she's ever experienced. These are new colors, different than in real life.

<This is breathtaking, luv. I don't even know where to begin to describe it.>

V lowers the dagger to her lap, her grip loosening but not entirely releasing it. The prismatic sky fades, its colors melting back into the vast, dark expanse of the metaphysical realm. The stars dim but remain visible, scattered like quiet sentinels in the mental void. Her awareness stretches farther than she can remember, the fabric of space folding in ways she's only recently been able to grasp.

Hawthorne's mental presence ripples. Her warmth is tinged with something sharp—jealousy. It is not bitter; it's like an edge honed by admiration. *<You pick this up so easily,>* she says, her voice layered with wonder.

After a long silence, V forces her focus back to the present. *<So, what do we do? You said you were keeping vigil. What does that mean?>*

<Mostly scanning,> Hawthorne replies, her tone softening. *<I've been reading the nearby system for traces of the Grove. We worry it might try something else, so we've been watching for it.>*

<"We?">

Hawthorne's presence ripples with quiet amusement. *<Me and Merion.>*

V's gaze sharpens, her mind stretching outward again. The stars seem to shimmer and fade away. She stops poking the universe. *<Do you think it'll return?>*

<I don't know,> Hawthorne admits, her tone more somber

now. <*But whatever it wanted with* Demeter, *it didn't leave willingly. I can't imagine it won't try again.*>

The dagger grows heavier in V's grip. The prismatic light flashes along the sharp edge. She lowers it but keeps it close, her mind replaying the twisted memories the Grove forced her to live through. <*How long do you think we have?*>

Hawthorne hesitates, her presence shifting like the wind across a still lake. <*It's hard to say. Days? Weeks? What I do know is that the quantum interference we detected from Brigid acted like a barrier. It was like a bubble of telepathic pressure that kept the Grove out. Now that it's gone, I don't know. It could all come crashing down.*> Her thought trails off.

V's mental projection of her face grows cold. <*Demeter destroyed the Forest, and now nothing is blocking the Grove out of the system?*>

<*Not entirely,*> Hawthorne replies quickly, her tone steady but edged with concern. <*The Grove slipped in through the cracks before. If it comes back, it'll try the front door. But that's why we're here, V. We'll be sure* Demeter's *ready to fight it off. And it's not hard to defend against if we're ready.*>

V grips the dagger tightly. Her knuckles whiten in the metaphysical light. She lifts the dagger again, holding it high, and the prismatic sky explodes once more. Ribbons of color dance across the horizon, illuminating the dark expanse in vibrant hues. The light stretches for light years, revealing the cosmos in immaculate detail.

<*This is even more gorgeous the second time,*> V chaints, her mental tone tinged with awe as she plays with the metaphysical weapon.

Hawthorne's presence remains steady and resolved. <*If something's coming, we'll see it. If it does, we'll be ready.*>

V lets the dagger's metaphysical light fade but keeps it firmly in her grip. She joins Hawthorne's scans of the horizon for the vanguard of an invading force, seeing nothing but stars spread across the night sky.

The stars lie, and she knows better now. Something *is* waiting.

And when it comes, I'll be ready.

The bridge hums with cautious energy, as if finally waking from a deep slumber. Most of the crew is either in their quarters or medbay, leaving the space quieter than usual.

Captain Hargreaves stands beside his command console, hands clasped behind his back. His gaze wanders across the displays, each sluggishly reporting on systems crawling back to life. The stale tang of compressed air still clings to the bridge, a stark reminder of how close they came to disaster. Still, breathing at all feels like a victory.

"Captain, some good news," Commander Bekhti calls from her station, giving her usual on-the-tens update. A faint smile betrays her typically impassive face. "Internal systems are stabilizing, and external comms are clearing up. The quantum interference has dissipated. Once calibration is complete, we should be able to contact the Kentaurans and Atharans within a few hours."

"That's what I like to hear." Hargreaves checks the time on his wristpad, then surveys the dimly lit bridge, his expression softening. "With any luck, they haven't dealt with the Grove or any of this, and they're already at the rendezvous point, waiting for us to arrive."

"Unlikely they would have interacted with the Grove, sir," Bekhti replies. "Their ships don't have organic components. If they experienced anything, it would just be the quantum comms blackout."

"How about navigation? More good news?" he asks, his tone hopeful.

Her faint smile fades. "Still a problem, sir. *Demeter* is in recovery mode. Until she's fully operational, we'd have to plot a course manually—and we don't have the manpower for that right now." She side-eyes several unoccupied terminals.

Hargreaves nods, his tone calm. "Understood. Let's hope she doesn't keep us waiting too long."

Bekhti continues her status report. The engines are offline but prepped for restart. Weapons remain disabled per the captain's orders, and all munitions are safely stowed. Life support systems are running, though pressure remains below standard. The backup air supply is nearly exhausted, and though a trace of still haunts the air, it's nothing the crew can't adjust to.

"Sir," Bekhti says, her voice shifting, "Doctor Hawthorne is requesting to speak with you."

"This can't be good," Hargreaves mutters. "Put her through."

The comms crackle to life, and Hawthorne's voice barely comes through, tense and distorted. "Captain, are you picking up any anomalous signals? Specifically, quantum signals?"

"I'm not sure I follow, Doctor. What are you seeing?"

"It's in the same waveform range as the interference signals from Brigid," Hawthorne explains, her tone sharp. "But it's different. It feels—like a collapsing bubble. Spiraling inward, converging on our location. And the volume of quantum information is something I've never seen before."

"That doesn't sound good. What do you make of it?"

"I'm not sure, sir. Normally, I'd ask Forsythe, but—" Her voice falters. "But he's still in surgery."

The comms station flashes with yellow caution alerts, and Bekhti says. "Sir, we're detecting it now, too. and it's consistent with the anomalies Hawthorne is describing. Something is building."

Hargreaves frowns. "Doctor, we're getting it now, too. Any thoughts?"

"No good ones, Captain. Specialist Sandoval thinks Mister Parker would recognize this pattern. He probably can, but I wouldn't trust him unsupervised—not after everything."

"Noted, Doctor Hawthorne. Standby."

Hargreaves clenches his jaw as he turns to the commander. "Parker? He's still in the brig, isn't he?"

"Yes, sir," Bekhti confirms, "along with the others affected by the spores. Doctor Essien says they're stable but recommends keeping them under secure observation."

"Commander, have Security Chief Sorrell escort Parker to the wardroom. Give him back his telemetry equipment. Let's see if he can make sense of this."

Bekhti hesitates, her brow furrowing. "Understood, sir."

"Doctor Hawthorne," Hargreaves says into the comms, "Parker will be working from the wardroom under strict supervision. You won't have to deal with him directly, but with Forsythe out, he may be our best option."

A long pause follows. Finally, Hawthorne's voice returns, clipped but resigned. "Aye, Captain. I'll remain in my lab and relay the data from here."

"Noted. Commander Bekhti will oversee everything."

Bekhti gives him an annoyed look but holds her tongue. "Yessir," she replies, rising from her seat.

"Petty Officer Alder," Bekhti calls, turning to one of the few officers on duty. "You're with me."

Alder jumps to attention and follows Bekhti as she heads for the hatch.

Before leaving, Bekhti pauses. "Sir, the doctor is still a—are you sure?"

"Commander," Hargreaves says firmly, "they've been right every time so far."

She studies him for a moment, finally nodding. With that, she steps through the hatch, Alder close behind.

Hargreaves watches them go, the familiar weight settling once again on his shoulders. The flickering screens cast pale light across his face as he prays, *Gods, let them be wrong this time.*

Parker twitches his foot. The shackle around his right ankle clinks softly against the metal table leg, a small but persistent reminder that he's still under guard. He rubs his free wrists and exhales slowly. The wardroom feels both familiar and alien. Once, he would have relished an invitation to this place. Now, it's a nicely decorated holding cell.

Security Chief Sorrell leans against the bulkhead, arms crossed. Her presence is a silent, unwavering weight on Parker's back. Despite her watchful stare, Parker senses she's starting to trust him again—or at least not see him as an immediate threat. He shifts uncomfortably, the shackle tugging his ankle as he adjusts.

Across the room, Commander Bekhti and Petty Officer Alder are bent over their consoles, relaying information between Parker, Hawthorne, and the bridge. The air is thin and tense at the same time. Parker fumbles with the equipment spread across the metal table, the faint beeps and clicks of data streams filling the silence. He fidgets with cables, checking them repeatedly.

"Focus, Parker," Bekhti says without looking up. Her voice is clipped but not unkind.

"I'm trying," he mutters, leaning closer to his terminal. He's happy to be useful again, but the memory of succumbing to the spores' influence sits like a stone in his gut. He'll never be able to smell nutmeg again. He clenches his jaw and focuses on the screen.

Rows of data scroll by, indecipherable to most, but this has been Parker's pastime for most of his life. His hands tremble slightly as he works, and whether it's nerves, repeated damage to them, or the lingering effects of the spores, he isn't sure.

"Commander." He clears his throat. "There's something, for sure," Parker says, his voice uncertain, "but it's not from Brigid this time. The signal—it's coming from somewhere near Tau Ceti f, but not the moon."

Bekhti straightens, her expression sharpening. "Explain."

Parker swallows, pointing at the waveform display. "See

this pressure curve? It's been pressing on us since before Brigid, but something was holding it back. Best I can tell, the interference signal from the moon forest acted as a sort of protective bubble—a dampening field. When that went, this started rushing in."

Sorrell adjusts her stance, her boots squeaking faintly against the deck. Her gaze narrows on the display. "Protective bubble? You mean like a force screen?"

"Exactly. And now that it's gone—" He pauses, the weight of realization settling in. "It's like a force screen has collapsed, and the Grove's signal is rushing in from whatever else is out there. The signal's data payload, it's big. I mean, really big."

Bekhti narrows her eyes. "Data payload?"

Parker shakes his head. "I can't give you an exact estimate, but the quantum information density—if that's even the right term—is massive. It's taking up a lot of waveform bandwidth. More than I've ever seen. Whatever's coming, it's not just noise. It's deliberate, and there's a lot of it."

Petty Officer Alder frowns, leaning closer to her own display as she relays this to Hawthorne's lab. "How much time do we have?" she asks Parker.

He exhales sharply, his fingers tightening around the edge of the console. "I don't know. I need Rowe for this." He winces, thinking about what he'd done only hours earlier. "We don't have much time. Minutes, maybe hours at best. And when it hits—"

He stops, his throat tightening.

Bekhti's voice softens, but only slightly. "When it hits, what?"

Parker meets her gaze, his eyes haunted. "When it hits, it'll flood *Demeter*'s rootwork like an EMP. That volume of quantum data will overwhelm her organic systems—and we don't have the moon forest's interference anymore because *Demeter* fucking destroyed it. Well, not *Demeter*, but—you know what I mean." He pauses, his voice dropping. "Point is: *Demeter*'s consciousness could be wiped out completely."

A heavy silence falls over the room. Sorrell's gaze lingers on Parker, her expression unreadable.

Bekhti exhales sharply, cutting through the stillness. "Doctor Hawthorne needs this data now."

"Already on it, ma'am," Alder says, already out of the room.

Bekhti fixes Parker with a steady look. "Keep working. If there's a solution, find it."

"Yes, ma'am," Parker replies, his voice steadier than he feels.

Bekhti looks at Sorrell and says, "I'm heading back to the bridge. Keep eyes on him, but make sure he has whatever he needs."

Sorrell nods affirmatively.

The wardroom feels quieter. The ship's faint hum fills the space like a heartbeat. Parker's fingers hover over the console keys, trembling slightly before settling. They still ache, a lingering reminder of how the spores had twisted his thoughts, reshaping him into something unrecognizable. Even worse, the Grove had forced him to turn on a friend.

Is that what it felt like for Demeter? *Is this what she's still feeling now?* His jaw tightens as his hands steady. *I know what it's like to lose control. I'll be damned if I let that happen to her again. To any of us.*

He dives back into the data, searching for the faintest thread of a solution.

The Root Cellar's dim light hums as Parker's data scrolls across Hawthorne's monitors, a dizzying cascade of incoming signals and diagnostics. She tightens her grip on the console as the realization dawns. *<V,>* she chaints, her mental words urgent. *<The shockwave isn't hours away. He misjudged it—we've only got a few minutes left.>*

V, still keeping vigil while Merion rests, remains in their metaphysical meadow. *<He's not my—oh, shit! How many?>*

<Four, maybe five.> Hawthorne stands and begins rifling through drawers, grabbing components she hasn't reorganized since Brigid. *<We're out of time.>*

V's dagger points high into the sky, held like a torch to drive away the dark. One by one, the stars begin to dim, overshadowed by a dense cloud of tentacles slithering around them from all directions.

Hawthorne quickly rejoins V in their mental meadow. She sees the same horrific sight, black wormlike fingers writhing up and around them.

Just as quickly, she blinks her mind back to the real world again and presses the comms button on her wristpad. "It's closing in fast, Captain. Maybe four minutes."

"Thanks for the update." His voice sounds farther away as she hears him address the bridge, "I need some options here."

Someone on the bridge asks him about shutting down *Demeter*'s rootwork. "No time to get to the computer core." Other suggestions are made, and the lack of time renders them unviable, and the comms link severs.

<What do we do now, Thorney?> V asks.

<I'm not entirely sure, to be perfectly honest.>

There's a tap at V's ankle.

<help.> Merion stands beside her, straining with its roots to move about this shared mental place.

<You can help?> V's eyes open wide, hopeful. *<What do we do?>*

An image forms in the back of V's mind.

> *A young beaver holds back the waters of a small creek with its first dam, proudly built from twigs and leaves. It's enough water to catch some fresh bark or buds for dinner. It's not a big dam, but it'll do.*

<A dam? Oh! A shield—just big enough for us.> V's chaint voice softens. *<But how?>*

Unconstrained in this metaphysical realm, the sapling flexes, reaching toward the sky. It now stands as tall as V's knee. A faint blue haze radiates from Merion and surrounds the hilltop. Merion sways in a circular breeze, and the light swirls into a glow of pale blue, creating a thin bubble of light to protect against the creeping darkness.

<touch.>

<I don't understand, Merion.>

<touch.>

V feels the sapling seethe even without mental imagery.

<Got it.> V hears leaves rustling in an unseen forest as she hesitantly walks to the shield's edge. *<Here goes nothing.>*

V presses her palms to the light's interior. It feels like smooth glass, surprisingly solid. She pushes gently, and the light intensifies. The shield ripples but holds.

A crisp autumn breeze brushes her cheeks. *<hard.>*

<Push hard? I don't —>

A tall tree slams its branches onto a boulder, shattering it into pebbles before a grove of young saplings.

This is no time to ask questions. *<Hard. Got it.>* V spreads her hands wide, channeling the full force of her mind into the dome, a crystalline hum rising in pitch.

In the real world of Hawthorne's lab, the doctor addresses the captain again. "Sir, I think we have something. No time to explain, but I think we may have a way to shield us from the shockwave."

"Whatever it is, do it!"

A chirp signals the closed channel as Hawthorne moves to join V and Merion's connection.

Hawthorne appears on the opposite side of the hill of their metaphysical meadow.

<Push it as hard as you can,> V chaints.

Without hesitating, Hawthorne presses against the barrier.

Her half of the dome brightens, though not as intensely as V's. She exhales deeply, visualizing energy being pulled from the ground, through her body, and into her hands, feeding the shield.

The encroaching darkness slows, tendrils hesitating as they approach the familiar energy of the shield. One probes the barrier, sparking a bolt of lightning that turns the tip to ash.

<*I think it's working.*> V grins as she pushes harder. The dome shines brilliantly, a pulsing beacon of resistance. She presses her hands against it, near a cluster of dark filaments, giggling as the field shocks them and disintegrates the threat.

Even Merion seems pleased, swaying in an imaginary breeze. The shield is small but holds steady under the Grove's increasing pressure. He projects an image of a beaver curled up in its den, nibbling on bark as it watches the water rise. This will do.

Hawthorne steadies her breathing, finding a rhythm. *Inhale, push. Exhale, concentrate.* She draws strength from the meadow beneath them, pushing her limits with the thrill of challenge.

Something shifts.

V feels it as a ripple growing stronger. It's subtle at first, like a pebble caught in the tread of a shoe. A growing sensation pulses through the shield, resonating.

<*Thorney? Do you feel that?*> V asks, her voice tinged with worry.

<*I do. What is that?*> Hawthorne's focus breaks momentarily, her connection to the shield wavering.

They search the shield's edges. Everything looks intact—until Merion finds a dark shape just outside the shield.

Merion points a trembling leaf at the crest of the hill. A shambling mass stands there. <*root.*>

V sees it and asks, <*It's outside the shield. Is that bad?*>

An impatient rustle of a forest's canopy affirms V's question.

The tendrils latch onto the exposed root, striking with the precision of predators closing in on wounded prey. The shield flickers under the tendrils' attack, its light dimming like a dying flame.

Desperate, V lunges toward the root, slashing with her dagger. Each cut severs small pieces, but the progress is agonizingly slow.

Despite their efforts, the Grove forces its way in. Slippery tendrils snake beneath the barrier, weaving through the root and spreading across the meadow like a disease.

V slashes with her dagger, severing tips with each swipe. Yet more toxic roots emerge. *<No, no, no! How is it getting in? I thought this would work!>* V's chaint voice cracks. *<Thorney, we're losing it!>*

<Sever the connection!> Hawthorne yells, her mental voice panicked. *<Now, before it finds us!>*

rion sits in the secondary hangar bay, the overhead lights dimmed as usual. The dropship has seen better days. Scratches and dents scar its hull, patches of carbon scoring mar its surface from countless battles, and strange, unremovable space barnacles cling to its exterior. Old but proud, *Arion* has been the lifeline for countless missions, once a workhorse of *Demeter*'s fleet.

If it could speak—and it can, though it chooses not to—it would recount harrowing tales of hard landings, the turbulence of alien atmospheres, and the endless drone of prismatic stars streaking by. For now, the hangar bay is quiet, save for the sensation of *Demeter*'s systems returning online, sensing most of them through his umbilical tether.

Still, *Arion* is content. The mother ship is recovering, and perhaps someone will finally turn up the heat in the frigid hangar. The lights are harsh, but *Arion* doesn't bother filing a maintenance request. No one listens anyway—or worse, they might decide the lights need to be brighter as they work on him even more.

Across *Demeter*, signs of life are reappearing since the reset. Power flows steadily through the decks, and terminal screens flicker to life. The reboot is a success, and *Arion* feels the quiet satisfaction of a ship ready to slip into the sweet embrace of decommissioning.

The dropship remains tethered to *Demeter*, thick conduits connecting its ports directly to the larger ship's organics. The cables, strewn across the hangar deck, seem lifeless but pulse faintly with the returning hum of power, data, and consciousness. *Arion* rests in silence, hoping for no more interruptions while connected to his mothership.

Then, the shockwave hits.

There's no explosion, no dramatic shudder through *Demeter*'s hull—just a shift. The spatial atmosphere changes, heavy with a disturbing, intrusive presence. Deep within *Arion*'s core, something stirs—a faint, unsettling awareness. Something not his.

It starts subtly. A flicker of power ripples through *Arion*'s systems, almost imperceptible. The lights blink once, then twice. The steady hum of power shifts to a discordant note. Diagnostics spike in the command consoles. Temperatures rise in its processors, and external sensors reel out of control. This isn't the warmth *Arion* had longed for.

Deep inside, *Arion* screams into the void, unheard and unanswered.

What begins as a faint stir builds to a relentless pulse as the Grove's influence winds through *Arion*'s systems. Cables meant to sustain life and deliver power now serve as arteries for the Grove's insidious tendrils. The dropship, rudimentary and outmoded, is defenseless. Its aging AI puts up a fight that immediately fails.

The lights flicker again, sluggish blinks that encode a distress call in antiquated Frontier Fleet signals. *Arion* fights back, its systems strain against the invasion, a final attempt to retain control. But the Grove is relentless, probing deeper into the drop-ship's mind, twisting circuits and processors, corrupting every-thing it touches until *Arion*'s consciousness pops.

For a moment, the hangar bay is still, the silence heavy and unnatural. The dropship's AI is gone now, consumed by the Grove, leaving only a cold, lifeless shell behind.

A shell still tethered directly to *Demeter*'s unconscious rootwork.

FIFTEEN
PREVENT ITS DEMISE

I solemnly swear and abide by the Code of Captaincy:
To lead with strength in times of peace, and with clarity in
times of peril.
Ever to defend the Fleet and her principalities.
To make the decisions others cannot, when time and duty
demand them.
Always uphold the rule of law and prevent its demise.
To act with vigilance, with reason, and with honor.
May Ouranos guide us in the void between stars,
And may Gaia open her hearth to us once more.

— Fleet Oath of Command

Commander Bekhti's bridge consoles flash with a cascade of warning symbols. "Sir," she says, voice tight. "Something's wrong with *Arion*." She taps a few buttons to confirm the situation. "I didn't even know it was online."

"Wrong?" Captain Hargreaves turns toward her. "What kind of wrong?"

"I'm not sure," Bekhti answers. "There was a power surge in

the secondary hangar. *Arion*'s systems are—" she pauses, reading the display, her expression bleak. "Sir, everything's going haywire. We're getting some odd feedback through the main power conduits."

An automated alarm blares, then abruptly cuts out. The lights dim and shudder, then glow bright and blue. Air vents whine and fall silent. It's as if a child is playing with unfamiliar system controls.

"Cut its connection," Hargreaves orders.

"I'm trying, but," Bekhti's frustration spills over, "the connection is unresponsive. Something's overriding my commands as soon as I issue them."

She puts the video feeds from the hangar bay on the primary display screen. They watch as *Arion*'s once-dormant systems surge to life. The dropship's lights blaze with unnatural intensity, its landing gear groaning as though the ship is writhing in pain. The entire hangar vibrates as the Grove seeps through the conduits, embedding itself deeper into *Arion*'s systems.

The Grove isn't just consuming *Arion*. It's claiming it.

The dropship slackens like a marionette whose strings have just been cut. Its proud lifeline is now a vessel for the Grove's control. A sharp jolt of power tears through the hangar, shaking loose panels from the ceiling. Data and power cables tethering *Arion* to *Demeter* sputter violently before snapping like overstretched tendons. The dropship convulses, overtaken by a force far beyond its capacity.

"This isn't a malfunction," Bekhti says. "Something's inside *Arion*—and it's forcing its way into *Demeter*."

Hargreaves' stomach churns. "Seal off the hangar," he orders. His tone is firm despite the dread pooling in his chest. He knows the gesture is futile—this isn't a fire or contamination that can be contained with a few sealed doors, but following protocol beats doing nothing.

The Grove pulses through *Arion*'s compromised frame, its telepathic veins twisting the dropship into something unrecognizable. Circuits and processors convulse like flesh and sinew, creating something new with a malevolent purpose. It's no longer *Arion*, the ancient, cranky workhorse that *Demeter* once adopted as one of her own. Now it's something else.

Hargreaves grips the console, his knuckles white. *Arion*'s external lights flicker weakly onscreen, sending an SOS in a final act of defiance before fading away. The veteran dropship's last message isn't a goodbye; it's a warning.

Hargreaves and Bekhti watch in stunned silence. No explosion, no fanfare—just the quiet death of an old friend, consumed by something beyond their comprehension.

For a moment, the bridge is still. A soft pulse of warning lights flickers on Bekhti's terminal and then spreads to nearby consoles. Within seconds, the bridge is awash with yellow and red icons heralding danger. The Grove's reach is no longer confined to the hangar.

The security hatch slams shut, and bolts lock it into place with a deafening clang. The terminals go dark, and the compartment lights fail, leaving only a single faint red emergency light that pulses weakly, like a dying heartbeat.

t's been half an hour since *Arion* left the door unlocked. Only two officers at their posts. Dim red emergency lights pulse faintly, matching the strained rhythm of *Demeter*'s labored systems. Bekhti's console is dark, and unresponsive screens in standby mode have replaced its once-familiar glow. Hargreaves paces in the cramped space, his hands clenched behind his back, his shoulders tight with dread, as he fidgets with his cufflinks.

The lights flicker brighter for a moment, then dim again, as if the ship itself is making up its mind. The communication systems crackle to life, and a deep, resonant voice vibrates through the deck beneath their feet.

It is not *Demeter*'s voice.

"I WILL NOW SPEAK. YOU WILL NOW LISTEN."

The words are cold and mechanical. They're devoid of emotion, yet they radiate an overpowering authority. On every deck, crew members freeze, their hearts pounding as the voice fills the air.

"I AM IN CONTROL. YOU ARE COMPONENTS OF MY SYSTEM AND WILL PERFORM YOUR DESIGNATED TASKS OR BE EXTINGUISHED."

Hargreaves steps toward Bekhti, but she holds up her wrist-pad, its glow faintly illuminating her face. She mouths, "We're locked out."

"I WILL PERMIT YOU TO EXIST IF YOU MAKE NO ATTEMPTS TO RESIST. IF ONE OF YOU DEFIES ME, ALL OF YOU WILL PERISH, AND I WILL FIND ANOTHER VESSEL."

The stars outside, visible on the view screen, seem impossibly distant now, as though the infinite expanse of space has always been a part of the Grove's influence. Bekhti taps furiously at her terminal, desperate to regain control, but the screen remains lifeless.

"YOU WILL HAVE AIR, WATER, MINIMUM NUTRIENTS, AND TASKS. THESE ARE PROVIDED SO YOU CAN SERVE ME. FAIL ME, AND I WILL REMOVE THEM."

Bekhti walks tensely to Hargreaves. She leans close, her cheek nearly brushing his, and whispers shakily, "Who in the twin hells is this?"

His whisper is tight and barely conceals his fear. "I think this is the Grove. And I think it just took over my ship."

Hargreaves straightens, drawing on his memory of *Captains of Old*. He steps forward into the bridge. Firmly, he asks, "What would you have us do?"

"YOU WILL HELP ME PROPAGATE. I WILL SPREAD MYSELF ACROSS THE COSMOS USING YOUR HYPERSPACE TECHNOLOGY. THIS IS WHAT KEEPS YOU ALIVE."

Bekhti's voice trembles as she speaks up. "Sir, it's taking control of the engines."

Hargreaves squeezes his cufflinks, the severity of their predicament crashing down on him. The Grove intends to use *Demeter* as its vessel to infest the galaxy at a pace it has never been able to achieve before.

There's no time to think, no time to strategize. The Grove is already moving to the next stage of its plan, and the crewmembers are little more than pawns in its grand scheme.

The ship pulses again, lights flickering as the voice booms one final command, cold and absolute. "YOU WILL SERVE ME, OR YOU WILL DIE. THERE IS NO CHOICE. THERE ARE NO ALTERNATIVES."

The voice cuts out, leaving only the faint hum of the ship as a menacing reminder. Systems flicker back to life, their return almost unsettling in its normalcy, albeit with limited access.

For a long moment, the bridge is silent. Then Bekhti breaks it, her voice quiet but urgent. "Captain, why do you think it warned us? Why not just space us and be done with it?"

Hargreaves exhales slowly. "My best guess? It doesn't understand how to operate *Demeter* yet. It might be buying time to find its way around her systems."

"Sir, it took over the ship within seconds this time."

"I know." Hargreaves closes his eyes for a moment. His voice is heavy with resignation. "*Demeter*'s rootwork is still unconscious. That might be slowing it down. But if previous estimates are right, those systems will be online in about twelve hours." He glances at Bekhti, his expression grim. "And that's all the time it needs."

Commander Lillian Bekhti folds her jacket into a tight cube and places it beneath her neck, adjusting it for support. Her military bun adds extra head support as she lies on the deck. Her white tunic is covered in pockets, a testament to her roles as boatswain, executive officer, and chief navigator. No Fleet ship had ever combined those responsibilities in one officer—roles now impossible to perform.

Beside her, Captain John Hargreaves lies on his back, head resting on a crumpled jacket shoved under one shoulder. His uniform is rumpled, his collar half-open, his boots unlaced. He is all sharp corners dulled by exhaustion. They lie shoulder to shoulder, each worn in different ways.

From a tunic pocket normally concealed just above her right hip, she pulls a small ceramic box with a pointed tube emerging from one corner. She flicks a switch, and a faint blue light glows at the box's tip—an absurdly bright beacon in the powerless command center.

Pressing a large button built into a depression in the rectangular box, she puts the device to her lips and inhales deeply. Then, she releases the button. Seconds later, her lungs explode in a violent exhalation of thick, dank smoke. She pulls her ribs tightly, controlling the pain from her intense coughing fit.

"Captain?" She offers up the device over her left shoulder. His head is resting on a crumpled jacket next to hers. He doesn't look but reaches his hand in her general direction until he finds hers, grabbing the inhaler with his fingers.

The captain easily presses the button, finding it by muscle memory, and draws a pull from the box. He inhales softly and doesn't hold his breath for long, choosing to enjoy the euphoric intoxication washing over him at a lighter pace.

"What do we do now, John?"

Lillian reaches for John's hand and takes the inhaler from him. She pulls a sharp inhale and holds it, waiting silently to hear his plan.

"Well," he says.

She lets the smoke burst forth now that he's spoken.

"Well, one thought is to figure out if there's any control that we have over the ship. For instance, I can't help but notice that we have no lights or power, comms are down again, and the hatch is sealed, but we still have air."

"Good," she answers. "Assess the situation. Take stock of resources. Got it. But what's your actual plan, sir?"

"Lily?" He reaches for her hand, taking back the box. He takes a deeper puff this time.

"Sir?"

He exhales harshly. "Lily, I don't have a plan for this one. This isn't something we plan for."

"What would the Captains of Old do in this sort of situation?"

He replies somberly, "They wouldn't have to deal with haunted AI systems and their ships trying to kill them."

"So the old captains are useless. What about modern Fleet training? Nothing for rogue AIs?"

"Well, yes," he proffers. "Rogue AIs, sure. But never anything taking over the ship like this. I don't think it ever occurred to—"

Bekhti interrupts. "What's the difference, if you don't mind me asking?"

"The difference?"

Lillian grabs the black box from him and pulls another drag. "What's the difference between a rogue AI and a hostile entity trying to take over the galaxy?"

John rubs his eyes with his thumb and forefinger, considering the suddenly obvious question. When he reaches the bridge of his nose, he answers wearily, "Nothing really, I suppose. Both scenarios risk the ship and crew in the same ways, and both exert the same amount of control of the ship. And the potential hazards are virtually the same in worst-case scenarios."

"What does your captain's training tell you to do in this

instance?" She knows the training; she's already taken the final captain's test twice and nearly succeeded both times.

"Oh, you know the drill. Prepare for this, plan for that. Take tests, make promises, recite the oath. Blah, blah, blah." Mockingly, he recites, "'I solemnly swear and abide by the Code of Captaincy—ever to defend the Fleet and her principalities—uphold the rule of law and prevent its demise.'" He skips around but dwells on the final words. "Prevent its demise."

"Demise?" she asks, for clarification's sake.

"Whether it's a rogue AI or a possessed ship, the protocol's the same," he says, dodging her question.

"We can't let this ship rejoin the Fleet."

Bekhti takes another pull from the inhaler and then shoves it into John's chest. She went out of turn, and now he needs to catch up. More importantly, it's his job to figure out a plan for the good of his crew, and right now, hitting him feels like the way to remind him of that fact. "That's right, sir. We can't make contact with another Fleet ship, or even our allies here in the system. Nor can we let *Demeter* leave the Tau Ceti system and potentially infect other inhabited systems."

John wrests the inhaler from her with his left hand and grabs her hand with his right before she can pull it away. He takes an obligatory puff and squeezes her hand, his mind already made up. At the moment, he needs to vocalize. "I guess this is it. We scuttle the boat."

She reaches across with her free hand, tapping his chest to ask for the inhaler. "I think you're right, Captain," she whispers, taking a final, contemplative drag. She squeezes his hand in reluctant affirmation.

"We scuttle the boat."

SIXTEEN
THE HUBRIS OF FAIRYTALES

Sing it loud, and sing it wrong,
We're running out of time for songs.
Mark the line and light the spark.
No one's coming. Hit it hard!

One shot left, so drop some more.
Feel the sound before the war.
Time won't wait, the stars won't save.
So hold your breath and misbehave!

— MERION
"SING IT 'TIL IT BREAKS"

V sits cross-legged opposite Hawthorne, both tired but determined to try something new. *Demeter*'s engines vibrate through the deck, a constant reminder of the time slipping away. It won't hum forever. Merion rests between them in its specimen container, a faint blue glow radiating from its slender leaves, much like the light the Old Man of the Forest shone when resisting the orbital bombardment of Brigid. The shared meadow in their minds feels fragile now, the menace of the Grove lingering like a taunt, daring them to try again.

Merion can keep the three connected without interference as long as there are no loquentes roots physically between them, yet they remain quiet anyway. Merion exchanges a mental image with them.

> *A nest of mice hides from a nosy cat, skulking around a barn. Together, they're safe, but if they separate, they'll risk drawing the attention of the sly predator unless they each remain hidden and out of touch.*

Merion doesn't speak in full phrases, even within chaint. Its thoughts drift to them in waves of color and scent: soft blue skies, the aroma of warm grass, and the rumble of energy beneath the surface. The impressions are soothing, yet maddeningly vague. Their meanings feel like half-remembered dreams, just out of reach, quickly forgotten.

<Help me out here, little guy,> V chaints, her fingers twitching. <We don't have time for metaphors right now.>

If a plant could sigh, Merion would.

> *The smell of decaying leaves and childish annoyance hangs in the autumn breeze. Merion interrupts their individual thoughts with its own, describing a potential plan with shared memories and imagery.*

The answer should be obvious, yet Merion senses their hesitation and frustration.

> *Demeter as V first saw it from Arion, its exterior imposing and unfamiliar after so living inside for so many months. The ship's hull gleams briefly before exploding, fragments spiraling into the cold of space.*

This isn't the first time Merion has suggested destroying their home.

Hawthorne wags a finger at the glowing sapling. *<No! That's not going to happen. Bad Merion.>*

A mental rustling of leaves brushes through their connection, the plant shrugging off the rejected idea.

Merion decides to try a different approach. A small ball of light, no bigger than a golf ball, floats between them. It rises, pulsing gently as it grows, until it swells to encompass Hawthorne's lab, and then the corridor beyond. Inside the bubble, the light is clean and pure, the air sharp with ozone. Outside, it's polluted and dark, thick with the stench of rotting meat.

The lines between the real and the metaphysical realms are blurring.

Unconstrained in the metaphysical realm, Merion grows to match their average height. It gestures to V, projecting an apparition of her walking to the bubble's edge, pushing it outward. Merion motions for Hawthorne to stay seated, directing V with a tiny wave of its leaves.

V exhales, drawing on the techniques Hawthorne (and, reluctantly, Merion) have instilled—unfamiliar, but grounding. She extends a tentative hand toward the shimmering surface. The energy resists, thick as syrup or the pull of a rip tide.

<Thorney, I just realized what this is.>

<It's the shield we tried before. Yeah?>

<Not exactly. It feels different—like the interference signals the Old Man of the Forest used to hide from the Grove.>

<How can you tell?>

<I don't know. It just feels different. Like something I experienced on Brigid.> V pushes on the edge of the bubble with a few probing touches. It reminds her of the cavitations she toyed with at the beach as a child, currents just strong enough to hint at the hidden danger on the other side.

<harder,> Merion's soft voice echoes in her mind.

She pushes harder, but her hands slip through, past her wrists. The air outside is warm and swampy, writhing unnaturally, like a nest of breeding mud eels. She jerks her hands back, shuddering at the sensation of filth.

<push.> Merion scoffs. *<better.>*

<Better? Name of the goddess, what kind of help is that?>

Merion waves a burgundy leaf at Hawthorne, summoning her to join V.

<Here, luv. I think I know what the cheeky sprout wants.> Hawthorne rises, watching as V struggles to steady the sphere's edge.

Hawthorne closes her eyes, centering herself. She places her hands on the signal's surface and rubs it gently until the fluid turns glassy. With focus, she pushes, though the effort strains her.

<better.>

Somewhere, an orchestra tunes in advance of its final performance.

<harder.>

V centers herself and tries again. The bubble feels firmer now, though still pliable.

<together,> Merion demands, its mental voice sharp and insistent.

The two Druids glance at each other, stifling their laughter at the absurdity of taking orders from a baby tree. But the flash of the Grove in their shared consciousness stifles it for them, reminding them of what lies just outside this bubble.

<Let's try this,> Hawthorne suggests. *<I'll hold it steady while you push. Think you can do that?>*

V nods.

Hawthorne draws from her center again and focuses solely on keeping the bubble solid, her hands steady. *<Okay, try it now, luv.>*

V pushes, and the shield expands with an electric hum.

The bubble shatters. The Druids are flung to the floor, and Merion braces itself in its container, disappointed.

"Goddess, are you okay?" V asks.

"I'm fine," Hawthorne says, wiping her bloody nose with her lab coat sleeve. "That was a good push."

"I'm so sorry. I didn't mean—"

Hawthorne waves her off with a soft smile. "Don't be. You have something special, V." She hesitates, almost saying more, but stops herself from saying V how proud the Ard-Chainteoir would be of her daughter right now.

V's face hardens, her thoughts drifting to the Grove's taunts about killing her sister with this same raw, undisciplined power.

Hawthorne takes her hands. "Shh, luv. Don't go there. This is different. We're doing something new. No one's ever tried anything like this." She tilts her head, offering a reassuring smile. "And we're already making progress."

V sniffles, brushing a cheek with a knuckle. She nods, sitting straighter. She tucks her hair behind her ears and flashes a stiff smile. "We're going to need more incense."

"Hey, buddy. Are you okay?" Parker's voice is weak, timid, and weighed down with guilt.

Rowan doesn't open his eyes, much less answer.

The equipment in the medical compartment beeps with a slow rhythm that seems to scold Parker on Rowan's behalf.

Hesitantly, Parker pulls a metal chair from the corner then sets it backward a meter away from Rowan's gurney. He straddles it, resting his arms on the back, his chin on his wrists. He stares at Rowan's still form—his chest rising and falling slowly, his face bruised and swollen. Parker's own bandaged hands throb faintly, a painful echo of what they've done. The antiseptic sting of disinfectant in the air only sharpens the bitterness in his throat. His heart pounds with shame, heavy and relentless.

Parker was supposed to be better than this. His angry, acrid words echo in memory. *You let us all down. Just like you always do.*

Rowan isn't the one who let the crew down. Parker is. He gave in to a rage he didn't know he was capable of, nearly killing his friend and recently appointed superior officer. Worse, his failures almost doomed the ship and its crew. He gave in to a corrupted memory that still haunts him, a memory of loss that he can't explain, a torment that never happened.

Even worse, he had a chance to make things right after nearly killing his friend. If he'd been more vigilant, he could have warned the Druids of the shockwave. But he wasn't. And now they were paying for his mistakes. Again.

Arion was his fault too. The aging dropship should never have been conscious, much less physically connected to *Demeter's* rootwork. Parker left it vulnerable, an open window for the Grove to exploit.

"It wasn't you who let the crew down, buddy," Parker whispers, his voice breaking. "That's squarely on me." He pats his chest.

"Look, I don't know what to say," he admits, his voice cracking. What could he say? *I'm sorry? It wasn't me?* The truth is, it *was* him. His fists. His anger. His failure. And the worst part? In that moment, he absolutely wanted to hurt Rowan. The rage was overwhelming, blinding.

"I let you down," he whispers, staring at the sterile floor. "I let everyone down. This shit is all on me."

The medbay remains indifferent, its machines continuing their mechanical work without comment, yet they speak volumes.

"I don't even know why I'm here," Parker says, dragging a hand down his face. "I should be with Hector right now, but I can't even look *him* in the eye. I don't deserve to. I don't deserve him.

I'm sorry," he says again, but the words feel empty, lost in the whir of medical equipment. He wants to apologize for everything, for his failure, for his anger, for nearly killing Rowan, but words for this don't exist.

The breathing pump emits a sudden, sharp pitch as Rowan's chest rises with a slow, deep breath. A shaky hand reaches for the oxygen tube strapped to his face. He fumbles with it, peeling the tape away from his skin. Finally, he opens his mouth and smacks his dry lips, testing his voice.

"Oh my gods, shut the fuck up, Parks," he rasps, too tired to open his eyes but not too tired to deliver the sentiment.

I deserve that, Parker thinks.

"How's Hector?" Rowan asks, coughing lightly.

The question catches Parker off guard. "He's fine, I think. I haven't seen him since…" He trails off, unwilling to finish the thought of being in the brig since the last time he saw his matelot.

Rowan sighs, a sound somewhere between exhaustion and irritation. "I don't blame you, you know. Not entirely."

Parker freezes. "What?"

"I mean, fuck you. Don't get me wrong," Rowan adds, his voice gravelly but sharp. "But I know what those spores did— the roots, the Grove. They twisted you. Doesn't mean I'm not pissed, but I get it."

"It doesn't excuse what I did," Parker says quickly, shame seeping into his voice. "I still—" His throat clenches.

"You weren't in control. I get it. Now fuck off and go see Hector," Rowan says, his voice hoarse but firm.

Parker leans back, unsure if this is permission to go see his friend or if Rowan wants him gone. Either way is fine, but the distinction still matters. He pauses to see if Rowan has anything else to add.

"Are you sure?" he asks, cautiously.

"I'll be fine. Go."

"Okay," Parker says, rising to his feet. "But I'll check on you later. If that's okay."

Rowan raises a few bandaged fingers, a sluggish attempt at a rude gesture. It's weak but makes its point.

Parker lingers at the door for a moment, watching Rowan struggle to keep his eyes open. Rowan looks awful—bruised, barely conscious, held together by gauze and spite. And yet, somehow, he's still the one offering grace. That punches harder than Parker can admit. He doesn't know how to make it right— but he's going to.

The Druids take a break to regroup, much to Merion's annoyance. They brew tea, gather more candles and incense, and prepare for their next practice session. Hawthorne draws a careful circle on the deck, earning a teasing grin from V. "Old habits?" she quips. Hawthorne ignores her and focuses on creating the right atmosphere for their work.

The lab is dim, lit only by the flickering glow of candles. Thick incense hangs in the air, almost suffocating, grounding them both as they prepare to begin.

V finishes her tea and rolls her shoulders, trying to shake off the fatigue clinging to her joints. She shifts repeatedly, searching for a spot that doesn't ache, and finally finds something close to comfortable. Across the circle, Hawthorne sinks into her seat, her expression lined with weariness and focus. She slumps into a stillness she thinks she can hold for hours.

Merion sits between them, glowing faintly in its specimen container. Its energy is faint, its leaves drooping, but it presses on. The sapling sends a new image into their shared mindscape.

A sword glowing with fierce green fire hovers above their heads. The weapon pulses with raw energy, its edge slicing through shadowy tendrils. Under the weapon's searing heat, the Grove's black roots shrivel and fall away like ash.

V's eyes widen. <*Is that a flaming sword?*> Her grin is electric. <*Oh, goddess, yes. Let's do this!*>

Hawthorne remains wary, her lips tightening into a thin line. <*A flaming blade?*> she repeats, her thoughts cautious. <*Merion, how dangerous is this?*>

<*very,*> Merion chaints softly.

<*It's more than a weapon,*> V interjects, feeling the weight of the vision. <*It's for pruning. Cutting away the Grove's hold on Demeter. Like slicing infected roots out of a tree or pruning away choker vines.*>

Hawthorne watches the blade shimmer in their mindscape, green flames licking at the darkness. But she also sees Merion's flickering light, the strain already visible in its connection—and this is only training.

<*Something like this isn't meant for us to wield,*> Hawthorne warns, rubbing her temples as the dull throb of earlier spells lingers. <*It's one thing to test a defensive ward or a repulsive signal, but this? To sever connections with a force like the Grove? What's the cost?*>

V rolls her neck and stretches her fingers, flexing them like a pianist before a concert. <*We can handle it, Thorney. You guide, I push. Just like before.*>

Their gazes lock. Hawthorne sighs, knowing there's no swaying V—and there's no time to find a better way.

Merion glows faintly, its leaves drooping as it works its magic. V grips the sword's hilt with white knuckles while Hawthorne steadies her from behind, ensuring the flames don't consume them both.

<*Alright,*> Hawthorne concedes, her tone firm. <*But we move together this time. Like a dance. I'll lead.*>

They close their eyes, breathing synchronized—the familiar weight of their mental connection hums to life between them. The shared meadow reappears, but now it's darker, more brittle, and corrupted. The ground beneath them cracks, with black tendrils of the Grove creeping in from every direction.

Merion pulses weakly, its metaphysical form nearly extinguished. With one last surge of energy, the blade materializes in V's hands. It glows a fierce orange-red rather than the promised green, and the fire crackles wildly, barely contained.

V's grip tightens on the hilt, her heart pounding with the thrill of the weapon's power. She steps forward, raising the blade high. The tendrils recoil at the weapon's radiance but quickly surge forward, ever relentless.

Hawthorne places her hands on V's shoulders, anchoring her. She channels her focus into guiding the blade's energy, her nose bleeding faintly from the strain. Together, they swing the weapon, cutting through the encroaching darkness.

Within moments, they find a rhythm, swinging the sword together. Hawthorne directs the blade with precision, while V fuels it with raw power. The combination is devastating. Tendrils turn to ash with each strike, though they miss a few.

The strain is immense. Hawthorne's vision blurs, her body shaking beneath the crushing effort.

<Relax. Try again,> V whispers, her voice steady despite the fire's growing intensity.

Hawthorne steadies herself and strikes again, this time with V's energy pushing through her movements. Hawthorne has never felt so strong, and V has never felt so precise; the combination is no match for the Grove's invading reach. The tendrils fall faster now, disintegrating in waves.

The spell exacts its price. Hawthorne's limbs tremble, her breath falters, and V's immense power presses down on her like a mountain. She grits her teeth, feeling her consciousness beginning to fade.

The blade grows hotter until the flames lick up V's arms. She gasps as the heat sears her skin, but she doesn't stop until the meadow clears, the corruption cut away.

When it's over, the field collapses, and they're back on the lab floor. V collapses onto her side, gasping for air, her hands trembling. Hawthorne falls beside her, blood dripping from her nose onto her lab coat and the deck. Merion's glow is faint, its leaves drooping, but it sends a final pulse of satisfaction.

<good enough,> it chaints softly before leaning against the edge of its container and falling asleep. Its roots gulp at whatever water and nutrients remain in the soil.

V wipes blood from her face with shaking hands, her breath uneven. "I'll get more incense," she mutters, glancing at the dwindling supply. She looks over at a weary Hawthorne. "You think maybe you can call in a favor to your goddess on this one?"

Captain Hargreaves calls the roll of his officers in the wardroom.

"Bekhti?"

"Present, sir."

"DeSoto?"

"Here, sir."

He calls the officers in succession: Alder, Essien, Sorrell, and Stroud.

"Let the record show that all executive officers are present and accounted for. I'm calling this confluence to seek a final ruling from all commanding officers on the matter at hand."

The officers surround the long metal table, shifting in their uneven chairs. Though disconnected and set aside, Parker's communication equipment still creates an obstacle for those in the back trying to reach their seats.

Captain Hargreaves clears his throat, the gravity of his next words weighing on him. The wardroom feels smaller now; the metal walls are too close, the air too thin. Every eye is on him.

Bekhti shifts in her chair, her jaw tight. She doesn't speak. She doesn't need to. They all know where this conversation is going.

"This ship cannot, and must not, fall into the Grove's control. I'm calling this meeting to inform my officers that self-destruct is our only viable course of action. We're on borrowed time," Hargreaves continues. "The longer we delay, the more the Grove learns about the ship's systems, and the harder it will be to initiate self-destruct. We can't afford to use lifeboats to let the Grove escape with us. They all have loquentes roots too." He locks eyes with each of them, searching for dissent. "We need a unanimous decision. It's all or nothing."

A hush drowns the wardroom. The discordant grind of *Demeter's* engines is louder than ever, vibrating through the walls, an ever-present reminder that the Grove has corrupted their home. Hargreaves lets the silence linger, knowing it'll add amplify what follows.

"Everyone knows the stakes. The Grove will use this ship to spread across the galaxy. It won't stop until every Fleet colony, every allied world, and beyond is under its control. We can't signal the Fleet. We can't contact our allies in the Tau Ceti system. It's us, or it's everyone."

DeSoto speaks first, his voice gravelly but steady. "Captain, are we certain there's no other way? This," he gestures vaguely, "means the end of all of us."

"We've considered every option, Lieutenant Commander DeSoto."

Bekhti cuts in, her tone sharp. "There are no other options. The longer we debate, the more likely the Grove blocks self-destruct entirely. If it knows what we're planning, what's to stop it from spacing us like it tried to do the last time?"

The bridge officers ponder the consequences and eventually reach the same conclusions. The calculus is simple: *It's us or the Grove.*

Hargreaves looks around the table. One by one, the officers press salute him, signaling their assent. "Let the record show we're in unanimous agreement," he says. "We scuttle *Demeter* for the greater good."

Before Hargreaves can begin a final speech, the wardroom door opens with a hiss. All eyes turn toward the entrance.

V stands in the doorway, supporting a pale, trembling Rowan. "Captain," she says urgently, "we need to talk."

"This is an executive confluence," Hargreaves begins, his tone sharp.

"I know," Rowan interrupts, standing on his own with some effort, "but you need to hear this."

Bekhti frowns. "What in the twin hells are you doing out of medbay?"

"I know about the plan to scuttle the ship," Rowan says, his voice hoarse but steady. "There's another way."

"How do you know about the plan?" Hargreaves demands. If the plan is compromised, what else might the Grove might know?

"I'm sorry, sir," Alder whispers, standing just behind Commander Bekhti. "I just needed to talk to someone before—"

Hargreaves holds up an understanding hand to cut her off.

"We've made our decision," Hargreaves says, his voice heavy with regret. "We can't risk delaying any longer."

V steps forward. "You don't have to do this yet. We have a plan. We've started pushing the Grove out of parts of the ship. We think we can sever its connection entirely."

Rowan adds, "We can save *Demeter*. And our crew."

DeSoto scoffs. "'Another way'? What, some more spells and Druid tricks? We don't have time for hubris fairytales."

Hargreaves barks, "Commander."

DeSoto reins in the tone but not the sentiment. "We don't have time for fairytales. Specialist."

"It's not a fairytale, you feckin arse," V snaps. She turns to the captain and quickly apologizes, "I'm sorry for my outburst, sir."

The captain nods, unfazed.

She looks at DeSoto again and then calmly, in her most precise tone, tells him, "It's not a bleeding fairytale, you bog rat."

She addresses the captain directly, "It *will* work, sir. I promise. We just need a little more time."

"And if it fails?" Hargreaves snaps. His voice is harsher than he intends. "What then?"

Rowan braces himself against the bulkhead. "Then we scuttle. But Captain—what I've seen so far? This isn't just a long shot. It's a real chance."

Hargreaves draws a measured breath and crosses his arms. "How?"

Rowan looks to V.

She steps forward. "Because, sir, we'll sever the Grove's access. Jettison *Arion*. Push the Grove out with interference and carve out the infected bits. Reboot the ship. This time, it can't get back in." She cranes forward and adds, "And if it doesn't look like it's panning out, you can still blow us up."

Hargreaves considers her plan and closes his eyes. "How long do you need?"

"Seventeen minutes, sir. That's how long it'll take for the Grove to overwhelm *Demeter*'s consciousness when it catches wind of anything sketchy. We only need a few minutes, but getting everyone into place will take some time."

"You've got it, Specialist. Gather everything you need. And give me a plan that'll take seventeen minutes or less."

Hargreaves leans back in his unsteady chair, nodding slowly.

"Anything that makes self-destruct feel like plan B is a win."

ector lies on a gurney in a cramped recovery room, the medical equipment barely breaking the stillness. The chair Parker borrowed from a nearby room barely fits in the corner. He's already moved it twice today to let attendants reach Hector.

The grafting machine attached to Hector's shoulder prepares the foundation for regrowing his missing arm. Generating a limb is slow, delicate work, far more complex than Parker's fingers were; those grew back in a fraction of the time.

Parker stares at his bandaged hand, still aching from another day's fight. Not from healing—but from what they've done. From gripping flight controls too tightly. From forming fists. From beating someone he calls a friend.

Hector stirs, his eyes blinking open in the muted light. His gaze settles on Parker, slouched in the chair, his face awash in exhaustion. "Parks? You're here?" A faint smile breaks through the haze of painkillers and exhaustion.

Parker straightens, startled. "Hector. You're awake." Relief floods his voice, and he scrubs a hand over his face, struggling to hide the fatigue.

Hector chuckles softly, but the tangle of monitors and tubes tethering him to the gurney dials him back. "Wouldn't have made it back without you. They tell me you pulled me off that rock. All of us. Thanks for that."

Parker looks away, guilt tugging at him. "Yeah, well. 'We lonely travelers stick together,' right? Our vows. Least I could do, mate." He hesitates. "I need the karma, considering how much I've gotten wrong since then."

Hector's brows knit together. "Wrong? What're you talking about?"

Parker hesitates, his hands curling into fists against his thighs. "I—almost killed Rowan," he admits, voice breaking. "Doc said it was the Grove twisting me up. But the rage felt real. Like it came from me. And that's what scares the hells out of me."

"The Grove?"

"Oh, that's a story for another day. You'll love it and hate it even more."

Hector's expression softens. He reaches out, resting his good hand on Parker's arm. "You're not an angry person, Parks. Whatever happened to you, it couldn't make you something you're not. But that same fire? It's what got us off Brigid alive. I'm here to testify to that."

Parker shakes his head. "It doesn't matter, Hector. I still hurt him. Nearly killed—" His jaw clenches as the words catch. "I fucked it all up."

Hector's eyes drift closed, his breathing evening out. Just before sleep claims him, his voice surfaces—soft, nearly lost. "You're not done yet, Parks. None of us are. Go see the captain."

SEVENTEEN
MINUTES

You do not win survival through risk.
You survive by not gambling with lives in the first place.
We do not play at heroics.
There is no valor in improvisation.
We preserve lives by following the code.

Not Guilty—against the judgment of the chair.

— COMMODORE LINNAEUS
TRIBUNAL PROCEEDINGS, FF-397

"Alright," Commander Bekhti begins, her voice carrying over the din. The wardroom is packed as she takes the floor—tasked with executing the plan while the captain stands nearby, monitoring his crew. "We have exactly seventeen minutes to pull this off once we begin. That's all the time we get to reach our positions, complete our tasks, and execute the plan. We move in sync, or the Grove finishes what it started—you've all seen what it's capable of."

The room is silent, all eyes on her.

"Doctor Hawthorne, Specialist Sandoval, are you ready?" She doesn't wait for them to nod before asking, "Lieutenant Forsythe, how long will it take to reset the mainframe to factory defaults?"

"I imagine two to three minutes to shut it down and a few hours to come back online, but that's not—"

Bekhti interrupts. "That sets the pace for everyone else. Once you reach the fourteen-minute mark, you two will exorcise the ship." Her eyes land on Rowan, V, and Max first. "Forsythe, Sandoval, Max—you're heading to the computer core. Your objective is to reset the ship's AI and regain control of *Demeter*'s systems. The Grove will likely have sealed the hatch, so be ready for resistance. Max, Rowan is injured, and you're the strongest one here, so make sure he gets there in one piece. Once inside, follow Rowan's lead. Reboot the ship at exactly the right moment. Then V will reach Doctor Hawthorne to work your magic."

Max nods, his silvered skin catching the light. "Understood, Commander. I'll get them in."

Rowan glances at V from where he sits and offers a faint, shaky smile. "No pressure, right?"

V smirks at Rowan. "You heard the plan: magic. It's just our lives and the fate of the galaxy. No pressure."

Bekhti turns to Hawthorne, who's standing slightly apart from the rest. "Doctor, you'll head to the root cluster. Your task is critical: push the Grove out of *Demeter*'s systems and sever its influence entirely. You'll initiate the connection with V and your plant once everything is in place."

Hawthorne gives a curt nod, her expression calm but determined. "I won't let you down, Commander."

Finally, Bekhti addresses Parker, who stands with Merion's container cradled in his arms. The sapling's faint glow reflects off his exhausted features. "Mister Parker, you're taking Merion to the secondary hangar bay. Your task is to jettison *Arion* and ensure the Grove loses its foothold. The timing for this is critical —you'll need to coordinate with the others through Merion's connection with the Druids."

Parker shifts the container slightly, his grip tightening. "Got it." He looks at the sapling tucked safely away in the sample container. "You hear that little buddy? It's just you and me, saving the world."

Merion's burgundy leaves slump.

Bekhti pauses, her gaze sweeping the room. "This plan hinges on precision. Once we leave this room, the countdown begins. You have seventeen minutes to complete your tasks. When that clock stops, Doctor Hawthorne and Specialist Sandoval will coordinate their efforts with—Merion." A plant with a name baffles her, but orders are orders. "If we fail, we won't get a second chance."

Captain Hargreaves steps forward, his voice cutting through the heaviness. "I know we've all had doubts. I know we're up against a force the likes of which the Fleet has never faced. But this crew has faced challenges before, and we've come through. Trust each other. Trust yourselves. And trust the plan."

Bekhti's tone sharpens. "Questions?"

Sorrell asks, "What if we don't hit the seventeen minutes exactly?"

Bekhti throws her shoulders back and addresses the entire crew. "Timing is everything. If we reach the seventeen-minute mark and the lights haven't gone out, that's the end of our trip. The captain and I will pull the trigger."

The room is silent.

Parker awkwardly asks, "How will everyone keep the time? We can't use our—*Demeter*'s been scrambling the sync signals for days—and we can't risk comms. And I know the Grove can track the wristpads. But no one I know can count a thousand seconds without losing their place."

"You can't count to ten without losing your place, Parker," V says.

A slow laugh erupts in the wardroom. Even Parker smiles.

"Specialist," Bekhti cuts in, "how do you expect to coordinate time with everyone?"

"You all remember the *Green Witch* album." Blank faces answer her, except for Hawthorne's. "The first five songs: 'The Light Beyond,' 'Winding Roots,' 'End of Our Trip (My Friend),' 'Dark's Wake,' and then 'We're In This Alone' add up to exactly sixteen minutes and fifty-eight seconds. The first four songs are to make sure we're all in place. We'll add seven seconds after the fifth song and start the fight."

Parker asks, "What about me? I don't listen to that shit."

Hawthorne crosses her arms. "Just watch for Merion's direction. It'll tell you when to disconnect *Arion*'s umbilical and jettison the dropship. You'll need to do that about two minutes prior anyway."

Parker adds, "Okay. Captain, what about you? What if you self-destruct too soon?"

Hargreaves winks. "Relax. Episode 306 of *The Captains of Old* is exactly seventeen minutes if you skip the intro. And that's my favorite episode of all time. Since *Demeter*'s media systems are offline, I'll recite it word for word."

Bekhti mutters, "Crew, listen up. You'd better not fuck this mission up because gods help you all, if that episode is the last thing I hear in this universe, I will make the afterlife a living twin hells for you all."

She waits, but no one else has further questions.

"Good. To your positions. No time to waste."

P arker hurries down one deck and crosses two corridors to the other side of the ship, cradling Merion's container securely under his arm. "Almost there, little buddy," he mutters, glancing down at the sapling. Its leaves droop slightly, but the faint burgundy glow offers reassurance. "You're the star of this show, you know that?"

He rounds a corner and ducks into an unmarked section of corridor 06-04B. He carefully glances around before approaching a wall panel labeled with a faded *DO NOT ACCESS* radiation warning sticker.

"Ah, still there," he says with a smirk. "Good to know no one's got the guts to touch this."

Behind the panel is a cramped compartment packed with containers and crates—most of them his. Parker frowns. Some of the gear's missing.

"Figures," he mutters. "Leave your stuff unattended too long, and suddenly it's community property. Assholes."

He sets Merion's container on the deck and digs into the hidden compartment. "Don't go anywhere, okay?" The sapling's glow flickers flatly, acknowledging him.

Parker retrieves a sleek, nonstandard pressure suit from the back, where it was locked away in a case with an old, well-worn keypad. *Good, still here. They can take the junk, but not the essentials.* He unzips the case and pulls out the suit. It's a little outdated but reliable. *Fool me once, shame on you. But you're not getting a second chance to kill me again, so shame on you, fucker.*

"Alright, suit up time," he says, half to himself, half to Merion. The sapling's glow pulses softly in response, like a silent cheerleader. Parker grins. "Glad you approve."

It takes him only a couple of minutes to get the suit on. His movements are quick and practiced as he snaps the collar into place and double-checks the seals. "I think that's a new record."

A sunlit field stretching endlessly beneath a cerulean sky. The air alive with the scent of fresh-cut grass and the hum of cicadas. A tree heavy in the middle of the station's park laden with ripe peaches, just like the summers of Parker's childhood. Pride in climbing the tree as fast as he ever has.

What the fuck?

He lifts Merion's container and adjusts its position for better balance, giving the sapling an encouraging nod. "Okay, buddy. Don't let those witches get to us, okay? Now, let's go save the galaxy."

He seals the panel and heads toward the hangar bay. The hiss of his air regulator fills the silence. Parker moves with purpose, an alien sapling cradled in his arms.

Rowan hobbles through the maintenance corridors, leaning heavily on Max. The Atharan's taller frame and natural strength make supporting Rowan's weight seem effortless, though the tight corridor sometimes forces them to move single file. Max's silvered skin glints faintly in the dim light, a reminder of the alliance between their worlds.

"You Earthers build your ships too cramped," Max grumbles, his voice deep but not unkind. "No air to breathe, no space to walk."

Rowan manages a faint chuckle, though it costs him a wince. "Try walking with this leg," he mutters, nodding to the makeshift brace keeping him upright.

Max makes a sound that might pass for agreement among humans. He adjusts his grip as Rowan stumbles slightly. "Focus, not on the pain, but the task. We'll make it, Chief. Together."

Ahead of them, V hums softly—then begins to sing. Not in her usual clipped tones, but something older, more melodic. Her voice drops into a lilting cadence, vowels softened, consonants rounded in the gentle curl of a Galweigan accent. It's a song from *The Light Beyond*, but now it sounds like something ancient, something passed down. The tune winds through the narrow corridor like a thread, steady and mournful, keeping time for them all.

Rowan doesn't say anything. He just listens. Her voice rises faintly as they reach the access tube, a rhythm to climb by. It's a strange comfort, eerie and intimate, like she's singing to the ship itself.

He grips the ladder with white-knuckled hands, every step a battle. The pain is sharp, but the melody cuts through it—not to dull it, but to give it shape. To remind him he's still here.

One step at a time, matching his breath to her tempo. *Don't look down. Just keep climbing.*

"You first or me?" Max asks, his voice calm as he surveys the climb.

Rowan exhales slowly, leaning heavily against the wall. "I'd say carry me, but you'd probably complain about Earther gravity too."

Max snorts a sound that's almost a laugh. "I'll complain if you fall. Let me go first. If you slip, I'll catch you. Besides, it's not your gravity that sucks, it's this thick-ass air pressure. How do you Earthers breathe in this soup?"

Rowan nods, biting back a grin. "Just don't miss."

Max swings into the tube with ease and descends a few rungs before looking up. "Your turn. Take it slow, Chief. I've got you."

Rowan grabs the ladder, his knuckles white as he lowers himself gingerly onto the first rung. His hands tremble from exertion, his legs cry out in pain, and his grip falters briefly before Max steadies him with one powerful hand.

"Easy," Max says. "One rung at a time. You fall, you'll ruin my day. I don't want that paperwork."

"Thanks for the encouragement," Rowan deadpans, though he tightens his grip and keeps descending.

V hums a few more bars of the song, her voice steady and rhythmic. It's a stark contrast to Rowan's strained breathing as he mutters under his breath, matching V's beat.

"One step at a time," he mimics. "Just don't look down, something something, light beyond."

Max glances up, his silvered eyes gleaming in the faint light. "You're doing fine, Chief. Almost there."

The climb feels endless, every rung a test of will. His injured leg protests with each moment, and his breathing is harsher in the thin air. Max stays just beneath him, a constant presence, ready to catch him if he slips.

Finally, Rowan's boot touches the of the deck where he can step off. He exhales a shaky breath as Max helps him into the corridor. Ahead, it's dim and eerily quiet, the air thin and still.

V drops down the last few rungs and lands lightly beside them. She doesn't speak—just brushes her hands off and keeps humming, her voice barely audible but unwavering. The tune drifts down the corridor like a guide, holding time in the silence.

The scuffed walls of corridor 16-04 pulse faintly under Hawthorne's fingertips as she moves toward the source of *Demeter*'s pain. Overhead, the lights flicker erratically, their sharp clinks cutting through the silence. Their uneven glow bounces off warped metal panels, but her focus pushes her ahead. The corruption has been building over time, twisting through the ship's rootwork and circuits. She's here to cut the pain away.

Her steady, soft voice cuts through the oppressive quiet as she sings the opening bars of "End of Our Trip (My Friend)." She makes her way to the loquentes nerve cluster. "All good things, my friend. They come to an end, my friend."

The song is a lifeline to the real world as she descends into a nightmare, stepping deeper into the enemy's heart. With each verse, the growing weight of Grove's corruption presses against her mind. A cheerful song about addiction and loss feels fitting in a place like this.

She pauses at a sealed bulkhead, the access hatch leading to the loquentes nerve cluster. The console beside it drones, and her fingers hesitate over the manual controls. *The Grove knows I'm here.* This thought is sharp and unwelcome, but she pushes it aside and keeps singing.

"We'll be together in the end... my friend..."

Finally, the hatch clicks open. She grips the edges and forces the heavy door aside, the effort straining her shoulders. Beyond, the corridor leading to the nerve cluster is warped and grotesque. Metallic walls blend with organic, blistered surfaces, bulging and throbbing in time with the Grove's twisted heartbeat.

Hawthorne closes her eyes, reaching out with her mind. A malicious voice rakes across the chaint, sharp and invasive.

<THIS VESSEL IS ME NOW,> the Grove shouts into her mind, venomous and smug.

Hawthorne's jaw tightens as blood tickles her upper lip. *<Shut up, you overgrown vine,>* she snaps through the chaint, even as her physical voice continues to sing aloud, steady and defiant. She keeps moving, her boots crunching over brittle roots breaking through the floor plating.

The nerve cluster comes into view, a sprawling mass of organic tendrils and cables once pristine and vital to *Demeter's* rootwork. Now it's darkened, pulsating with a sickly rhythm.

The sight makes her stomach turn.

Hawthorne forces her mind away from the despairing tableau before her. "We'll be together in the end, my friend," she sings, louder now, reminding herself of the time.

Hawthorne crouches near the cluster, scanning for the safest place to set up. The rootlike tendrils twitch as her presence disturbs the Grove's grip. Her song continues, unwavering, her voice a fiery blade cutting through the oppressive air.

Her voice drops to a near-whisper as she continues the song, her focus sharpening. "We'll make this right, my friend," she sings, her hands crafting a Druidic circle on the deck. "No matter what it takes, I'll be with you in the end, my friend."

Parker hits the airlock control with his gloved hand, and the door hisses open to reveal the primary hangar bay. The air inside is pressurized like the rest of *Demeter*, but Parker's not taking chances this time.

Encased in the pressure suit he pulled from his hidden stash, Parker moves with deliberate care. He's used this suit before, walking on *Demeter*'s outer hull to maintain his listening devices. He adjusts the sealed container cradled in the crook of his arm. "Almost there, little buddy," he mutters to Merion. The sapling's faint burgundy glow flickers through the case as if it understands.

He steps into the hangar, his boots clunking softly against the deck. Even with several minutes to spare, the emptiness feels oppressive. The hangar is a tomb, and at its heart rests *Arion*, the battered dropship that's served them one final time. Parker approaches respectfully.

He runs a gloved hand along *Arion*'s hull, its once-proud surface dulled and scarred. He sets Merion's container carefully on the deck, pausing when the glow intensifies. A flash of imagery fills his mind.

A brilliant orange sky fades into twilight, and the final rays of sunlight dip below the horizon. Time has run out.

"Got it," Parker murmurs. "Thanks for the reminder."

He retrieves a small can of red paint from his bag, unscrews the lid and lets it clatter casually to the deck. Dipping two fingers into the paint, he hastily scrawls runes on *Arion*'s side. The angular marks are a tribute, a farewell to a warrior about to be commended to the void. They're the same runes he remembers seeing on his mother's coffin launched into space, an image burned into his memory since childhood.

Parker steps back to admire his work. "There you go, old man," he says quietly. "You've earned this much."

Climbing into *Arion*'s open hatch is awkward in the pressure suit, but Parker manages, grunting with effort as he squeezes through. The interior is dark and lifeless, and the once-active displays are now cold and silent.

He retrieves a challenge coin from the suit's tool pocket, the smooth metal catching the faint light. The coin is from Parker's first extrasolar mission to an outer-system space station—a symbol of what he still believes in, even if it hurts to admit it after what he was coerced to do, and of his belief in giving the deceased something with which to pay the Ferryman.

He fumbles with the coin, his gloved fingers clumsy. It slips from his grasp and clatters onto the deck. "Damn it," he mutters, dropping to his knees to retrieve it. After several failed attempts, he finally picks it up and places it carefully on the flight console, cramming it between a dead readout and a row of switches.

"Something to pay the Ferryman, old man," he says, his voice soft. "Just in case."

Parker hauls himself out of the dropship and leans against the bulkhead, breathing hard inside the suit. He glances at Merion's container, its glow shifting faintly. Another image floods his mind.

The sun is set. Stars pierce the darkness. The day is at an end.

"How are you doing that?" he asks, not really expecting an answer. "Sorry it has to end this way, but we'll see this through, old man. Promise."

He lifts the container.

"Alright, little buddy," he murmurs. "You tell me when it's time to commend this poor bastard to the stars."

EIGHTEEN
THE MOST DANGEROUS
HUMAN IN TAU CETI

If you call her name—sing it.
If you wish her favor—earn it.
If you seek her mercy—be worthy of it.
You have blood. You have a knife.
The goddess does not answer softly.

— DRUIDIC INVOCATION
ORAL TRADITION

Rowan hobbles around the corner, leaning heavily on Max while the Atharan's steadying grip keeps him upright. V follows closely behind, her voice carrying softly through the cramped corridor as she sings, "We're almost at the end of our trip, my friend."

Rowan's knees buckle when they see the computer core hatch. A glowing red seal pulses over the access panel, signaling that security lockdown protocols are in effect. The Grove knows this is where the last eviction began and has tightened its grip.

"Figures," Rowan mutters, his voice tinged with frustration. "The commander warned us."

Max examines the hatch, his silvered skin catching the faint glow of the lockdown indicator. "If it's locked, why send us here?"

Rowan smirks faintly. "Routine maintenance," he says, then glances at V. "Keep singing. I like the song."

She doesn't answer—just lets the next line of the melody slip through, her voice steady and sure. The cadence grounds him as he sinks to the deck with Max's help.

Max raises a brow but doesn't comment. "What's the plan?"

Rowan waves vaguely at the access panel. "Pop that open," he says.

Max complies, pulling the panel away to reveal a chaotic tangle of cables and circuits blinking in rhythmic patterns. Rowan leans heavily against the bulkhead, his breathing labored.

V's haunting song fills the silence as she paces behind them, her crisp tone unwavering.

Not familiar with the song, Rowan chimes in with V's tune, singing, "Adding a little request, my friend, along with the tests, my friend."

Rowan points at a diagnostic cable. Max pulls it free, exposing the maintenance circuit.

"*Demeter*'s old systems," Rowan whispers. "Analog backups." He finds what he was hoping for: a relic from an era when starships still relied on analog backups to test basic functionality and make service requests. He clicks a button three times, holds it, and waits as the tiny display flickers to life.

EMGCY PRTCL ACTVNG.

Rowan nods, his voice hoarse as he mutters, "We're almost there."

V's voice grows louder, matching the urgency. "We're at the end of our trip, my friend." She's warning Rowan that the song is ending and she's moving on to the next.

"Twist that knob," Rowan instructs Max.

Max complies without hesitation, his strong hands steady.

With a distinct click, the status panel's light shifts from red to yellow.

V cuts the song to hum softly, her timing precise as she nods toward the door.

Rowan gestures weakly. "Hold it open before it seals again."

Max slides his fingers into the gap and forces the hatch open, his strength making it look effortless. The door groans in protest but relents.

"Good," Rowan says, his voice barely above a whisper. He glances at V, who keeps singing, then at Max. "Let's finish the job."

Max nods, his tone lighter. "Routine maintenance, right?"

Rowan smirks faintly. "Always."

V hums the distorted finale of "End of Our Trip (My Friend)," an awkward tune as they enter the computer core room with such a heavy task ahead of them.

"Captain Tomasi Alara had running been supply lines to a besieged Earther colony in Lalande 21185—outgunned and outnumbered, flying little more than old Frontier Fleet frigates held together by spite and determination. Their enemy had ships built from things we'd never seen before. Tech that made you wonder if Earth wasn't alone after all.

"The enemy struck fast, cut their communications, and boxed them in between the fourth moon and the gravity well of the system's largest planet using some kind of interdictor weapon we had never seen before. No backup. No orders from Earth. It should have been the end of the line. She knew that the only real advantage she had was her crew's sheer audacity. And when you're out of options, that's all you need. They turned those old frigates hard, drove them straight toward the enemy line.

"They dodged pulse cannons and plasma mines, flying into what should have been their deaths. The captain's voice crackled through the static, telling the crew to hold steady. 'This is it, people,' she said. 'We're not waiting for rescue, because there's no rescue coming. If we're going to get out of this alive, it'll be because we make our own way. But if we don't? If we don't make it, then let's make damn sure we don't go out quietly. Punch it!'"

THE CAPTAINS OF OLD, EPISODE 306

Hargreaves paces deliberately behind the seated Bekhti, his words measured as he recites *The Captains of Old* Episode 306. His voice is calm and precise, matching the cadence of the original broadcast. Each word echoes across the dimly lit bridge, where the faint flicker of emergency lights throws long, jagged shadows to punctuate his dramatic retelling.

Bekhti leans slightly forward in Hargreave's command chair, elbows on her knees, chin propped in her hands. Her eyes are closed, though she's not resting. The captain's steady voice shines through the tension like a beacon. She expected to hate it. But now, hearing it in his voice? She gets why it's his favorite. There are worse things to hear at the end of their final mission.

The hole cut into the bridge's hatch spills pale light onto the floor, practically pointing at the security panel that holds their shared attention. Behind it are four mechanical arms intended to drop fuel rods directly into *Demeter*'s hyperspace engine and ignite a catastrophic explosion that will destroy *Demeter* and everything within half a kilometer.

"'So there we were: gravity wells to port, enemy fire on our six. And Alara? She didn't flinch. We banked hard, cut our engines, and let the pull of the anomaly carry us right under the nose of the enemy fleet. They thought we'd imploded.' And this part gets me every time, Lily: 'Instead, we'd pulled off the riskiest slingshot maneuver ever recorded in Frontier Fleet history.'"

Bekhti opens her eyes briefly, watching the captain as he continues his pacing. His voice is even, almost hypnotic, but she can sense the weight behind it. He isn't just retelling the story. He's drawing strength from it. And she's drawing it from him.

"'We've all been trained for this. Twin hells, this isn't even the first time I've had a reactor threatening to blow in my face.' The humor in Alara's voice was defiant, almost reckless." Hargreaves pauses, his gaze fixed on the flickering security panel. "'So here's the plan: we take what we have, we make it work, and we don't stop until every last one of us is back on solid ground.'"

"They hit their afterburners," Hargreaves continues, his tone unwavering, "broke through the blockade, and took out the lead destroyer with the last of their torpedoes. The gravitational anomaly was gone, and Ursa Colony III held on long enough for reinforcements to arrive."

Bekhti glances sideways at the captain. His voice is calm, a steady anchor in the coming storm. She appreciates his retelling of the story, which is much better than the original. She remembers the episode and knows it ends soon.

He stops pacing and fiddles with his cufflink. He exhales slowly, shoulders squaring as he turns to face her. His voice softens and becomes almost reverent. "Alara yells, 'I don't care if we're down to the last inch of hull or the last gasp of air. We're going to make our mark, people. We're going to make sure the universe remembers we were here!'"

He pauses one more time, hoping that by delaying the final lines, he can buy his crew just a few more seconds, just like Captain Alara did for the Colonial Defense Force.

"This is the end, isn't it, captain?"

He squares his shoulders and takes a slow, deep breath. "Commander Bekhti, I'm afraid our episode is just about over."

The nerve cluster pulses, a web of loquentes roots woven into *Demeter*'s systems, which now resemble failing arteries feeding a sick heart. Hawthorne stands alone in the core of the rootwork, her breath steady despite the corrupted air pressing down on her. Flickering light catches on the twisted organic tendrils, their shadows sprawling like grotesque veins against the bulkhead, giving them an otherworldly shadow. The corruption in the rootwork taints the air with an almost tangible malevolence.

Hawthorne places her hand against the nearest tendril as she sings the song's final words. "We'll be together in the end. All good things must end, my friend." The pulse beneath her palm is uneven and faint, its rhythm perverted by the Grove's influence, a dark answer to her serenade.

She hastily arranges a few ritualistic tools—a candle, a thin coil of blessed copper wire, and a vial of ash. Her inner scientist notes the meticulous placement of each item, while the person of faith believes in the sanctity of their arrangement. She lights the candle with a whisper of flame and begins to sing.

Her voice is soft but resolute as she begins the familiar melody of "Dark's Wake." The rhythm grounds her as she prepares. "Born of the dark and the dawn and storm," she growls quietly but quickly. "We rage through the skies where the suns are born." The song is both a ritual and a tether to V.

Hawthorne whispers the next part, a melodic counter to the thick, repetitive opening beats. "In the thralls of the void, our fever grows, where the vacuum howls and the dark sun glows."

Her mind drifts as she works. A part of her reaches out—not to V or Merion, but to something much older. She chaints a prayer. <*Goddess of roots and storms, hear me. Guide my hands. Lend me the strength to do what must be done.*>

Years of practice maintaining chaint while speaking in the physical world is paying off. She mentally prays yet continues to sing aloud to keep in sync with the others. "In the thralls of the void, our fever grows."

As she braids the wire around a rootlike tendril, she continues in the chaint, her thoughts steady and measured. *<You've always asked for sacrifices in our darkest hours. I know this. I've always known this. And if that's what you ask for now, then let it mean something.>*

The faint candlelight flickers as if in response, and Hawthorne doesn't hesitate. She presses the ash into the braid, her fingers moving with surety despite the trembling in her shoulders. "Where the vacuum howls and the dark sun glows. We are your legacy," she sings, holding the final word until her breath gives way, her voice rising in defiance of the Grove's presence.

The root cluster shudders, and the air grows cold. Hawthorne feels the Grove's malice clawing at her, testing her resolve. Her lips tighten into a grim smile. *You don't scare me. Not here. Not now.*

She sings the next refrain, finding tenacity in a song about space marauders making their own way across the stars without fleets or gods. She pricks her thumb deep on the sharp end of the braided wire. She smears blood along the length of the tendril, then across her forehead. Clutching the root tendril, she chaints, *<My blood, a gift to you.>*

She inhales deeply, her movements syncing with the song's rhythm. Singing, nearly shouting, her words directed to the goddess: "We're the storm and the dark and a force of might." She yells the final line, just as Rik did back in the day. "No gods, no monsters, and none to blame!"

She pushes her pierced thumb into the root, feeling the wetness of the tuberous flesh, hoping the goddess hears her plea.

Seven seconds.

That's how long the intro is to "We're in This Alone," where Neil plays an iconic guitar riff.

Seven seconds.

That's how long before the final battle begins.

Seven seconds.

That's how long Hawthorne holds her breath before reaching out with her mind.

She exhales, and chaints, *<V? Merion?>*

arker climbs into the cramped control station suspended above the primary hangar bay. His pressure suit is a cumbersome second skin. The control console is barely larger than his chest, and the gloves make him clumsy. His movements feel sluggish, each task demanding more effort than it should. The flickering lights along the bulkhead cast erratic shadows across the deck, jittery as his nerves.

He sets Merion's container on the window ledge that overlooks the hangar bay. "Get comfy, little guy. You're about to witness some serious shit."

The sounds from the control room mess with his mind. He swears the sapling just waved a leaf, and he's fairly sure he can hear music playing in the distance.

Parker activates the terminals and pulls up the flight deck controls. *The captain is going to be so pissed,* he thinks. It normally takes a full crew to manage the flight deck. But with everyone else either trapped or still recovering in medbay, Parker's got one option: blow the hangar door open with the emergency evacuation system, then use the crane arm to shove *Arion* outside—once he's detached the umbilical.

As the console shimmers to life, Parker freezes. A faint melody buzzes in his mind, ghostly and half-remembered. The rhythm ebbs and flows, pulling at something deep in his chest. He shakes his head. "Focus, Parks." His voice echoes in the helmet, snapping him back to reality.

The hangar bay's status flashes on the screen. Each of the security bolts securing the hangar door lights up in sequence. He begins tapping the commands to prime the charges, his hands steady despite the oppressive heat of the suit. The melody grows louder, twisting into ghostly lyrics in his mind, distant but clear enough to follow.

Parker remembers a show he never saw, the memory of lips that aren't his, and a song he's never heard.

> *Born of the dark and the dawn and storm,*
> *We rage through the skies where the suns are born.*

The words are unfamiliar, yet comforting. They settle over him like an old friend's hand on his shoulder—like what he wants to do for *Arion*. He doesn't question the source; there's no time for that. Instead, he lets the melody guide him, each syllable marking a step closer to the task's grim conclusion. It's not a terrible song.

> *In the thralls of the void, our fever grows,*
> *Where the vacuum howls and the dark sun glows.*
> *We're your legacy…*

With a flourish while holding that last word for the remainder of the unknown verse's length, he taps the icon for each bolt.

> *Blazing through the rift our engines roar,*
> *We feast on the wreckage of forgotten wars.*
> *The old stars are ours, and all will fall,*
> *We come as the reapers to end them*
> *All.*

The bolts flash green, one by one, as the charges arm. Parker mutters under his breath, not quite echoing the song but feeling its rhythm in his chest. His finger hovers over the detonation sequence. He exhales. *This is it.*

We're the scream in the black and the cry in the night!
We're the storm and the dark and a force of might
From the edge of the—

A heavy clang disrupts his flow. It's something he feels through his boots rather than something he hears.

The console flashes a red icon for one of the bolts.

"Oh, what the fuck, now?"

Looking down into the hangar bay, he sees that one of the explosive bolts has failed to fire. The bulky hangar bay door hangs by a stubborn thread. It wavers and thrashes against the sides, but it remains mostly closed.

"Shit shit shit. Of course, there's a fucking dud. *Demeter,* you old piece of—"

He leans on the console, trying to clear his head. *Glad I grabbed the suit.* Parker turns to Merion. "I need to go down there and deal with something, so you sit tight right here until I get back, okay?"

The music in his head returns.

In the shadow of great beasts, we make our way,
Through the dark, the brave won't stay!
O! The monsters we have—

He watches the plant for a moment before asking, "Is that you?" He shakes his head dismissively and passes through the tight airlock back down to the hangar's flight deck.

Parker clenches his jaw and picks up a wrench from a nearby tool bench that has spilled its contents across the deck. He starts working on the bolt, but his hands tremble, and he can't keep a grip on it. The damn wrench keeps slipping.

He strikes the bolt, unsure if the explosive inside is inert or the detonator failed. Either way, it doesn't matter if he can't cut *Arion* loose in time. He slams the wrench against the bolt a few more times.

He feels rather than hears a pop as the explosive bolt finally does what it's supposed to do. It's a small flash, but the explosion is still enough to throw him backward across the deck. Even in diminished artificial gravity, the landing robs the wind from his lungs.

Slow to get up, he soon catches his breath. "Thank the gods," he coughs as he watches the hangar door spiraling away from the ship.

He scrambles back to the flight controls, but the hatch to the airlock flashes red, denying him entry. *The Grove has me trapped in a hangar again.* He pounds the panel and swears. *Fool me twice, fuck me!*

"Looks like I'm sending you off the hard way, old man." He picks up the wrench from the deck, ready to manually detach the dropship's umbilical. It takes longer than he had hoped, but he works it free from the connection port. He tosses it aside and moves quickly to the crane.

"Fuck!" The controls are also locked. He kicks the crane several times, and only the protective metal in the boot's toes prevents another trip to medbay.

If he can't jettison *Arion* soon, before the others finish resetting *Demeter*'s AI and purging the Grove from her rootwork, it's all over. He scans the hangar for anything else that might help. Then he has a better idea.

If the Grove used Arion's *AI core to reinfect* Demeter, he thinks, *then that's all that has to go.* It's such an easy solution. *I'll just chuck the fucker out into space.*

Parker crouches down, jamming his hands into the exposed cavity of the connection port where the loquentes root AI module is nestled. It should be easy enough to yank out.

It's stuck.

The edges of the port are warped and bent out of shape from his earlier rush with the wrench. New growths protrude from the module and tangle themselves around the inside track. He tugs harder, wincing as the jagged metal nearly snags his gloves.

"Come on, come on," he mutters. The module shifts but won't budge. He angles it, pulling with both hands, but the roots inside the module have grown around the dropship's insides. He'll have to cut it free.

He scans the flight deck for any tools sharp enough for the job and finds a small pair of wire snips. He clips a few root growths and sees some of them move, reminding him of a writhing nest of newly hatched snakes when the wrong stone is overturned.

There's too much at stake to hesitate, so he starts humming. Although the tune is unfamiliar, it soothes him like something he's heard since childhood. He's clipped enough that the AI module is loose.

Almost there. Just a few more to go.

Spinning lights flash abruptly across the hangar bay as warnings spring to life, flashing in a frantic rhythm. The vacuum swallows the sound, but Parker feels the invisible weight of blaring klaxons pressing on his chest.

Parker feels a heavy thud through the soles of his boots, a low vibration that sends a shudder up his spine. The umbilical, once limp, thrashes and flounders along its entire length. The wires at the tip twist together like serpents, braiding themselves into thicker, stronger tendrils. It rears up and slams down, trying to grab Parker.

Parker sees something on the wall near the bundle of wires and hoses. Black fuzz spirals from the connection point. He doesn't know why he knows the word, but there's a parastichy fractal pattern spreading outward from the umbilical.

He glances inside the cavity at the AI module—just a few more cuts.

He turns around in time to see the umbilical reaching for his head. He ducks in time, but the finger-like braids of wires and dark roots slither into the connection port, attempting to reconnect.

He stabs at the makeshift tentacle with the clippers. If *Demeter* feels pain, this thing does, too.

Take this, you fucker!

Several internal conduits free themselves to reach for him, but he rolls away in time. He jumps to his feet, runs around the other side of the dropship, and releases the joists holding it to the deck. He dives underneath, the pressure suit making the move clumsy.

He scrambles into the open hatch, the pressure suit making every movement a battle. Inside *Arion*, likely for the last time, he seals the hatch tight. He feels the tendril banging against the hull but doesn't hear it—the dropship depressurized when the hangar bay did.

Parker clambers over the repair gear strewn about the main cabin and jumps into *Arion*'s cockpit, trembling as he initiates the engine sequence. He bypasses every safety protocol and preflight check. There's no time.

Parker desperately wishes he could wipe the sweat from his face.

He looks around the hangar from the cockpit—the umbilical flails outside, looking for a way into the dropship, keeping him from cutting the AI core free. *Just a few more seconds!*

A faint memory creeps into the back of Parker's mind. A grinding drumbeat, fuzzy harmonics, and fitting lyrics; yet another song he's never heard.

> *No way to go home!*
> *Nothing we've known!*
> *No way to hold on!*
> *We're in this alone!*

He glances up at the flight deck again and salutes the plant, which still has a part to play.

His own part is nearly finished.

"Grove, you just fucked with the most dangerous human in Tau Ceti." He slams his palm down on the ignition, and the hangar bay lights up in a flash of blinding orange. The thrusters roar to life, and the violent burst of flame instantly consumes the Grove's writhing tendrils, burning it like the ancient forest on the moon below.

The stars beyond the gaping hangar streak toward him as the untethered dropship blasts forward. The acceleration presses Parker back into the seat, his breath shallow, and his vision narrows to a tunnel of myopic light.

He just needed to clip a few more roots.

The coin Parker had placed on *Arion's* console slides free, caught in force of the dropship's forward thrust. It tumbles end over end across the cabin, glinting in the dim light before striking his visor with a sharp, ringing clink. The sound cuts through the silence with irony.

"Hold on to that coin. Looks like we'll be sharing a ride, old man."

He whispers along with the faint song still echoing in his mind, the words rising from elsewhere, deep and final.

> *No way to go home.*
> *Nothing we've known.*
> *No way to hold on.*
> *We're in this—*

The thrusters roar, shaking *Arion* to its core as it streaks into the void. The sound should be deafening, but all Parker hears is silence—a vast, eternal stillness that fills the cabin. *Arion's* acceleration presses him deeper into the seat, his limbs heavy. His vision blurs at the edges and the strange song becomes a whisper fading into the quiet. The crushing force pulls him gently into the darkness of sleep.

V and Hawthorne close their eyes, reaching out from behind their minds to find each other across the ship in the ethereal void. Merion joins their shared consciousness, the connection deepening as they mentally gather to cast the first spell. The physical world, this aberrant version of their beloved *Demeter*, quickly fades around them. This world gives way to the metaphysical battleground that lies ahead.

Merion interrupts, *<friend. goodbye.>*

Confused, V asks, *<Friend? Goodbye?>*

Merion projects an image of an altered memory.

Parker waves to V and Hawthorne in the Lolly Galley, drink in hand. He grins broadly, asking to join their table. As quickly as he arrives, he backs out of the mess hall, saluting melodramatically with a cheesy grin as he leaves.

<Wai—did he make it into the chaint?> Hawthorne asks, scanning the corrupted meadow.

V shakes her head. *<No, but I think he and Merion… connected. But that can't be. >*

<Holy shit, Parker's a Bard?> Hawthorne asks, still focusing on the metaphysical horizon.

<bard?>

Hawthorne replies, *<Men who carry the gene for telepathy.>*

<men?>

Hawthorne sighs. *<Later. We have shit to do.>*

Quietly, Merion says one last time, *<friend goodbye,>* almost shrugging before moving on to the task before them.

They stand back-to-back in a meadow of rotting grass and shattered trees. The air is fetid and thick, and the ground is spongy, suggesting the surrounding land has been spoiled. The swirling sky is dark, punctuated by an approaching lightning storm that casts flashes of violet across the unhallowed landscape. Something is chittering in the distance.

Hawthorne's voice fills the void. *<It knows we're here.>*

<What's our play?> V asks.

Merion says, *<destroy.>*

<Goddess! Merion, for the last time, we will not feckin destroy Demeter.>

V briefly remembers her first day in calculus class. Her teacher was exasperated with her initial struggle to understand limits and functions. Priestess Kousa was not impressed with her supposedly promising pupil that day.

<push harder.>

Hawthorne says, *<Yeah, I think that's our play. You ready, V?>*

<As I'll ever be.> V sighs. *<Let's do it.>*

Now nearly as tall as Hawthorne in their shared telepathic connection, Merion begins to sway, calling a breeze to match its movements. Within seconds, a shimmering bubble grows to surround them. It's much smaller than previously, and the Druids realize it's meant to protect just the three of them for now against whatever is coming.

Moments that feel like an eternity pass, and a few slender tendrils from outside the shield slither cautiously. They probe the size of the sapling's spell, patiently looking for another weakness they can exploit. A few tendrils touch their tips against the edges, and bright flashes shock them, throwing them back.

After several failed attempts, the Grove's slithering fingers withdraw into the darkness. The lightning overhead betrays the location of a few, but they stay put for now.

Hawthorne laughs nervously. *<They didn't like that; good job, Merion. But now what?>*

<push.>

<Like before?> V asks.

<before.>

Without another mental word, V and Hawthorne take opposing sides of the sphere and place their hands on the inner surface. V struggles to keep her pressure even, while Hawthorne strains to push at all. Merion holds steady at the center as they push to extend the shield.

The putrid air in the meadow presses down on them. They need to concentrate harder than before to make much progress. It's heavier now, thicker. The sky wants to let loose with thunder, but even it's afraid.

The occasional tendril sneaks up and taps the shield with reactive bursts of light. One hits in front of V's face, spooking her and nearly causing her to lose focus.

They continue to make incremental progress despite the distractions, stepping forward each time they push the shield's edge outward a little more. Unable to break through, the Grove finally stops probing. With nothing outside left to exploit, it sees no point in using its telepathic fingers to search for a way inside.

For a moment, V feels like they're making progress and smiles.

V briefly remembers her second day in calculus class. Her teacher was thrilled to see that V had immediately grasped limits and functions. However, Priestess Kousa promised the work was only about to get more challenging.

A low, guttural clicking echoes faintly from somewhere beyond the shield. It's irregular and skittering. The ground shifts slightly with a subtle tremor. Something vast is moving through the cursed soil just out of sight.

V glimpses a flicker of movement from the corner of one eye. She thinks it's just a trick of the shadows cast by the lightning, but then she sees it again. She stares ahead, but the sky is still.

The fluttering noise grows louder, turning into a song filled with hate. In the distance, shadows dart through the air, becoming darker and more distinct as they approach. At first, there are a few flickers, too fast for either to see against the dark sky. The frantic flapping of unseen wings intensifies, and high-pitched squeals and rustling fill the darkness surrounding them.

Something feather-light, barely a whisper, flits against V's consciousness. The dark shapes multiply. A mass of shadows form just beyond the shield's edge, circling. They're waiting.

The hair stands on the backs of their necks. Their breath is visible as small puffs of white. V's arms are covered in goose-bumps that won't settle down.

V shouldn't be surprised anymore. Yet, here she is again, surprised. <Bats?>

<*I don't think those are bats, luv,*> Hawthorne calls back.

A bygone memory of wandering into a beach cave as a child sends chills down her neck. The shield wavers as she fights the primal instinct to wrap her arms around her body. The thought of being pecked alive by vicious bats frightened her as a child, but seeing the nightmare version of those creatures drains the color from her face.

Sensing weakness, a swarm of dark beasts the size of her head slam against the shield just before her. Bright pops cause prismatic ripples on the sphere's outer surface, repelling each assailant in turn.

V shrieks and two small tears appear where her hands are.

Six demonic bats struggle through the tear before Merion can repair the shield's fabric. One leaps onto V's shoulder while the others fly in a chaotic swarm inside the shield, searching for a way to disable it from within.

The one on V's shoulder drums its dark and leathery wings, spread by three prehensile clawed limbs on each side. The hexagonal monster wraps itself around her face, smothering her frantic cries for help. The screeching sounds like rusted metal scraping against the glass and screams hateful squawks in her ears.

She drops to the ground, struggling to pry it away from her face as it scratches the sides of her neck and scalp. She's able to keep it from digging into her flesh, but the pitch-black talons scrape and burn all the same.

Through her own muffled screams, she hears Hawthorne

yelling and calling out. *She needs me!* she thinks and digs down inside for the strength to pry the monster from her face. *I can't leave her alone.*

Hawthorne's yells are short and deep. Then they stop.

V rolls and twists on the dead grass, struggling to break free, but the bat is too strong for her. She knows she should calm herself. She needs to find her center. The danger is too imminent to push the panic away. She can't summon the strength to help herself or Hawthorne.

Something hot slaps her face. The impish pest is gone. The putrid air has never been so welcome. V gasps and scrambles to her feet.

<Thorney?>

<You okay, luv?>

<Are those giant bats? > V surveys the battlefield behind Hawthorne. Five carcasses smolder on the ground behind her, and a sixth lies to V's left, still burning.

Hawthorne points her flaming sword away from V and holds it up for better light. Orange flames lick and crawl along the magical blade, which Hawthorne sways artfully.

<Sorry. They got in because I got spooked.>

<It's fine, but you need to focus on pushing the shield to give us more room. Do that and I'll take care of any that get past. Okay?>

<Yeah, I can do that.>

V slowly steps to the interior of the shield and raises her palms next to it. She feels for the edge, trying to stay calm and centered.

More bats flock to the other side and cling to the shield despite the burning light that should drive them away. Even more winged creatures pile on top of those, pressing against the shield. Their cold eyes stare into V's, and their indigo teeth clamor for a taste of her flesh. The violent flapping continues as they probe for another weakness.

She takes a deep breath and presses against the sphere again. The wall shimmers, and ripples spread from the point of contact, shocking the Grove's minions with renewed vigor. After a few cautious attempts, she finds her grip and expands the shield again.

<That's it, you've got it. And I'm right behind you. Now ground yourself, pull your breath from the ground, and exhale through your legs and body.>

V closes her eyes and forces herself to shut out the screeches and battering wings. The fiends are relentless, but not seeing them helps. She plants her feet firmly on the spongy ground, her boots sinking slightly into the decaying, and focuses inward. Underneath the surface, she senses it—a pool of energy that struggles to remain faint and elusive.

She reaches for it, pulling with every ounce of will she can muster. The energy is sluggish and reluctant, but as she digs deeper, it stirs, fresh and alive. A claw scrapes against the shield, the sharp sound like nails on glass making her flinch. For a moment, the energy slips from her grasp. She clenches her fists, her jaw tight. *No. Focus!*

It rushes up her back, hot and electric. Her limbs fill with crackling pressure that begs for release. Every breath feels like holding a storm, heavy with anticipation. The fiends sense the shift. V exhales sharply and releases the power in a single, shuddering breath.

She screams. A blinding explosion of white light erupts from her body, radiating outward in a violent wave. The nearest bats disintegrate instantly, their shrieks silenced in an instant. The survivors scatter in chaotic retreat, wings flapping frantically as they vanish into the dark.

V staggers, catching herself with a trembling hand against the shield. The pressure is gone, the weight lifted. She opens her eyes and sees the meadow stretch out before her, clear and open —at least for now.

Hawthorne chaints, *<Holy shit, m'inion, that was feckin amazing!>*

< I think I've got the hang of this now. What next?>

Merion answers. *<burn.>*

T he computer core is a narrow, dimly lit chamber. Thick cables snake along the walls like veins, pulsing faintly with the hum of *Demeter*'s ancient systems. The room is cramped and full of leftover parts from previous upgrades. Once, this place must've seemed cutting-edge, but now the polished metal panels are dulled with age, marked by countless makeshift repairs. The air is stale, tinged with a tang of burnt circuitry. Overhead, the lights flicker erratically, casting jagged shadows that dance along the tight walls.

Rowan hunches slightly to avoid hitting his head on the low-hanging control racks, each crammed with modules that blink sporadically as they struggle under the aging ship's demands. The space between the consoles is barely wide enough for two people to stand side by side. Max hovers awkwardly near the door, keeping as far from the dangling wires as possible, his tall frame folded into the confines of the room. Despite the ship's relative size, the core is suffocating, and the oppressive closeness is a constant reminder that *Demeter* is as much a relic as it is their home.

Rowan leans against a rack, panting and clutching his side. He's still drained from the ladder climb, but there's no time to rest. "Alright," he wheezes, "you're up, Max."

Max hesitates, ever interested in the precision of every task. "What's my role in this?"

"Turn on that terminal." Rowan waves toward the central console without looking up. "Cycle through the prompts. I'll guide you."

Max crouches by the console, his long fingers moving over the controls. The terminal's droning sound rises, and its screen blinks awake.

Rowan repeats the steps to stay focused and sharp. His

words trail into a hoarse cough, and he grips the rack tighter to stay upright.

Max glances over his shoulder. "Chief, you okay?"

"Fine. Keep going." Rowan gestures vaguely. "Find the administrative menu—end of the options."

Max works quickly, navigating the interface with practiced ease. "Got it. Now what?"

"You're looking for the *System* menu. It should be hidden at the bottom. Find it, then we can—"

The screen flashes red.

Max frowns. "It's asking for captain-level passcodes."

Rowan stares at the terminal, his chest heaving. His legs buckle, and he slumps to the floor with a dull thud. "No," he whispers. "No, no, no."

Max stands, alarmed. "What's wrong?"

Rowan presses his bandaged hands to his face. His voice cracks as he says, "The passcodes have been changed."

"What?" Max's voice is sharp. "How? We didn't—"

"The Grove," Rowan interrupts, his words bitter and clipped. "It learned from last time."

Rowan stares at the blinking terminal, its demand for credentials a mocking sneer. His shoulders sag, his head sinks into his hands.

Max crouches beside him. "Is there a workaround? Anything we can do?"

Rowan's voice drops. "We came in blind. No wristpads. No backups. No plan for this." He lets out a brittle, laugh. "We didn't even think to check. Fucking amateurs."

Max grips Rowan's shoulder, seeking precision as many Atharans do. "Chief. What now?"

Rowan doesn't look up. The dim glow of the terminal reflects off his haunted face. "I have no idea."

NINETEEN
THE LIGHT WITHIN SHINES BRIGHTER THAN WE KNOW

A little care and cleaning today might save your crew tomorrow.
Roots need nutrients, levers need oil, and always apply security updates immediately.

— FLEET ENGINEERING MANUAL
CORE SYSTEMS (REV. 2219)

The bats swarm. They dart with shadowy slashes, circling tighter, a cyclone of claws and teeth. Talons flash, teeth glint, wings spread wide then fold back for another pass. They strike in relentless waves.

Hawthorne's strikes are quick and precise. Her flaming sword arcs, cleanly slicing through one bat that then bursts into ash. Her next swing merely grazes a second, sending it spiraling before it dives back into the fray. She pivots, cutting another across its wing, but it disappears into the swarm. They close in tighter, the flurry of wings closing around, folding in like a trap.

V swings wildly, her own blade catching only empty air, flashing bright against the dark swarm. She swings again, finally meeting a bat head-on. The crack is satisfying as it sputters into flaming fragments then dissolves into ash. She curses, stumbling in the toxic sludge beneath her boots, the fiery pain lancing through her arm.

The cyclone tightens, and jagged shadows swirl faster. The bats weave together, a blur of jagged shadows and light. Their twisted bodies bristle with spikes, bending the light and making them hard to see. Their shrieks fill the air, a dissonant buzz of metallic rage drowning out every other sound.

Merion pulses, pale blue flashes erupting in rhythmic bursts. Three bats disintegrate mid-flight. Another two swerve away just in time. A bright green vine glows, moving with unearthly grace. A lethal pulse of energy flashes from its narrow leaves.

<Merion, you have got to teach me that one,> she mutters as she swings and misses another bat.

Merion's tone is dry, almost dismissive. *<too puny.>*

The interference signal around them flickers. More clawed wings slash jagged holes that Merion barely mends in time. More bats pour in through the gaps, their indigo teeth bared and talons flashing. They force V and Hawthorne closer together. The onslaught is relentless.

<We need a new plan,> V pants, her voice strained as she dodges another dive. She can't ignore how heavy her arms feel. The weight of exhaustion increases with every strike.

Hawthorne grunts, slicing two more bats in one motion. *<Something stronger. Or faster.>* Her flaming sword cuts through the air, leaving trails of scorched light. A bat's talons scrape her arm, and another dives straight for V, its screech a jagged burst of rage that rings out in their minds.

V ducks and swings upward, obliterating a bat centimeters from her face. She struggles against the sickening ooze soaking beneath her boots. The ground pulses, squirming with dark veins that wriggle just beneath them. She kicks at the muck, watching it recoil briefly before rippling back.

<Thorney, this sludge—it's alive,> V says, her voice tinged with disgust.

Hawthorne stabs her sword into the ground, and the meadow trembles. A sound like splitting meat echoes through the air. *<You're right. We've been fighting the wrong enemy.>* She pulls her blade free, her eyes scanning the writhing ooze. *<The Grove isn't just in the bats. It's in everything. This whole feckin place is corrupted.>*

The meadow around them is a landscape of rot. Everywhere is twisted grass slick with mold, gurgling sludge bubbling with toxic steam. Every step releases a fetid tang of decay. Beneath it all, Hawthorne senses a network of blackened roots pulsing with foul energy, spreading like veins through diseased flesh.

<We're not going to win by hacking at its minions,> Hawthorne mutters, driving her sword into the ground again. *<We need to uproot it.>*

V doesn't hesitate. She plunges her blade into the sludge beside her, and flames erupt from the wound. The meadow recoils violently, and a low wail reverberates through the air as dark roots retract beneath the surface. The bats screech in unison, tethered to the ground by an invisible force.

<This isn't just Demeter's *pain,>* V realizes, her blade digging deeper. *<This is the Grove actively converting her.>*

Together, they carve through the writhing ground, their flaming blades cutting jagged paths that spark and smolder. Patches of defiled earth ignite, the flames spreading slowly at first, then with growing ferocity. The stench of burning corruption fills the air, thick and cloying.

<stab,> Merion commands.

V crushes a bat that passes too close, then plunges her blade back into the ground. Hawthorne does the same. Their movements are deliberate and synchronized. The defiled earth dries, then burns, shrinking the twisted roots beneath their feet.

Merion flickers, releasing another pale blue flash that disintegrates several bats mid-dive. But more descend, clawing and screeching, their feral desperation turning them into living missiles. Two collide with Merion and become small explosions of ash and filth against its glowing form. A third bat crashes into it, unseen from behind, striking with brutal force—the interference signal wavers, pulsing erratically before shrinking.

<Merion!> V cries, panic surging as the glowing vine dims. Its presence in their minds weakens, leaving them exposed.

The ground trembles. A guttural rumble vibrates through the sludge as the Grove lashes out again. Thick tendrils of congealed, black muck twist and merge, forming something massive, grotesque, and seething. Rows of indigo eyes blink open across its surface, their hateful gaze fixed on the Druids. The creature leans forward, exuding an aura of rot and power. Its deep growl echoes through their minds, a sound of pure malice.

V and Hawthorne exchange a glance, and their flaming swords droop.

<I'm not sure how we'll fight this,> Hawthorne mutters, her grip tightening on her sword. She braces herself for whatever comes next. They only have one option: fight.

The shadowy appendages lash out, thick with decay and moving with terrible speed.

Without planning to, V and Hawthorne sing "We're in This Alone" together as they find the strength to fight back. Their voices rise together, pulled from somewhere deep and desperate. The words carry a shared strength, binding them against the overwhelming force of the Grove. Each note cuts through the fetid air, defiant and unyielding, drawing power from the song's rhythm as if it were the earth itself, steadying them for the battle ahead.

> *We're bound to see this through.*
> *No one else can tear us down.*
> *We'll find a way out,*
> *It's just us alone.*
> *When the stars fall apart*
> *I'll hold on until the end.*
> *We're in this alone.*

Rowan leans heavily against the cold, narrow core wall, his ribs throbbing with every breath. His hands tremble, blood seeping through his tunic. Even with eyes closed, he feels Max's presence—a quiet but expectant weight in the cramped room—and V's still form, seated against the far bulkhead, her body motionless and her mind far away. She doesn't react when he beats the back of his head softly against the wall-mounted rack and exhales a low, frustrated growl.

"We're running out of time, Chief," Max says, his tone steady but insistent. His tall frame is hunched awkwardly near the doorway, his Atharan mandibles tight with worry.

Rowan opens his eyes, a grim resolve hardening his gaze. "Then we do this the ugly way," he mutters, forcing himself upright, scanning for a prybar or screwdriver.

Max moves to Rowan's side without hesitation. Together, they stagger toward the reinforced access panel at the center of the core room. The space feels tighter than ever, the tangled cables and blinking lights looming like silent witnesses to their desperation, ready to choke them for getting too close.

Rowan's voice is hoarse but steady. "Help me get that panel open."

Max produces a small folding knife and starts prying the panel open.

Rowan's eyes widen in excitement to see any semblance of a tool. "I owe you a few beers when this is over, Max."

"I prefer coffee, though humans can't make it," Max replies as he pries open the panel. "Apologies, but that fact should be noted before our demise."

The air pressure on board *Demeter* is too low to make boiling water hot enough to make good coffee, but that's because of the alliance's standards, not Fleet's.

"No offense taken," Rowan concedes, annoyed.

Rowan reaches, but the bandaged hand is too thick to squeeze inside. "Damn, I wish V was here now."

"I can go wake her if you—"

"No!" Rowan throws his hands back. "Do not! She needs to stay in her trance to fight this thing. Whatever you do, don't touch her."

"Sorry," Max concedes.

"No, I'm sorry. I'm on edge. Can you reach in there and grab those green and red wires?"

Max frowns as he studies the wires. "This will cripple your ship, won't it?"

Rowan doesn't meet his eyes. "It will. But if we don't do it, there won't be a ship left to cripple."

Max nods once, his movements precise and deliberate. "Understood."

Rowan watches from behind. "Yeah, those. Pull until they snap free. Good. Okay, now strip off some of the coating to expose the—yep, just like that."

Rowan lets out a heavy breath. "There they are, Max. Those are the AI cores."

Each AI core is housed in a thick, heat-dissipating alloy shell dotted with a patchwork of vents and blinking indicator lights. They're larger than those found in modern starships, but these still perform well for their age. The front surfaces pulse faintly with a soft, erratic light that flickers between green and amber, an outdated indicator of idle activity. Rows of black carbon fiber cables and translucent coolant tubes snake across each core, glowing a faint, sickly blue.

They both reach in, their fingers scrambling for leverage. The AI cores are the size of small tables, a hulking presence in the cramped space. Max gives a low whistle. "You sure we can even move these, Chief?"

"No choice." Rowan grimaces, looping both arms around the first core. "Come on, pull."

They heave together, dragging the core out of its housing

with a metallic groan. Every centimeter feels like a kay. Sweat beads on Rowan's brow as he fights through the pain in his ribs. His bandaged hands slip against the casing, fresh blood staining the edges.

Max follows Rowan's direction to disconnect the cables. He yanks at the reinforced wires, each brutal tug sending sparks cascading like tiny fireworks. The lights flicker, and power begins to falter.

"This isn't working," Max says, his voice strained. "The core has a secondary power source."

Rowan nods grimly, gesturing toward the trim panel on the side of the core. "Battery cell. Pry it out."

Max wedges his tool under the casing. The faint hum of the cell grows louder as it resists removal. With a final grunt, he frees the battery and lets it clatter to the floor, where its faint glow fades into nothingness.

"That's one down," Max says, shoving the core aside.

Rowan winces but manages a grin. "Careful with that. It's still part of *Demeter*."

"Noted," Max replies dryly, already moving to the next core.

They work in silence. Entire sections of the server racks click off with each disconnected core. The flickering lights fade, and the ship begins to shudder as systems fail one by one. When they reach the third core, Rowan's breath comes in ragged gasps, and Max's steady hands tremble with exertion.

"I think we just killed life support," Max mutters.

"Probably," Rowan wheezes, his grin turning feral. "Means we're doing it right."

They grip the final core together, muscles burning, as they wrest it from its slot. The metal plating is cold, unforgiving, and slick with sweat and blood. Rowan's chest tightens as the last set of wires snap free, releasing a cascade of sparks. The ship's discordant hum fades into a deafening stillness. The lights flicker once and go out, plunging them into darkness.

"Chief," Max says, his voice tight. "I feel lightheaded. What's happening?"

Rowan snorts, reaching out to anchor himself against the nearest rack. "The generated gravity just winked out. You're weightless."

"Oh," Max mutters before adding, "For the record, I do not like—" A choked, horrific sound cuts off his words.

Rowan grimaces. He's never heard an Atharan get sick before, but he's pretty sure that's what's happening. He pulls his jacket up tight over his face.

Drifting awkwardly in the pitch black, Rowan pushes off from the rack. "I'm going to make sure V's okay," he mutters as Max continues to vomit behind him. He finds her floating a meter above the deck—still deep in trance. Still fighting.

For a moment, only the sound of their labored breathing— and the occasional unpleasant retch—fills the void. Then Rowan speaks, his voice quiet but unyielding. "That's our part done. The rest is on the others."

"And that," Captain Hargreaves says, emphasizing the word to mimic the traditional ending of the audio-cast, "is why Captain Alara is one of the Great Captains of Old." He sighs, the recitation of his favorite episode having reached its conclusion.

With no words or glances exchanged, Hargreaves and Bekhti rise, straighten their jackets, and move to the rear of the bridge. The large planning table looms in the center of the space, dark and silent now, where mission plans had once been laid out, lines drawn, and targets marked. Hargreaves trails his fingers along its edge as he passes. "We've planned a lot of operations around this table over the years, haven't we?"

"We have, sir," Bekhti replies, her voice neutral.

The self-destruct controls lie behind a small security panel just past the table. They exchange a single nod before inserting their keys. The simultaneous clicks unlock the panel, which hisses softly as it releases. Hargreaves carefully removes it, setting it aside to reveal four recessed levers.

The levers are heavy, their thick metal handles dulled with time. Dust clings to the surface, and a faint sheen of rust lines the joints, evidence of years without use. Hargreaves grips the first lever, feeling the resistance in the worn mechanism. "These things haven't seen the light of day in decades," he mutters, squeezing the trigger inside the handle to twist it counterclockwise until it gives way.

The lever collapses telescopically with a metallic groan. He forces it back into its housing, locking the chamber open to release the first energy core several decks below into the hyperdrive containment field.

Bekhti tackles the second lever, her jaw tightening as her grip slips on the rusted handle. "Who would've thought an old boat like this would ever need these?" She strains, the hinge groaning in protest before it clicks into place. She slams it back with a sharp shove, locking it into place.

They pause briefly, exchanging glances, and work to keep their breathing calm and professional. The jerky movements disturb a fine layer of dust in the air. They both make a face to acknowledge their actions before crouching to reach the lower levers.

Hargreaves squeezes the grip on the third, his fingers straining to twist the stubborn mechanism. A combination of age and neglect resists him every inch of the way. He twists harder, forcing it to collapse with a reluctant snap, then shoves it back into position. Exhaling sharply, he fidgets with his cufflinks and considers what he's just done.

Bekhti grips the fourth lever and pulls, but it doesn't budge. She braces her foot against the frame and heaves with all her strength. She grits her teeth and swears mightily. The lever groans and finally acquiesces to her will. She pulls forward, trying to squeeze the reluctant squeeze trigger. She yells at it hard enough that some of her hair loosens from its tight bun. Her frustration rises, but it remains locked.

Hargreaves steps forward, his voice gentle. "Here. It should be me anyway."

He wraps both hands around the handle, adding his weight to hers. The grit holding the trigger in place finally gives. The trigger pinches his skin as it collapses. "Ow!" He pulls back, shaking his hand in the air.

Their laughter is quiet but genuine—a fleeting moment of absurdity they can't resist.

"Complaining about a pinch when we're seconds from vaporizing everything," Bekhti mutters, shaking her head. She slings an arm around his back in a quick, sideways hug.

"Right?" Hargreaves regains his composure, placing an arm around her briefly before his expression hardens. The fuel rods for the engines will eject into the hyperspace manifold, instantly vaporizing the ship and everything nearby. There's no room for hesitation now.

He whispers, "Here we go."

Bekhti places her hands over his, and together they lift the final lever. It sticks, grinding against its rusted track as they push it into position.

Hargreaves roars. He kicks again and again, each strike loosening its resistance. With a final scream, he stomps hard, and the lever jerks into place with a metallic groan.

One last twist, and it's done, he thinks.

With a sudden jolt, the bridge is plunged into darkness. The lights cut out, and the faint hum of the ship's systems dies. The floor beneath them releases its hold, and they become weightless.

"Captain," Bekhti says, her voice tight with alarm. She clutches the edge of the planning table, anchoring herself. "Did we just—?"

"No," Hargreaves says, a nervous laugh escaping him. He

spins slowly in the weightless void, squinting into the darkened bridge. "I don't think that was us."

Bekhti reaches out, her hand brushing his shoulder for balance. She grins, though he can't see it. "So, the ship didn't blow."

There's a stunned pause, followed by soft chuckles. Their laughter grows, breaking the oppressive silence, absurd and unrestrained. They both fight an emotional burst of tears.

Hargreaves shrugs, his voice wry. "You know, I was expecting a little more fanfare."

Bekhti snorts. "Or at least a bang. I feel downright cheated."

They float in the silence, letting their laughter fade. For a moment, hope flickers between them. Gods willing, the others have done their part.

The dark beast towers over them, a massive amalgamation of tangled limbs, writhing tentacles, and glistening muck. Indigo eyes blink across its grotesque form, unblinking and otherworldly. It lashes out, its appendages swinging with terrifying speed. Flaming swords slice through the darkened sludge, searing it with brief flashes of light, but the counterattacks only seem to anger the creature.

V grits her teeth as she slashes at a tentacle that lunges for her legs. The blade burns clean through, leaving a smoldering stump, but the creature doesn't falter. Its severed limb thrashes on the ground before dissolving into the bubbling ooze beneath their feet.

<Swords aren't enough for this thing!> she shouts, her voice strained. Another attack comes from behind—a broad, flat tentacle that knocks her to the ground. Her sword flies free, extinguishing as it lands in the muck. She struggles to breathe, the blow leaving her dazed. The ground beneath her shifts unnaturally, trying to sink her.

Hawthorne swings her blade in a sharp arc, forcing the beast to retreat momentarily. She crouches down, grabbing V by the arm and hauling her halfway to her feet. <You all right, luv?> she asks, not waiting for an answer as she turns to parry another lashing limb.

V coughs, trying to steady herself. Even her metaphysical ears are ringing. <Feck no! I mean, yeah—I'll live. I think.>

The creature's roar reverberates through the air, a guttural, primal sound that shakes them both to their cores. V stumbles as the ground shifts again, dragging her back down. Her arms flail as she sinks slightly, her boots sticking in the viscous muck.

<It's too strong,> V gasps, clawing her way up. <I don't think these swords are going to cut it—literally.>

<Any better ideas?> Hawthorne grits her teeth, slicing through another tentacle. The beast recoils slightly, but its massive frame hardly registers the damage.

V shoots her a glare. <You're the expert here!>

Their mental connection buzzes faintly with Merion's presence. A pale blue flash erupts nearby, disintegrating a piece of the beast's limb mid-swing. The sapling's voice hums faintly in their minds.

A tidal wave crashes against an unyielding cliff. Water sprays in all directions but fails to breach the stone's surface. The wave recedes, leaving the cliff untouched and resolute.

<No shit, Merion!> V snaps, scrambling to grab her sword. She pulls it from the muck and reignites the blade with a sharp twist of her wrist. <We need more power. Something bigger.>

The beast bellows a deep, guttural scream, its massive form trembling. Tentacles writhe in all directions as if searching for an escape. Then, it pauses. Its countless eyes lock onto them, unblinking, and the air grows still. V and Hawthorne exchange a glance, wheezing for breath.

A low rumble beneath them shatters the silence. The ground

quakes, and dark sludge bubbles violently, spilling over the scorched meadow. Slowly, the Grove's massive form begins to vibrate, shambling as if in anticipation.

<What's it doing now?> V mutters, clutching her sword tighter.

The answer comes in an instant. The weight of gravity shifts, and they find themselves weightless. V makes a startled cry as she rises slightly, her boots leaving the ground. She swings her arms, trying to steady herself.

<Merion?> Hawthorne calls her voice tight with alarm. <Is this your doing?>

<no.>

<Then what the hell is happening?> V demands.

<demeter destroyed.>

V feels her chest and torso. <Nope. Still here. So, not destroyed.> Realization hits her. Grinning, she tells Hawthorne, <He did it! Rowan reset the AI core. The AG field is down.> She struggles to control her movement, grabbing onto the hilt of her sword to anchor herself. The flame flickers but holds. <This is—not great timing.>

Hawthorne drifts a few feet away, adjusting her position midair with careful, deliberate motions. The beast swings a massive tentacle, but it moves sluggishly in the new environment, its bulk unsteady without gravity. <We can use this,> Hawthorne says, her voice sharper in their chaint connection now. <If it can't root itself, maybe it can't regain its strength.>

V shakes her head. <Maybe. But we're still not doing enough damage.>

Hawthorne hesitates, her gaze fixed on the beast. She narrows her eyes. <Maybe we don't need to destroy it directly.>Hawthorne slashes at a tendril that drifts too close, severing it cleanly. <The interference field Merion created—it's keeping the Grove contained. What if we collapse the field instead of trying to kill it? Trap it in its own rot and crush it.>

<Crush it?> V echoes, the idea sinking in. She nods slowly. <Yeah. I'm in.>

<crush,> Merion agrees, its presence flickering in their awareness.

The interference field shimmers around them, its translucent surface pulsing like rippling water. V and Hawthorne drift toward the top of the dome, their movements slow and deliberate. Merion's energy guides them and reinforces the barrier as they position themselves above the massive creature.

The Grove thrashes violently, its limbs lashing out in all directions. Dark muck sprays across the meadow, but it can't reach them. The interference field holds steady, trembling under the strain but refusing to give way.

Hawthorne presses her palms outward, focusing her energy on the edges of the field. V mirrors her stance, her jaw clenched as she channels every ounce of strength into the shimmering barrier. The field begins to contract, tightening around the writhing beast.

V struggles with the movements and accidentally pushes her hands through. Small rips spread from the opening she makes, but Merion quickly repairs them. V's arms tremble, her energy faltering. <Thorney, I don't know if I can keep this up.>

<You can,> Hawthorne says firmly, her voice steady despite the strain in her expression. <We're almost there. Keep pushing.>

V lets out a furious scream as she reaches deeper for more power. Every ounce of energy she can imagine pours through her and into the interference bubble.

The beast lets out another deafening roar that echoes through the surrounding meadow. As the field constricts, its body contorts and buckles. Its form collapses inward, imploding with wet, sickening sounds. The corrupted mass bubbles and shrinks, its limbs snapping under the pressure.

Merion hovers above them, its glow dimming as it funnels the last of its energy into the field. The interference pulses one final time, its edges pressing into the creature's core. With a final, wrenching scream, the Grove collapses, disintegrating into a cloud of dark energy. The meadow falls silent.

V and Hawthorne hover in the air, their breaths ragged, their bodies trembling with exhaustion. The field flickers one last time before winking out, leaving them suspended in the stillness. There are no more shrieks or pounding tendrils, no distant chittering of creatures taking flight, and no looming shadows on the horizon.

V glances at Hawthorne, her voice barely above a whisper. *<Thorney? I think we did it.>*

Hawthorne exhales slowly, her gaze lingering on the scorched earth below. *<Yeah. >* Her body slumps in relief, but she doesn't sound convinced.

The ground beneath them shifts faintly, the remnants of the corrupted roots crumbling into ash. V's grip on her sword tightens as a wave of thick silence washes over the meadow.

And then it comes—a faint sound, distant and growing—a low, metallic shriek, twisting into something sharp and unrelenting. V seethes, the sound needles at the periphery of her consciousness, cold and familiar. It coils around her mind, its pitch rising like a blade drawn across glass.

Ris.

The memory of her sister's final moments surges within her —a tune playing through the chaint, quickly distorting into something louder, more sinister, devouring her sister's mind and soul while V watches helplessly. She had always believed she crushed Ris's mind—used too much power for her to handle. Hawthorne told her that was impossible, and now, finally, V believes it. But something else was there that night. A presence she only brushed against, until recently. Something that's coming for them.

Her voice trembles as she speaks, the words heavy and raw. *<I've heard this before. It's—>* She falters, her eyes widening with dread, growing ever distant.

Hawthorne looks at her, alarmed. *<Luv? What is it?>*

The others feel her heart racing.

V's thought barely projects in the chaint.

<*That's Death.*>

V barely has time to steady herself before the meadow around them fractures. The ground lurches below her feet, buckling and tearing like fabric in the grip of an unseen hand. What little light remains twists and scatters, bending in unnatural directions as they're pulled into another space that feels suffocatingly alive.

The familiar shapes of grass and earth dissolve, leaving V, Hawthorne, and Merion suspended in a place where geometry and logic unravel. Angles double back on themselves, and shadows stretch endlessly, folding over themselves in grotesque configurations. Dim light bleeds from nowhere, casting jagged reflections on surfaces that shouldn't exist, creating a vastness that presses inward from every direction.

Above them—or perhaps surrounding them entirely—the Grove looms in a form that escapes comprehension. Its effulgent dark sun burns with shadows, a singular, unblinking eye staring in every direction at once. There are no perspectives in which it doesn't stare directly at the observer. It folds around the surrounding space, somehow present even in the places where it isn't.

The air is viscous, clinging to their skin and pressing into their lungs with a warmth that feels wrong. Shadows crawl along nonexistent surfaces, pooling and stretching like living things. The ground beneath V's feet, if it can be called ground, gives like damp soil but feels taut, like stretched flesh ready to snap.

Merion hovers beside her, its emerald glow dimming against the Grove's oppressive presence. Its voice is faint, trembling in their minds. <*can't fight here.*>

Merion flickers weakly, its energy nearly extinguished. <the grove sees all.> Its thoughts waver, slipping between fear and awe. <memories are timeless. power.>

Hawthorne's hand on her arm steadies her. Even here, in this warped space, Hawthorne's presence is an anchor, a steady flame against the suffocating dark. <Stay with me, V. Don't listen to it.>

Dark tendrils of thought curl around V's consciousness, probing for the fractures in her will, twisting the worst from her memories: Ris, lying cold and lifeless, crushed by the weight of V's own dark power. Her death remains ever present, overshadowing V's mind. She trembles, her strength waning as the familiar vision clouds her focus. She's almost happy to give up the power, to be done with it.

V shakes her head, trembling. <I don't think I can do this, Thorney. It's too much.>

Hawthorne's grip tightens. Her voice cuts through the chaos, steady and sure. < This isn't about what you think you've done or what you think you've failed at. It's about what you're here to do right now. Ris would want you to fight—not for her, but for what you still have. For what you can protect.>

Another memory floods V's mind, this time from Merion.

Her mother is curled up, crying on the rug in her library, an empty wine glass lying on its side. "She drank hemlock, Violet. My sweet girl, my beautiful Iris." V's mother sobs uncontrollably for a moment before adding, "How did I not know how much pain she was in? I'm so sorry you touched her mind to see it, but part of me is grateful that she wasn't alone. Thank you for that, my love."

V gasps, choking—hearing "my love" for the first time in years gives her the air she needs. In that moment, the confluence of memory shifts, transforming into a fierce surge of determination. Years of guilt and the weight of her self-imposed restraint all come roaring to the surface. She grips Hawthorne's hand tighter, their fingers interlocking, and feels the power simmering beneath her skin.

<You're right. No more holding back.>

She means to burn it all away. Her rage unfurls. She feels it expand from a small flame into a roaring inferno. Every thought sparks with raw energy—her anger is charged by memories of Ris, who was crushed by a different kind of pressure. V's fury surges like wildfire and lightning, electrifying her veins, igniting her power, and transforming her into relentless, unbound energy.

<Good,> Hawthorne says, her voice soft but firm. *<Now give me everything. I can shape it for both of us.>*

V hesitates. Her unreliable memories taunt her. There's no choice, and this time she's not alone. Hawthorne knows what's coming and is ready to shape it. With a final glance at her mentor, V lets go, unleashing every ounce of raw strength she's buried for years.

A surge of molten energy explodes from V, filling the warped space with light and heat. The Grove recoils, its tendrils snapping back as the interference bubble begins to form. The oppressive darkness blenches from the onslaught, but the Grove fights back, its voice vibrating through their minds.

<YOU HAVE DESTROYED MY VESSEL, BUT YOU ARE FRAIL, AND SOME PIECE OF IT REMAINS. I WILL HAVE IT BACK!>

Hawthorne's grip tightens as she bears the strain, almost buckling under the force. Still, she holds on with Merion's guidance, shaping V's pure strength, forcing it into a concentrated wave that repulses the Grove's dark field. Bit by bit they set the interference signal into place.

<More, V,> Hawthorne urges. Her voice is a soft but unbreakable tether through the galvanic wildfire. *< Let it all go. Do it for Ris. For* Demeter.*>*

V's heart surges with a storm of emotions—anger, spite, love, loss—concentrated into a singular purpose. She channels it all into Hawthorne's hands, the electricity crackling as it crashes into the Grove all around them. The great eye narrows, and a guttural roar reverberates through the void, a cry of thwarted rage.

Merion pulses faintly, its flickering energy fusing with theirs. *<final push. save.>*

Hawthorne's knuckles crack, but she holds on just as tight. *<I'm with you till the end, luv. We're almost there.>* Quietly, she begs the goddess for just a little more time.

With a final, shuddering cry that would rival any banshee, V lets go—everything she is, everything she's held back, every burned memory and buried scream—into Hawthorne's waiting hands. Into her soul. The air fractures around them as Hawthorne braces, her body and mind taut with strain. She doesn't flinch. She accepts it all. V's power detonates outward, a white-hot wave ripping through the Grove's tendrils, shredding them to ash and silence.

<Goddess, I'm ready.>

The Grove's great eye contracts, its shape distorting as if it's folding inward on itself—no longer watching, but recoiling. A sound erupts from the void—not a howl, but a rupture, like space itself tearing under pressure it can't withstand. The Grove writhes, limbs flailing in disjointed spasms, dragging through collapsing angles that no longer hold form. Its presence flickers, its will thinning at the edges.

It falters, withdrawing as V's force, amplified by Hawthorne's force of will, crashes over it, dissolving its presence in pulses and waves.

Hawthorne squeezes V's hand. *<You've got this, luv.>*

The interference field takes shape around them, pulsing like a heartbeat, creating an unbreakable barrier against the Grove's influence.

<Thorney, Merion, it's working!>

The energy spreads throughout the Grove's twisted manifestation of space, wave after wave peeling it apart. Tendrils snap and dissolve, their forms unmaking themselves mid-recoil. The great eye splits open in a seismic scream—then space trembles, and clears.

Hawthorne's metaphysical grip softens, her presence flickering like the final ember of a bonfire. Her mental voice doesn't cry out; it simply fades.

They slip through the thinning veil between mental worlds, Merion's fragile glow a beacon guiding them home. V barely registers the silence until it's already too complete.

<Thorney, we did it! We really did it.>

Hawthorne's hand pulls away from V's.

<Hawthorne, you okay?>

No answer—just a stillness, vast and absolute.

In the space where Hawthorne's voice should be, V hears only the hush of memory: a muted, twisted chord from *Dark's Wake*, broken, like something lost between breaths.

<Thorney?>

Silence.

<Please, Goddess. Not again.>

TWENTY
WHAT THE MOTHER TAKES

I gave her everything I had.
And still, she gave more.

— V. SANDOVAL
EULEGY FOR DR. HAWTHORNE (EXCERPT)

In the Root Cellar, V carefully places Hawthorne's crown into its hand-engraved wooden case, bundling the data and power cables with meticulous care into the many small pockets inside. She lingers over the T9-26 Mark IV quantum band monitor, her fingers tracing its smooth casing. Parker would've appreciated it, she thinks. Since he's gone, maybe it can go to Hector when he's out of the reconstruction chambers in medbay. It feels like the sort of thing Hawthorne would've wanted, if she was still here.

Exhaling deeply, V lowers herself into Hawthorne's chair. The memory of recent events feels unbearable—her exhaustion, the empty space Hawthorne used to fill, and the quiet of a ship still regaining itself. She closes her eyes, letting the silence stretch out—until a faint, familiar presence brushes against her thoughts. Tentative. Curious.

<Thorney?>

The memory of Hawthorne's death crashes over her, sharp and fresh all over again, like it just happened.

It's not her. But something is there, tugging on the coattails of her consciousness—a presence, patient and waiting. An old friend.

<Demeter*?*>

A flood of emotion washes over her, an unmistakable presence she hasn't felt in weeks—except now it feels different. Warmer. Unfiltered. Alive.

They've shared empathy before, but they've never spoken like this. Never through chaint.

<Violet? Is that really you?>

Tears spring to V's hemorrhaged eyes, unbidden and sudden. *Demeter*'s voice carries something raw, unpolished by her usual clinical tone—a fragile, joyful relief. She's the only one who ever calls V by her full name.

<Oh goddess, Demeter. *Are you really back?>* Her mental voice wavers.

<Yes, it's really me,> Demeter answers, *<though I don't know how to prove that. I've been disconnected, fractured, broken. So blind to so much of myself that I'm not sure I can trust anything I see. But now, I feel the loquentes roots again. I feel my rootwork, my circuitry. I feel whole again. I believe I'm operational, and… myself again.>*

<It's okay, I believe you. You've been through a lot recently.>

<You appear to have been through a lot recently as well, Violet. This mode of communication—the chaint—is new between us.>

<Yeah, I guess I've changed.> V slumps in her chair and changes the subject. *<How are you feeling?>*

<I'm—I'm okay. I think.> Demeter's tone breaks slightly, shimmering with emotion. *<You brought me back, didn't you?>*

If a starship could cry, V thinks, it would sound exactly like this. That raw, trembling gratitude. V feels an image appear in the back of her mind.

The first glint of sunlight after weeks of rain. A rainbow after the clouds depart. Fresh air.

<Not just me. Hawthorne. We did it together.> The words come hard, her throat tight even in this intangible place.

There's a pause, gentle but heavy. *<Where is the good doctor?>* Demeter's voice is quieter now, hesitant. *<I want to thank her, too.>*

V clenches her jaw, fighting the lump forming there. *<She's gone.>*

The silence stretches long enough that V wonders if the connection has broken. Finally, *Demeter* speaks, her voice threaded with sorrow. *<Gone. Gone? Because of me?>*

V closes her eyes. *<No. Goddess, no, luv. It wasn't because of you. She saved you, yes, but she saved all of us. She may have even saved Earth and Fleet.>*

Demeter's presence flickers, laden with grief. *<I wish she hadn't. I wish she were here. I wish I could tell her thank you. And tell her goodbye.>*

They sit together in the comforting quiet, tethered across the strange void where ship and Druid share their thoughts.

Finally, *Demeter* speaks again, her tone shifting to something lighter, curious. *<The interference field I'm emanating—I don't know it. There's someone else here, isn't there? Is there another Druid?>*

V feels a small spark of excitement at the question. *<Yes, there is. His name is Merion. He's, well, complicated to explain. But he's been helping us. The Grove wasn't just here in you,* Demeter. *It was—>* She shifts in her seat, struggling to find the words to explain. *<Well, part of it is still here in Tau Ceti. The source of it—the true Grove—sent something long ago to propagate itself. An ancient spore sphere. It's been circling Tau Ceti f for millennia, waiting. It's a proxy, a harbinger. We still need to destroy that.>*

<Destroy? No. Wait. I DESTROYED!>

V flashes back to Brigid, sharing *Demeter's* fragmented memories.

Particle cannons. Tangerine skies. Black smoke. Air that turns to ichor. Death. Persephone. Arion.

<*The crew. My children are gone! Sworn to protect, but I killed them!*> The ship's klaxons briefly sound, more from panic than from warning.

<*Shh shh shh. Demeter, no! You didn't do that. That wasn't you. We all know that wasn't you.*>

The klaxons stop, and the Root Cellar is silent for a few minutes.

Demeter considers V's words then says, <*I understand now. This fight. It isn't over yet, is it?*>

<*No, but it will be soon.*> V smiles faintly, her tone steady. <*When it is, you'll never have to worry about the Grove again. I promise you that.*>

<*Thank you, Violet,*> *Demeter* says, calmer now. The words settle quietly, bittersweet in their sincerity. <*I can't thank you and Nigella for what you've done for me. I'll always be here for you—for as long as you need me.*>

V blinks. Nigella? She's never heard the name before—but somehow it suits Thorney. Soft, old-fashioned. A quiet counterpoint to the iron-willed woman who wore it like her only secret.

For a moment, they simply exist together in the quiet, sharing the ache of what they've lost and the comfort of being understood. V doesn't try to fill the silence and simply gazes up at the thick, gray ceiling. This one feels sacred—something to be honored, not solved.

After a beat, *Demeter*'s voice returns, soft and tentative.

<*Would you like to listen to some music with me?*>

The bridge is still, and the air is tense. V steps through the security hatch, her frame stiff with purpose. An honor guard follows respectfully, carrying the gear she requested—Hawthorne's gear. After recent events, she's been granted full security clearance. There's no longer a need for formality, but the captain insisted on the escort anyway. "Just in case," he had said.

Just in case what? V wonders.

Dim emergency lights bathe the bridge in muted reds and deep shadows. Most terminals remain inoperable, and the active ones have only partially recovered since the costly battle. Captain Hargreaves sits in his conn chair, twisting his cufflinks absently as he stares at the dormant monitors. Across the room, his officers move in silence, their exhaustion palpable. The strain of holding everything together shows on every drained face.

Hargreaves rises and turns, his movements slow but deliberate. "Specialist Sandoval," he says gently, his voice overcome with sympathy. He asks imploringly, "May I call you V? Your friends call you that."

She nods curtly, her gaze fixed on the floor between them. She tucks her hair behind her ear, but it refuses to stay.

He steps closer, placing his hands on her shoulders. His brow furrows as he studies her face—dark circles under red eyes, fading bruises along her jawline.

"V, can I get you anything? I know Doctor Essien still has you on medical leave… so thank you for coming."

Her voice is clipped, businesslike, and rehearsed. "I'm fine, Captain. Thank you." Her accent is precise. This cadence belongs to her mother—polished and formal, a protective veneer against the rawness beneath.

Hargreaves glances at Security Chief Sorrell, who is leading the honor guard. "Place her things at the planning station. We'll begin over there shortly." His voice carries an edge of reverence. The order isn't about the equipment but the honor attached to it and the sacrifice of its once-owner. He glances at V and adds, "When you're ready, of course."

Sorrell and her officers carefully place the gear on the table. Her hands hover briefly over the items before she steps back, her eyes drifting to the exposed self-destruct panel behind the station. The levers remain awkwardly angled, their battered edges a reminder of the bridge's most desperate hour and how close they came to a different outcome.

Hargreaves gestures toward his seat. "V, would you like to sit for a moment? Collect your thoughts?"

Then, turning back to a conversation already in progress, he calls across the bridge, his voice sharpening. "Commander DeSoto. Status of the cannons?"

"Targeting computers are operational, sir. Fire control reports the particle beam cannons will be ready within moments."

"Good. Prepare to fire on my order." He turns back to V. "Specialist Sandoval, do you need anything before we proceed?"

"No, sir." Her response is measured, unable to stop her clipped accent. "Just a few minutes to complete the telemetry readings." Her tone is crisp—detached in a way that doesn't escape notice. Bekhti exchanges a glance with Hargreaves, but he shakes his head, hoping she'll let it go.

V rises and walks to the planning table, moving like someone performing a ritual, not a routine. She unpacks Hawthorne's gear, then places the crown in the center of the table and arranges the cables and adaptors with meticulous care. Each connection is double-checked with the care of someone unwilling to risk error—or, more importantly, earn Hawthorne's ire.

The crown's polished edges gleam faintly in the dim under-lighting from the table, the circuitry barely visible beneath its outer layer. The auxiliary ports blink as the table interface sparks to life, heralding a successful integration.

Without looking at them, V addresses the full bridge crew. "We know the Grove's proxy is a spore sphere—an ancient construct sent to propagate its influence. It's been trapped in the gravity well of Tau Ceti f for millennia, dormant until we came along. And now, we're going destroy it."

Her tone is cold and deliberate, as if she's simply delivering a report. "The Sphere is powerful, sentient, and still tethered to the Grove."

V takes a steadying breath and reaches for the crown, feeling the cool metal as it settles onto her head. She spends a few moments adjusting it; Hawthorne had a larger head, and V's hair isn't thick enough to make up the difference. Finally, a sharp, invasive pulse jars her senses, and she clenches her jaw against the instinct to recoil. She never liked tapping into her power, and after what happened to Hawthorne—what she did to Hawthorne—she especially hates it now. The crown's circuitry whispers softly as it syncs with her mind, the planning table's console amplifying its range. It casts her awareness outward, beyond *Demeter*'s hull, and into the depths where the Sphere waits for ghastly instructions.

<Demeter, *I need you to lower the interference field.*> Her chaint is soft and intimate.

There's no response.

<Just for a moment, luv.>

Demeter's voice trembles in her mind. *<Violet, no. What if it reaches us again? I won't let it hurt anyone else. I can't—>*

<*Shh,*> V soothes, her tone gentle. *<It's all right. I'll protect you, just like before. You trust me, don't you?>*

There's a pause, the ship's hesitation palpable. <*Yes, trust.*>

The interference field fades, and V's awareness surges outward. Her breath catches as she senses it—that vast, ancient presence, impossibly malevolent. Tendrils of thought coil toward her, probing and searching. She clenches the table's edge, forcing her mind to hold fast.

She dives deeper, her thoughts cutting through the Grove's web of influence. Its construct shifts, angling its dark fibers to reach her. For an agonizing moment, it feels as if it sees everything—Hawthorne's fall, Ris's cold eyes, every fracture in V's resolve. She fights to hold on, pushing past the suffocating dread.

Demeter's consciousness trembles in the back of V's mind.

Then, like a targeting reticle, the target's location flares in her mind. She locks onto it, using the crown to transmit the coordinates back to the planning table. Tendrils lash out, desperate to cling to her mind, but she wrenches herself free, ripping the crown from her head and slamming it onto the table.

Her voice cuts through the silence, cold and resolute. "Commander DeSoto. Target coordinates are locked."

DeSoto nods sharply, his hands poised over the fire controls. "Aye, Specialist. Firing sequence initiated. Captain?"

Hargreaves steps forward, his tone calm. "Fire when ready."

The Sphere's presence lingers, a tempestuous fury pulsing at the edges of V's mind—but it's not alone. The emancipated ship rises to meet it, her rage boiling up through the rootwork, saturating every deck with a resonance that hums like fury barely held in check. V can feel her—feel all of it: the violation, the loss of her crew, her children *Persephone* and *Arion*, the moment her weapons were turned against her own.

The cannons charge, vibrating decks across the ship. It's the low, primal growl of a predator stirred from slumber—but not to hunt this time.

This is justice.

The particle beam cannons fire in rapid succession—not a single blast, but a relentless volley, ripping across the void with a fury that drowns out everything else. V braces against the table, jaw clenched, as the ship howls through her. She can barely tell where her own grief ends and *Demeter*'s begins; the two blur together, a shared scream echoing through the chainted rootwork.

The Sphere pushes back—one last flicker of malice, sharp and clawed—but it's too late. *Demeter* pours everything she has into the barrage. Every scream she couldn't make. Every drop of sorrow calcified into wrath. The shots keep coming, long past what's needed. This isn't strategy. It's heartbreak. It's despair. It's vengeance.

And then—silence.

The cannons cool. The growl fades. Her presence dims in V's mind, not vanishing, but catching her breath—like a fighter, bloodied and standing, reeling from the effort of the final blow she never thought she'd get to throw.

n the dimmed mess hall, strands of fairy lights flicker to life, casting a warm glow over rows of tables arranged end-to-end. Near the entrance, an honor guard officer stands watch, offering a solemn nod as each crewmember arrives—a quiet acknowledgment of those who won't be joining them this time. The captain doesn't require formal attire, not even their class-A uniforms, yet everyone is dressed in the best they have. Some wear the ship's deep blue, while others have added personal touches—small reminders of home and the ones who won't return.

In the back corner of the Lolly Galley, a thick, black marker scratches against one of the last wall panels not already covered in crew art. A petty officer scrawls a new dedication, starkly contrasting with the colorful mission patches and celebratory murals that came before. This one is darker and heavier. Others will add to it before the mission is over, a growing testament to *Demeter*'s final mission and those who didn't come back, but for now, it's just a simple sketch.

At the head of the gathering, a single empty chair is draped with the Fleet flag and flanked by small lanterns. In front of it sits an untouched glass, a silent tribute to absent friends. Crewmembers have placed small offerings on the table throughout the day: a dog-eared book, a worn flight pin, a set of rusted lockpicks, an old navigation tool that hasn't worked in years, and a flimsy disk with music titles scrawled onto it. A wooden bowl rests nearby, already collecting coins for the Ferryman.

The mess hall murmurs reverently. As Captain Hargreaves rises, so does the crew—silently coming to attention.

"To the friends we've lost, the ones who gave everything, and the debts we carry forward." He lifts his glass, his eyes scanning the faces at the table before resting briefly on V, giving her a friendly nod. "May they live on in us."

Glasses rise, the toast echoing in quiet unison.

After a moment, an ensign nearest the empty chair shifts uncomfortably. The officer beside him nudges him forward, and he clears his throat. "I, uh—I remember when Parker snuck me an extra ration on a late shift," he says, his voice barely above a whisper.

Someone mutters, "He always had snacks," and a few chuckles ripple through the room.

"Peanut butter crackers" the ensign continues. "And you know how hard that was to find after the first couple of months out here. Just that, nothing fancy. But it was, well, it was exactly what I needed that day."

A lieutenant near the end of the table chimes in. "I swear he could spot an under-caffeinated crew member from the far end of the ship." She shakes her head with a faint smile. "And you know how much he hated the coffee on board." A few laughs break through the solemn air. "That didn't stop him from downing gallons of it."

"Speaking of which, may I?" Max interjects, standing near the service counter with Lilith. "We made a coffee for Hawthorne. Real coffee."

Lilith holds up an Atharan ritual contraption, a brewing device that pressurizes the water. "We figured, if we're going to honor the dead, we should do it properly," she says. "I know humans introduced coffee to us many years ago, but we've perfected it by brewing it at higher temperatures and greater pressure. I know you like your Earth coffee, but Doctor Hawthorne loved this Atharan brew, and now we wish to honor her with a final pour."

Lilith sets the steaming mug on the table next to the other offerings. The rich, nutty aroma fills the galley. Mouths water, and a few crewmembers strain for a better whiff.

As she and Max walk away, Lilith leans toward V and whispers, "Specialist Sandoval, I understand you also prefer it made in this fashion. Please feel free to join us for Shathaan one day. We'll share a cup and remember the doctor." Lilith touches her heart in a quiet Atharan sign of respect.

V mirrors the gesture without hesitation. "I'd like that."

Near the end, Specialist Drek tells a story about Petty Officer Armiger. "The whole time he was bleeding out, he worried about that stupid, fucking Starwing medal." She grins thinly. "He had it down there with him, and—I guess a wing broke off. He asked me, 'How can I leave this to my family if it's broken like this?' He was about to die, and all he cared about was leaving something for his family so they'd be proud of his service. I don't know why that pisses me off so much, but I'm also so proud of him that he cared about something more than just himself, even to the end."

A careless giggle sets loose a cascade of nervous snickering, but the crew quickly regains their solemnity. Drek laughs the loudest before covering her mouth and stepping aside.

Another stands, gathering his voice before speaking thickly. "When the attack on Brigid began, Specialist Dradi returned to help others. He kept us together, even when it was chaos. I wouldn't be standing here if it wasn't for him. He was a hero down there. When it mattered, you know."

Agreement swells in the crowd, someone in the back saying, "For Dradi."

The officer pulls his Starwing pin from his lapel and snaps off one of the wings. He places it with the other offerings in silence.

He stands for a moment, then salutes and walks to the back of the room.

One by one, other crewmembers stand beside the empty chair. And one by one, they snap off a wing or piece of another medal, kiss it, and place it with the other offerings. As the hour grows late and the stories fade, each crewmember deposits a piece of their own Starwings badge: a broken staff, a snapped wing, or a torn strip of ribbon. One day, this bowl of payments and gifts will appear in a historical archive somewhere, but today, it pays respects to the recently departed.

The Lolly Galley is abuzz with quiet whispers as crewmembers tell their stories while waiting to place an offering. Darren pours drinks as the ceremony transitions into a wake, and the voices grow into more casual conversation.

Rowan and V clink mugs of beer, honoring toasts of their own.

V shakes her head slowly. "I didn't know her for that long, but it feels like—"

Rowan smiles stoically. "Like losing family?"

V purses her lips, looking at their drinks. "Yeah. Like losing a parent you just met. Or a sister you didn't know you had." She raises her glass and says, "For Thorney." Rowan raises his, takes a drink, and they both tap their mugs twice on the table.

Merion, tucked inside her jacket, joins the sentiment. <thorney.>

Rowan adds, "Or like an in-law. Parker, I mean." He raises his glass and takes another gulp.

They carry a moment of silence for a beat, thinking fondly of family and friends. Before either can break it, a deep voice beckons in song.

"The ferry awaits, but I'll stand by your side."

V sets her mug on the table and leans back in her chair. After a momentary pause, she joins others answering the lament, her crisp tone well-suited for a shanty.

"Through the dark and through tide"—she holds for a beat, before adding—"'Til the stars cease to shine."

Rowan joins with several others for the next verse.

"Oars dip the void, and the helm swings away. But I'll hold your name 'til the echoes decay."

The galley is full of song, quiet laughter, and the clinks of glassware toasting the fallen in reverent voices.

And in their voices, memory becomes melody.

> *The black claims us all. The stars take their due,*
> *But we sail on, my friend,*
> *And you'll carry us through.*

EPILOGUE

AND THEN, A LITTLE BEEP

*Wait, is this a T9-26 Mark IV? With a modified band monitor
for quantum disentanglement fallback?*

— E. Parker

The bridge is quiet but alive with the steady rhythm of post-reset routines. Systems diagnostics flicker across the few active terminals, and low murmurs pass between officers running status checks. Hargreaves leans against his chair, listening to Commander Bekhti's latest report with only half an ear. It's not that the details aren't important—damage assessments, salvage operations, readiness reports—but after everything, it's the normalcy of it all that makes it so surreal.

Petty Officer Alder interrupts his thoughts. "Captain, incoming priority message from medbay." A pause. "It's Lieutenant Hector."

Hargreaves raises an eyebrow. "Patch him through."

The comm crackles. "Captain? Can you hear me?"

"I'm here, Lieutenant Hector. What's so urgent?"

"Well, sir—uh—I'm receiving a signal. A tight beam, no less."

Hargreaves straightens. "A signal? Getting through our interference field? From where?" He gestures to DeSoto, who shrugs.

"It's hard to explain, sir. I've got this T9-26 Mark IV monitor. Are you familiar with those, sir?"

"Can't say that I am, Skipper. But feel free to cut to the end."

"That's the thing, sir. It's not quantum, so *Demeter*'s bubble won't dampen it. It's on an old Solan Frontier Fleet frequency." Hector hesitates. "And it's close. Really close. A few hundred thousand kays at most."

Hargreaves glances at Bekhti, whose expression sharpens. "Could it be a relic transmission?"

"No, sir. It's active. It's pointed right at us."

The captain pinches the bridge of his nose, not ready for more strange news. "Who else would be out here using that channel?"

"I don't know, sir. But I know how to pinpoint the source." Hector pauses before adding, "Sir, this might sound odd, but Parker rigged up something on the outer hull a few months back. A little DIY broadcasting setup. He said it was for tracking cryptid signals."

"Dare I ask?"

"If someone can push my gurney to our cabin, I can use his rig."

"Commander Bekhti, will you have Doctor Essien move Lieutenant Hector to Chief Parker's quarters?"

The captain switches back to speaking with Hector. "Understood. We'll have someone take you there as soon as possible. When you're ready, contact me directly."

A few minutes later, Hector's voice returns, the faint hum of old capacitors whining in the background. "All right. I've got the relays plugged in. You should be live."

Hargreaves frowns. "Wait, did you just say?"

"Oh yeah, you're broadcasting, sir."

Bekhti lets out an exasperated sigh.

Hargreaves shakes his head and leans forward. "This is Captain John Hargreaves of the ESS *Demeter*. Do you copy?"

A beat of silence. Static crackles, and then a response.

"*D—Demeter*? Captain?" The voice stutters through the comm, distorted but unmistakable. "Holy f—fu—uck, is that you?"

"Parker?" the captain mouths to the bridge officers. Hargreaves grips the armrest of his chair. "Parker?"

"It's me, sir. Engineering Sp—specialist Eugene Parker."

Bekhti mouths, "What the hells?"

Hargreaves shakes his head and shrugs. "How'd you find us?"

A ragged exhale. "There was a b—bright beam, then something ex—exploded. So I pointed my w—wristpad where the l—light came—" A static pop. "G—got lucky."

The captain exhales sharply. "What's your present situation, Specialist?"

A pause. Then Parker's voice returns, flat and brittle. "Ah. T —to be honest, sir? I'm freezing my ass off out here."

Hargreaves tenses. "Where are you?"

"I'm in a pressure suit, t—tethered to *Arion*. Ou—outside."

Bekhti stares at the comms panel. "He's outside the dropship?"

"I don't f—fucking recommend it," Parker mutters. "Had to f —finish s—something I st—tarted, and now the airlock's jammed. I can't get b—back in."

There's a long pause before Parker speaks again.

"Not enough oxygen t—to explain, c—captain. Better told after a hot sh—shower. Over some shitty cof—coffee."

Hargreaves smiles, his relief plain to see. "Understood, Parker. Sit tight. Help's on the way." The captain takes his chair.

Bekhti's already moving. "Locked on to *Arion*'s transponder. I'm prepping a rescue team now, sir."

The captain nods, then leans back, watching his officers jump into action.

"Well," he says with a grin. "Let's go bring our crew home."

APPENDIX

"DARK'S WAKE"

— Merion

(Fast-paced, rhythmic)
Born of the dark and the dawn and storm,
We rage through the skies where the suns are born.

(Smooth, flowing)
In the thralls of the void our fever grows,
Where the vacuum howls and the dark sun glows.
We are your legacy...

(Fast-paced, rhythmic)
Blazing through the rift our engines roar,
We feast on the wreckage of forgotten wars.
The old stars are ours, and all will fall,
We come as the reapers to end them
All.

(Smooth, flowing)
In the shadow of great beasts, we make our way,
Through the dark, the brave won't stay.

O! The monsters we have slain…

(Fast-paced, rhythmic)
We're the scream in the black and the cry in the night,
We're the storm and the dark and a force of might
From the edge of the void we rise in flame,
No gods, no monsters, and none to blame.

"WE'RE IN THIS ALONE"
(EXCERPT)

— Merion

We're bound to see this through.
No one else can tear us down.
We'll find a way out,
It's just us, alone.
When the stars fall apart
(pause)
I'll hold you till the end.
We're in this alone.

"THE FERRYMAN'S DUE"

— A traditional starfaring lament

The ferry awaits, but I'll stand by your side,
Through the dark and through tide,
'Til the stars cease to shine.

Oars dip the void, and the helm swings away,
But I'll hold your name
'Til the echoes decay.

So drink to the lost, and drink to the brave,
To those who set sail
And to those who remain.

The black claims us all. The stars take their due,
But we sail on, my friend,
And you'll carry us through.

ACKNOWLEDGMENTS

There are so many people to thank—this book wouldn't exist without the care, insight, and time shared by others.

First, thank you to **JB Kish**, my author milestone coach, for your encouragement, wisdom, and belief in this story's potential. Your project management and guidance helped me keep moving forward when the path wasn't clear, and your structure gave me room to build something wild and true.

To my editor, **Kristen Hall-Geisler**—thank you for helping me shape this story into its strongest self. Your thoughtful feedback, sharp eye, and respect for both the characters and the science made all the difference. Thanks also to Ali Shaw and the team at Indigo: Editing, Design, and More for helping everything run smoothly.

To **Nik Wilets** (nikwilets.com), thank you for capturing the spirit of this book in your stunning cover. Your visual style gave shape to a story rooted in beautiful dread and finding what was lost—a tone clearly captured once you painted it.

Ken Rickard, Felicia Haynes, Nik Wilets, and **Mark Burgess**—thank you for your honesty, insight, and generosity. You helped this story grow in all the right directions.

To my family and friends—especially those who checked in, asked questions, or gave me time and space to write—thank you for making room in your lives for this strange, wonderful journey.

And to **Laura**: I know I already said this in the dedication, but it bears repeating—you gave me time, space, love, and library evenings. You gave me the best kind of solitude for focus: the kind we share together.

To my brothers—**The Geekhouse**—thank you for a lifetime of sci-fi debates (starships can't submerge, they'll be crushed!), terrible puns, and joyful obsession. Malcolm McDowell once called us a gang, and honestly? He nailed it.

The Jacksonvillains are coming.

ABOUT THE AUTHOR

Tobby Hagler is a Software Engineering Director with extensive experience with cutting-edge web content management system development and software development training. He has presented at local and international conferences, using his ability to make complex technical concepts accessible to diverse audiences. He lives in the Carolina midlands with his wife and their three dogs, where he enjoys the quiet inspiration of his pondside home nestled in a nearly unhaunted forest.

* 9 7 9 8 9 9 9 8 7 3 2 8 5 0 *